Memory and
Desire

A Novel of Mystery and Romance

D0829524

Memory and
Desire

A Novel of Mystery and Romance

Lillian Stewart Carl

WILDSIDE PRESS
Berkeley Heights, New Jersey

First Wildside Press edition: January 2001

Memory and Desire
A publication of
Wildside Press
P.O. Box 45
Gillette, NJ 07933-0045
www.wildsidepress.com

FIRST EDITION

For my friends on "the loop":
Annette, Deni, Garda, Harriet,
Pam, Sherry-Anne, and Terey

Chapter One

*C*laire was so badly jet-lagged from her transatlantic flight she felt as disembodied as a ghost. When Detective Chief Inspector Blake strode across the lobby of the police station and crushed her fingers in a handshake she was faintly surprised. She'd half expected him to walk right through her.

"Miss Godwin," he said. "The sergeant tells me you're here about the Melinda Varek case."

"Yes, I am. She was my foster-sister and best friend. I need to know what happened to her."

"I'd like to know what happened to her myself. But the longer a case goes unsolved the less likely it will ever be solved. And it's been a year."

"I know. I'd still like to talk to you about it, please."

Blake's expression was polite, although the twitch of his moustache suggested he wouldn't be sorry if she vanished into thin air. But Claire persisted in physical existence. A conservatively dressed young American wearing glasses, she had to be the least threatening apparition the detective had seen all day.

Conceding defeat, Blake gestured toward a door beside the reception desk. "Come through. I have a few moments."

"Thank you."

He ushered her into a small office. The fluorescent-lit and linoleum-lined cubicle probably looked just like a cell downstairs, except for a computer and several thousand pieces of paper. Through the window the city of Derby was as damp and dark as a scene in a film noir.

Claire sat down and clasped her hands in her lap. They were trembling. At last. She was here at last.

"It's been a year," repeated Blake, settling behind his desk.

"The first I heard Melinda was missing was when your officer went through the return addresses on her mail and contacted me. I wasn't too concerned then — she was always taking off on spur-of-the moment treks to odd parts of the world.

"Which is what I told your officer. And what her brother told him. And what her former husband told him. It was six weeks, well into August, before I was sure something was wrong. By that time school was starting. I'm a media specialist — fancy name for a librarian — in a big high school, I couldn't just walk off the job to look for her. And I had some other things I had to deal with." Not that Steve had actually moved out until December, she added to herself. But once he'd "put his foot down," in his words, and told her she couldn't go running off to England on a wild goose chase, she'd known the relationship had reached its sell-by date.

"The trail is a lot colder now than it was then," said Blake.

"I know that. But if the professionals couldn't find her, what could I have done?"

"We had other problems to deal with, too," Blake stated. "You're speaking of Miss Varek in the past tense. You think she's dead, then."

"Yes." Claire didn't flinch. She'd had a long time to think about it. "Don't you think she's dead?"

Blake nodded agreement.

"So where's her body? You found her car parked by Ladybower Reservoir and dragged the lake. You searched the surrounding country-side. You searched Somerstowe itself, on the off chance her car was stolen. Nothing."

"She scarpered, then. Ran off to make a new life."

"Why?" returned Claire. "She was a very successful journalist. She went to Somerstowe to research her first novel — she already had a couple of publishers interested. Nothing was missing from her room except her laptop and her camera. The tools of her trade, yes, but . . ."

"Maybe she wanted to hide from her ex-husband."

"Melinda never hid. She felt success was the best revenge."

"Did she, now?" Blake took off his glasses and polished them with a handkerchief. He was almost bald, the expanse of his skull shining above a tidy fringe of brown hair, while the lower half of his face was almost concealed by the luxuriant moustache.

Here was a man, Claire thought, who had all his bases covered. Or perhaps, being English, he had all his wickets defended. But he'd think she really was nuts if she asked him if he played cricket.

"Miss Varek might have thrown everything over," Blake went on, "because she committed a crime."

Claire had cataloged every possibility. "I can't see that. I know her better than anyone else, probably, and she's not — she wasn't — the criminal type any more than she was the suicidal type. Do you have any unsolved crimes you could pin on her?"

"No," Blake admitted, but his voice hinted that anyone could be either criminal or suicidal, take your pick.

"Maybe she went walking," Claire suggested, "and, say, fell into an old mine shaft and is still lying there. Maybe she hit her head and has amnesia — although I'm not sure that ever really happens. But why go out walking alone, at midnight, away from the village, instead of enjoying all the attention she must've gotten after the play?"

"The play. 'A history of . . .' What was the title again?"

"'An Historie of the Apocalypse as Visit'd upon Summerstow.' The true story of a seventeenth century witch trial."

"Ah, yes," said Blake. "Costumes and melodrama. Miss Varek played the lead, the girl who was a witch. Odd, that they'd choose an American for the role."

"The girl, Elizabeth, was only accused of being a witch," Claire amended. "What if the play had something to do with Melinda's disappearance?"

"You never know about actresses." Or Americans, Blake's grimace seemed to say. "We rang up hospitals. We placed notices in newspapers. We sent her photo to Interpol. Nothing."

"In Melinda's last letter she told me she had a new lover, someone connected with the play, but she didn't name names. Maybe he . . ."

"We interviewed everyone connected with the play and a fair number who weren't. They all had quite a few things to say about Miss Varek, some complimentary, some not, but none of them told us anything helpful." Blake replaced his glasses. His eyes were the dull gray of flint. "I think we can agree, Miss Godwin, that the amnesia, suicide, and running away theories are right out. Illogical and too dramatic. It could be that Miss Varek was murdered, if that's not too dramatic as well."

"Yeah, well, Melinda was a pretty dramatic person, play or no play."

"There are any number of motives for murder," Blake pointed out.

"Yes there are. A fatal accident would be simple, wouldn't it? But a murder, that's another matter entirely. That would be complicated."

Blake glanced at his watch and stood up. "I'm sorry, Miss Godwin. I'd like nothing better than to find Miss Varek, alive or dead. Unless some sort of evidence turns up, though, her case is as good as closed."

Claire envisioned a portfolio slamming shut on Melinda, flattening her into two dimensions like a playing card. If this had been a poker game, Blake would've just called her bluff. And her hand was empty.

Blake handed her a business card and summoned a sympathetic smile even as he eased her from her chair. Muttering something about a pleasant holiday, he ushered her out the door of the office and abandoned her in the corridor. It smelled of cigarette smoke, disinfectant, and sausage.

Claire hadn't expected her visit to the Derbyshire Constabulary to prove anything. It was merely a formality, like securing the end of a strand of yarn before she began stitching. Because she wasn't on holiday.

She was on her way to Somerstowe to volunteer at the Hall just like Melinda had done last summer. She was going to discover her friend's body and a means of death, whether accident or murder.

Uncovering a murder, she reminded herself, would mean uncovering a murderer.

Her hands were still trembling. *Jet lag,* she assured herself, *not fear,* and she walked out into the rain.

*T*he black, rain-slicked country road seemed no wider than the sheep path it'd probably once been. Its shoulders were stone walls whisking by inches from Claire's left side mirror. Beyond them the green countryside of the Peak District was soft-silvered by the rain, hazy and unreal as a dream. She groped after an appropriate quote — "this earth, this realm, this England," or "England's green and peaceful land," but all she could think was, *I've fallen down a rabbit hole.*

A roar and a whoosh made her clutch convulsively at the steering wheel. A missile disguised as a red Jaguar came up behind her and without slowing veered around her and vanished around the next curve. The drivers here, she thought as she started breathing again, either had x-ray vision or steadier nerves than hers.

She crawled around the curve. There was the village at last, a group of slate roofs nestled beneath those glorious English oaks and beeches which always gave her a crick in her neck, imprinted as she was on stunted Texas trees. She relaxed her death-grip on the wheel.

The road became a street lined by stone buildings. On her right stood a pub: "Druid's Circle" read the sign swinging over the narrow sidewalk. Its lighted windows were warm and welcoming. So were those of the tea shop down the street. The shapes inside were no doubt those of the mad hatter and the march hare taking tea.

The Jaguar had either gone on through the town or turned aside — Claire didn't see it or its smoking wreckage anywhere. But she had other things to do than worry about crazed local drivers. Her letter from Richard Lacey, the National Trust's conservation architect, said to report to Somerstowe Lodge, outside the Hall, which was visible from the village.

Yes, it was. *All right!* Enchanted, Claire peered up at the sixteenth-century mansion perched atop its embankment. Tall multi-paned windows stared blankly toward the horizon. While rain streaked the pale golden stone of the façade, the carved balustrades edging the roof stood up as proudly as an Elizabethan's starched ruff. The old house might be afflicted with age and damp rot, but it was determined to keep up appearances.

A driveway turned off to the right. So did Claire, stopping beside a little house just outside the gate in the stone wall encircling the Hall. A dark green Rover, its door emblazoned with the oak leaf of the National Trust, sat beside it. Through the gate Claire saw a man strolling along behind the columns of the Hall's portico. The rain sifted silently down.

She was here. She was really here. She got out of the car, inhaled deeply of the cool damp air, and started toward the house. As Melinda always said, nothing ventured, nothing gained.

The door was set in an alcove, sheltered from the rain. Claire lifted the huge iron ring of the knocker and let it fall. The door opened so quickly she almost fell inside. She took a quick step forward.

The man in the doorway was younger than she'd envisioned, about her age, high twenties pushing thirty. He had chiseled lips, flexible eyebrows, and dark hair cut in a thick, soft brush. When Claire lurched toward him he juggled the rolled blueprints he was carrying and caught her elbow in a grip so firm she winced. "Miss Godwin, I presume?"

"Claire, please." She regained her balance. "Sorry."

He released her, his casual attitude indicating that strange women fell over his doorstep every day, a furtive sparkle in his eyes revealing that they didn't. "Richard Lacey. Please come through."

"Thank you."

Richard ushered her down a short hallway into a sitting room. A tiny fire burned in a grate, making the room look warmer than it really was. Furniture emerged like boulders from an overgrowth of books, magazines, and newspapers. A CD player, TV, and VCR sat on a stand beside the fireplace, the box to *Shakespeare in Love* gaping on top. Rows of neatly labeled notebooks — "Plaster," "Roof," "Planning Permission Forms" — filled a bookcase. A stone gargoyle smirked from the mantelpiece.

Richard dumped his drawings onto a table already piled with a computer, printer, scanner, and fax. A stack of charts avalanched onto the carpet. He considered them gravely.

Claire considered him, surreptitiously smoothing her canvas skirt. *Great.* Here she was, goofy with jet lag, and the Trust's caretaker and conservator turned out to be a hunk. But then Melinda, writing about the village's cast of characters, had said something about "Adonis" Lacey.

With the toe of his running shoe Richard nudged the papers beneath the table. Housekeeping accomplished, he looked around at Claire. His eyes were those of a tiger, brown flecked with gold, alight with perception, reflecting rather than revealing. Appraisal ran both ways, didn't it? Claire ducked.

The whistle of a teakettle came from the next room. Richard smiled ruefully, as though only too aware of — and not exactly comfortable with — his effect on the opposite sex. "Would you care for a cuppa?"

"Yes, please," Claire said.

He vanished into the kitchen, where he apparently started throwing dishes on the floor. She stifled any offers to help and warmed her hands at the fire. The gargoyle shared the mantelpiece with a penknife, two drawing compasses, a burned-down candle in a silver holder, duct tape, a floppy disk, and a swatch of brocade.

Heat rushed to Claire's cheeks. The wad of velvet half-concealed a color postcard. Glancing toward the kitchen, she moved the cloth aside.

She didn't have to see the entire picture, though, to recognize it. It was a distant shot of the Texas State Capitol looming at the end of Congress Avenue in Austin. She turned the postcard over. Her own handwriting jumped out at her. "Hey Melinda, Here's something to remind you of home. I put the ring in my safe-deposit box. Happy antiquating! — C."

Last summer, the night before Melinda left for England, she'd stopped by Claire's house for pizza and Chianti and a post-mortem of her marriage to a London solicitor. Taking off her wedding band, she'd inspected it with archaeological detachment. The engagement ring with its three exquisitely cut diamonds had stayed on her hand.

"Nige told me to keep the diamonds. He was glad I didn't want the cottage in the Cotswolds and the BMW. But what good would they do me? Money doesn't mean happiness. Neither does marriage. It was nice while it lasted. But it's over now. Finito. Kaput." She'd thrown the wedding ring up in the air and laughed when she couldn't find it.

Two weeks later Claire had turned up the ring behind her couch and e-mailed the good news. "Keep it for me," Melinda returned. And now that ring, an engraved gold band inscribed "To Melinda from Nigel" was in Claire's jewelry case in the car, a talisman for her quest.

Melinda's bittersweet laugh had always been directed mostly at herself, Claire reflected. She knew herself altogether too well. No wonder she sometimes made less self-aware people uneasy. Claire tucked the postcard back behind the velvet. She hadn't planned to find a clue quite so fast — she hadn't unpacked her deerstalker and magnifying glass. And yet there it was.

She'd wondered before she met him if Richard was Melinda's new lover. Now she put him at the top of her list. He'd not only known Melinda because she'd worked at the Hall, but he, too, had had a role in the play. According to the playbill Melinda sent, Richard played the role of Phillip Lacey, who'd written the melodrama in 1775 and who appeared as narrator in its production.

Richard emerged from the kitchen carrying a tray loaded with teapot and cups. Claire reminded herself that after her broken engagement she was supposed to be cynical about men and looked at Richard more critically.

The angles of his face were almost too severe, she decided, as though freshly-sculpted and not yet weathered. He was tall and slender as a Corinthian column and carried himself as straight — which could just as well indicate arrogance as self-esteem. In contrast to the domestic disaster of his house, his RAF blue sweater with its dashing nylon patches on the shoulders and elbows was as clean as the jeans it was draped over. Did that imply a contradictory nature?

"Are you related to Phillip Lacey?" Claire asked.

"Author of The Play?" Richard replied, his careful enunciation capitalizing the letters, his velvet voice enriching the words. "I'm a descendent, right enough."

"Is that why you were chosen to be Somerstowe Hall's conservation expert?"

He elbowed a pile of magazines off a coffee table and set down the tray. Speaking to the teapot rather than to Claire, he said, "My presence here is a bit more than cosmic coincidence, yes. But it's been donkey's years since a Lacey owned the place. Phillip was the family wastrel. His sons had to sell up to the Cranbournes and their descendents left the place to the Trust. One sugar or two?"

"One please."

He sloshed milk, tea, and sugar into a cup and handed it over. Claire sipped at the steaming caramel-colored brew. Should she try cleverly worded leading questions about Melinda or should she simply ask him outright? Her blood-sugar level probably wasn't up to cleverness.

With a fine disregard for the temperature of the tea, Richard drank deeply. "Tea thick enough to trot a mouse across, my mother always says. Mind you, she's Scottish."

"You make that sound like a confession."

"In some quarters it might be." His smile was like the sun coming out after forty days of rain.

Dazzled, Claire reminded herself once again to be cynical. This man was a suspect.

"Is this your first trip to the UK?" Richard went on.

"Oh no, I've been here several times."

"So the driving on the left's not too bad, is it?"

Claire groaned. "When you can concentrate, no. I probably made a public menace of myself today, renting a car as soon as I stepped off the plane. The motorway wasn't so bad, with three lanes of traffic going the same way. But the interchanges, and the smaller roads — I kept repeating, *keep left, keep left, keep left*, like a crazed communist bureaucrat."

He laughed. "I've driven in America. It's all backward, like stepping through the looking-glass, isn't it?"

"Tell me about it," she said, and couldn't help a Cheshire cat grin in return.

He set down his mug and strolled over to the fireplace, where he prodded the burning chunks of wood into a pile. His efforts released a few more BTUs into the room.

"The last time I was here," Claire went carefully on, "was two years ago, for Melinda Varek's wedding. You met her last summer. I was hoping to find out what happened to her. Along with my volunteer work, of course."

Richard was leaning to the side, putting the poker back in its rack on the hearth, when the magic name passed her lips. She couldn't see his face, but even his back was expressive. He straightened very slowly. His hands tightened into fists at his sides. His shoulders squared themselves beneath the sweater. Claire waited for him to turn around and say something along the lines of, "Oh yes, Melinda. Quite the baffling mystery. So you're here now, how can I help you?"

He spun around. The blaze in his eyes knocked Claire back against the couch. She'd sneaked up on him. He was resentful, angry — maybe even, oddly enough, frightened. "That's your game, then," he said, his voice clipped to the minimum. "I've been wondering ever since your application came in why your name was so damnably familiar."

"It's no game," retorted Claire. "I'm trying to find out what happened to Melinda. You knew her. You have a postcard I sent her on the mantel."

"The police couldn't find her. Why do you think you will do?"

"I knew Melinda."

"Well, we all knew Melinda, didn't we?" Richard turned back to the mantelpiece. In one swift gesture he threw the postcard into the fire. It flared with yellow flame and then shriveled into black crepe paper. He assumed a pose that was obviously meant to appear casual, but was closer to the stance of a man before a firing squad.

"Do you know anything that could help explain her disappearance?" Claire persisted. "Maybe she said something about making a quick trip somewhere."

"I assure you I was thoroughly interviewed by the police. I couldn't help them. I can't help you."

Claire scowled, then reminded herself that discretion was the better part of valor — or foolishness, as the case might be. She put down her cup and stood. "What time do you want me to report to work tomorrow?"

"Nine," Richard said to the gargoyle's carved leer.

"Thank you for the tea."

"You're welcome."

She let herself out. The afternoon had lightened. The rain had stopped, the fields glistened an ethereal fairy green, and through the massed ranks of gray and white clouds a sunbeam shone like a searchlight. Crows called harshly from the trees behind the wall. The windows of Somerstowe Hall glinted as though with sudden inspiration.

Claire was more puzzled and indignant than inspired. So much for the direct query. She should've opted for leading questions, made friends with Richard, won his confidence . . . No. She was cautious, but she wasn't sneaky. Not on purpose, anyway.

If Richard had been Melinda's lover, wouldn't he be just as frustrated at her disappearance as Claire was? Wouldn't they be allies? But what he was was defensive. Why? Because of a guilty conscience?

Yes, there'd been a spark of mutual attraction. Big deal. Richard's handsome face might just as well have been the gargoyle's for all she was attracted to him now. He knew something. She was positive he knew something.

Sheep stood like bundles of cotton candy in a distant field. Two boys on bicycles splashed by on the road. Claire tried closing her burning eyes, but when she opened them they didn't focus any more clearly. She'd waited a year and now everything was happening too fast.

She climbed back into her car and slammed the door. Someone had stolen the steering wheel . . . No, she'd gotten in the wrong side. With an aggravated snort she crawled across the emergency brake to the driver's seat.

Claire could be certain of only one thing. Whether Richard had been Melinda's lover or not, whether he knew anything about her disappearance or not, his attitude was going to make him the very devil to work for.

Chapter Two

In the suddenly bright evening Somerstowe was picture-postcard quaint. There was even a village bobby ambling down the drive from the Hall, his hands folded behind his back.

Claire expected a director to shout "Cut!" and crews to rush forward and disassemble the false fronts of the houses. But the village remained solid, damp stone glowing, gardens winking in multi-colored floral fantasy. Richard or no Richard, she told herself, Melinda or no Melinda, I'm going to like Somerstowe.

Across the street from the Druid's Circle was the village shop, a red post office sign on its bay window. Claire turned into its tiny parking lot, parked, and hefted her suitcase and carry-on bag.

The shop smelled of newsprint and exotic spices. Behind the counter a plump woman with sleek black hair pulled into a bun stood sorting a pile of letters and magazines. She wore a loose dress in a lush paisley pattern, belted with an apron of dazzling whiteness. When Claire stepped through the door she looked up smiling.

"Mrs. Nair?" Claire asked. "I'm Claire Godwin. I've booked your efficiency apartment."

"I am most certainly Sarita Nair," returned the woman. "Welcome to Somerstowe. Your journey was a pleasant one, I trust?"

"I don't relish playing a sardine for several hours, but I arrived safely, that's the important thing."

Sarita looked a bit puzzled, but didn't ask for an explanation. She swept the mail into a tidy stack and pushed through a swinging door in the counter. "First you must see your flat, then you will be taking dinner with us."

"Why, thank you." Food, Claire thought. She remembered food. Her stomach growled.

Sarita led her into an old-fashioned but spotless kitchen and plucked a key off a rack by the door. A man with the smooth round features of a teddy bear, adorned with a moustache that made Blake's look underfed, sat at a table with newspaper and tea. "This is my husband Roshan, Miss Godwin."

"Greetings, Miss Godwin," said Roshan, standing and bowing. "Your journey was a pleasant one, I trust?"

Claire abandoned her sardine metaphor. "Yes, thank you, Mr. Nair."

"That is very good. I am minding the shop now." He vanished toward the front of the house.

Claire followed Sarita across a bricked yard and up a stairway clinging to the outside of a low stone building. Former stables, Claire estimated, now inhabited by a car and a red mail van.

The apartment was just about what she'd anticipated, a long low-ceilinged room furnished with haphazard bits of furniture. A small television occupied one end of a bookcase filled with tour guides, old paperback novels, and Reader's Digest magazines. A miniature kitchen nestled in a curtained alcove. Sarita demonstrated a foldout bed and the complex controls of the shower, which took up most of the floor space in a cupboard-sized bathroom.

The apartment was as spotless as Sarita's apron. Slipcovers, pillows, and tablecloths were made of bright Indian fabrics. Everything else was drab and serviceable, including a wall to wall carpet of an institutional muddy green. Claire hoisted her suitcase onto a rack by a huge wardrobe and dumped her carry-on and purse to the floor. Odd how much heavier her luggage was on this side of the Atlantic. "It's very nice, Mrs. Nair."

"Thank you very much. I have placed a few food items in your kitchen, and such things are always available at the shop, but I'm sorry to say there is no telephone connection for your computer."

"I didn't bring one. My friend Melinda Varek stayed here last year and told me about having to scrounge for a place to plug in her laptop." This time Claire had her witness squarely in her sights as she spoke.

Unlike Richard, Sarita shook her head. "Now that is a puzzle. Such a — well — lively young lady. You are her friend Claire, then?"

"Yes. I'd like to find out what happened to her."

"I opened the flat to the police, I packed her things when she could not be found. It seems as though she ran off still wearing her costume from The Play, taking her computer and her camera only. Miss Godwin, I can offer no explanation."

"Claire," Claire murmured. "Just Claire."

"She had many admirers, did Melinda. I thought perhaps she had gone away with one. But they are still here, mystified as are we all."

"Was Richard Lacey one of her admirers?"

"Oh, certainly, yes. Melinda spent much time with him at Somerstowe Hall. The Hall is Richard's passion. His family built it, his family enacted the story that became The Play — memories are long here, I'm thinking."

"I bet they are," Claire agreed. "Was it Richard who chose Melinda to be Elizabeth Spenser in The Play? Melinda said last year was the first time someone not from Somerstowe had been chosen to play the lead."

"Oh yes, that was most unusual. It is not Richard, however, who does the choosing of parts."

Claire interpreted the slow wave of Sarita's eyebrows as a seismological response to social shock waves. "Then . . ." she began, only to be interrupted by a shout from the yard below.

"Mum! Mum! Derek's pinched my biro!"

"It's never hers, Mum!" protested a similar but deeper voice.

"Please excuse me," said Sarita, gliding toward the door. "Dinner is at seven."

"Thank you." Claire watched as Sarita wafted down the steps to intervene between two teenagers who were facing off like gladiators. The boy's black hair was cut in a shaved-nape helmet that wouldn't have looked out of place on the Bayeux tapestry. The girl's poufed upward from her forehead in testimony to the power of gel and spray. Their colorful clothes were either skintight or three sizes too big.

Sarita read the riot act in dulcet tones, restored the pen to its rightful owner, and sent the children to their separate corners of the house. Claire was impressed. Coping with squabbling adolescents was one of her occupational hazards, but she never managed anywhere near so much poise. She was usually tempted to restore order with a two-by-four.

She shut the door, tripped over a wrinkle in the carpet — it wasn't tacked down, she saw — and started to unpack.

Of course Melinda had had admirers here, too. She took cruises to romantic palm-fringed isles and carriage rides in Central Park. Claire had matter-of-fact relationships in her own bedroom. Yeah, maybe Melinda had eloped with someone, although, given her ambitions, that wasn't likely. Her ambitions had contributed to the breakup of her marriage.

From her carry-on bag Claire took a small jeweler's box. She opened it, peeked at Melinda's wedding ring glinting impassively on its bed of cotton, and hid it in the back corner of the wardrobe.

That Richard was passionate she could well believe. His over-reaction to Claire's mention of Melinda was probably basic masculine touchiness, not a guilty conscience. Maybe he was resentful Melinda had chosen someone else for whatever post-divorce therapy she'd had in mind. Maybe he thought she'd trashed him to Claire.

She hadn't, though. She'd never had a chance to. Her notes and letters were only quick stream-of-consciousness anecdotes. As always, she'd been saving chapter and verse until afterwards.

Claire stacked Melinda's letters — most printed out from e-mails, a couple hand-written — on the desk by the window. Beside them she set the playbill. "An Historie of the Apocalypse as Visit'd upon Summerstow" was printed in antique script across the outside of the folded paper. No wonder everyone simply referred to it as "The Play." Tucked inside was a snapshot of Melinda in her costume, a long blue dress with the puffy sleeves and broad collar of the 1660's. She was smiling, challenging the lens as she challenged life, with a direct, uncompromising look.

Beside the letters Claire placed a thin book, its red construction paper cover imprinted with the same title as the playbill. "A True Story dramatized by Phillip Lacey" was added on a lower line. And had he ever dramatized it. Claire had ordered her own copy of The Play and studied it as carefully as she'd studied Melinda's letters, as though some word or phrase would leap from the page and announce, "I'm a clue!" But she'd found nothing in the florid dialog that even smelled of red herring.

She found a place for her CD player on the bookcase, then turned to the bathroom, arranging her cosmetics and lotions on a glass shelf above the sink. In the mirror her face looked like slept-in corduroy, her brown eyes muddy with weariness. Melinda never looked tired. Claire knew how much maintaining her blonde and beautiful image cost — and why the security that image provided made the cost worthwhile.

Claire wasn't sure she had an image. Her features were symmetrical, functional, respectable. Maybe her lips had recently started pinching just a bit at the corners, and a frown line was threatening to appear between her eyes, but today the rain had incited her auburn hair to rebelliousness. Rebellion, she thought. Sidekicks of the world unite!

But she'd never been Melinda's sidekick any more than Melinda had been hers. They'd been more than friends. They'd been sisters. Claire peeled off her wilted clothes, adjusted the water in the shower, and remembered.

"Everyone knew Melinda," Richard had said. Well, once upon a time everyone at Crockett High knew Melinda. She was pretty. She was popular. She belonged to all the clubs and she organized all the dances. Shy, awkward, introverted only-child Claire had hated her. Then she'd found Melinda sobbing in the girl's locker room, her tears washing away enough of her artfully applied make-up to reveal the bruise discoloring her cheekbone. To this day Claire could see Melinda's look of terror and belligerence melt into relief when she said only, "How can I help?"

The situation at Melinda's home, the alcoholic mother, the abusive stepfather, grew so bad that Child Protective Services intervened. Claire's parents, who she'd always thought were stodgy beyond all redemption, became state-mandated foster parents so that Melinda could spend her senior year with them instead of with her distant and much older brother.

Since then they'd won their own scholarships, gone to their own colleges, pursued their own careers and their own romances. If at times Claire felt like she was standing on the curb watching Melinda's parade, there were other times she felt like she was sitting cozily before a warm hearth with Melinda's face pressed against the window behind her. Yes, she'd known Melinda all right. Without her, Claire wouldn't be who she was.

And now she was a solo act. She had to re-define herself. Maybe once she found out what had happened to Melinda, and, even more importantly, *why*, she could get on with her life. But not before then. If that's what the psychology pop-word "closure" meant, so be it.

The shower slapped her back into if not alertness at least wakefulness. She dressed in chino pants and chambray blouse and cinched her belt snugly, hoping it would create a waistline where none existed. Not that she was overweight, her figure simply owed more to Kansas's topography than to Colorado's. Melinda's figure, on the other hand, looked like a relief map of San Francisco.

Claire had run out of tears a long time ago. Now she blew her nose, cleaned her glasses — which Melinda had made sure were fashionable enough not to be cliche librarian accessories — and walked out into the evening. She arrived at the Nair's back door just as a clock inside the house struck seven.

The dining room was warm and bright. Light reflected off brass trays, polished china, and the smooth mahogany complexions of the teenagers, who were introduced as Derek and Trillian. They were now standing demurely behind their chairs waiting for the adults to sit. Claire smiled at them and received gleaming white grins in return.

Sarita filled Claire's plate with a lamb and tomato stew scented with onions and spices. Her taste buds snapped to attention. She helped herself to generous portions of the side dishes, lentils, cauliflower, brussels sprouts, and boiled potatoes. Using a crispy pappadum to scoop food onto her fork, she ate almost without breathing. Delicious!

It wasn't until Sarita had served a sweet, milky rice pudding that Claire managed to re-boot her brain and ask questions about the village and its long memory.

"Some of the families in Somerstowe," Roshan answered, "have been here for generations. To other families, though, Somerstowe is a dormitory suburb of Derby and Sheffield only."

"The people with roots here are the ones who put on The Play?"

"Yes indeed," replied Sarita. "For many years Diana Jackman played Elizabeth, and before her Heather Little — right back to the first production. We have just begun rehearsals for the fifteenth. I am wardrobe mistress again, and this year Trillian will be playing Elizabeth."

Trillian dimpled mischievously, looking not at all like the modest servant girl Elizabeth had been. Period clothes and a less assertive hairdo would make a big difference, Claire thought. "It isn't Richard who chooses the roles? He doesn't get points for his name?"

"He's only lived here a year," answered Derek.

"I am understanding, though," Sarita added, "his family spent summers here when he was a boy."

"Yeh," said Trillian. "It was his dad sussed out the manuscript of the The Play in the attic at the Hall. We study it in school now." She rolled her expressive dark eyes, obviously wishing scholars would stop adding items to the curriculum.

Roshan went on, "Richard Lacey was dispatched by the National Trust after the elderly Mrs. Cranbourne left the Hall to them. She also assigned the income from The Play to a trust fund to maintain the Hall. Very tidy arrangement, I'm thinking. For the Trust, not for her relatives who wanted the Hall for themselves."

"You will be mending the old textiles, as did Melinda?" Sarita started gathering the dirty dishes. "As did Elizabeth, for that matter."

"Yes," Claire answered. "I've been doing needlework for years, but I've never had the chance to work on anything as old as Somerstowe's canvases. I'm the one who taught Melinda how to . . ."

"Tally ho!" shouted a cheerful voice from the shop. "What light through yonder doorway breaks?"

"Hello, Elliot," Roshan called, and shoved himself away from the table. "I shall fetch your letters." He disappeared toward the front of the house.

A face that displayed its long nose and prominent front teeth like the marquee of a movie theater looked around the doorframe. "Please, don't let me disturb you — I was simply perishing for the days' post — conference at Shepherd's Bush, don't you know, a new movie deal — the commute to London's not quite as bad as commuting in Los Angeles — oh, I say, hello there! Elliot Moncrief. And you?"

"Claire Godwin," Claire replied, somewhat dazed. So this was the producer and director. If not a household name he was at least a neighborhood phrase. Melinda had mentioned him more than once — he had a cottage in Somerstowe and had directed The Play for several years now. Claire, Melinda, and her then-husband Nigel had seen Elliot's production of "Don Juan in Hell" in Covent Garden year before last. He'd dressed the actors as punks and scored Shaw's prose with heavy metal music. Melinda had thought it was all a great joke. Nigel had been shocked rigid.

Elliot sauntered through the doorway and pressed Claire's fingertips in his smooth, cool hand. "Is that one of your inestimable pappadums, Sarita? May I? Lucky you, Miss Godwin, to be treated to such a repast."

As he leaned over Claire's shoulder to snare the last pappadum she caught of whiff of his musky cologne. Or polish, as the case might be. Is this guy for real? she asked herself. Judging by his tanned, finely lined complexion, he'd spent a lot of time in Hollywood. Maybe he was used to playing Noel Coward for the colonials.

Elliot was staring at her while he munched his pappadum. Sorry, witty repartee was beyond her benumbed brain. She defaulted to her usual topic. "Melinda wrote me about your directing The Play."

"Ah, you're *that* Claire, late of the Lone Star State. You haven't, by some chance, any idea what became of Melinda, the dear girl?"

"No, I don't."

"She made an excellent Elizabeth." Elliot extracted his handkerchief and wiped his fingertips. "One of my more inspired choices. Even though choosing a foreigner was, shall we say, a bit of a controversy."

Oh. That answered the question of who did the casting for The Play. "Melinda is — was — very talented."

Elliot's pale blue eyes crinkled at the corners. "Oh yes, that she was."

Was he implying what she thought he was implying? Elliot could just as easily have been Melinda's lover as Richard. More easily, maybe. At least, a lot more casually.

"You're hoping to find her, then?" Elliot went on. "She's leagues from here, I should think. And what is your specialty, Claire? Treading the boards? Scribing deathless prose? Breaking hearts?"

"Mending needlework," replied Claire. She should rent a billboard outside of town, she thought, and put up a twenty-foot-high notice: *It's no coincidence Claire Godwin is in Somerstowe! She's searching for Melinda Varek!* So much for her vision of herself as the compleat sleuth.

Sarita shooed the children to their feet. Roshan reappeared with several letters and a large brown envelope. "Ta, most kind," Elliot told him. "Must run, expecting an important phone call — just between you and me and the gatepost, Andrew Lloyd Webber is having a look at The Play — it'd make a lovely musical, don't you think? Raise it several levels above the village production — which is charming and all, but, well . . . Later?"

He disappeared out the door, his parting "Later?" seemingly directed at no one in particular, and yet, Claire felt, really aimed at her. *I'm not your type,* she wanted to call after him, but after the last year she wasn't sure any more just whose type she was.

Not good old Steve's, that was for sure. After the relationships with the scatter-brained music teacher and the yuppie with the cell phone welded to his ear — both of which had still had more possibilities than some of Melinda's affairs — Steve's quiet steadiness had appealed to her. All too soon Claire discovered the difference between steady and petrified. An engineer, he'd done his best to reduce the relationship to flow charts and logic diagrams. And he'd never been comfortable around Melinda, always making little barbed comments under his breath about her travels, her clothes, her sex life.

But just because Claire was feeling as though she'd fallen into a movie set didn't mean she could re-write the past. What she wanted was to write the future.

She stood up. "Thank you very much for the dinner. May I help clear things away?"

"Oh no," Sarita assured her. "Derek and Trillian always do the washing up."

Judging by the clatter of dishes and splashes of water coming from the kitchen, they were doing it as an Olympic water polo match. "I think I'll turn in," Claire went on. "I have to be able to work a needle tomorrow morning."

Roshan and Sarita murmured pleasantries and showed her out. Claire climbed the steps to her door. From her vantage point on the landing the village and countryside looked like a watercolor, soft greens, golds, and grays streaked by the dark horizontal of the street. The bobby was leaning against the wall outside the pub, chatting with an elderly man. Beyond several green-edged slate roofs rose the spire of a church. The shadow of Somerstowe Hall reached toward the town as though the old house wanted to join in. Somewhere a lamb was bleating, "Muuuum! Muuuum!"

Elliot strolled along the sidewalk and into a suitably picturesque cottage. As he passed a red Jaguar parked in the driveway he patted its hood affectionately. Aha! So the car was his. That was no surprise. What Claire wondered was why, if he'd been in such a hurry to get his mail, he didn't pick it up hours ago when he'd first blasted into town.

Melinda had driven like that, passing bats out of hell on her way, and was perpetually taking defensive driving courses to wipe the tickets off her record. Claire, on the other hand, had never gotten a traffic ticket. There was some basic imbalance there. There was a lot about her relationship with Melinda that'd been unbalanced. It was like Claire had always played it safe because she'd had Melinda to take the risks for her.

Maybe, she thought, Melinda had been able to take risks because she'd had Claire to be her anchor.

Frowning, Claire unlocked the door. Her leaden feet stumbled over the edge of the carpet. At least she had the carpet as an excuse this time, she thought, remembering her undignified stutter-step toward Richard.

The door wouldn't shut — the carpet was bunched beneath it. She went back out onto the landing and grasped its edge to pull it smooth. Her fingertips touched paper. From beneath the heavy material she pulled a small envelope that had once been white but was now gray with dust. The word "Melinda" was pasted on its face in block letters cut from a newspaper.

The back of her neck went icy cold. Claire jerked the carpet flat, leaped inside, and slammed the door behind her. She took the envelope to the kitchen and slit it open with a paring knife.

The message inside was also cut from smeared newsprint. "Somerstowe shall not suffer a witch to live. Hie you hence, evil one, or your own demons will pick your bones." Folded in the paper was a snapshot of Melinda in jeans and T-shirt. The photograph was punctured repeatedly by pinholes. The pin itself, an ordinary dressmaker's pin, was tucked into the center of the picture. Its head and its point framed Melinda's face with cold steel.

Claire clapped her curry-scented hand over her mouth, pressing a gasp into her lungs. *Sympathetic magic.* A pin stabbing, a knife stabbing, witchcraft . . . Those were the words one of the townspeople addressed to poor Elizabeth Spenser. According to both history and drama, Elizabeth had not hied herself hence. And she'd paid the price for her stubbornness, not by steel but by rope.

Someone slipped the letter under Melinda's door for her to find. It'd gone beneath the carpet instead. She hadn't found it. There might have been others she'd laughed off, or this might have been the only warning before someone carried out the threat. A death threat.

"Good God," Claire said aloud. And the concept of "murder," which had been a word in her vocabulary, an item on her list, suddenly became a sharp point lodged in her own heart. "Oh my God."

Blake would only re-open the case if he had new evidence. Here it was. Wide awake now, Claire thrust the letter into her purse and headed out to look for a telephone booth.

Chapter Three

*T*he engines of the huge jet rumbled in her ears. She wriggled, trying to escape. She was trapped in her seat, surrounded not with sleeping but with dead bodies, each murdered by a dressmaker's pin between the eyes. . . .

Claire jerked awake. Above her a nubbly plaster ceiling shimmered with reflected sunlight. That pounding in her head was someone knocking at her door. Groaning, she rolled out of the hide-a-bed and pulled on her robe.

"Who is it, please?" she called from her side of the door.

From the other came a calm male voice. "Police Constable Alec Wood, Miss Godwin. DCI Blake rang me and asked me to call round."

"Oh, sure — just a minute."

Claire charged into the bathroom, dragged a comb through her hair, and found her glasses. Her travel clock read 8:10. She'd set the alarm for 7:30 and never pulled out the knob. That figured.

At least her message of the night before had reached Blake. Claire folded the bed and tightened the sash of her robe. She was hardly wearing the proper clothing for a gentleman caller, but policemen were like doctors, they had to take what they could get. She opened the door to find the same bobby she'd seen twice last evening. No, three times — he was the man who'd been strolling through the portico of the Hall.

He took off his hat, revealing a head of curly brown hair. "I'm sorry to knock you up."

Claire gurgled, suppressing her laughter. She knew perfectly well what that expression meant here, she simply hadn't been prepared to encounter a transatlantic malapropism quite so soon. "It's a good thing you waked me up, I have to be at the Hall at nine and I didn't turn on my alarm clock. Come on in. Would you like some coffee?"

"Thank you," Alec stepped inside and closed the door. "It's good to meet you at last, Miss Godwin. I'm sorry about the circumstances, Melinda going missing and all."

Claire's reputation had certainly preceded her, hadn't it? "I just wish I'd been able to come sooner," she told him.

"DCI Blake said you found a threatening letter addressed to Melinda."

"Yes. It was under the carpet just inside the door."

"Someone slotted the letter beneath the door and legged it, then, didn't know his scheme had gone wrong."

Alec, thought Claire, sure wasn't the country bumpkin cop beloved of stage, screen, and television. He was maybe a couple of years younger than she was, tall enough to have to stoop coming in the door, his broad shoulders square and yet not at all tense. A tremor at the corners of his mouth suggested it was accustomed to smiling. He had a good face for a policeman, his even, open features as reassuringly matter-of-fact as his uniform.

He had a good face, period. She filled the teakettle, set it on the hot plate, and took two cups and a jar of Nescafe from the cabinet. "I wonder whether Melinda even knew she was being threatened. She sure never told me."

"Would she have done?

"Taking it as a joke, maybe."

Alec nodded in agreement. "Yes. She'd think it was a joke, being a bit of a joker herself."

Claire pulled the letter from the desk drawer where she'd locked it last night and offered it to him.

"Put it down there, please." The letter safely on the scarred wooden top of the table, Alec pulled a pair of tweezers from his pocket and teased the letter and the photograph from the envelope. He bent over them.

Claire poured boiling water over the instant coffee and added milk and sugar. She set the steaming cup on the table, far enough away from Alec's hand he wouldn't accidentally knock it over onto the evidence. But even though his hands were as large and strong as the rest of his body they moved with deliberate delicacy.

"The words are from The Play," he said. "A load of rubbish about witchcraft and all. Are you familiar with it?"

With witchcraft? Oh. "The Play? I've never seen it performed."

"Whoever did this has done. The words are changed slightly from the script as per Elliot's direction."

"You played Walter Tradescant last year, didn't you?"

"I've played him for three years now, since Rob Jackman gave up the role. He was getting a wee bit long in the tooth for the role of the male ingenue. And I'm a bachelor, to boot. More suitable, so some would think."

Really? Who would think? Melinda? Walter had been Elizabeth's lover — in the old-fashioned sense of the term, not in the modern trash your inhibitions and get down to it sense. Claire drank, grimacing not at the heat of the coffee but at finding yet another candidate for Melinda's real-life lover. She'd find men hanging in the wardrobe next, arranged neatly on hangers.

Alec frowned. "Now, that's no good. I made this snap myself. Richard tacked it up on the bulletin board in the entrance hall."

Melinda's miniaturized face looked up from the table. She'd taken on the expression of a fashion model, eyes slightly crossed, lips parted, expression vacant. And yet the angle of her brows mocked her pose. Claire could hear her asking, "Why is it that in order to look glamorous you have to look brain dead? Why is it you have to be glamorous in order to be taken seriously by the good-old-boy Establishment?"

"That stone wall in the background," Claire said, "looks like the Hall's boundary wall."

"That's what it is, right enough. Melinda, Fred, and Janet were on lunch break, picnicking in the garden, when I made the snap."

"And the pin?"

"Ready to hand, I expect. Every year Sarita uses up a box or two of pins, with the costumes and all."

"How could Blake's people have missed the letter beneath the rug?"

"He only sent a couple of men, not an entire investigative team. No body, you see. No probable cause." With his tweezers Alec turned the picture over and looked narrowly at the date printed on the back.

"Why would anyone threaten Melinda, try to get her to leave? Did you see anything going on?"

"The usual behind-the-scenes ego trips. Melinda was an outsider, but only a bit more so than, say, Elliot himself."

"Or Richard?"

"Richard has an impeccable pedigree," Alec said with a hint of a chuckle.

"And Melinda didn't," said Claire. "She wasn't into ego trips, but she was no shrinking violet, either. She could've rubbed someone the wrong way. Or maybe someone was envious of her looks and her talents. Not that resentment or envy or anything else justifies murder."

"Murder?" Alec glanced sharply up. "Is it murder then?"

His eyes were a striking gold-green, the color of sunlight in an English forest. Oberon, king of Faerie, must have eyes like that. "I don't see how she could've died in an accident and not been found. So that means someone else was involved. But . . ." Claire sighed. "Now that it looks like it really was murder, well — it's kind of anticlimactic. Melinda wasn't an anti-climax. She should've gone out with a clash of cymbals and a lightning bolt. It's not fair. She deserved better than just — disappearing . . ." Alec's clear gaze had loosened her tongue, Claire realized. There was a useful talent for a policeman.

He looked back at the letter. "Were you envious of her?"

"Sometimes. I know what was below the surface gloss, though. Hers was a real ugly duckling story. I think she was always afraid she'd wake up someday and find herself an ugly duckling again."

A slight movement of Alec's mouth and eyebrow annotated her statement with what might have been a personal memory. "It might have been envy. It might have something as ordinary as greed — she had that diamond ring, remember. But every murderer thinks he's justified, doesn't he?"

"I don't know. Murder has only recently become part of my vocabulary."

"I'm sorry it has done, Miss Godwin."

"It's Claire."

"Claire." Alec drained his coffee and set the mug down. From his pocket he pulled a plastic evidence bag. He shoved the letter, the picture with its macabre pin, and the envelope into it. "I'll send these along to Derby. Blake won't be half narked when he learns it was here all along. He'll have your carpet up, I reckon, and start interviewing all over again."

Claire contemplated constables in the hands of an angry Blake. "I hope he won't be mad at you."

"I wasn't the one assigned here." And suddenly the smile broke through the uniformed solemnity, a pearly crescent that made her feel as though matters were properly in hand. "Ta, then. See you again soon." Replacing his hat, in three long strides Alec went out the door and shut it behind him.

Whoa. A charming and empathic public official. And a good-looking guy . . . Another suspect, Claire reminded herself. Just because Alec was nicer than Richard and less fake than Elliot didn't mean he wasn't hiding something about Melinda.

He hadn't expressed either like or dislike for her, let alone implying a more-than-friends relationship. And yet he'd known Melinda well enough to agree with Claire's ugly duckling comment. Was he just more perceptive than some people or had she opened up to him, too? Melinda didn't tell many people about her past. Why should she? She'd worked hard polishing her manner, her mind, and her appearance. She deserved the good fortune she'd made for herself. She hadn't deserved death threats, let alone murder.

Murder, which demanded a murderer, and means, and motive. Not to mention a corpse. Judging by the malice in the anonymous letter, the diamond ring was, at most, a side issue. What the real issue was, though, Claire could only imagine. And she had a vivid imagination. What she didn't have were facts.

She drank the rest of her coffee and fixed herself some toast. Okay, she'd found a clue. Even if she'd fallen over it by accident. Whether Blake picked up on it or not, she wasn't going to stop asking questions of the volunteers and the local people. Melinda always said Claire was stubborn beyond all reason.

She cleaned up the kitchen, dressed in jeans and sweatshirt, and locked the door of her flat behind her. The morning was bright and clear. Fluffy clouds floated in a blue sky, innocent of rain. Somerstowe village looked more than ever like a postcard, the telephone booth and Elliot's Jaguar adding artistic dashes of red. Claire took a deep breath of the cool breeze, willed herself not to look over her shoulder, and set out for the Hall.

She'd done her homework. She knew that the Hall's stone perimeter wall considerably pre-dated the house. The hill which it crowned was partly artificial, the remains of an eleventh century Norman motte built by one Baron de Lacy, a minion of William the Conqueror. By 1592 the country had been peaceful enough for the Laceys to tear down the old Norman keep and build an up-to-date mansion from its stones. It hadn't been peaceful enough to take down the Norman bailey wall.

Which still showed scars from Cromwell's cannon fire during the English Civil War. Royalist Somerstowe had at last fallen to treachery – a time-honored method if there ever was one, Claire told herself. Cecil Lacey had surrendered his house and its grounds, only to have it restored when Charles II regained the throne in 1660. Five years later Cecil had presided over the trial of Elizabeth Spenser, showing Puritan zeal worthy of Cromwell himself. Phillip Lacey offered a motive for Cecil's actions – Elizabeth had turned down his advances. As Alec had said, every murderer thinks he's justified.

The Lodge had once been the estate's gatehouse. Claire cast a wary glance toward its door, half expecting the most recent Lacey, Richard, to emerge with teeth and claws bared. But the door remained shut. It was five after nine – he was already at the Hall, no doubt glancing at his watch and tapping his foot. Claire hurried through the archway.

A flagstone walk cut across the green lawn. Against the enclosing walls lay banks of flowers. The Hall stretched its Elizabethan chimneys toward the sun. Behind it mammoth oaks and beeches made cascades of green lace against the sky.

The Play was always presented in the forecourt of the Hall, within the enclosing wings of the E-shaped building. Each pane of glass in the vast windows reflected the light at a slightly different angle, making them wink and flash in perception. Claire imagined those windows watching the dramatization as they had once watched the real events, like a sleeper caught in a cycling nightmare.

A calico cat was sitting primly at one end of the columned portico, its head tilted to the side, watching her. The *genius loci,* no doubt — the spirit of the house. Smiling at it, she stepped through the open door and into a still, dim interior scented with old stone, damp wood and potpourri.

"Good of you to join us, Miss Godwin," said the crisp male voice she'd been both expecting and dreading.

Richard was standing before a huge fireplace that gouged one wall of the two-story entrance hall. A group of people was ranged in a semi-circle before him. A bulletin board made an anachronistic note to his right. "I hope you weren't waiting for me," Claire replied.

"Not a bit of it." He turned back to his audience and gestured with a clipboard toward the painted plasterwork crest above the mantelpiece. Its armorial bearings were taller than he was. "The leopard and the stag of the Laceys were unashamedly adopted by the Cranbournes, solid bourgeois industrialists that they were, when they acquired the Hall in 1786. Fortunately the later Laceys didn't have the money, nor the Cranbournes the imagination, to mess the place about. What the Cranbournes did was make a good fist of keeping it watertight, leaving us with a brilliant late Elizabethan house. Come along."

He started off across the black and white tile floor, steps ringing. His flock followed, Claire in the rear. Included in the group of volunteers were half a dozen college students and several elderly people looking for something interesting to do on vacation. And then there were the serious hobbyists like Claire — well, no, she thought, not like me, I have an ulterior motive. Even so, she gazed hungrily upward at the tapestries lining the upper part of the hall. Seventeenth century Brussels, she decided. *Wow.*

"Great tapestries, aren't they?" said a plump young woman. "I'm glad I'm not working on them, though. All those tiny stitches would drive me crazy."

A tapestry was woven, not stitched. Needlepoint stitched on a very fine canvas only looked woven. But Claire wasn't going to play know-it-all. "Actually I find all those tiny stitches very relaxing. Each one is an accomplishment, I guess. I'm Claire Godwin, needleworker."

"Oh, hi! I'm Janet Harlow, painter, detailer, and gold leaf freak."

Janet? An American named Janet was here last year. And this woman's voice definitely had the flat buzz-saw whine of an American accent.

Richard took a hard right onto a staircase and started to climb. Its windows framed the area behind the Hall — topiary shaggy with new growth, weathered statuary, and a walled rose garden at the foot of a green lawn. "The Elizabethan house," Richard said over his shoulder, "is a continuation of the late Gothic and Tudor brick or stone structure, with French and Italian Renaissance triangular pediments and decorative motifs such as the curved Dutch gables. The windows are a defining feature, large, regular, mullioned and transomed. The horizontal proportions and symmetrical façade look toward classicism."

Janet's round rosebud face was fixed on the back of Richard's sweater. "I was here last year. You gotta watch your step — he's a real perfectionist. I bet he'll be sitting pretty with the Trust if he can carry off the restoration of Somerstowe Hall."

"Not restoration," said a young man with the droopy brown eyes and awkward gait of a giraffe. "Remember his lecture on restoration being in the eye of the beholder and doing more harm than good? We're here for, quote, 'conservation, preservation, and maintenance.'"

Janet turned to Claire. "This is Fred Siebold. Mason and gadfly."

"Hello," Claire said to Fred, who was obviously another American. "If anyone needs a gadfly, Richard does. How did it go last year?"

"Fine, until our needleworker went AWOL," Fred answered mournfully. "The police asked around, but this is England, after all. Civilized country. Richard was in a real aristocratic snit. I expected him to get up and give a speech about blood, sweat, toil, and tears. He didn't, though, just put away the tapestries and never said another word about it."

All right, chatty witnesses! But she'd better be honest with them or they'd never trust her. "I was a friend of Melinda, the woman who disappeared. I guess that's more or less why I'm here." Claire tried a casual wave of her hand that didn't seem at all convincing to her, but might have fooled her compatriots.

Fred was a head taller than Janet. Even so they managed to exchange a significant look Claire couldn't interpret. Caution? Or was she reading too much into ordinary puzzlement?

"I thought maybe Melinda left as a joke," said Janet. "She had a weird sense of humor. One time she found a newt in the garden and put it on my lunch plate. There it was, curled up next to the pickled onion."

Fred made a face. "A ploughman's lunch with pickled newt. Sounds like some kind of witch's spell."

"When she and her husband broke up he gave her her luggage and reminded her that the terrace house in Chiswick was his," Claire said. "She moved out all right, but before she left she dialed the time and temperature computer in Tokyo and left the phone switched on. He didn't find it for three days."

Fred and Janet laughed. Claire couldn't manage more than a rueful smile. Melinda loved to gut stuffed shirts, true. And yet the same day she'd moved out of Nigel's house she'd called Claire and cried bitterly at the failure of her marriage.

"To tell you the truth," Janet went on, "we thought Melinda simply got tired of slumming with us artisans. She had so many other projects — the travel articles, the TV shows, the novel. Not that she wasn't nice. A lot of fun. And that smile of hers — you felt it was for you alone, didn't you?"

The staircase rose through the house like Ariadne's thread transformed to stone, tying together block after block of sunlight and the bars of shadow between them. Several doors were ranged around the third story landing. The one Richard pushed open responded with a piercing squeak. "This is the high great chamber. The plaster frieze, the tapestries and needlework, the mantelpiece were all designed to complement and contrast with each other. The Elizabethans loved drama, not subtlety. Their houses were stage sets."

Oh yes, Claire thought with a sigh of delight. The colors had faded, the plasterwork was chipped, and the tapestries — Mortlake, obviously — were threadbare. Still the huge room had a lusty exuberance that suggested Francis Drake had just stepped out to defeat the Armada and would walk back through the door at any moment.

She had to force herself to focus. "I knew Melinda was here researching a novel about the Elizabeth Spenser story — she even got here a week early, just to poke around — but I didn't know she told anyone else about it."

"Oh yeah," Janet said. "She mentioned it to several people, I guess to explain why she was constantly asking questions."

"She was curious as a cat," said Fred. "Nothing got by her."

Claire waited a beat, but he didn't add, *curiosity killed the cat.* "She was a journalist. Questions were her stock in trade." And had Melinda's curiosity bordering on hyper-vigilance rattled a few skeletons in closets? Everyone had skeletons — well, Claire herself didn't . . . Someone sure had a skeleton in his closet now. Literally.

Richard led the way through a withdrawing room and two bedchambers. The rush mats on the floors squeaked faintly beneath the numerous feet, but not as loudly as the floors themselves creaked. One expanse of planks sagged perceptibly. Richard made them walk across it one at a time, explaining that workmen were installing steel jack posts beneath it.

In the next room a false wall was framed a foot in front of the original. "Sometimes there's no other way to install wiring. I once worked at a medieval manor house where we tied a cable round the neck of a ferret and lured it through a conduit by waving a dead rabbit at the far end."

A ripple of amazement greeted that statement. Either Richard knew his stuff, Claire told herself, or he could bullshit for Britain.

His audience well in hand, he guided them down a back staircase and past more bedrooms. Broken-down bedsteads lined the walls. Racks held embroidered and appliqued linen hangings whose dilapidation filled Claire with both anticipation and anxiety. Empty picture frames lay propped in corners, bits of furniture were shoved together and covered with drop cloths, wooden crates were labeled in the same precise hand-writing as Richard's notebooks: "Delftware," "Prints," "Curtain Fittings." In more than one room segments of ornate wood paneling had been peeled away from its lathe and daub backing. A couple of bath-rooms nestled in odd corners, their Victorian porcelain looking obscenely bald.

Richard threw open a double door. "The low great chamber, made into a library by Phillip Lacey in the 1770's, redecorated by the Cranbournes in the 1880's."

Between the tall shelves loaded with books, the room was papered with a William Morris Arts and Crafts print. The blue-green leafy patterns spoke to a more modern taste, making the library seem intimate rather than intimidating. The house as stage set, thought Claire, had gone out of fashion, as perception scaled itself down from theatre to television.

Next door was a chapel. Its walls were partly painted with Biblical scenes, partly sketched in charcoal. "Here's where I'm working," Janet whispered. "We're having to recreate the original pictures — the plaster was too cracked and damp to save."

Down more stairs they went, and along a narrow, twisting hallway. Richard waved at the doors as they passed. "Lumber room, public loos, cellar. That's the butler's pantry where we store the cleaning supplies, paints, and so on. Don't go messing about in there, some of the chemicals are right dangerous. And here's the kitchen."

A long vaulted stone chamber was lined with cabinets and cooking implements. At least Claire assumed they were cooking implements. The brass pots and pans and assorted dishes she could identify, but some of the more arcane items might just as well have belonged to an Inquisition torturer. A set of relatively modern appliances was grouped along one wall, behind a trestle table as long as a bowling lane.

Richard was thoroughly warmed up. His eyes shone and his face glowed like those of a worshipper in a medieval religious painting. "The plaster decorations, the marble mantelpieces, the wooden paneling, the diamond panes of glass in the windows were made for the play of candlelight and shadow. Imagine how Somerstowe Hall once looked, glass glittering, shadows dancing, the 'lightsome, airy, and spiritous' rooms filled with lute music and the laughter of folk wearing velvets and brocades. The house is a time machine."

Under her breath Claire muttered to Fred and Janet, "Imagine how the rooms smelled. No one took baths in those days, you can't wash velvet and brocade, and the flush toilet wasn't even a gleam in Thomas Crapper's eye. No wonder the inventories are full of perfuming pans and pomander cases."

They grinned. A couple of other people looked around. Richard opened another door and waved the group out onto the forecourt. He must have a tiger's ears as well as eyes, Claire told herself. He'd heard what she said. As she passed him he fixed her with a long look, one brow arched, a corner of his mouth tucked, stifling a laugh.

With a wry smile and a shrug — so he had a sense of humor after all — she swept past him.

"Mr. Lacey," called one of the older women. "How thrilling it must be for you to come back to your ancestral home. No wonder you love it so."

Richard's face went blank. "Ah yes — just that, Mrs. Zielinski. On around to the back, please. Mind the scaffolding."

Mrs. Zielinski looked puzzled. Fred and Janet rolled their eyes indulgently. Claire suppressed a smile. Richard did love the old house. But it wasn't the done thing to admit to passion, was it? Cool was in.

The sunlight was warm after the chill inside. Bits of ancient mortar littered the mud and gravel at the back of the house. Pulling a pen from his clipboard and pointing to the interstices between building stones, Richard launched into an explanation of rising damp and weatherproofing. The masonry was being repointed with mortar made to his own recipe of lime, sand, and cement, copying the compound originally used. "Portland cement not being compatible with an early house like this one," he concluded.

Claire suspected that the silence of his audience was less respect for his knowledge than bewilderment at his topic.

"Remember," Richard went on. "The main principle of conservation is the retention of as much of the original historic fabric as possible, with the least amount of intervention."

A respectful murmur answered him, although no one actually raised their right hands and swore.

"One last thing. Only a few doors inside the house have locks, the door to the cellars in particular. That's for good cause. The house was built atop the Norman dungeons, which were later expanded into a series of grottoes. The caves are none too stable today. And since there's a gate to the outside, bats roost there during the day. The Trust require that the volunteers stay in the main house."

He'd glided over that one very nicely, thought Claire. The grottoes had been built in the 1750's by Phillip Lacey in imitation of his friend Francis Dashwood's caverns in West Wycombe. Dashwood and his gentlemen friends — only aristocrats needed apply — amused themselves staging rites he called occult, but which were really excuses for orgies. They weren't so picky about the social status of their female "guests." No wonder Phillip had died broke, so that his heirs had to sell the Hall.

What intrigued Claire was how this same cynical wastrel Phillip had managed to write the rational and yet sentimental "An Historie of the Apocalypse as Visit'd upon Summerstow." Although if Cecil Lacey could change his philosophical colors in only a few years, she told herself, then why not his descendent Phillip? Whether their descendent Richard had inherited a tendency to multiple personalities she couldn't say. Not yet, anyway.

He glanced at his watch, lifted his clipboard, and tore off a couple of lists. "Very good, then. Fred and Janet, you were here last year, would you be kind enough to show everyone to his place?"

Obligingly Janet and Fred sorted the group by ability and enthusiasm, from carpenters, joiners, and glaziers to gardeners and masons to those people who were simply muscle power, put to work sweeping and scrubbing.

Everyone filed away. Claire stood her ground, watching Richard as he jotted down a few notes. If he hid any other secrets as poorly as he hid his love for Somerstowe Hall, even her meager detecting abilities should figure out why he'd turned on her when she said Melinda's name.

He looked up. They locked eyes, exchanging — what? Speculation? Challenge? She blinked. "Ah, they went on without me."

"You'll be working upstairs," he replied, without commenting on her inability to play follow the leader. "Come along."

He steered her into the back door of the entrance hall, up the stone staircase, and into the gallery, a room several times as long as it was wide. The first time through, Richard had commented on how the long gallery was peculiar to England, a place to take one's exercise in the rain and cold. Today though, the room was sunny. The paneling glowed like silk and the elaborate mantelpiece over the empty fireplace was a riot of the light and shadow Richard had spoken of so feelingly.

He indicated a tapestry frame and a chair next to a window. "You can have a go at one of the new canvases, see how you get on."

"So I can establish my credentials?" Claire asked.

"Yes."

Well, give him one point for honesty. Claire bent over the frame. A new canvas? This is a William Morris 'Strawberry Thief' pattern, at least a hundred years old. It matches the wallpaper in the library."

"It's the newest we have. Some Cranbourne showed a bit of imagination by supporting the Arts and Crafts movement. Rather uncharacteristic of the family temperament. Unless it was Vincent, the black sheep."

Claire sat down next to the frame and checked out the supplies arranged on the broad, whitewashed windowsill. Numerous colors of tapestry wool — Paterna Persian, good — crewel wool and embroidery cotton for detail, blunt-end needles in a pincushion, a box of straight pins, a tape measure, and a graph and pencil so she could record what she'd done and where. Had Melinda left everything this tidy last year? Or was it Richard who'd sorted all the yarns by color and smoothed them into tidy rows? What she asked him was, "Did you know any of the Cranbournes?"

"I met Maud, the last of her generation, a time or two before she died. My father did some research for . . ." Something caught Richard's eye. He reached into the pocket of his jeans, extracted a penknife, climbed onto a paint-spattered step stool and probed the decorative end of a ceiling beam.

So exquisite was his touch, so intense his expression — eyes narrowed, teeth sunk into his lower lip — that his long, slender hands might just as well have been exploring a woman's body.

The pit of Claire's stomach went hot with the image. Quickly she looked down at the faded but still saucy colors of the canvas, telling her hormones, yes, cool is in.

"Just a wee bit of dry rot. Mercuric oxide in methyl alcohol, that'll set you to rights." Richard stepped down, replaced the knife in his pocket, and made a note on his clipboard. "I'll leave you to it, then. Don't forget the chart." And he was gone, the rush matting creaking faintly behind him.

Exhaling, Claire bent over the canvas. Even though it smelled of mothballs, moths had still snacked on it, leaving quite a few frayed places. Half a dozen spots had already been mended, efficiently if not expertly. Melinda, no doubt, who regarded only finished work as an accomplishment. With a wistful smile, Claire picked up a length of red yarn. Thank goodness she hadn't been handed too difficult an assignment her first day on the job. She already had a difficult assignment.

She matched the yarn to a sewn strawberry and threaded a needle. Carefully she caught the frayed end of the broken yarn and secured both it and the end of the fresh yarn with her first stitch.

Seated next to the window Claire was no longer chilly. The musty odor of the lower stories was here more a faint scent of dust and dried rush. If she listened carefully she could hear a distant voice or the clink of trowel upon stone. But the sounds were filtered through the thick walls of the house. Filtered through time, as though from the corner of her eye she might see Elizabeth Tudor herself standing in the doorway.

Someone was standing in the doorway. Claire's shoulders prickled. Melinda had said something about a ghost — that was just one of her jokes, though . . . She looked sharply around.

A body as lean as the leopard in the Lacey crest, clothed in RAF blue, armed with a clipboard, disappeared from the door almost before she saw it. Richard hadn't been simply walking by. He'd been standing there watching her, even his hair on the alert. She could still feel his heat of his eyes searing her back.

Leopards, tigers they were predators, not prey, she reminded herself. Anyone who went hunting a tiger had better be damn sure she wanted to catch him.

Right now Claire wasn't sure of anything, except that she wasn't leaving Somerstowe without finding Melinda. Setting her jaw, she scooted the tapestry frame and the chair around so that her back was to the window, and continued stitching with yarn as red as blood.

Chapter Four

*F*rom the corner of her eye Claire watched the sunlight change from a clear gold tinted with green to a hazy white. When at last the cry of "lunch break!" echoed from the depths of the house she stood, stretched, and cleared her throat of the part-smell, part-taste, of mothballs.

Outside the mirror-like morning sky was now fogged blue-gray with humidity, as though the sun had breathed on it. Claire unlatched the window and swung it open. Only the faintest breath of moist air, heavy with the scents of grass, roses, and mud, entered the house. About time for a storm to clear the air, she thought.

Three times that morning her neck had puckered and her shoulder blades twitched, sensing a very physical presence in the doorway. So Richard was a control freak. If he wanted to check up on her work he could come into the room and look, already. But no. He was watching Claire just as surely as she was watching him.

Maybe he thought Melinda was guilty of dereliction of duty. Fine. Claire wasn't guilty by association. And if he'd harmed Melinda, or even sent her the threatening letter, wouldn't he be trying to deflect suspicion, not attract it by skulking around? He knew why Claire was here . . . Yeah. He knew why she was here.

She stabbed her needles into the pincushion, shut the window, and headed downstairs. The silence in the house was so deep that the sound of footsteps in the entrance hall echoed up the staircase.

She rounded the corner. There was Richard. He stopped dead on the expanse of checkerboard tile, hunched over as though someone had hit him in the stomach, and cupped his hands before his face. "Damn!" he said, softly but distinctly, and peered down at the floor.

Oh. "Lose a contact?" Claire asked.

Richard leaped straight up and spun around like Baryshnikov. He glared at Claire standing on the bottom step. Of course he'd glare at her for startling him, not be embarrassed for being startled. His eye glittered just as tigerishly whether he had a contact lens in it or not.

"Sorry," she said. "Can I help you look for it?"

"No thank you," Richard returned. "It's disposable. I'll fetch another."

"Okay." She looked at him. He looked at her. "I tried to wear contacts once. My eyes are too sensitive."

"Are they?"

"I hear the disposable ones are easier to wear, but I guess I'm set in my ways. Wearing glasses and everything."

"Old habits die hard."

His voice was dry, his manner distant. At least he was polite. Maybe it was time for entente. She went on, "I guess everyone except us has already gone to lunch."

"You can catch them up at the pub or the tearoom, like as not. If you'll excuse me?" With a slight inclination of his head, almost a formal bow, Richard made an about-face and walked off toward the door.

Not that she was all that anxious to have lunch with him, Claire told herself, it was just that he was a witness. He was intelligent. He was dedicated. He filled out a pair of jeans very nicely. And he was hiding something, maybe something about Melinda.

Frowning, she turned and saw the cat again. It was sitting on the hearth of the huge fireplace, washing its face with a paw. "Kitty, kitty?" Claire called.

No, even he — she? — wasn't feeling communicative, but whisked away into the shadows. Wondering if she should change her deodorant, Claire walked out into the glare of noon. After a quick reconnaissance she discovered a narrow gateway in the surrounding wall that opened onto a row of back gardens in the village. Good — she could get in and out of the Hall without going past the Lodge. She zigged around a line of washing, zagged down an alley, and emerged on the high street.

Claire didn't have time to go looking for Alec and news about the threatening letter. Instead she bought a sandwich and a newspaper from Roshan and took them up to her flat. She sternly told herself she didn't have time to look through any of Melinda's letters, either, on the chance that a casual word or two might take on new meaning now that she'd seen the Hall.

The bottom line was that someone had wanted Melinda out of the way. *She was constantly asking questions. Nothing got by her.* And her computer and camera had disappeared with her. "Did you find out something you weren't supposed to know?" Claire asked the letters. They didn't answer.

She ate and scanned the newspaper. A speech by the Prime Minister. A train derailment. A Muslim policeman suing the Derbyshire Constabulary for discrimination. A photo of the Chief Constable showed an older man whose tucked-in chin and clipped moustache had been time-warped in from World War Two. Claire wondered if he carried a swagger stick, and how a contemporary cop like the shopworn Blake felt about working for him.

When she headed back to the Hall she met Fred and Janet next to a bedraggled flowerbed just inside the postern gate. His clothes were bedaubed with mortar, hers with paint. "Sorry we missed you," Janet said.

"I'll catch up with you tomorrow," replied Claire.

Fred eyed the flowers and their companion weeds as though contemplating metaphors of beauty and sin, and returned to his work. Janet went back to the chapel. Claire greeted a couple of other workers on her way upstairs. In the gallery nothing moved but dust motes.

The air was as deep and still as a warm pool. She opened the window, admitting a bumblebee that buzzed up and down the sill like a drinker uncertain of his way home from the pub. Smiling, Claire reached for a length of green yarn.

By the time she'd mended several leaves she was mesmerized by her repetitive stitching and by the buzzing of the bee. Only the occasional voice from outside or downstairs jogged her brain out of a timeless, spaceless, fugue state. Until the hair rose on the back of her neck.

In spite of the warm day, she felt a distinct chill. Every nerve suddenly alert, she glanced toward the far doorway. Nothing. Or was it nothing? She might be seeing a reflection of the sunlight through the windows of the high great chamber next door, a sinuous shimmer in the air. And yet she could swear the shimmer had a shape. Long skirts and puffed sleeves sketched themselves in light upon nothingness. A faint rustle of cloth tickled her ears as the shape moved in utter silence down the room toward the far door. She caught a whiff of some kind of pomander, a floral fragrance much lighter than the scents of earth and mothballs. Her hands, her head, her body felt like dry ice, steaming into the afternoon warmth.

She blinked. Nothing was there. *Oh wow.* Melinda had mentioned a ghost. She hadn't been joking or trying out some plot twist for her book. There was something there. Someone. Elizabeth Spenser?

Steady footsteps came from behind her. Claire spun around. Alec came pacing down the gallery as calmly as he'd pace down the sidewalk outside. "Oh, well then," he said, as though it was seeing Claire that was startling. "How're you getting on?"

Did you see that? she wanted to ask. He must've just missed it. "Ah — er — fine, thanks."

He walked on by and disappeared out the far door. More footsteps rang across the high great chamber. Richard walked briskly through the door. He halted at her elbow and started inspecting the needlework canvas.

Claire forced herself to take a stitch and then another. Warmth rushed into her face and hands. *So,* she imagined saying, *tell me about the ghost.* But that was one question she wasn't sure she wanted answered. She'd almost dozed off, yes. She hadn't dreamed that unworldly presence. Apparently Melinda hadn't dreamed it up, either.

She cleared her throat. "Alec walked by here a minute ago. I guess the house is on his beat."

"He grew up here in Somerstowe, knows the Hall better than just about anyone, I should think." Richard stroked the new stitches with a long and no doubt very sensitive forefinger.

Claire caught herself leaning toward him, pulled by some subtle gravity, and inched away. Pheromones, she assured herself. A simple scientific phenomenon. And it wasn't as though she was on the rebound or anything.

"That's fiddly work," Richard said, "Not everyone has the patience to do it well."

"Did Melinda have the patience?"

"Not especially, no. But then she was after bigger and better things, wasn't she, with the book and all?"

"I taught Melinda how to do needlework. There was nothing she wouldn't try. She had a voracious appetite — figuratively speaking," Claire added. "For education, for experience. For living. That's why she wanted to try her hand at a novel."

Richard's gravitational field seemed to fluctuate, as though disturbed by a passing moon. "Your work is much finer than Melinda's," he said, and was gone before Claire could look up at his expression.

She sat, needle aloft, yarn dangling, staring after him. So was the compliment his way of making nice or was he simply trying to lull her suspicions? She turned the canvas on its frame so she could see its underside and sewed the end of her thread through the stitches.

Richard meant "finer" in the sense of smaller and more delicate. The ends of Melinda's stitches were rammed through the tightly woven threads on the back of the canvas in typical damn-the-torpedoes fashion. With a shake of her head, Claire untangled one or two of the knots.

The bee was still bumbling around the windowsill. She got up and with a length of yarn brushed it through the window into the air. It made an indignant loop-the-loop, then winged away. Below the window stood Richard and Fred, arms folded. Fred was eyeing Richard as though the architect was a headsman sharpening his axe. Richard was eyeing the wall. From the row of tools on the ground he chose one that looked like a thin spoon. With it he smoothed the fresh mortar packed between the stones. Then he gave the tool to Fred and watched as he repeated the motion.

Claire pulled her head back into the room. Richard was an artist, no doubt about it, unkempt house and all. But when it came to the Hall he was a martinet with his swagger stick. It was a matter of priorities, wasn't it?

So, then, where had Melinda come in his priorities? Claire couldn't see them as lovers. Melinda dealt in broad pictures and bottom lines. Richard had a keen eye for subtlety and detail. He probably had a girlfriend, too, even though she'd have to be something to compete with the Hall. Melinda was something, yes, but while she'd have wanted attention, physical and otherwise, she wouldn't have demanded a commitment.

Claire threaded her needle with gold yarn and began filling in the frayed decorative border at the edge of the canvas. She kept her back to the window and glanced from doorway to doorway more than once. But not even the bee returned to interrupt her reveries of plot, motive, and character. The one time she saw a movement in the doorway it was the calico cat, which considered her gravely for a few moments and then went on its way.

At quitting time she closed and locked the window, stowed her supplies, and turned the face of the canvas away from the sun. Several other volunteers walked her out this time. She did not see Richard.

Every window in the high street displayed a poster advertising The Play. PERFORMANCES AT EIGHT P.M., JUNE 20 AND 21 — ten days away. A red Jaguar was parked half on, half off the curb in front of the shop. Through the window Claire saw Elliot Moncrief buying a newspaper from Trillian Nair. His sweater was loosely draped over the shoulders of a polo shirt as though he was on his way to a tennis court, unlikely as Somerstowe was to have one.

Weighing tea and scones against beer, Claire ducked into her flat to tidy up and then headed across to the Druid's Circle. Perfect timing, she thought when she saw Alec coming up the street.

He was dressed in a rugby shirt and khaki pants, off duty. "It'll rain within the hour," he said with a glance at the increasingly cloudy sky. Opening the door of the pub for Claire, he added, "I recommend the local ale. And Diana makes a cracking shepherd's pie, if you've an appetite."

"I wasn't exactly doing hard physical labor," Claire answered, "but yes, I have an appetite, and I sure didn't come all this way to drink Coors Light."

From the gloom her eyes resolved a low beamed ceiling, a fireplace complete with electric fire, floral wallpaper hung with faded landscapes, and a bar backed by a kaleidoscope of beer advertisements. Above it hung a television tuned to a talk show. A public telephone occupied the far end. A slot machine sparkled and chimed in a short hallway to one side. Beyond it a stairway overflowed with the largest German Shepherd Claire had ever seen. His huge brown eyes gazed benignly, almost sadly, down at her, as though she wasn't a big enough mouthful to make it worth his effort to bite her.

Behind the bar a stood a middle-aged man, his belly protruding coyly over his belt, his scalp peeking through his graying hair. His craggy features — those that were visible above his bristling beard — and shoe-button black eyes made Claire think of Rumpelstiltskin.

"Claire, this is Rob Jackman," Alec said.

"Hullo," said Rob, striking a note between bored and belligerent.

"Nice to meet you," Claire said. "I'd like some ale, please."

Rob recited, "Marston Mercian Mild, Owd Rodger, Winkle Ivanhoe, Sheffield Best Bitter."

Envisioning dusty casks filled by elves, Claire looked up at Alec. "What do you suggest?"

"Two Marstons and two shepherd's pies," he ordered.

Wordlessly Rob put down the glass he was polishing and disappeared through a swinging door.

Alec and Claire sat down at a table in the corner. Except for the obligatory horse brasses by the fireplace, Claire noted, the Jackmans had resisted tarting their pub up for the tourist trade. Being the only pub in town must cut down on competitive expenses. A couple of elderly men sat at other tables, but so far the place hardly resembled happy hour at Chili's.

"The name 'Druid's Circle,'" said Alec, "comes from the ancient stone circle just beyond the Hall. People used to believe the Druids went about building stone circles, when in reality the circles were built by Neolithic tribes long before the Druids arrived."

"The Druids being the priests of the Celtic tribes who were here at the time of the Romans," concluded Claire. "Not that they couldn't have used the circles for ceremonies."

"Oh, I should imagine the circles were used for centuries, by many different people." Alec's gleaming smile rewarded Claire either for her knowledge or for her not playing dumb-female games.

As much as Claire enjoyed academic discussions, this was not the time for one. "What did Blake say about the letter?" she asked.

Alec shrugged. "He rang me at half past three, said he'd give the forensic chaps a go at it, and asked me to have a shufti beneath your carpet. Sarita let me in, hope you don't mind. All I found was dust."

Even Sarita wouldn't clean beneath a carpet any more often than necessary. Claire kicked herself for not noticing someone had been in her room. "That's all? Blake's not going to re-open the case?" she asked, lowering her voice as though keeping Melinda's murder a secret would cancel it out.

"He didn't say."

Rob appeared at Claire's elbow and plunked down two heavy mugs brimming with dark liquid and froth. The door opened, admitting a thick ray of sunlight and several more customers. From the room behind the bar shouted a female voice, "Rob! Get a move on!"

The publican stamped away, the floor protesting beneath his feet. "Think you can order me about, eh? And where were you yesterday afternoon when I was after chopping the fruit and veg?"

Funny how fast relationships can go downhill, Claire told herself. She lifted her mug and drank. The ale was cool on her tongue, filling her nose and throat with summer fields, autumn smoke, and the bite of winter. What was that verse of Tolkien's, something about cold water being all well and good, "but beer is best when drink we lack." Appropriate — Alec reminded her of a giant economy-sized hobbit.

When he put down his mug it was half-empty. He wiped a bit of froth from his upper lip. That lip then compressed itself against the lower, showing proper concern for the situation. "It's right embarrassing. Here you are, come all the way from America to look for her, and I let her go missing."

"You had no idea she was in danger, did you? She didn't know."

"So it seems," he conceded.

"I'm sure you investigated thoroughly." Claire tried to make that a statement. It came out more like the question it was.

"The last performance of The Play was on the Saturday. No one saw Melinda after the cast party in the entrance hall — and it took a fair bit of questioning to settle that. Blake or one of his lads or I talked to everyone in town and quite a few of the day trippers who came for The Play."

"When did you realize she was missing?"

"Monday morning. I was walking about the Hall and Richard told me she hadn't come to work." Alec grimaced. "I know — someone should have missed her before then, but she usually spent the weekends away."

"With some man or another?" Claire couldn't help asking.

Alec raised his glass, drank until it was empty, then gazed into it as though the foam scraps on its sides were prophetic tealeaves. "Maybe. I saw her myself a time or two — mind you, for nothing more than a few laughs. When I realized she'd gone missing I rang Blake. His lads found her car by the reservoir. That's all I know, little as it is."

His hazel eyes were clear and guileless. No, Claire thought, she shouldn't expect Alec to have been immune to Melinda's beauty. Neither should she take him off her list of suspects, pleasant though it was sitting next to him . . . Rebound, she reminded herself.

The delectable odor of beef stew filled the air, warring with an aroma of perfume and hair spray. A woman set two casserole dishes capped with browned mashed potatoes onto the table. Tomato and cress salads and thick slices of bread edged the plates beneath. She nudged Alec's elbow with her hip. "Hullo, Constable. In mufti tonight, I see."

With great presence of mind, Alec lifted his eyes from the low-cut blouse right in front of his nose. "Diana, this is Claire Godwin. Claire, Diana Jackman."

"Hullo," Diana said, with an up and down appraisal that counted every freckle and measured each curve. She folded her arms beneath her impressively cantilevered breasts. "You're the needleworker, then. Melinda's pal. Sarita told me you were letting her flat."

"Yes, that's me. Nice to meet you." Claire craned her neck to look Diana in the face. So this was the woman who'd played Elizabeth Spenser before Melinda came along. Melinda might have been ten years older than the nineteen-year-old Elizabeth, but Diana was twenty years older, and those years were gaining on her. Although growing older gracefully was not a concept she seemed to place much faith in.

Her hair was permed into an anxious blond frizz. She wore as much eye make-up and lipstick as a Kabuki dancer. That the cosmetics, like her tight blouse and pants, only emphasized her middle age seemed not to have occurred to her. Wishful thinking at its best, Claire thought. Not that it was any business of hers what face Diana chose to present to the world.

"I've mended a few tapestries meself over the years," Diana said. "Went to work for old Miss Cranbourne when I first came here to Somerstowe, before Rob and me opened up the pub. She said I did the finest work she'd ever seen, including Elizabeth Spenser's. Have you met the Hall ghosts yet?"

Claire's brain lost traction for a second. "Ghosts? Plural ghosts?"

"Proper ghosts they are, and no mistake. Sometimes just a bit of light in the air, sometimes solid as this table. Elizabeth Spenser and her cat. Her familiar. Little calico beggar."

"Her cat?" *Come on*. But why should the ghost of a cat be any more unbelievable than the ghost of a human being? And Claire knew darn well she'd seen both the solid cat and the shimmering woman, even if she wasn't quite ready to admit either was an actual ghost. "You aren't pulling a tourist's leg, are you?"

Diana laughed. "You've seen them, haven't you? I can smell the fear on you."

"Not fear, exactly. Just — surprise. I mean, if the Hall didn't have a ghost then some supernatural registry agency is missing a bet."

"There's nothing to be frightened of," Alec said. "Old places like Somerstowe Hall have ghost stories because the human mind senses the emotions that are trapped there. And there were enough emotions during Elizabeth's day to provide stories for a dozen houses. The question is whether the ghost is simply a — well, a psychic video playing inside your head, or whether it's an actual external presence."

"Whether the ghosts can see you back again, he means. I think they can, they've come on more substantial recently."

Alec picked up his fork. "No surprise there, with folk in and out of the Hall all day long. Stirred them up a bit, I expect."

Okay, Claire told herself, everyone believes in ghosts here. Until she got a better explanation — joke, illusion, whatever — she was just about ready to believe in them herself.

"Elizabeth did needlework for that bitch Lettice Lacey," Diana went on. "Learned from her grandmother, who worked for Bess of Hardwick. Now there's a woman. Money, class, the lot."

"I always liked her," Claire returned. "Married and buried four husbands, getting richer each time. She built gorgeous houses and even meddled in politics. Queen Elizabeth gave her and one of her husbands the job of keeping Mary, Queen of Scots, under house arrest. Legend has Bess and Mary sitting together over their needlework, probably saying nasty things about the bloody-mindedness of men."

"Well, then, you're quite the scholar, aren't you?" said Diana.

Oops, Claire thought. She'd been playing the know-it-all. There had to be some way of splitting the difference between dumb and overbearing.

The door opened and several more people came in, including Richard. Rob started rapping glasses onto the bar and glared daggers at Diana.

"Enjoy," she said to Alec and Claire. Tossing her head, she thrust her bosom out like the figurehead of a ship and turned to the table where three of the newcomers were sitting down. They greeted her with several raunchy comments. She upped the ante with some of her own and took their orders.

Richard ordered a bitter from Rob. As he walked by Claire and Alec's table he offered them a reasonably affable nod.

Claire smiled warily back. Alec said, "Sit down, Richard. Have a natter."

"Thanks, but I've some letters that need seeing to just now." He found a chair by the fireplace and pulled several envelopes from his pocket.

You know, Claire thought toward him, *if I was the suspicious type I'd think you were avoiding me.* She turned to her plate and started forking up the meat and potatoes. The pie could have used more pepper, but the vegetables were nice and fresh. She waited until Alec was mopping up the last of the gravy with his bread before prodding him into conversation again. While the ghost stories were fascinating — would she have some good tales to tell in the faculty lounge! — right now Melinda was more important. "So you talked to a lot of people about Melinda's disappearance. You didn't know it was a murder then, so I guess your procedures were different."

"We're still not positive it's a murder," he warned. "The first rule in any case is to talk to the people closest to the victim. So we talked to the Nairs, the volunteers at the Hall, the cast and crew of the play. Blake even sent his sergeant to London to interview her ex-husband. No one admitted to anything."

Someone who wasn't a cop, Claire reflected, would have said no one knew anything. "So you have records of everyone's alibi, then."

Alec shook his head. "We need a time of death to establish alibis. We need a cause of death to search for weapons. We need a motive before we can consider suspects. We don't have any of those."

"No. You don't. A body would help, wouldn't it?"

"Oh yes, it would indeed. Although after all this time. . . ." He let the sentence evaporate, like Elizabeth's ghost had evaporated this afternoon.

Not just anyone's body, but Melinda's. Melinda's physical shell, ripped untimely away from her humor, her intelligence, her spirit. Was her ghost, too, wandering around the Hall? Claire hoped not. If anyone deserved to rest, it was Melinda.

Suddenly Richard's chair crashed back against the wall. He stood up. His scowl of rage and resentment hit Claire, and only Claire, like the slap of dueling gloves. His hand crushed the envelope he was holding, one with a big red and yellow commemorative stamp.

Claire felt her eyebrows and mouth constrict from bewilderment into a frown. *What the hell is it now?*

The spigots for dispensing beer and ale peeked over the counter like a row of spectators. Rob counted change into the cash register, each chink of coin against coin ringing loudly. Diana leaned forward, every glass on her tray quivering with eagerness.

Richard wasn't about to oblige anyone with explanations. His expression slammed itself shut and barred its door. Cramming the letters back into his pocket, he stalked out of the room without looking again at Claire, even though she turned around in her chair to watch him leave.

The door slammed. One of the customers said, "Didn't know the pub did cabaret, Diana."

Pursing her lips, Diana sashayed over to the table of customers and distributed the glasses. "Our Mr. Lacey's always been something of a nutter, him and his old house."

Alec looked more worried than puzzled. He stood up. "I'll have a quick word with him, see what he was on about. Half a tick."

"He's not so keen on American lasses, is he?" Diana went on. "That one last year, they didn't half have a row at the cast party, did they? And now this one's got up his nose as well."

Alec walked away. Her chair, Claire decided, was the most uncomfortable piece of furniture she'd ever been associated with. She, too, stood up. *American lasses.* Melinda's year-old threatening letter. Richard flipping out while he was reading a letter. If anger was all he'd been feeling. Claire could have sworn that his resentful glare had something in it of a cornered animal. Or was that wishful thinking on her part?

He'd had a fight with Melinda at the cast party. The last place she'd been seen alive. So much for entente. So much for lulling her suspicions.

She picked up her billfold, thanked Diana, and walked up to Rob and the cash register. Every eye in the place watched her pay the bill and leave.

Chapter Five

*C*laire emerged from the pub to discover the evening had dimmed. Clouds filled the sky and the breeze smelled of rain, just as Alec had predicted.

The bobby was standing with his hands folded behind his back, gazing down the street. Elliot leaned against the hood of his Jaguar, looking curiously past two volunteers of the young and female variety who were either admiring him or his car. Richard was nowhere to be seen.

"Here," Alec asked, "you didn't pay for the food, did you?"

"Sure," replied Claire. "No problem."

He reached into his pocket and thrust several pound coins at her. She batted his hand away. The coins fell jangling onto the sidewalk. Alec scooped them up and stuffed them into the pocket of Claire's windbreaker. "There you are. When the new pound coins came out my cousin, a wee lad, thought they were sweeties. We caught him nibbling at them, trying to take off the gold paper and get at the chocolate inside. My mum washed his mouth out with nettle tea."

Claire smiled. "Next time the food's on me. We can skip the nettle tea."

"If it's Richard you're wanting," called Elliot, "he set out toward the church at a rattling good pace. Shall I put on my boots and spurs and form a posse?"

"Thank you, Elliot," Alec returned equably. "No need." His hand in the small of Claire's back urged her down the street like a sail a sailboat.

She glanced back to see Elliot looking after them, hands braced on his hips, head tilted to the side, expression less puzzled than calculating. The polo shirt showed his chest and shoulders to be broader than they'd looked in his Italian-cut suit. Claire knew she was going to have to talk to him eventually. But one suspect at a time.

"Did you get the impression," she asked Alec, "that Richard was upset over one of those letters he was reading?"

"I did do, yes. Not like him to get the wind up."

She'd take Alec's word for Richard's usual barometric pressure. To her he was like a fall day in Texas — warm and sunny enough for a light sweater in the morning, a navy-blue sky spitting sleet by five. "How did he get along with Melinda? Before the argument at the cast party, that is."

"They were at sixes and sevens a bit," Alec replied. "He noticed her — who wouldn't? He'd just broken off a relationship with a woman in London, though, and I doubt he was ready to tangle himself up again."

Claire wanted to ask, *don't you have a relationship with someone?* She said, "Melinda wouldn't have wanted him to tangle himself up."

"No, I daresay she wouldn't have done," said Alec, with a reminiscent half smile which raised Claire's brows. "She wound him up good and proper, but then she wound us all up. Even so, it was Richard who was a bit shirty with her."

"She teased him," translated Claire, "and he was irritated. No surprise there."

"When she disappeared he was just as baffled as the rest of us."

Was he? Innocent until proven guilty, Claire reminded herself.

They turned a corner and walked down a street so narrow the sidewalk took a third of its width. Where the street made an acute angle to the right a large mirror was mounted on the building opposite, so the hapless motorist could see how much competition he had for the corner. "Let me guess," said Claire. "This used to be a medieval gutter."

"That it was."

Dodging three children on skateboards, Alec and Claire stepped out onto a wide grassy area. Ahead rose the church, its spire reaching heavenward like a hymn in stone. To its left was a grove of trees, foliage rustling in the cool breeze. The well below them was capped by a tangle of Victorian metalwork. Judging by its weathered and chipped stone, its base was considerably older. Next to it was a painting propped on an easel and surrounded by several camera-toting tourists.

Claire squinted. No, it wasn't a painting. It was a picture formed of leaves, petals, moss, berries and beans, outlined by dark twigs and strips of bark. She turned toward it.

"It's the well-dressing," Alec explained. "The custom probably goes back to ancient Celtic ceremonies of blessing the wells and is peculiar to Derbyshire. One picks out the pattern in damp clay and fills it in with flowers, seeds — the first fruits tradition goes back a long way. Supposedly the custom died out in the Middle Ages, then was revived with a Christian theme during the seventeenth century."

"Between the Civil War and the plague in the seventeenth century," Claire said, "I would've wanted all the help I could get."   .

"Even though the well's capped now, we still do up the picture. Elliot wanted to adjust the date to coincide with The Play, but Rob pointed out by spacing the events two weeks apart we get the tourists twice, and twice the quid."

"Commerce meets tradition?"

"Uneasy bedfellows, I expect."

Claire looked up at him. "Alec, when you were searching for Melinda, did you check the well?"

"Yes, we had the lid up and poked about. Got a right pile of muck and a fair number of coins we put in the collection box at the church."

"Oh. Okay." The picture showed an old man greeting a ragged youth. Tiny botanical bits provided amazing detail, the folds of the men's garments waving in the breeze, the dark eyes of the calf in the background rolling piteously. "The return of the prodigal son," said Claire. "I always felt kind of sorry for the fatted calf."

"A guiltless victim," Alec agreed. "Like Elizabeth Spenser."

"Is this the well she was accused of poisoning?"

"Yes. And the gibbet was just there. Grass won't grow on the site."

Claire followed his gesture and saw a cement post emerging from a patch of bare ground. "Superstition? Or the feet of tourists?"

"Evidence that Elizabeth was innocent. Just as the many thousands — tens of thousands — of witches done horribly to death across Europe were innocent." Alec's face went hard as the stone coping of the well, mouth thin, jaw set. "They murdered her cat, too. Said it was her familiar."

"Now that's sadistic," said Claire. "Although why killing a cat would be any worse than killing a young woman . . ." So this was where Elizabeth died, the victim of a judicial murder. And yet if her ghost walked, it walked at Somerstowe Hall, where she'd stitched away the long summer afternoons, foolish bumblebees and the scent of roses wafting in the window. "She's haunting the Hall? And the cat? It's a ghost, too?"

"I know it looks like a real cat, but many's the time I've seen it vanish into thin air. Whereas Elizabeth . . ." His face softened. "She has more complex emotions than the cat, I reckon. Her image is not always distinct. She's sad and lonely, not frightening."

"No, not frightening. Just — unusual. And cool, too. I mean, I can suspend my disbelief. The ghosts are probably appearing to me anyway because I'm such a soft touch for ghost stories. They wouldn't be so quick to appear to Melinda. She'd laugh . . ." Claire looked sharply up at Alec. "Is that what she teased you about? Your believing in the ghosts?"

"In a way." Alec cleared his throat. "Well then. The first church was built here in 732 or thereabouts. This one is late Gothic. It's had its modifications over the years, of course. Richard calls it a 'slow growth' church. Ah, there's Trevor. Hello!"

An elderly man in a black coat and dog collar was just stepping out of the wide western doorway of the church. He looked up at Alec's call and waved vigorously.

That was a quick change of subject, Claire thought. So Richard wasn't the only one who had a bone to pick with Melinda. She filed those factoids away and turned to the church.

The churchyard was surrounded by a stone wall. Its base was overgrown by white and pink blooms that might have been either wildflowers or weeds. Its gate was a wooden one, below a shingled roof supported on four posts. One of the tourists started adjusting a camera on a tripod, determined to capture the charming scene.

"This is a lych gate," said Alec, opening it for and closing it behind Claire. "Or a resurrection gate. Where the pallbearers would rest the coffin and wait for the vicar to arrive."

The vicar came bustling up to them. "Hello, you must be one of the new volunteers."

"Claire Godwin."

"Oh yes, yes, of course. Melinda's friend. I'm Trevor Digby." His handshake was light and dry. His smiling face was creased like fine parchment and his pale blue eyes danced behind his glasses like angels dancing on heads of pins. His fine white hair made a perfect halo around his head, his bald spot as tidy as a monk's tonsure.

"I'm very pleased to meet you," Claire told him, and she was, having always had a soft spot for the otherworldly — clerics, scholars, artists — and village bobbies with ghosts on their beats. "Alec was just starting to tell me about the church."

"Well then, come inside." Trevor shooed Alec and Claire up the gravel walk. Behind them the camera clicked.

The grass in the churchyard was a deep, translucent green, like some ideal of green rather than the ordinary palette color. From the turf sprouted a multitude of gravestones, the old ones weathered to feature-less lumps, the new ones sporting shiny gilded letters. This silent congregation was no doubt larger than the living one.

"Jackman" read the name on one stone dated 1832 — ancestors of Rob and Diana, Claire guessed. Other grave markers read, "Brandreth, Little, Stafford, Hardinge." She could only imagine living in the same town where her ancestors had lived and died.

In the far corner of the churchyard was a squat stone mausoleum adorned with vases, statues of angels gesticulating heavenward, and several plaques of no doubt maudlin Victorian sentiments. The name incised over the door was "Cranbourne." The last private owners of the Hall stooped to occupy the same sacred ground as the peasantry, but still made sure they were set apart, entering heaven with suitable dignity.

Trevor opened the ironbound wooden doors and ushered Claire and Alec into the interior of the church. Claire smelled the odor of sanctity, dust, candle wax, and decay. Tall stained-glass windows glowed sullenly in the darkening afternoon, leaving the nave and its two columned aisles in deep shadow. Below the silence of the church was a subtle resonance, as though the songs and the prayers uttered there over the centuries had seeped into the walls.

"The church is dedicated to St. Thomas Becket," Trevor said with his best tour guide's diction. "I'm not sure which early saint he displaced. The traces of the first two churches are almost gone, just a bit of Saxon foundation and some Norman columns in the crypt. This structure is mostly Perpendicular with some Early English remnants. The roof is late fifteenth century, older than the Hall."

Claire looked up. The ceiling was a tracery of carved and gilded wood, huge beams interlaced like toothpicks and apparently suspended from heaven. "It's beautiful. Such workmanship!"

Columns and arches led her eye down from the roof to the aisles, where human shapes — stone effigies — lurked in the shadows. The monument at her immediate left depicted a knight and lady lying side by side, he with his sword, she with her little lap dog. Claire deciphered the words, "William de Lacy," half-hidden in scrollwork around the tomb.

"Died at Crecy, that one did," said Alec. "And that one there, he died fighting for Warwick the Kingmaker in the Wars of the Roses."

Claire thought not of the knights dead in no doubt particularly messy ways on the field of battle, but of their wives sewing their samplers in drafty castle halls, waiting for a hoof beat at the gate. Chafing in their chastity belts, except chastity belts were a mordant Victorian fantasy.

They moved up the aisle to the monument of an earlier Richard Lacey, the builder of Somerstowe Hall. His effigy was more lifelike than those of his ancestors. He lay on one elbow holding a mason's compass, his stone-blank eyes gazing almost defiantly from below supple brows. Runs in the family, Claire told herself.

The monument to Cecil Lacey and his wife Lettice was a proper Puritan one. Busts of man and wife, their eyes lowered and hands folded piously, were framed by oval cutouts. Phillip Lacey's monument was a baroque extravaganza, swirling cupids and draperies carved from marble slick as butter. Phillip himself reclined on his tomb in a Roman toga, as though he were attending a banquet instead of trying to explain his way into the Pearly Gates. *The orgies were just games, St. Peter, Sir. Just a bit of a lark.*

Suppressing a smile, Claire turned away from Phillip. One of the monuments stepped out from behind a pillar of the opposite aisle. She gasped and recoiled.

The living Richard Lacey leaned against the end of a pew, raised his clipboard, and started sketching an intricate conjunction of roof beams. His features were even less expressive than the stone ones.

"Oh dear," said Trevor, "I'm dreadfully sorry, I should have told you we were not alone."

"No, no," Claire stammered, "I mean, we're never really alone in a church, are we?"

That was lame, but Trevor smiled broadly. He stepped across to Richard and starting speaking some arcane language. "Hammer posts. Pendant bosses and angel finials."

"Scissor trusses," replied Richard.

"Purlins and spandrels?" Trevor countered.

"Arch-braced cambered tie-beams," Richard concluded, and the men nodded as though they'd successfully worked their way through a complex litany.

"The ceiling," Alec explained to Claire.

"Ah," she answered. She wondered what Richard felt like, returning to the home of his ancestors, whether skeletal shapes leaned over his shoulder as he worked. She promised herself she'd do a little genealogical research of her own sometime soon. Probably she'd find a bunch of serfs named Godwin touching their forelocks to some armored Norman baron named Lacey.

Trevor called, "Would you like to see our other treasures?" and guided Claire past Richard's perch. Alec lingered, eyeing his drawing.

She admired various carvings in wood and stone, polished memorial brasses, medieval chests, and a wonderful embroidered altar cloth that had been saved from Puritans who equated piety with destruction. All the while she kept glancing over her shoulder, trying to interpret Alec's and Richard's body language.

Alec, nonchalant inquiry. Richard, throwaway shrug and terse sentence or two. Alec, skeptical nod followed by a serious, murmured question. Richard, quick glance at Claire, then at Alec, then a negative shake of his head and painstaking attention to the drawing.

When Alec caught up with Claire at the door she already knew how he'd answer her question. But she asked anyway, quietly, while Trevor was fussing over a vase of flowers by the visitor's book. "What was all that in the pub?"

"Says he got a past-due notice on a bill he'd already paid."

"So why did he glare at me?"

"He wasn't glaring at you, he was angry at the bill."

"Yeah, right," Claire said under her breath. Even Alec didn't look as though he believed that.

Trevor turned from the flowers and opened the door. "Would you care to join my wife and me for a coffee?" he asked.

"Thank you," Alec and Claire replied simultaneously.

"Richard?" Trevor called. "Coffee?"

Richard hesitated, then said, "Yes, thank you." He holstered his pencil.

Okay, Claire told herself, the more I hang around him, the more I'll find out about him. About Melinda and him, she amended quickly. She wouldn't be interested in him otherwise.

Yeah, right, she thought again, with the uneasy feeling Richard was thinking the same thing about her. She knew what she wanted from him. What was it he wanted from her?

Chapter Six

*T*he heavy door of the church opened with a muted squeal and shut with a solid thunk. The sky was now a lumpy gray. A mist of raindrops spun down the chilly air and tickled Claire's cheeks. Trevor, Alec, and Claire, with Richard bringing up the rear, tramped around the buttressed side of the church, through another gate, and into the garden of a graceful Georgian brick house.

Mrs. Digby met them at the door. She was the perfect foil for Trevor, the element earth to his element air. Her sturdy body was clothed in a modest house dress, her gray hair was cut in a no-nonsense style, and her face was touched only lightly with cosmetics, unashamed of having been lived in for sixty or so years.

"Priscilla," Mrs. Digby introduced herself, and led them into a sitting room that was all the more comfortable for being rather shabby. There was even a cat — an ordinary corporeal one, Claire assumed — dozing on the hearth. It glanced up when everyone walked in and fell promptly back to sleep.

"How are your parents?" Trevor asked Alec. "We miss them hereabouts."

"They're getting on well," Alec answered, and explained to Claire, "My mum's from Somerstowe, my dad's from the Isle of Man. They moved house a couple of years ago, to help out with the family museum and shop there."

"I bet you miss them," she said politely. "Blessed be the ties that bind and all that."

"Please, sit down." Trevor sorted Alec into a wing chair and Richard and Claire onto a sofa. They inched toward the ends, leaving the cushion in the middle a no-man's land. By the time Trevor walked Claire through ranks of photographs of their children and grandchildren, Priscilla had returned with the coffee tray.

"As you can see, we're amateur antiquarians." Trevor gestured at shelves crammed with historical tomes, notebooks and folders, and the odd artifact.

"Who wouldn't be, in Somerstowe?" asked Priscilla. "Did you see the well? The panel is very nice this year. Richard designed it for us." She poured coffee and passed cookies.

Claire made a noise of agreement and glanced at Richard. He stirred his coffee, his pose saying, *Oh that old thing? Just something I slapped together.*

Trevor said, "It was Richard's father, Julian, who discovered The Play whilst doing ancestral research. Mind you, he held a chair in Seventeenth Century History at Oxford."

Claire nodded, impressed. Her father was a professor of Economics at Texas A&M University. Economics would've been at the top of her list of non-romantic professions, except engineering had it beat.

"Maud Cranbourne," said Priscilla, "asked Julian to explore the old box rooms and attics at the Hall hoping he'd find valuable antiques. We expected he'd find furniture and vases, not a literary treasure."

"It must have been quite a thrill," said Claire, "for Julian — Mr. Lacey — to get a look at his ancestors' home."

"Oh, he'd been here many, many times. He and Dierdre and Richard used to spend their summer holidays here. Our children would play with Richard and Alec in the gardens of the Hall — Cavaliers and Roundheads was one of your favorite games, wasn't it, Alec? Richard?"

"That was a long time ago," Richard said through his teeth. Which were long and carnivorous, Claire noted. Yes, his being here was considerably more than cosmic coincidence. It was fate woven tightly with free will — which, when you came right down to it, was why she was here, too.

She tuned back in. Trevor was saying, ". . . genealogical research follows on, of course. I give the odd lecture from time to time. My folk are originally from Kent, but Priscilla's a Brandreth, they've been here in Somerstowe almost as long as the Littles, the Fosters, and the Jackmans. Diana came here when she married Rob and the Nairs came to us ten — or was it twelve — years ago from London, looking out a quiet place to raise their children. Then there's Elliot Moncrief, who has no family here at all. He says he likes the country air."

"And a chance to lord it over the country folk," said Alec.

"I'm afraid so," Trevor said with a gentle smile. "But we all have our foibles and follies, don't we?"

Claire wondered if Elliot's superior attitude quite fit under "foible."

"The Laceys, now," Trevor went on, "well, you find 'de Lacy' baronies all over the country, at Ludlow on the Welsh Marches, for example, not to mention the great houses at Kingston Lacy in Dorset and Polesden Lacey in Surrey. Then there are the Cranbournes, who were originally tradesmen from Birmingham."

Such a dull, conventional family the Cranbournes must have been, thought Claire, compared to the volatile Laceys they displaced. "Modern cash-flow aristocrats compared to the traditional landed type?" she essayed.

"Very much so," said Trevor.

Priscilla topped up his cup. "If Julian had been working on his own I doubt he would have offered The Play for production. He was a meticulous scholar, probably would've spent years researching every detail of language and style. But Dierdre — she'd been one of his students, mind you — Dierdre Callander that was, never lost her lovely Scotch accent — Dierdre was quite the scholar herself and kept Julian's feet on the ground as well. She transcribed the manuscript for Maud, and calmed Julian's concerns when Maud sent it to the British Library to be authenticated. You were just a lad, Richard — twelve, thirteen? — I seem to remember you helping out even so."

"Yes," he replied. "I helped out."

"Unfortunately, Julian didn't live to see how successful The Play proved to be," Trevor added, "Not only here, but overseas."

"We do miss Julian," said Priscilla with a sigh. "And Dierdre as well. Thankfully Richard has found his way back to us."

"Dierdre," Alec explained parenthetically, "remarried and moved to Canada, is teaching at McMaster University, I believe."

"Yes." Richard considered each cookie on the plate and selected a shortbread petticoat tail.

Claire couldn't imagine how he'd pry his teeth far enough apart to eat it. You'd think the Digbys were spilling some ghastly family scandal instead of chatting pleasantly. But Richard's parents had never met, never even heard of, Melinda.

Priscilla was asking, "Are you familiar with 'An Historie,' Miss Godwin?"

"Claire," she responded automatically. "I've read it, and I'm looking forward to seeing it performed. I can see why it's popular — drama, romance, and based on a true story to boot."

"Ah, yes," said Trevor. He leaned back in his chair and set his cup on a nearby table. The cat opened both eyes, saw his opportunity, and leaped into his lap. Cool, Claire thought. The little guy was a Manx, with only a stub of a tail. A gift from Alec's dad, maybe?

Trevor stroked the cat's back while he spoke. "Cecil Lacey was a wool merchant. He owned half the town and was its leading citizen, not to mention its magistrate. Elizabeth Spenser was chief needleworker for his wife Lettice. By 1665 Cecil and Lettice were beyond their youth, well into that disillusionment that happens to us all . . ."

Oh yeah, Claire agreed silently.

". . . aggravated, no doubt, by the wounds he suffered fighting with Charles II during the Civil War. After the restoration of the monarchy in 1660 Charles gave Somerstowe back to Cecil, as well as other preferments, but Lettice never believed he received enough to compensate him for the constant pain he suffered — and made her suffer as well. Gradually they found themselves moving toward the Puritanism they had once rejected. Or so Phillip wrote a hundred years later. Certainly the contemporary evidence supports his conclusions."

Alec sat back in his chair, cup and saucer resting on his knee, listening with the grave attention of a child hearing a favorite story. Richard held his saucer in his left hand and his cup in his right, lifting the one from the other and putting it back again as though trying to fit two puzzles pieces together. If he was bored he was too polite to show it. His eyes were downcast, the shadow of his lashes softening the almost harsh angle of his cheekbones, revealing nothing. But his hair was still standing to attention, rippling in the breeze from the open window beside the couch.

The cat's purr droned gently beneath Trevor's voice. "In 1665 the Black Death — the plague — once again came to England. This area had a rough time of it. The villagers thought the water from their ancient and perhaps sacred well would keep them safe. It didn't. Panicked, they searched for a scapegoat. Elizabeth had no family to protect her, only a younger brother."

"And what was worse," said Priscilla, "she was young, unmarried, and very pretty, attracting a few too many glances from the men of the village. So she was accused of witchcraft, specifically of poisoning the well."

"The young vicar," Trevor went on, "Walter Tradescant, appealed to the villagers' reason. His efforts might have succeeded except for the Laceys. In Phillip's play Cecil nurtures a guilty passion for Elizabeth, but she spurns him. And Lettice is jealous of Elizabeth's youth and beauty. Such things have happened all too often in the course of history."

"Cecil condemned Elizabeth to death," concluded Alec sadly. "On grounds that would be laughed out of a court of law today."

Trevor nodded. "For his support of her Walter Tradescant narrowly escaped charges of witchcraft himself. After Elizabeth's death he took her brother — who but for his youth would have suffered as well — and left the village, never to return."

Through the window came a damp gust of wind and a spattering of rain, perfectly timed for the climax of the story. Stagehands were probably stationed outside with hoses and wind machines, Claire thought.

Priscilla got up and shut the window. "More coffee?"

Everyone accepted except the cat, who was blissfully snagging his claws on Trevor's pants leg.

"Was there really a romantic relationship between Walter and Elizabeth?" Claire asked.

"That was probably poetic license on Phillip's part," replied Trevor. "It does add another dimension to the story. Richard? You're the expert."

"My parents were the experts, Trevor," Richard replied, his tones so academically dehydrated he might just as well have been discussing the marginal productivity theory of income distribution. "I'm more familiar with The Play and with Phillip's life than with Elizabeth's death. The historical record is sketchy at best."

"Melinda asked that same question about Walter and Elizabeth," said Alec. "She was a very curious person, in both senses of the word."

It seemed to Claire as though the name fell into the midst of the group like a grenade and lay on the hearthrug ticking. But neither of the Digbys leaped up to throw their bodies over it. Priscilla sighed, said "How terribly puzzling about Melinda," and passed around the cookies.

Trevor shook his head, said "I often pray for her. I hope she's well and happy somewhere," and petted the cat. Richard's lips went thin and tight. He said nothing.

Had Alec introduced the topic deliberately? Claire asked herself. His expression was as composed as ever, as though his mind and body were filled with the same evocative silence as the village church. "Melinda was after starting her novel with Phillip Lacey playing at the occult and writing his play," he said, "then going back to Elizabeth and how she was charged — wrongly — with devil worship."

"She probably told y'all more about the book than she did me. Usually she did her research, then worked it into a pattern by bouncing it off me. She'd have done a great job, maybe even had a bestseller." Claire intercepted a quick darting glance from Richard.

"Fictionalized history," Trevor said, "is quite popular these days."

"That's what The Play is, actually," added Priscilla.

Richard set his cup and saucer on the table. He stood up. "Thank you very much for the coffee, Trevor, Priscilla."

"Must you be going?" Priscilla asked, rising as well.

"Needs must," answered Richard. "Rehearsal tonight, and I've not swotted up my lines yet. Cheers, Alec. Claire. No, please, Priscilla — I'll show myself out." And he was gone. The front door opened and shut, admitting a brief sound of running water.

Maybe getting rained on would soften him up a little, Claire thought. Although the prospect of Richard soft was a little discouraging, like seeing one of the old stone memorials cracked and chipped by acid rain. Had he bailed out abruptly there or was she simply sensitized to his behavior? No one else seemed to notice. Even the cat dozed peacefully on.

It could be that while Americans were often kind of tickled to find horse thieves dangling from the family tree, Richard was embarrassed about Phillip and Cecil. . . . No. If it was embarrassment that was making him downplay his family connections to Somerstowe, why act in The Play?

What was more likely, Claire thought, was that he felt a proprietary interest in The Play. Melinda's novel might have been a burr under his saddle. Maybe he'd offered his help and she brushed him aside. Maybe he thought she was going to sensationalize the story, even though it was pretty sensational as it was. Whatever, she was intending to cash in on his family's history and his family's scholarly work as well. And he had no way of stopping her — The Play's historical basis was in the public domain. . . . Richard had no legal way to stop her, rather. But murdering someone for writing a novel seemed a little drastic.

"Claire?" Alec asked, and she jumped.

"Oh, sorry, just . . ." *Wondering about motives.* "The Nairs were telling me that the National Trust gets the income from The Play to maintain the Hall." Maybe she was making a social blunder by asking about money, like suddenly exposing her underwear. The three faces before her smiled indulgently — she was American, after all.

"That's the provision in Maud Cranborne's will," answered Trevor. "Her relatives weren't best pleased — they'd intended selling the Hall to a corporation which builds new housing. Which would probably have meant the destruction of the Hall and most certainly quite a change for us here in Somerstowe."

"I see," Claire said, and she did, wincing at the vision.

"Because of the Hall," Priscilla went on, "and because of Elliot's good work representing The Play, I should add, we've been able to get grants for other work that needed doing here — a children's playground, for example. And two years ago we installed central heating in the church."

"That was fascinating," said Trevor. "The workmen had the floor up and opened the crypt. Gave us an opportunity to study the church's history."

Alec leaned forward, hands cupping something invisible, eyes focussed on something distant. "Beneath the altar lie the bones of a young woman. The archaeologist couldn't say for certain whether it was Elizabeth. In the last scene of The Play Walter cuts down her body and lays her to rest in consecrated ground. I'd like to think Phillip's vision was true, even to Elizabeth and Walter being lovers."

"Nothing like a little romance," Claire agreed, adding silently, *when it works.*

"The Play has certainly brought business here," Trevor went on. "And it's returned some community spirit that was leaching away, I'm afraid, in these busy modern times. The Play helped Maud Cranbourne to leave the Hall to the National Trust and the Trust to take up the challenge of preserving it — although the Hall would be of great interest even without

The Play."

"Of course." Claire was beginning to wonder just what she'd had in mind by asking the question. Money was a time-honored motive for murder, but she couldn't for the life of her see how Richard or anyone else — such as Elliot, in his role as literary agent — would've profited monetarily by Melinda's death. In fact, her novel would have encouraged even more interest in Somerstowe and The Play.

Claire's brain felt as though it was doing wind sprints. Either she'd gathered a body of evidence today or she'd gathered a few nail parings of insignificance. Maybe if she sat down by herself she could figure out which. She stood up. "Thank you very much for your hospitality."

"Our pleasure, my dear. I hope we've not bored you with the history and genealogy." Priscilla started gathering up the dishes.

"No way, it's very interesting." Whether it had anything to do with Melinda or not, Claire told herself.

Alec brushed a few crumbs from his pants and helped. His large, steady hands didn't so much as bang a cup and a saucer together. Claire visualized an entire city police department — that of New York or Los Angeles, for example — filled with officers of Alec's disposition. Whether that would allow more crime or prevent it, she couldn't say.

Trevor put the cat on the floor, where he settled back down on the hearth, and he and his wife escorted their guests to the door.

A bell rang in the church steeple, marking the ending of the day. The gray curtain of the rain blurred the houses and trees across the now deserted green. The solitary cement post seemed like an obscene gesture.

"Have an umbrella," Trevor said to Claire. "No, no, please — people are always leaving them in the church." He gave her a long black umbrella with a hooked handle and a pointed tip.

Alec and Claire stepped from the porch into the rain. He offered his arm and she took it. His body was firm and reassuring, like a tree. He held the umbrella low, resting on his own head so it'd shelter hers.

Across the damp grass they went, and through another alley. They passed the police station, its blue light shining bravely through the murk. "I live there." Alec motioned toward a stone cottage next to the stucco box of the station. A gorgeous garden, flowers and drifts of green leafy plants, filled the front yard and added a subtle herbal/floral undertone to the wet cement smell of the rain.

Once back in the high street Claire glanced into the lighted windows of the pub and the tearoom. But she was too full of ale and gravy, coffee and cookies, jet lag, doubt, and confusion, to suggest another culinary expedition. "Here," Alec said, when they reached the stairs leading to her apartment. "Have the brolly."

"You have to go to rehearsal, don't you? Where is it, at the Hall?"

"Yes, in the entrance hall. You're welcome to sit in, Elliot loves an audience."

"Maybe tomorrow. Sure you don't want the umbrella?"

"I shan't melt. I'm a native. Waterproofed." Saluting her with a smile, Alec waited at the bottom of the stairs while she unlocked the door.

Safely inside, Claire collapsed the umbrella and hung it over the doorknob to drip dry. Her flat was silent except for the almost inaudible swish of the rain outside, like long skirts in the next room. Had Melinda died still wearing her long-skirted costume? God, Claire thought, please let her have died fast and clean, not like poor Elizabeth.

She hung up her windbreaker, then went around the room pulling the curtains. At the front window she froze. Alec was still standing in the yard below, gazing up at her door, one hand in his pocket. In the dim light she couldn't make out his expression. But he must've seen her, because he turned abruptly and hurried away.

Great. Claire didn't so much sit down on the desk chair as fall into it. Let that be a lesson, she told herself, not to get fixated on Richard. If you wanted to murder someone and hide her body, being the local cop would certainly help. And yet opportunity sure as heck didn't mean motive.

Neither did acting suspicious. Maybe Alec simply was attracted to her. Fine. He was a personable person. But right now she had neither the time nor the energy for romance.

She had to use both getting methodical. Across the top of a clean piece of paper she wrote "Motive" and "Opportunity." Down the left side she wrote, "Richard. Alec. Fred and/or Janet. Other volunteers. Elliot. The Jackmans. The Digbys. The Nairs. Other townspeople." So far only Richard had jumped when Claire mentioned her connection with Melinda. Word gets around fast in a small town, doesn't it?

She threw the pen down. It rolled to a stop against the stack of letters. "Why, Melinda, why?"

Melinda would come breezing in, scented with suntan lotion, and toss a salad — arugula and sprouts, never iceberg lettuce — while Claire stirred a pot of her raise-the-dead chili. Melinda would listen gravely to Claire's stories of dropped stitches, overdue books, and troubled students. She'd say, "Those kids need something to do. How about a photography program? I'll round up some cameras." Melinda would pile stacks of photos and notes on the coffee table and say, "Should I open with that story about the old hippie running the hostel in Darjeeling?"

Surely Trevor's prayers were far more effective than Claire's own nebulous intentions. Surely Melinda had entered into heaven with all the ruffles and flourishes she'd have loved and was finally, at last, at peace. It was Claire who'd forgotten what "peace" meant.

She took a shower, checked the lock on the door, and turned off the light. With a determined if somewhat wobbly smile she went to bed and pulled the covers over her head.

Chapter Seven

A soft cottony mist lay over the village. The top half of the church steeple had disappeared and the imposing lines of the Hall were smudged, as though a crazed architect was trying to erase it.

The only architect Claire knew at the moment didn't appear, at least, to be crazy. Preoccupied, yes. Nursing some sort of grievance. Conflicted, even. But not crazy.

Frowning, Claire walked down the staircase and across the muddy and puddle-strewn yard. Even though the mist would probably thicken into rain at any moment — she could feel droplets gathering in her hair — she didn't bother with the umbrella. It'd been good to have in last night's downpour, though. And Alec had been very attentive. Maybe too attentive.

Claire had waked up at five a.m. and sat over coffee and toast making notes. She'd concluded she didn't have any real evidence, just a soufflé of assumptions and impressions garnished with one or two parsley sprigs of fact. Her mission today, then, was to collect more facts. First on her list was the village post office, tucked away in a corner of the Nairs' shop.

Claire dodged around the corner of the building and went in the front door. The shop was scented with floor wax and curry. Somewhere in the back of the house a heavy metal band screamed at a blessedly low volume. Sarita was sorting the mail. "Good morning, Claire!"

Claire produced the postcards she'd scribbled a few minutes earlier. "Good morning. I need to send these home. Do you have any pretty commemorative stamps?"

"No, not for post cards. I am having commemoratives for letters only."

"Could I see some, please? My nephew collects stamps."

"Certainly." Sarita reached under the counter and produced a battered notebook. Inside were waxed-paper envelopes containing stamps of all sizes and descriptions. "Here are stamps with little bits of ordnance maps on them. Here are those picturing the poet Tennyson. Here are a few only of the Scottish Parliament stamps issued last year."

Each red and yellow stamp was emblazoned with the rampant lion of Scotland. The tiny cameo of the Queen in the corner was turned away from its open-mouthed roar of defiance, not particularly amused. "I like those," Claire said. "I saw one yesterday, on a letter Richard was reading."

"Yes, I noticed that one myself. Square envelope, Scottish Parliament stamp. Altogether like his letters last summer."

"Last summer?" Claire repeated lamely.

"Oh yes. I am very much afraid I offended him by asking about his London correspondent, if it was his former girlfriend wanting to join him up again. But the post is private, after all. And the addresses were typed, so they were probably not a woman's letters at all."

So those letters upset him, too, Claire told herself. Judging by that evil look he'd given her last night, they had something to do with Melinda . . . *Don't push your luck.* "Speaking of Richard, I need to get to work. I'll take the postcard stamps and a plate block of the Parliaments, please."

"Thank you," said Sarita, making change. "Place the cards in the basket on the counter. Roshan will be taking them away to Derby very soon now."

Claire stuck the stamps on the cards and left them in the basket. Then she started off up the street, telling herself that it'd be useless to ask Richard point-blank about the letters. Whatever they were, they weren't bills he'd already paid. She'd caught him in a lie.

And what had she just done by telling Sarita she had a nephew who collected stamps? Testified that the end justified the means? That two wrongs made a right? On top of any ethical issue, she now had to remember she'd said she had a nephew when she didn't even have any siblings.

The Lodge was silent. The gardens before the Hall drooped gently. A light or two glinted in the windows, but most of them were dark, abstracted, as though the mist emanated from the damp stones themselves. The Gothic air of the place was not only appropriate to a haunted house, it almost demanded that the house be haunted. Which came first, Claire asked herself, a ghost or a place for it to walk, the artifact or the template?

She strode into the entrance hall, exchanged greetings with several people, and discovered Janet waiting for her on the staircase. "How about lunch in the tearoom today?"

"Love to."

"See you then." Janet bustled away and collided in the back hall with Richard, who apologized for getting in her way.

When he saw Claire standing on the steps he called, "How are you getting on with the Morris canvas?"

"I should finish it tomorrow."

"Don't take it off the frame on your own."

"Okay." She bit her tongue to keep from returning, *Aye, aye sir.*

The long gallery was much darker today in the mist than it'd been in yesterday's sunshine. She found a light switch hidden in a corner and looked dubiously up at the bulbs spaced along the ceiling. They spilled only a few watts into shadows that could have been either romantic or sinister. Claire voted for sinister.

She moved her chair and adjusted the frame so she could sit with her back to the wall. Only once did she sense Richard's silent acetylene gaze from the doorway. Odd how she actually missed it, even though it was like working with burned fingertips.

She glanced up at every odd creak or rustle in the room. Only Alec, though, came strolling by. He nodded amiably but said nothing, very much the cop on duty. By the time the cry, "Lunch break!" echoed through the house, Claire was ready to go. She tucked her needle into its pincushion, turned off the lights, and promised herself she'd ask for a lamp. And maybe a space heater — sneaky little drafts played up and down the room even after she'd scooted away from the window. Maybe she should bring her CD player and earphones . . . No, that just wouldn't fit.

On the staircase she met Janet, her face and arms sprinkled with dots of gold like fairy dust. With her were Fred and Mrs. Zielinski, who introduced herself as Susan. Outside the mist had thinned a bit, but still both sky and ground were low on definition, open to impression, not quite real.

The tearoom was a brighter version of the pub, its windows larger and its ceiling higher. The four Americans found a table in the corner and ordered from a waitress wearing a starched uniform and blond corn rows. Claire's hands were cold. Fred, the only one of the group working outside, had hands that were red and raw with chill. And with scrapes, Claire noted. "Having a rough time with the masonry?" she asked.

"No worse than usual." He wrapped his fingers around a warm cup of tea.

"Richard bought the stone from a couple of old houses that were being demolished," Janet explained. "So it'd match the Hall, right? That's what he was doing when we first got here last year, waving the truck down to the foot of the lawn by the rose garden."

"He wanted to use the same stone for the garden walls," added Susan.

Claire closed in. "So you were here last year, too."

"Oh yes. I just fell in love with Somerstowe, had to come back this year. Do you know I'm one of the few people who've actually seen the ghost of Elizabeth Spenser? Not just a kind of sparkle in the air — several people have seen that — but the actual woman, long dress, collar, and all."

"In the gallery?" asked Claire.

"No, in the portico late one night. Very pale and spectral. I went off in the other direction pretty fast, let me tell you!"

"She told Richard about it," Janet said, "and he just gave her one of his Mr. Spock 'fascinating' looks."

"Richard doesn't fuss at me. I'm old enough to be his grandmother." Susan's dark eyes twinkled in a face furrowed deep with long experience and well-earned knowledge. Her hair was a teased crown of a mauve color Claire had never seen in nature. If Diana Jackman fought her age, and Priscilla Digby accepted hers, then Susan Zielinski declared to the world, *if this be age, make the most of it!*

Claire waited while the waitress distributed soup and sandwiches, then said, "So you knew Melinda Varek."

"Claire's a friend of hers," Janet put in. "She'd like to find out what happened to her."

"We wondered if she just ran off," said Susan. "But her leaving her things behind, that didn't look good. You must be very worried."

Claire spooned up thick pea soup and nodded. "Yes, I am. Maybe you can help. Sarita tells me Melinda had a lot of friends here."

"She was friendly," muttered Fred into his sandwich. Something in his tone suggested that "friendly" wasn't quite the word he had in mind.

Janet shot a sharp look at him. "Yeah, she was friendly, all right. And stunning. I'd say I disliked her — sorry Claire — but she was so nice, with such a great sense of humor . . . Well, you can't blame all the men for flocking around her. Bees and flowers, you know."

Susan fished a packet of artificial sweetener from her fanny pack and poured it into her tea. "Every night, almost, Melinda would sit in the pub with her laptop and ask questions about Somerstowe, Elizabeth, and the Hall. There're several families who've been here so long they must've evolved right on the spot. She could've written five books."

"All these people with the huge family trees," Janet muttered. "My great-grandparents came through Ellis Island and some official wrote the name down as 'Harlow.' Big deal."

And now Melinda's laptop was gone, Claire told herself. "I guess she took lots of pictures, too? She had one of those digital cameras that'd download right into the computer."

"It looked to me like she was mainly interested in the Hall, that stone circle, and the church," Susan said. "Not that I was with her all the time."

"She was taking pictures at the cast party, last time anybody saw her," said Fred. "Showed me how to use the camera. High-tech. Really cool."

"If kind of dislocating to see a woman in a seventeenth-century gown taking pictures with a digital camera," Susan added.

"She didn't change her clothes right after the show?" asked Claire.

Janet shook her head. "No. Not everybody did. Just having fun playing dress-up, I guess."

"Melinda told me she liked that dress," Claire went on. "She only hinted, though, that she had something going with one of the men here."

"Wouldn't surprise me one bit," said Susan. "I was cleaning the fireplace in the long gallery one day, right before she disappeared, and we got to talking. She pretty much ran down the list. She said Elliot was so fake he was charming. 'A hoot,' she said. 'Lots of laughs.' They spent a lot of time together since she had a major role in The Play. Could've been him."

Yeah, Claire thought, and Elliot isn't volunteering any information, is he?

"Hey," offered Fred. "I saw Melinda drive off with Rob Jackman once. He's married, yeah, but I mean, look what he's married to."

"Rob has to run all the errands for the pub," said Janet. "Diana can't drive, and I don't think she's much help any other way, either. He was just giving Melinda a ride, like you did that time. When you got lost and stopped for a beer and everything?"

Fred pulled himself up, dignity wounded. "*I* didn't have anything going with Melinda, okay?"

"I imagine it was all very — well — innocent," Susan said. "I can't imagine Rob appealing to her, he's pretty rough around the edges."

"Having someone else do the driving," said Janet quickly, "you can't beat that."

Susan nodded. "Melinda drove all over the place, no problem. It takes intestinal fortitude to drive on the wrong side of the road and negotiate those roundabouts, but she had plenty of that. You drove here, didn't you, Claire?"

"You gotta do what you gotta do." Maybe, Claire worried, one of the volunteers from last year had killed Melinda and not returned to the scene of the crime . . . No, it had to be someone who was in The Play — the letter shoved under the door pointed to that. It was someone Melinda had known. "What did she say about Alec?"

"I saw them in a heck of a clinch in the upper great chamber one night after rehearsal," said Janet. "He's so tall and she's so petite she looked like a rock climber working her way up a cliff face."

Claire nodded. Alec had said right up front he'd "seen" Melinda.

"Not that a kiss means much in this day and time," Susan said. "She told me she liked Alec just fine, that he was 'sweet,' but then she added, 'his heart belongs to another.' Not that I've ever seen him with anyone. Some sort of long-distance relationship, I guess."

Oh? Claire asked herself. That was interesting. Who was the lucky woman, then? Someone on the Isle of Man? "And Richard?"

"She said Richard was a real looker and damned smart, but too honest."

Too honest? Richard? Claire let her spoon drip soup back into the bowl. "Alec told me Melinda used to tease Richard."

"Oh yes, she did. She teased everyone. There was some sort of static between her and Richard, though. She'd twit him about being descended from Cecil and Phillip and acting like such a pill about the house. Just trying to get him to lighten up, I guess. Not that he's all that grim, just a little — intense."

"Even so," said Janet, "Melinda told me she had a date with Richard at the Lodge right after the cast party. But they got into a real knock-down drag-out upstairs while the rest of us were still partying."

Again with the argument. Claire put the spoon down. "What were they fighting about?"

"Who knows?" asked Susan. "They weren't shouting, it was just their voices, you know. Very sharp. Alec walked over and turned up the volume on the boom box — it was playing the Rolling Stones right then, that would've covered up anything short of a train wreck. After a few minutes Melinda came sweeping down the stairs, smiling as though nothing was wrong, and started dancing with old Jimmy Hawkins. Then Richard came down. You could've cut stone with his face. He said good night and took off. Soon after that the party broke up."

"So did she actually see him later that night, do you know?"

Susan looked at Janet and shrugged. Janet looked at Fred and shook her head. Fred looked at Claire's half-empty bowl. "Do you want the rest of that?"

"Ah, no. Help yourself."

Fred pulled her bowl toward him. Claire shoved the last quarter of her sandwich at him, too. If Melinda met Richard after the party, he might have been the last person to see her alive. . . . She reminded herself that only on TV detective shows was the most likely suspect always innocent. In real life it was the other way around.

She waited until after the waitress had taken away the plates and produced gooseberry tart with cream to ask, "I guess the police questioned everyone in town when Melinda disappeared."

"You'd better believe it," Janet replied, rolling her eyes. "That Blake, and his sergeant, Pakenpork . . ."

"Pakenham," corrected Susan.

"Just a joke," Janet told her. "Blake and Pakenham grilled everyone between here and the reservoir where they found Melinda's car. Even Alec, who's on their side. Talk about leaving no stone unturned, or no turn unstoned, or something."

"Nothing," said Fred, and burped gently. "Sod-all. Sweet Fanny Adams, as the Brits say."

Susan took out her change purse and started counting out pence. "Me, I think she's dead. Sorry, Claire."

"I'm sorry, too," Claire replied, without expanding the issue to include murder.

She paid her portion of the bill and walked back to the Hall a few paces behind the others, wondering whether Melinda had accidentally tripped over Fred and Janet's relationship. Ditto Rob and Diana, who seemed to be on somewhat less than the best of terms. But then, running a business was stressful.

And did it even matter who Melinda had had her eye on? Someone could've killed her because, say, she'd uncovered some financial plot. The international illegal antiquities trade was booming, and the villagers were in a good position to be selling off bits of the Hall to wealthy and unscrupulous collectors — it happened all the time.

Just as Claire started up the stairs she remembered to ask Susan about the lamp. "I'll find Richard and ask," Susan returned. "Can't have you ruining your eyes."

Claire expected Richard to bring a lamp himself. He had a slight problem delegating responsibility — possessive perfectionists usually did. But it was Susan who returned with an angle-arm lamp about thirty minutes later. "He sent me down to the Lodge for it," she explained, and helped Claire clamp it onto the tapestry frame.

At quitting time Claire had only a few stitches left, so she went on working as the house emptied. When at last she cut off the last bit of yarn and finished filling in the chart, Somerstowe Hall was so quiet her own heartbeat thudded in her ears. The gallery seemed even draftier than it had this morning. Shivering, she switched off the lights and turned to go.

Thin rays of sun shone through the windows, illuminating blocks of the slightly undulating floor. And there was that reflection through the windows of the great chamber next door . . . The hair rose on the back of Claire's neck. Something shimmered through the shadows between the blocks of light, followed by a swirl of dust particles as though long skirts brushed them up from the floorboards. Elizabeth.

The — *ghost*, Claire articulated — passed out the far door of the gallery. Claire's torso twisted toward the main staircase and the mundane outside world. Her feet, though, carried her in the opposite direction, so that she sidled along like a crab and slipped sideways out the door.

There was the shimmer-shape, gliding silently along the corridor and up a narrow set of stairs. Curiosity killed the cat, Claire reminded herself. And yet the uncanny shape, the quasi-physical memory of a life ended too soon, called her to follow. Melinda would've followed in a New York minute.

Claire tiptoed up the staircase, each step squeaking gently beneath her athletic shoes, and emerged in another hallway. This one was smaller and darker than the one downstairs. Servant's territory, she thought. Where Elizabeth had lived.

There she was, the skirts and the sleeves of her dress glowing faintly in the gloom like a supernatural wedding gown. Now Claire could see the curled hair, the cap, the wide collar. And Elizabeth's molded porcelain face, small nose, full lips, blue eyes glancing inquisitively over her shoulder. *Whether the ghost can see you back again . . .* Claire stopped dead at the top of the stairs, not wanting Elizabeth to acknowledge her presence. What do you say to a ghost? *Haunted anyplace interesting lately?*

Elizabeth glided into a room at the end of the hall. Taking a deep breath of the cold, musty air, Claire followed. And reached the door just in time to see the ghost walk right through a wall.

Well, they were supposed to do that, weren't they? Claire crept forward. No, it wasn't a wall. It was a closed door next to the massive brick side of a fireplace. A cupboard, probably.

With an almost audible pop the chill in the air dissipated. Claire looked around, at the window scummed with dust and yet still admitting light, at the wide equally dusty floorboards of the bare room. A row of smeared footprints led diagonally through the dust from the door to the cupboard, edged on either side by the small paw prints of a cat.

So ghostly feet made paths, Claire told herself. Or were some of the feet that'd made that path very human? She couldn't have been the only person ever to follow Elizabeth. Maybe some of the prints were Melinda's. Maybe Melinda was . . .

Oh my God. Claire sprinted across the floor and threw open the door of the cupboard. Nothing was inside the small room, little more than a cell, except dust and cobwebs.

For a long moment she leaned against the doorframe, her knees shaking, her heart doing aerobatics inside her chest. Come on, she told herself, some of those prints were made a lot more recently than last year. Melinda might have come here alive, yes, but she wasn't — here now. As for who had been here. . . . Well, it was time to tackle Richard again. You gotta do what you gotta do.

Something vibrated almost subliminally in the wood against Claire's shoulder. A purr. A cat's purr. Strange, how soothing that was.

Chapter Eight

*S*lowly the purr faded away. Claire's knees firmed up and her heart landed safely behind her breastbone. She made her way back to the door wondering why Elizabeth would walk into a closet. Had that once been the door into another room? Fine, but that didn't explain the prints of living feet. Unless everyone who worked in the house had to follow the ghost, like some sort of hazing ritual.

She'd have to ask Richard. Try to ask Richard, depending on whether he'd gotten over yesterday's letter-and-stamp episode, whatever that was all about. She could segue cleverly from Elizabeth to Melinda. *She took a lot of notes for her book, didn't she? Was she at the cast party?*

Claire retraced her — Elizabeth's — path back to the gallery and then headed outside. Her steps rang hollowly across the entrance hall. The cellars, she thought, were an obvious place for Blake and his men to have looked. She sure wasn't going to tackle them.

This time when she knocked at the Lodge door Richard didn't appear like a genie out of a bottle. She was about to give up and go back to the Hall to look for him when he at last opened the door. Only his brows slanting up his forehead betrayed his surprise. Claire could imagine what he was seeing with those guarded eyes — her hair curling every direction at once, no lipstick, only a perfunctory dab of mascara. Melinda wouldn't have gone out to get the newspaper looking like this.

Now that was annoying, to care what she looked like to him. Claire said briskly, "Thank you for the lamp."

"The anglepoise?" replied Richard. "Turned the trick, did it?"

"I can see to work better now."

"Good." They looked at each other, actors without scripts. "Ah, I was just off on my afternoon recce." Richard vanished into the interior of the house leaving Claire on the doorstep.

That was probably a dismissal. But she hadn't asked him about the cupboard yet, let alone Melinda, and at the moment he wasn't openly hostile. If she could just get her brain to stop emitting white noise whenever she was around him.

Tightening her jaw — Claire suspected that after the last couple of days her teeth were beginning to squeeze out of shape — she stepped inside. A long table filled one side of the hallway, so heavily layered with papers it looked like an archaeological mound. Two volumes of Pevsner's *Buildings of England*, a spiral-bound sketchbook, and an assortment of pencils perched on top.

When Richard emerged from the living room armed with his clipboard, Claire asked, "May I join you?"

After a long searching look, he replied, "If you like."

They jockeyed for the door and, in avoiding each other, brushed against the table. Papers and books avalanched onto the floor. "Sorry," said Claire.

"My fault," Richard said.

She started to retrieve lists, letters, and the odd grocery receipt. The pencils emerged from the pile like pungee sticks. Several pages of the sketchbook were creased. Claire tried to smooth them out and saw that some of the sketches were expert line drawings of the Hall and the church. Two depicted a vaulted room stacked with coffins. "The crypt beneath the church?" she asked. "Where Elizabeth Spenser was supposedly buried?"

"Yes." Richard held out his hand for the book.

Claire flipped to the next page. And there was Melinda in her seventeenth-century gown, unbuttoned, so that the collar slipped provocatively off her shoulders. Her splayed fingers pressed the gathered material of the bodice against her breasts. Her head was tilted back, so that she was looking at the viewer — at the artist — from beneath her eyelashes. Her half-smile was an engraved invitation. And yet the drawing also caught perfectly Melinda's edge of irony, the way she mocked her actions even as she acted.

Claire looked around at Richard. His extended hand froze in mid-air. Nothing else on his body moved, not his eyes, not his mouth, not even the usually animated strands of his hair.

Then, all in a rush, he snatched the sketchbook, shuffled it into a pile of papers, and wedged them all back beneath the books. "If you're coming, come along then."

She was tempted to say sarcastically, *Only if you promise not to talk my ear off,* but that wouldn't help. She whisked out behind him as he shut the door, wondering whether Melinda's sitting for him had ended as she obviously planned, with her lying down for him. Whatever, something had gone wrong. Not that wrong meant murder.

And here she was walking off with him. . . . There was Derek Nair, strolling across the forecourt carrying a pair of rollerblades. There were a couple of volunteers taking pictures on the lawn. Claire waved at them all — *look, I'm with Richard.* He didn't seem to notice.

The clouds were giant gray puffballs sailing through a blue sky. The sun peeked out, hid, then peeked out again, each shaft of light drawing sparkles from grass and stone. The windows of the Hall winked inscrutably. Richard, Claire at his heels, took a path around the side of the house.

Clipboard at the ready, he eyed the progress of the mortar-and-stone squad. He sighted toward the roof, considered the angle of a chimney, and then took off through the gardens, noting flowerbeds, stone walls, trees, and hedges. At the end of a long stretch of greensward, just beside the gate into the walled rose garden, stood a mound of building stones the same soft honey color as the house. Crowning it was a hand-lettered sign reading No TIPPING "What does that mean?" asked Claire.

"This is not a rubbish tip. Throw your litter someplace else."

"Oh. Of course. For a minute there I thought it meant you weren't allowed to tip the masons. You know, give them a few extra coins or a pint of beer or something."

Richard shot her a mildly exasperated glance, as though wondering why she had to complicate matters by having a sense of humor. She hadn't meant that as a joke, but if he took it that way, fine, it defused the tension.

He clambered up on the pile of stone and turned to survey if not his realm, at least the realm he was responsible for. Without waiting for an invitation, Claire followed and promptly stumbled over a loose rock. Only Richard's lunge and grab kept her from falling. His firm hand held her forearm until she was balanced beside him, then dropped it like a hot potato.

Her forearm tingled. And just why did *he* have to complicate matters? She said, "Thank you," and looked out over the countryside.

Behind the rose garden the land sloped away into a green and gray quilt tufted with sheep. Just opposite was a hillside. On it stood a circle of ancient megaliths, all but one of them lying face down in the grass like worshippers prostrating themselves before a religious image. And yet there was no image there, only the solitary tall stone and the hillside leading the eye up to the sky. Claire was reminded of the steeple of the church pointing heavenward. Interesting, how the church was built as far away from the stones as possible, playing tug-of-war with the village.

"Derbyshire was one of the last strongholds of the Druids," Richard said behind her. "Phillip Lacey called his games Druidic rituals, even though they were nothing of the sort. Elizabeth Spenser's accusers were expressing some long-held prejudices against non-Christians."

"I imagine her accusers were also expressing some long-held prejudices against independent women." Claire turned around.

Richard's brows were at neutral. His windblown hair softened the angles of his face. "Elizabeth had no family. Which seems to me less like independence than loneliness."

"True. I mean, you could make a feminist tract out of the story, but historical revisionism only goes so far."

He blinked, as though he'd expected her to come out fighting. Melinda would have. Melinda would've asked him about that sketch. If Claire had learned anything at all the last couple of days, though, it was that getting in Richard's face was counter-productive.

He picked his way down from the pile of stones. At its foot he turned and extended his hand, but Claire made it safely down by herself. Side by side they walked back toward the house, if not companionably at least mutually tiptoeing around any minefields. The bracing air and the cool vistas of the countryside did have a mellowing effect, Claire thought. She wished she could bottle them for the library.

When they arrived at the back door of the house Claire defaulted to her original topic. "Ah, I found something interesting a little while ago."

"Yes?"

"Diana and Alec were telling me the house is haunted. By Elizabeth Spenser, who else? I think I've — er — seen something myself a time or two."

"I should think you have done," Richard returned matter-of-factly. "Most old buildings have a ghost of some sort, ranging from apparitions that look quite real to, well, a ripple in space and time. Like music, or the memory of music. Susan Zielinski once saw Elizabeth completely manifested, although most people see the cat."

He was holding the door open, but Claire stalled out on the threshold. "Oh. I didn't think you'd — I mean, I didn't know . . ."

There went his brows again, one down, one up, repeating the angle of his mouth. "You followed her from the gallery to the little room upstairs, I take it? No, you've not gone crackers. I'll show you."

Okay. Exhaling, Claire waited while Richard locked the door and then followed as his long legs took the stairs to the top floor. He walked right across to the cupboard and threw open the door, then turned to the wall that paralleled the side of the fireplace, did some sort of hocus-pocus, and slid a wood panel jerking and scraping to the side.

"Voila!" he announced. "A secret room. It's fitted in between the back of this chimney stack and the one on the other side. If you try matching the windows with the floor plan you'll find there's one unaccounted for."

"Cool," said Claire, and stepped through the wooden frame into the room.

The walls to her right and left were brick. Straight ahead, the wall was a crumbling lathe-and-plaster lined stone. Its narrow window was no doubt hidden on the outside by a decorative figure — well, hidden to everyone except Richard with his sharp eyes. Ceiling beams slanted close overhead. The room was warm, suffused by year after year of English summer sun and rain, roses and mold. Something about the light filtering through the uneven but polished glass of the window reminded Claire of Alec's eyes.

A polished window? And the floorboards were swept clean, even though traces of silvery dust lingered in the cracks between them. A spotless nineteenth century Shaker-style bench sat to one side. Below the window stood a long, narrow table, of wood so old and dry it looked like paper mache. Atop the table lay a rolled piece of cloth, somewhat squashed and hollowed in the shape of a sleeping cat.

Richard was saying something. ". . . a priest's hole. Some day I'll ask Trevor about the religious tenacity of my ancestors. I don't recall them being devout enough to keep a priest, let alone hide one from the authorities. This priest's hole might be a status symbol, like a moat around a manor house."

"Artillery made moats useless," said Claire. "Religious prejudice is perennial, I'm afraid. What's that on the table?"

"An embroidered cloth."

"May I look?"

"Have a care, it's very old."

She didn't remind him that that's why she was here, to handle old textiles. Gingerly she unrolled the fabric. It was a long linen panel, a little dusty, embroidered with trees and plants, stars and mythological figures. "It's like that altar cloth Trevor was showing me — the one that was saved from the Puritans. Similar shape and fabric. And the border is the same pattern, a Tudor barley-sugar twist. But that one was stitched with religious symbols. This can't be seventeenth century, it's in way too good a condition. Look at these leaves, they're a little frayed, and yet . . ."

Richard leaned over her shoulder. She could sense his breath on her cheek, making her skin thrill. She went doggedly on. ". . . the natural dyestuffs used to color early yarns contained chemicals that eat away the fibers of the cloth as they oxidize. But some of these greens have faded to blue is all."

"Did Trevor tell you the altar cloth in the church was stitched by Elizabeth Spenser?" Richard asked. "Cecil wanted to burn it, saying it was blasphemous, but one of the villagers hid it. It was passed down in the family, and given to the church around 1800 or so. After the beginning of the Age of Reason."

"You think this cloth is her work, too?"

"Yes, I do," he told her. "I know its provenance."

"The villager hid this one, too? His family deserves a reward for keeping it dry and out of the air — they even knew not to fold it . . ." She turned around, almost knocking her nose on Richard's. He took a hasty step back. "Or are those 'villagers' named Lacey? Is that why you're keeping this room — Elizabeth's room — as a museum, some sort of multi-generation guilt trip?"

Richard's body stiffened. "You're the canny one, aren't you?"

Not really, she thought. But she wasn't going to get in his face about his sensitive under-belly, either. . . . Floorboards creaked in the room outside. Light footsteps came toward the door. As one Claire and Richard spun toward the sound.

The steps stopped in front of the closet. The sunlight reflected through the closet door darkened slightly and then brightened again, as though something not quite substantial had walked through it. This time we're going to see her, Claire thought. This is Elizabeth's room and we're intruding and we're going to see her.

She could feel dust settling on her eyeballs, but she couldn't close her eyes. A breath was caught in her chest, but she couldn't exhale. Richard's arm was pressed like a live wire against her shoulder, but she couldn't inch away. The walls of the room seemed to cave slowly inwards. The air was cold, as stiflingly cold as the grave.

Something moved in the doorway. Several dust motes, maybe, or a reflection from an old window with warped glass . . . Or nothing. Claire deflated. She ordered herself not to grab Richard's arm and cling like some stupid soap opera heroine.

He jerked himself away from her and strode across the room, peering from the door like a soldier from his bunker. "There's the cat," he said, somewhat breathlessly. "Sitting in the sun . . . No. It's gone, too."

"Oh," Claire croaked, for lack of anything better to say. She rolled the cloth and set it respectfully down. She wiped her clammy palms on her jeans. The room was warm again, and yet she hadn't imagined the cold.

"Well then," Richard said. "We should be going."

"Yeah. I think so." Brushing by him, Claire stepped through the opening. She walked on into the hall, where she waited while he replaced the secret panel and shut the closet door. "Melinda," she said deliberately as soon as he caught up with her. "Melinda said something about a ghost at Somerstowe. She would've made one up, if necessary, for her book."

"She'd have made up quite a bit, I daresay," Richard returned, and at her quick look up at him raised both hands to fend her off. "All right then, we'll have us a chat about Melinda. But not now. Not today."

What? Claire asked herself, you need to get your story straight? Planning to skip town tonight? And yet the more she saw of Richard the less she saw him as a criminal.

In silence they walked back down through the house, Claire, at least, stepping as lightly as possible so as to make no noise. If the house decided to play any more numbers from its temporal and spatial hit parade, she wasn't up to hearing them.

Richard locked the front door of the Hall behind them. When they reached the Lodge he excused himself and went inside. With a long look at the blank face of his front door, Claire walked on toward her flat.

The worst thing about this — this case, she thought, is what it's doing to me. The lie to Sarita, small as it was. The sarcasm. The irritability. The paranoia, for God's sake. Being with Richard in particular was like walking a tightrope, a constant struggle to keep her balance, energizing and exhausting at once. Her quest for Melinda threatened him, didn't it? He was afraid, and like any frightened man he'd come out fighting. The question was, why was he threatened?

And the second question was, was her own hormonal flux blinding her to Richard's possible guilt?

Muttering four-letter words, she unlocked the door of her flat, stepped inside, and stopped, her hand still on the knob. Some instinct even deeper than the one that responded to ripples in time and space was now responding to an almost palpable scent of danger.

Leaving the door open behind her, Claire picked up the furled umbrella and rushed the bathroom. No one was there. She threw open the doors of the wardrobe. No one was there. No one was crammed into the kitchen cabinet or was huddled behind the neatly folded sofa bed. She even looked out all the windows, but none of them was close enough to a drainpipe or a roof for anyone to hide outside.

Shaking her head, Claire released the umbrella and flexed the blood back into her whitened knuckles. Now who was being hyper-vigilant? Nothing was wrong, nothing was disarranged . . .

Wait a minute. She'd left the doors of the wardrobe open. Now they were closed. She'd left Melinda's letters stacked to the right of the desk blotter. Now they were stacked in its center, next to her notes.

Claire ran to the wardrobe and groped in its back corner. There was the box with Melinda's ring, safe and sound. There was her own jewelry case, holding a pearl necklace and earring set and a pair of tiny diamond studs. Theft, then, was not the motive.

As if she didn't know what the motive was. She spun around to the desk and sorted through the letters. One dated June 10 was in an envelope postmarked June 17. The second page of her notes was on top of the first. Someone had searched the apartment and read everything. Someone wanted to find out how much Claire knew, just how much of a threat she was.

Everyone in town knew she was looking for Melinda. God only knew how many people in addition to the Nairs had keys to the flat. She hadn't seen Richard all afternoon . . . *Don't get fixated on Richard.* Only Alec, for example, knew about the letter beneath the carpet.

Except for the person who'd sent it.

She couldn't trust anyone, she reminded herself, not even the Digbys. Who else was more likely to know which village closets were rattling with skeletons? Or the Nairs, who from their shop-and-post office nexus would know everything the Digbys didn't. And Alec and Richard were childhood buddies, weren't they? Not that she was ready to indulge in conspiracy theories. Not yet, anyway.

So now what? Running away wasn't an option. She had to tell Alec someone had searched her room. Even if he'd done it himself he'd expect her to report it. She had to keep one jump ahead of the evildoer, whoever it was . . . Right, she thought. One jump ahead, where she could feel his hot breath on the back of her neck.

Claire was frightened. And she was sure as hell going to come out fighting.

Chapter Nine

After the evening sunlight outside, the pub seemed murky. So much smoke hung in the air Claire wondered if Rob and Diana were grilling sausages over an open fire. But no, the smoke was from several burning cigarettes. Since she could hardly ask for scuba gear, she told herself she was sacrificing her lungs for a good cause and waded in.

Tonight the huge animal, part dog, part Shetland pony, was lying at the foot of the stairs. He looked up as Claire passed. His morose brown eyes reminded her of Fred Siebold. No, she thought, Fred wasn't Melinda's lover, actual or projected. Just not her style.

Alec was sitting near the bar, idly watching a soccer game on the TV. Claire zigzagged among the tables, said hello to several volunteers, and sat down beside him. "Hello, Alec."

He looked up with a smile. "Hello there. Fancy a Taddy Porter? Have you eaten?"

"I'll try the porter, thank you. And yes, I've eaten." She'd heated up a can of soup and crumbled crackers into it, if you could call that eating.

But she wasn't going to let Alec pay for another meal.

He made arcane gestures at Rob. Rob drew off a glass of rich brown liquid topped by creamy foam. Without waiting for Diana to bring it — she was flirting with someone on the far side of the room — Alec reached a long arm to the bar and handed Claire the glass. With a beetle-browed glower at Diana's back, Rob moved on down the bar and greeted Fred and Janet with a, "What'll you have, then?"

Claire took a deep drink of the porter. Its sharp and yet sweet tang scoured her throat of dust, mold, and acid. False courage, maybe, but she'd take any she could get. "Alec, when I got back to my room tonight I found some things disarranged — mainly my letters from Melinda and some notes. Sarita says she didn't see anyone go inside."

"Bloody hell!" Alec's face went from sociable to steely. He enveloped her hand with his own and squeezed. Her bones squealed. "I'll get on to Blake so as he can lay on some more constables. Can't have you in danger."

"I don't know enough to be in danger," Claire asserted, with more conviction than she felt. She only had to be perceived as a threat to be in danger. Melinda's disappearance might have been forgotten if Claire hadn't come to Somerstowe, asking questions and finding letters beneath the carpet.

If Alec had put the letter there himself he was a superb actor . . . That's just it, thought Claire. Everyone in town is an actor. She was just going to have to play along.

She extracted her hand from his and wrapped it, too, around her glass. "What did Blake say about the letter I found?"

"No joy. Both envelope and paper were covered in too many finger-prints, in too poor a condition, to identify any one in particular. The paper itself is nothing special. The flap was sealed with water, not saliva. The letters were cut from the Derby daily. The last I saw the snap it was on the notice board at the Hall — anyone could have taken it. The letter is helpful, Blake says, but what needs finding is Melinda's body."

"Then we need to look for it. Blake wasted a lot of time and effort searching the reservoir where her car was found. I think she's here."

"Blake had his lads going door to door," Alec pointed out.

"Did he bring in dogs? I have a friend at home who works with search and rescue dogs — they'll turn up human bones that are fifty years old or even older."

"No, no dogs. You're right, Claire. We should have another shufti round the village. And I might could . . ." Alec frowned. "Well, no, not that. I'll get on to Blake about another search."

She tilted her head quizzically. Whatever he'd almost let slip, it was gone now. Hoping it was nothing significant, she went on, "I'm sure y'all checked out the cellars of the Hall. What about the crypt of the church?"

"We searched the cellars, right enough, though another go wouldn't hurt. They're a proper maze, they are. But the crypt, well then . . ."

"Everyone in town knows about Trevor opening the crypt to install central heating. Where else would you hide a dead body except among other dead bodies?" Claire saw Richard's sketches of the crypt superimposed on the drifting smoke in the room like a cinematic dissolve effect. "I just thought it'd be worthwhile looking. No stone unturned, and all that."

"I'll get on to Trevor, too, then," said Alec, his firm nod indicating that matters were well in hand.

Claire only hoped they were. If the truth be told — not that it was being told, not by a long shot — she didn't want Alec to be the murderer any more than she wanted Richard to be. She didn't want any of these people to be a murderer. She didn't want Melinda to be dead, period. But she was.

A flat American accent whined beneath the British-inflected babel. Janet and Fred were still leaning on the bar. Fred's face was even longer than usual, while Janet's was slightly shriveled. "Come on," Fred said to her. "I was only making conversation."

"He didn't mean it," Janet said to Rob, who was hovering nearby rinsing glasses. His face looked like a garden gnome's, round and blank. No telling what Fred had said or why Janet was defending Rob. He was short, and yet he was broad enough he could probably pick up a battleaxe and defend himself with one hand tied behind his back.

No, he wasn't Melinda's type either. Even if he'd been, she'd never have gotten it on with a married man, no matter how rocky the marriage.

Diana worked her way through the crowd and wedged herself between Alec and Claire. "You'll be needing a refill then, eh, Alec? All the better to sort out our Yank invaders." She jerked her head toward Fred and Janet and managed to include Claire in her gesture. Claire smiled, taking her comment as a joke even if it probably hadn't been meant as one.

"Yes, thank you, Diana," said Alec. "Claire?"

Knowing she couldn't afford to get fuzzy headed, she said, "I'll have lemonade this time, please."

"Right." The bottom hem of Diana's crop top hung like a curtain several inches from her midriff, exposing its gentle bulge over the waistband of her stretch pants. The woman was solidly built, Claire thought, but it was the tight, clingy clothes that made her look overweight. Although if Diana was typical of her sex, buying something in a larger size was the equivalent of pulling your own teeth.

The chair at Claire's elbow scraped and she spun around. Elliot Moncrief folded himself gracefully into a seated position. He was wearing a tweed jacket and an ascot. The tooth marks of a comb were visible in his thinning hair. Claire expected him to launch into a Monty Python routine. Instead he shed a charming smile on her and Diana both. "Bring me a Bristol Cream, Diana, that would be lovely."

"Right," Diana said again, and ducked behind the bar.

"You may be playing the detective just now," Elliot said to Claire, "but I hear in civilian life you're a librarian."

Another suspect — good. She smiled. "My title is media specialist, which translates into librarian."

"Thought we should have a bit of a chin wag — I'm dying to know if what I've heard about librarians is true."

"You mean," Claire said, "that librarians are uptight, upright, and inhibited creatures? I'll have you know that sometimes I lose all sense of decency and go two days without flossing my teeth."

Elliot brayed with delight. "And yet you're Melinda's pal, and she such a tearaway. How can this be?"

"Oil and vinegar make a tasty salad dressing."

"May I assume, then, you and Melinda have similar tastes? I mean, she was quite the original — in many ways. We grew to be very good friends indeed." Elliot winked and his elbow nudged Claire in the side.

It was all she could do to keep herself from groaning aloud. So Elliot was volunteering for the role of the mysterious lover. No, Melinda's taste wasn't infallible, and yes, she had a touching faith in the benefits of recreational sex. Elliot was safer, emotionally speaking, than anyone else — an amusing lightweight compared to Nigel, her husband . . . Why believe Elliot's version of events any more than anyone else's, Claire asked herself. "What do you think happened to Melinda?"

"Fluttered away, as butterflies eventually do." He shrugged. *Who me? Care about someone other than myself?* "I hope the dear girl didn't harm herself. I made it very clear that it was all for grins."

Melinda wouldn't have given herself a hangnail over a poser like Elliot. "Did you have a fight?"

"Oh, no, no. But I was her director. Most of these well-meaning amateurs simply haven't a clue. Melinda had her own little ideas about how the part should be played. We — shall we say — had our disagreements?"

"I'm sure you did." Especially since Melinda's ideas had probably been very good ones. "Why did you choose her to play Elizabeth?"

"The bones found in the church were of a small woman," replied Elliot. "Isn't that so, Alec?"

Alec was leaning on his elbow, looking at Elliot the way you'd look at a television sitcom in its third rerun. "Some say people were smaller in the seventeenth century."

"Ergo, we need a small woman to play the part. And not before time, may I add. That's why I chose Trillian Nair this year. Willowy sweet young thing and close to the right age, for once."

Diana materialized at Claire's elbow and slammed three glasses onto the table. Ouch, Claire thought. She'd played Elizabeth herself, hadn't she? And she probably hadn't been a small woman since puberty. But Elliot held his sherry to the light as though inspecting it for impurities, indifferent to Diana's glare on the back of his neck.

"Fine draught of ale, Diana," said Alec, the peacemaker.

Diana nodded truculently and turned away. Claire considered her own glass of what she would have called 7-Up. It was cool enough to condense on the outside, but without a shred of ice. She drank.

"I say, Diana." Elliot beckoned her back with a hailing-a-taxi gesture. "I've decided to add an extra dimension to The Play this year. Instead of simply implying that Elizabeth was involved in witchcraft, we're going to stage a real Black Mass. *Pater noster qui es in coelis, maledicatur nomen tuum, destruatur regnum tuum* — and so forth and so on."

Whether or not Diana understood the Latin of the bastardized prayer, she certainly caught the drift of Elliot's — it was a joke, wasn't it? Her eyes widened. "Oh, Elliot, you mustn't. You never know what you might call from out that stone circle."

"You named your pub the Druid's Circle," Elliot riposted. *"In nomine diaboli et servorum suorum. . . ."*

Alec's voice was like a lid clamping down on a grease fire. "Elliot, don't be stupid. The name of the pub is for the tourists, you know that. There's nothing evil in the stone circle, despite what Cecil says in The Play when he sees Elizabeth picking flowers there. Witchcraft was the last survival of the old nature religions, whilst the Black Mass is Satanism, an invention of the Middle Ages. They're not the same at all. He's only winding you up, Diana. Don't pay him any mind."

Diana's features puckered. "Bugger off, Elliot," she said, and flounced away.

Elliot laughed. "Not two brain cells to rub together, our Diana. Witchcraft, Satanism — it's all rot, only good for a giggle. You know that, Alec, there's a good chap."

"You wouldn't have thought it was rot three hundred years ago, if it had been you in the dock and not Elizabeth. She was innocent of all charges and yet they found her guilty and killed her even so."

"Well excuse me, Constable," Elliot returned. "Didn't mean to cast aspersions on your Elizabeth."

Alec did have a thing about Elizabeth, Claire thought. He himself had said witchcraft was rubbish, but he was right — Elizabeth was just as dead. Was it worse to die for an illusion than for a cause?

Alec looked down at his glass. His cheeks were slightly flushed. If the cliche librarian was an inhibited spinster, then the cliche cop was a just-the-facts tough guy. Alec, though, spoke more like a scholar. More like Richard, who was certified a scholar — and yet who had a yen to be an artist and craftsman, like Claire herself.

Suddenly she thought of the little room at the top of Somerstowe Hall, Elizabeth's hideaway in life and in death as well. Alec had come strolling along the gallery just seconds after Claire first saw Elizabeth's ghost. He'd lived here all of his life. Richard said he knew the Hall better than anyone else.

It was Alec who was caretaking the room — and Elizabeth's innocence as well. Melinda was right, Alec was sweet. In a very masculine way, of course. Claire smiled at the top of his head. But she wasn't going to say anything to him about the room. His feelings were his own business. Which Richard was respecting, to let her think he was the one tidying the room. Yeah, there was a sensitive guy lurking inside Richard's crust. Go figure.

"Diana made quite a good Elizabeth, once," Elliot was confiding in Claire's ear. She winced at his alcoholic breath. "Then she lost her girlish figure and peaches and cream complexion. She could hardly outrun time's winged chariots, could she?"

"None of us can," Claire returned tartly.

Elliot raised his chin, tightening the wattle hanging beneath. "The play must go on, mustn't it? Diana wasn't best pleased, mind you, to be replaced in the role. Especially by Melinda. It took Miss American Pie perhaps five minutes to see how solemn Diana is wont to be — positively grim — and to start winding her up good and proper."

"Melinda wound us all up." Alec's mouth softened into a wry smile. "We all have chinks in our armor. She didn't mean anything by it."

"Every now and then she'd go a little bit too far," Claire conceded. "She was never malicious." *Like you,* she added silently to Elliot.

He was neither sweet nor sensitive, was he? A lightweight, but with a cruel and callous edge. Yes, Melinda would've thought he was a hoot. She might even have gotten a kick out of sleeping with him — Claire couldn't be positive one way or the other. If not, though, then she'd caught Elliot in a lie. Unfortunately it was one so typical of the male sex she couldn't count it against him.

Elliot continued his monologue. "This year's production of 'An Historie' is scheduled for June 20 and 21. We've been rehearsing for ten days already. I know three weeks is a dreadfully short time, but I'm a professional, I can move mountains and aging actresses as well."

Diana strolled by, murmuring, "We're so lucky to have a big name toff like Elliot to help us along."

"I'm even thinking of purchasing my humble abode here in Somerstowe," Elliot went on, with a cheery wave at Diana's departing backside. "I do so like quaint things — antiques, old houses, two hundred year old plays."

"Elliot's been one of the trustees of Somerstowe Hall since the Cranbournes willed it to the Trust," said Alec.

"Has he," Claire returned, wondering whether that gave him a chance for any cozy financial deals.

"So, Claire," Elliot went on. "How can we get you involved? Richard is reprising his role as Phillip — our blue-blooded narrator and chorus. Alec is faithful Walter once again. When Diana gave up the role of Elizabeth Rob went from playing Walter to playing Cecil, the villain, and he's back as well."

"And Diana played Cecil's wife Lettice?" Claire dimly remembered seeing her name on Melinda's playbill.

"Grudgingly, letting us know she was much too good to cut off her nose to spite her face. Although in her case that would be an improvement." He laughed. Claire and Alec didn't. "If you ask me — and you did, didn't you? — Diana was born for the part of Lettice. As for you, well, we have a few small parts you could play quite nicely. Those lovely curls would look a treat in a period cap." Elliot reached out to touch her hair.

Claire, with visions of casting couches, evaded his hand and said quickly, "I'm no actress. Didn't Sarita say she was wardrobe mistress? I could help her. I wield a mean needle."

If Elliot was disappointed at her not rising to his bait, he didn't show it. "Just so. Sarita would be delighted. And you could turn the pages for Priscilla, who provides musical accompaniment during the show itself. If you read music, that is."

"I can read music, I play at the piano now and then. I'd like to help. Thanks for asking." Claire drained the last of her lemonade, congratulating herself for working her way into an inside look at the production.

"This year is the fifteenth performance," said Alec, half to himself. "I began by playing Elizabeth's young brother. Time's winged chariot indeed."

Claire scooted her chair back. "If y'all will excuse me, Alec, Elliot, I really need to get my beauty sleep." Not to mention that her bladder was about to burst.

Immediately both men were on their feet. Elliot was the quicker with a handful of change, throwing it onto the bar like a duke distributing coins to the peasantry. With a grimace, as though fondly imagining dukes trundled off to the guillotine, Rob scooped up the money and counted it into the cash drawer.

Claire sighed. Next time she'd slip Rob a few pounds in advance . . . On a shelf just below the cash drawer sat a camera. A new digital camera, the same model as Melinda's. No way, she thought. But she had to ask. "Ah, Rob — that's a nice camera you've got there. Melinda had one like that. She tried to teach me how to use it. I never quite caught on, though."

Rob looked from her to the camera and back. "Yeh."

Alec said behind Claire's shoulder, "Melinda showed you some tricks with her camera, didn't she, Rob? That's why you went and bought yourself one."

"Yeh." Rob's black eyes drilled into Claire's. He knew exactly what she was thinking and dared her to make something of it.

Never mind. Alec vouched for him. "Thanks," she said, to Rob, to Elliot, to Alec. "Good night."

Elliot gripped Claire's hand and lifted it to his lips. "Parting is such sweet sorrow, and so forth and so on. Until we meet again."

"Yeah. Sure." Wiping her hand on her jeans and nodding at Fred and Janet, Claire headed for the door. Only to find Alec beside her, every line of his face set in police procedure mode. He was going to walk her home and scare away the bogeyman beneath the bed. *Great.*

Don't get fixated on Alec, either, she told herself. He was going along with all her bright-eyed detecting ideas because it was his job, not because he was the bogeyman himself. For one thing, he didn't have a motive for killing Melinda any more than any one else did. Well, Richard resented Melinda for some reason, and Diana resented her for better reason, but so what?

So, Claire answered, what if Diana had written the threatening letter? Or what if Elliot had done it to stir up even more trouble between the women than he already had? That would tickle his sense of humor, such as it was.

The evening was clear, the sun flirting with the horizon and casting long shadows across the street. "Is Elliot always like that?" she asked.

Alec nodded. "Always on stage, isn't he? I suppose we could hire him to play the village idiot."

Elliot is no idiot. Claire led Alec up the steps and opened the door. It took him all of two minutes to check the place out. "Well, carry on," he said with a smile. "Give me a shout if you have any more scares."

"I will," Claire promised.

He hesitated just a moment, then leaned down and brushed her cheek with his lips. The light kiss left a pleasant glow in her skin. Funny how touching Alec was comforting and touching Richard was anything but. "Remember," he murmured, "I'm keeping an eye on you."

Like you were last night, down in the yard? He didn't mean that as a threat. Surely he didn't mean any of it as a threat. She offered him a brave smile of her own. "Thanks."

Claire locked the door and stood with her back against it. Alec was no idiot, either. He knew she suspected him. She wondered what else he knew.

*C*laire walked into the Hall yawning. She couldn't remember what she'd dreamed, only that her dreams had been anxious and left her more tired than when she'd gone to sleep. She resolved to stop watching old horror movies at bedtime, even though she knew darn well what the problem really was.

Outside the sun shone blissfully on village and Hall, but inside Claire needed all the illumination she could get. She turned on the overhead light in the gallery and was reaching for the lamp when Richard appeared. So he hadn't skipped town last night after all. Not that she'd expected him to.

Today he was wearing a handsome Fair Isle sweater whose heather grays, greens, and blues complimented the ivory tones of his clean-shaven cheeks. With a cordial, "Good morning," he started inspecting the canvas and the completed chart. She tensed. His face cracked into a smile. "Well done." He started pulling out the tacks holding the canvas to the frame.

"Thank you." Claire felt as though she'd ducked an egg hurled in her direction only to discover it was filled with confetti. She went after the tacks on the other side of the frame. Together they released the canvas, rolled it up, and carried it to a spic and span storeroom on the ground floor.

For a few moments Claire oohed and aahed over the treasures piled on shelves spaced around a dehumidifier. She peered closely at a set of bed hangings with needlepoint applique slips, the motifs worked on thin canvas, then cut out and sewed onto a linen backing. The stitches of the couched thread around the edge of each motif were so fine and even they must've been sewn by fairies with hands the size of thimbles.

Richard indicated a bundle of what looked like tapestry. "This one is a bit older. Are you up for it?"

"Why not?" Claire checked over one end and in her best professional voice said, "Late sixteenth or early seventeenth century. Needlepoint, not tapestry. Tent stitch. Cushion cover, probably. Some kind of mytho-logical theme. There's a monogram in the corner. . . ."

She bent closer to the fabric, bending closer to Richard at the same time. Beneath the mildew and mothball smell she sensed another, a fresh aroma that reminded her of the breeze through the Hall gardens. Every fine hair on the back of her neck twitched like antennae. That gentle humming was either the dehumidifier or her own unruly senses strain-ing toward the envelope of energy around Richard's body.

Wrong time, wrong place, wrong guy, she told herself, and went on, ". . . initials ES — Elizabeth Spenser? No, wait. A crest with two stags, the symbol of the Cavendishes. Elizabeth Shrewsbury, also known as Bess of Hardwick. Did she make this one herself, do you think?"

"It was probably made at Chatsworth or Hardwick by her embroiderers." Richard stepped back and bumped into a shelf. "You'll have a go at it, then?"

"If you'll let me," she returned.

"Why not?" He smiled again, a quick sardonic flash of tooth and eye, and gathered the rolled canvas into his arms. Lugging the bundle upstairs, he draped it over the frame and announced, "This needs basting, not tacking."

"I'll take care of it," Claire returned.

He balanced on the balls of his feet as though contemplating a quick getaway. "Well then. About the — ah — the chat I promised you . . ."

"Richard!" called Susan's voice from the stairs. "The new paint samples are here!"

"Later," he said, and vanished out door.

So was he going to try and wriggle out of it, Claire asked herself, or was he actually going to talk about Melinda? And if so, was he going to be honest or was he going to do a smoke and mirrors routine like Elliot?

She turned to the cushion cover. A linen border had already been stitched to it. Judging by the yellowed thread, the border had been attached at about the same time some ham-handed person darned a few moth holes. Soon after the turn of the century, maybe, the Cranbourne daughters dutifully doing their mending instead of begetting heirs to keep the Hall in the family. Maud had been what? ninety? when she asked Julian Lacey to search the premises for valuables.

Claire found some heavy thread in the box of supplies and started basting the linen border to the frame. She'd have to pick out those old darns, she estimated, re-stitch some mangled areas, and even splice in some new canvas where there were actual holes in the fabric. At least the needlework had been cleaned fairly recently. It probably illustrated the myth of Venus and Adonis, with a woman reaching pleadingly toward a man who was more interested in a pack of dogs. The watching courtiers were dressed in the ruffs and pantaloons of high Elizabethan fashion.

This canvas was much more tightly woven than that used for the Morris canvas. The stitches were minuscule. Light or no light, by noon Claire's eyes were crossed. No matter where she looked all she could see was stitches, as though her retinal nerve was done in petit point. Elizabeth Spenser and her cat could've danced a pavane down the long gallery and she wouldn't have seen them.

How nice, she thought, to be so absorbed in her work she'd been able to *not* think about Melinda's murder mystery for a couple of hours. "No offense," she said quietly into the air.

After lunch she'd ask Richard about that embroidery from the attic. It was a valuable historical artifact that needed to be cleaned and stored properly. Besides, she was curious about Elizabeth's handiwork, and wanted another look at it, as though some dynamic of cloth and thread would give her insight into the seventeenth-century woman's slandered soul.

Funny, Alec hadn't come by this morning. Surely he wasn't embarrassed about that peck on her cheek last night. She'd give him the benefit of the doubt. He'd been trying to reassure her, not threaten her, not even come on to her — even though his long distance relationship could be last year's news.

Shaking her head, Claire walked down the stairs and looked around for Janet or Susan or any available lunch partner. But it was Richard who was loitering with apparent intent on the bottom step.

"Claire," he stated. "I'll be popping over to Haddon Hall this afternoon to view a tapestry. Would you care to ride along?"

Claire looked at him. His expression was sober, his eyes direct and guileless, and he wasn't smiling. If he intended to knock her over the head and leave her body in a hedgerow, he'd at least be smiling. And he could've committed any kind of mayhem on her person yesterday afternoon. All he'd done was keep her from cracking her skull on the rock pile.

He was, she hoped, as tired of playing games as she was. "Sure. Let me run back to my apartment and freshen up."

"Half past twelve, then. I'll collect you." He walked off with a grimace he probably intended to be a winning smile.

Collect me? Claire saw herself chloroformed and dumped into a bottle labeled, "Annoying American woman, genus *frienda Melinda*," and laughed out loud. Hey, the day was going well. Maybe she was on a roll. She hurried down the street to her flat, declined Susan's invitation outside the tearoom, and grabbed a meat pie from Sarita's warming cabinet. The newspaper headline, she noted, was of some new political scandal back home.

While she paid for the pie she told Sarita where she was going and with whom. Sarita nodded. "You will like Haddon, it is altogether a fine old manor house. And since you are going with Richard, here is a letter for him. From his London lady friend, I am thinking."

Sarita grinned. But the letter Claire took from her hand was no joke. The Scottish Parliament stamp was a patch of crimson and gold against the white envelope. The London postmark looked like a bruise on fair skin. RICHARD LACEY, THE LODGE, SOMERSTOWE, DERBYSHIRE S31 4BR was actually typed, not printed. It might be a solicitation from an exclusive charity, except there was no return address.

"I'll see that he gets this," Claire croaked, and walked out of the shop with the letter a live ember in her hand. She would see that he got it, all right. As Elliot had said, the play must go on. And it wasn't even remotely a game.

Chapter Ten

*C*laire stood in her cool, quiet room, senses alert. No one had been there, she decided.

She eyed the teakettle. In novels investigators steamed open letters. She knew if she tried opening Richard's, though, she'd end up giving him a soggy mess. Better to just hand it over and see how he reacted.

The meat pie was lukewarm in the middle and she managed to choke only half of it down. Quickly she changed from her jeans into a cotton blouse and khaki skirt, brushed her teeth, and locked the door behind her.

Across the street stood Richard's Rover with its National Trust oak leaf emblazoned on the door. Some nice perks came with his job, Claire told herself. She opened the passenger side door and climbed in.

He looked around with a nod. "Bang on time, I see."

She started to reply with some dazzling display of verbal ability when the back door of the car opened. Diana Jackman dumped two empty shopping bags onto the seat and followed them inside. Damn! Claire said to herself. She twisted her face into a smile. "Hello, Diana. Going shopping?"

"Yeh, market day in Bakewell. Have to keep the customers fed, don't I? Thanks for the lift, Richard."

"No problem." He started the car and drove off.

Claire glanced around. In the light of day Diana's make-up looked even thicker . . . Was that a discoloration along one cheekbone, a bruise hidden by an extra layer of blusher? She hoped not. "Ah — that's right, Fred or Janet said you don't drive."

"All because that bloody rozzer was too bone idle to chase after criminals and did me instead. Mind you, I'd only had a couple of pints."

"Oh," said Claire. A couple of pints of strong ale would leave the Terminator tipsy — and cost him his driver's license, too.

Expressionlessly, eyes front, Richard negotiated the high street and sped out into the countryside.

Huge dark clouds sailed across the vast Derbyshire sky, making Claire feel as though she was at the bottom of a bowl. It was going to rain again. She'd be disappointed to come to England and find it warm and dry, but she was willing to give it a try.

Richard plugged a tape into the cassette player. The bagpipes, electric guitars, and thick dialect of a Scottish folk-rock group filled the car. That figures, Claire thought. She'd finally found someone else who liked rock 'n' reel and it turned out to be Richard.

"What are they saying?" asked Diana.

Richard, the son of a Scot, smothered a grin. "It's a code used by the Scottish Nationalist Party to alert their operatives here in England. They're plotting to put the Jacobites back on the throne. Assuming they can find any."

His grin led Claire into temptation. "It's like playing Beatles songs backwards for the secret messages."

"Richard!" Diana exclaimed. "Do Scotland Yard know about this?"

"It wouldn't be much of an uprising if they did, now would it?"

For a moment Diana was silent. Then she said, "You're winding me up."

"Yes, I am. Sorry."

"Me ancestors weren't Scotch," she muttered. "Me people have been in Somerstowe a long time. Me grandfather was a proper gentleman."

Elliot had Diana pegged right in one way, Claire thought. She was humor-impaired. But then, domestic abuse wasn't exactly a joke.

They dropped Diana off in Bakewell, Richard making sure Rob would be picking her up. As soon as they pulled away Claire asked, "Was that a bruise on her face? Any chance she just walked into a door or something?"

"Not bloody likely," he said with a sigh. "Alec and Trevor both have had words with Rob. Diana stays with him, though. There's only so much they can do."

Yeah, Claire told herself, sometimes you just can't see any alternatives.

Once at Haddon Hall, she set aside her feminist indignation and helped Richard check over a slightly decayed but still gorgeous Flemish tapestry. He jotted statistics in a small notebook and told the caretaker he'd recommend the Trust buy it for Somerstowe. "It'd look a treat in the main bedchamber, same motif as the bed hangings."

Then, mission accomplished, they set off on a busman's holiday tour through the house. Richard commented on paneling, glass, mantelpieces, and the quality of the restoration. Claire gaped appreciatively. By the time they reached the Technicolor rose gardens terraced above the River Wye they were chatting as companionably as though they were on a successful first date.

What they were on was their best behavior, Claire thought as they walked back to the car. They were trying not to rub each other the wrong way. Not that rubbing each other the right way was an option. A good detective wouldn't be responding to her suspect's erotic vibrations. What if Richard had gone from vinegar to honey simply to distract her from her quest?

As they turned out of the parking lot the rain began, first a few drops, then torrents of cats, dogs, and other furry animals. The countryside blurred into a gray-green smear. When a building sign-posted THE DEVONSHIRE ARMS loomed through the streaming water Richard announced, "Time for tea."

They raced through the downpour to the entrance, ordered tea from the receptionist, and found a table next to the fireplace in the deserted bar. Even while she mopped her glasses Claire could see that Richard's hair was damp enough to lie down flat, as though it'd suddenly gone shy. She knew her own hair was curling like a medusa. Maybe that's why he was staring stone-faced at her.

Or maybe it was because they were hanging between breaths, between heartbeats, time suspended, waiting for a director to yell, "Action!" But they had no director, they were making it up as they went along . . . "I suppose you thought Melinda was the attractive one," Richard said.

Here we go. Claire replaced her glasses. "Sometimes I felt sort of eclipsed, like a star by the sun. Glamour was her thing, though, not mine."

"Glamour can wear a bit thin, even start to look dishonest."

"Not necessarily. Melinda was one of those people who polished the outside to hide what she thought were imperfections inside."

"And you knew what was inside."

"Yes. I did. I liked her all the better for knowing."

"Did you now?" Richard asked. There were the tiger's eyes again, evaluating, questioning, doubting. Claire ducked, and kicked herself for ducking.

An aproned woman emerged from the kitchen door. She was carrying a tray loaded with tea, scones, and dishes of thick cream and strawberry jam. "It's a proper spate outside, isn't it?" she asked cheerfully.

"Yes." And there was going to be a spate inside too. Claire poured tea, gulped, and cauterized most of the mucus membrane in her mouth, so that she could barely taste her scone. Across the table Richard cradled his cup in his hands and gazed at the fire. "A penny for your thoughts," she said at last.

"I'm wondering where I should begin."

"With this." Claire pulled the letter from her pocket and scooted it across the table.

"Oh, for the love of. . . ." Richard grabbed the letter and tore it open. "I almost had myself convinced that Melinda wasn't doing it. That you weren't taking up where she left off."

"Doing what?"

"You hand me another demand and then play stupid? Come off it."

"Sarita gave me that letter to give to you," Claire retorted. "If it has something to do with Melinda then you'd better fill me in, and now."

He threw the letter at her and fell back into his chair, arms crossed, face averted. Time plummeted onward, filled with hammering heartbeats.

The paper crinkled in Claire's hand. "Lacey," read the typed text. "Time to ante up again and keep that secret safe. Cash this time. One hundred quid. You know the drill. Affectionately, an admirer."

"Blackmail," Claire said.

"Snap," returned Richard. "Blackmail it is."

"You opened one of these in the pub, didn't you? And you had some last summer — I, ah, I got that out of Sarita. You think Melinda sent those? You think I'm sending the ones now?"

"I have a clue, don't I?" he said tightly.

"Oh yeah, right! Like I'm going to just give you the letter, here, alone with you . . ." She veered away from that. "You think Melinda told me something to blackmail you with, don't you? Well she didn't. And if I'm not sending the letters, then Melinda wasn't, either."

"She was working with someone else, then."

Claire had to let that one go. "Why Melinda?"

"The letters told me to send small antiques from the house to an address in London. I sussed it out — it's close to Nigel Killigrew's office. He collects antiques. He's a trustee of Somerstowe Hall. Melinda worked for publishers in New York and London. The letters stopped coming when she disappeared. Until you arrived." Richard's accent was migrating north, away from the Oxford-Cambridge axis toward a Highland hillside covered with thistles, diphthongs, and glottal stops.

The cool, damp air from an open window at Claire's back made the nape of her neck crawl. The warmth of the fire on her face made her cheeks burn. Yes, Nigel was a trustee of Somerstowe Hall. That was why Melinda chose it for her summer's project. But . . . "You were taking things from the house?"

"Of course not. I bought items in antique shops and posted them."

"Oh. Good move."

"Melinda had a motive to blackmail me," Richard went stubbornly on. "She was in a position to — well, to know how to go about it."

To know your secret, Claire added to herself. Or anyone else's, for that matter. Melinda was very good at smelling out buried embarrassments, sensitized as she was by her own. No wonder she'd become a journalist. "The blackmailer threatened to publicize your secret, right? I guess you couldn't exactly say 'publish and be damned.'"

"No."

"You haven't gone to the police with the letters?"

"Melinda's blackmailing me seems to give me a motive to kill her, doesn't it? If I started helping the police with their inquiries in a murder case, then I'd hardly be keeping up appearances with the Trust."

"You think she was murdered, then?"

"Don't you?"

"Yes, I do," admitted Claire.

"I didn't kill her." Richard glared at the fire, his expression repeating that of the lion on the stamp. It would have helped if the innkeeper had appeared at that moment carrying thumbscrews, but she brought only fresh scones and hot water for the teapot.

Richard uncrossed his arms, refilled his cup, and scooped blood-red jam onto his plate. He ate another scone, doctoring each individual bite with jam and cream. Even though his teeth glinted between his lips, his incisors didn't seem to be any longer than usual.

Claire refilled her cup, halved her scone, and smeared each side with cream and jam so that the colors mingled into a rosy pink. She took a big bite of the rich, sweet, buttery treat. Richard could be lying up one side and down the other. And yet his story hung together. As far as it went.

Melinda's sense of humor would every now and then run a stop sign and leave skid marks. She joked and teased to keep everyone except Claire at arm's length, frightened of intimacy even as she looked for intimacy in various love affairs. And in a marriage that failed miserably. With that much pain distorting her perceptions she could well have gone too far. And that come-hither sketch suggested why.

"Okay," Claire said. "Melinda played jokes. She didn't do anything illegal. Especially not for Nigel. And he's not the only trustee. What about Elliot? He likes antiques, and a spot of blackmail sounds just like his idea of fun and games."

"I've thought of him, right enough. But he had at least one letter, too. I saw Sarita hand it him."

"So he sent one to hims . . ." Claire stopped. "Wait a minute. Yours weren't the only ones?"

"You didn't ask Sarita, whilst you were prying into my affairs, if there were any others?"

"No, I didn't." Rats, she added to herself. "That makes it even less likely Melinda was sending the letters. She might have had a motive to play a joke on you. She might've somehow fallen over a secret of yours. But how does that translate into her going after other people, too?"

Richard's jaw twitched. "All right. Like Alice in the looking glass, I try to believe at least one impossible thing every day. Today I'll believe in your innocence. In Melinda's innocence, if you like."

"You're acting as if it's up to you to decide. It's not impossible, though, it's a fact."

"I'm sorry, Claire. It's the best I can do." His bright golden-brown eyes were fixed on her face again. Looking into those eyes was like looking into twin fireplaces, shape after shape forming and re-forming in the flames. He wanted her to believe him. Claire wanted to believe him. Not that that was at all logical. But her coming to England to begin with hadn't been logical.

"If Melinda was blackmailing you or anyone else, she meant it as a joke," Claire said with a sigh. "She would've apologized, given you back the antiques, and treated you to dinner at the most exclusive restaurant in London. But she didn't have the chance, did she?"

"It wasn't that I disliked Melinda," insisted Richard. "We actually got on quite well. She pushed my buttons a bit, no harm in that. Even if she'd confessed to being the blackmailer, I'd hardly have killed her."

Time hiccuped. The room was faintly smoky, more from their own friction, Claire thought, than from the fire. "I try to believe at least one impossible thing every day, too. So today I'll believe you didn't kill Melinda."

"You're acting as though it's up to you to decide."

"I won't be sure I can trust you until you trust me. And I suppose you're not real motivated to do that."

His eyes fell at last. He looked down at his cup and slopped the tea back and forth like a do-it-yourself lava lamp. "Claire, I'll tell you what I can. Not what my secret is, though. Because it's not my own."

Oh. Claire heard Susan repeating Melinda's description of Richard: "He's too honest." Honest with himself. Sparing himself nothing. Demanding honesty from others even as he honorably protected some-one else's secret . . . Which only made him even more appealing, damn it all anyway.

Averting her eyes from his chiseled profile, she said, "Richard, you've got to go to the police with your blackmail letters. They must be tied in with Melinda's disappearance. For all you know, she was getting letters, too."

"Sarita might know," he returned, obviously trying to be helpful.

So either he didn't know about the letter beneath the carpet, or . . . He didn't know, Claire told herself, trying the concept on for size. She warmed up her tea and his, and gave him the last scone — she had enough to chew on. "So why did you make a date with Melinda the night she disappeared?"

"I'd decided she was the blackmailer. I wanted to sort it with her."

"But you had a fight instead."

"Alec and I were having one last look round the house, making sure everyone was away. She leapt out at us in the upper great chamber still wearing Elizabeth's gown and all, trying to frighten us. And I did jump.

Alec went dead white and then told her in no uncertain terms how little he appreciated her winding him up like that."

"Alec has a temper?"

"When he's stressed. He simply doesn't stress as easily as most."

Alec had snapped at Elliot in the pub last night, hadn't he? Nothing like an unsolved murder on your beat. "I guess The Play is stressful on everyone," Claire said neutrally.

"Oh aye, that it is. For whatever reason, Alec told Melinda off and then went on down the stairs, leaving me alone with her. And we rowed."

"Did you accuse her of blackmail?"

"I never had the chance. She told me she was breaking our date, she'd made other plans. I assumed she meant Elliot, though she put every man in the village through his paces. I said something about keeping commitments. I should've remembered her divorce and put it some other way, but I didn't do."

"Being stressed out yourself," Claire said dryly. "Yeah, that was hitting below the belt. She tried to make that marriage work."

One of Richard's brows annotated that statement. All he said was, "Melinda came back at me, saying I had no — well, she called me a eunuch."

"Oh boy. I figured we were going to get around to that sketch. What happened? Not that I want to hear any gory details," she added hastily.

"There are no gory details, that's just the point. It wasn't until I was actually making the sketch I realized she'd misinterpreted my intentions. I ended by having to refuse her advances, as they say in Victorian novels. I thought she'd shrugged it all off, more fool I."

"You rejected her?"

"I wasn't in the mood."

"She wouldn't have wanted a relationship, you know."

"If you're having sex, you're having a relationship." Richard stared at Claire as though daring her to make something of it.

What Claire would have liked to make of him was a bronze statue for posterity — a man who realized there was no such thing as free sex. "Somebody said you'd just broken off a relationship," she hazarded.

"Can't hide from your past in a village, can you?" Richard asked, dry in turn. "Yes, I'd broken it off with a woman in London. She was quite like Melinda in some ways, caught up in her work. She wouldn't come with me to Somerstowe, I wouldn't miss out the job at the Hall. The relationship was dying in any event, Somerstowe simply put the nails in the coffin."

"Yeah, I just ended one of those, too."

"Oh?"

"Things were starting to come unglued anyway, and when Melinda disappeared, well, that was it." Her view of Melinda, and Richard's view,

or Elliot's, or Nigel's, or even Steve's, for that matter, shifted kalei-
doscopically each from the other. Melinda probably intended it that
way. "You didn't mean to hurt her. She didn't mean to hurt you. Or
Alec, either. Even if she was the blackmailer, she meant it as a joke."

"I suppose so." Richard tried a smile, but it didn't quite work.

"Why," Claire went on, "did you keep that postcard I sent her?"

"She gave it me as an example of American pretentious architecture.
I bunged it onto the mantel and forgot about it. Housekeeping's not
my forte. Melinda would joke about that, too."

"She'd joke on the way to her own funer . . ." Claire stopped. "I came
here to find Melinda and her murderer. Now I want to find the
blackmailer, too. I bet they're the same person."

"Not a bit of it. The killer is someone else who thought Melinda was
the blackmailer."

"I don't like that version. That would mean the blackmailer is trying
to set the killer on me, too."

"You've already called more than a little attention to yourself,"
Richard told her. He swallowed the last morsel of scone and ran his
tongue between his lips.

The sight was as unsettling as his words. Of all the things Melinda
could've called him, Claire thought, asexual was as far from the truth
as calling him a Martian. And yes, he was too damned honest.

He looked up at her. "Are we allies, then?"

"I think a mutual cooperation treaty is called for, yes," she said, and
stopped before she said something about strange bedfellows.

The innkeeper strode across the floor, beat sparks out of the fire,
raised the window further, and turned to the table. "Anything else?
Sherry?"

"No, thank you," stated Claire.

"We'd better be away," Richard said, his voice regaining its usual crisp
Oxbridge inflections. He produced several coins and threw them on the
table, not protesting when Claire chipped in a few of her own and then
jammed the blackmail letter into her billfold. Not that she had any
coherent plans for dealing with it. Their chat had raised more issues
that it'd settled, but then, raising issues *was* Richard's forte.

Outside the rain had stopped. The world was filled with the scents
of damp earth, grass, and wool. Brilliant shafts of sunlight broke
through the clouds like Jacob's ladder joining earth to heaven. The wet
highway hissed beneath the wheels of the car. Funny, Claire thought as
the miles passed in silence, how neither of us has anything else to say.
Now.

By the time they made it back to Somerstowe the countryside was
steaming softly in the sunshine. Two police cars and a van sat in the
car park beside the shop. Rob Jackman stood outside the Druid's Circle,

the smoke of his cigarette drifting straight upward in the warm, humid air. "At the church," he said to Richard's query. "Opened the crypt."

Together Richard and Claire double-timed it up the street and around the corner. "The crypt?" he asked.

"Alec," she returned. "Looking for Melinda's body."

Between the quick and the dead, the churchyard was swarming. Villagers and tourists milled among the tombstones and stood outside the fence. The locals muttered to one another. The day-trippers took pictures of dusty, shirt-sleeved policemen moving like ants in and out of the church. Priscilla Digby carried a basket from kibitzer to kibitzer, hitting each one up for some charitable fund. Alec and Trevor stood at the lych gate as awkwardly as an old married couple who'd just had a tiff. With them was a rotund man in an expensive dark suit, inspecting his fingernails.

"Well, well," Richard said. "It's the second coming of DS Arnold Pakenham."

Now Claire understood Janet's reference to "Pakenpork." The detective sergeant looked, unfortunately, like Porky Pig. When Trevor motioned to Richard and Claire, Pakenham pulled his attention away from his manicure and turned toward them too, his colorless eyes taking vital statistics.

Richard he already knew. Alec introduced Claire. Pakenham shook her hand delicately, as though he wished he were wearing latex gloves. "Clever, Claire, to suggest a likely hiding place for the body. Since the excavations two years ago the crypt has been readily accessible by a trap door beside the altar. A passerby wouldn't know that."

"Thank you, but it wasn't my . . ."

"However," Pakenham went on, "Miss Varek's not there. Pity."

Trevor's tonsure was damp with perspiration. "May I set it all to rights now, Detective Sergeant? I'm sorry, Alec, Claire, I wish you'd asked me, I could have told you. Richard . . ." Sputtering gently, he bustled off.

"Could have told us what?" Claire asked Alec.

"The night Melinda disappeared Trevor held a vigil in the church. Prayers for starving African children. I knew several people attended, but I didn't know that some stayed all night. No one could have hidden her body in the crypt."

"So Digby says," stated Pakenham. "Someone could have left her there later, couldn't they? The church is always open."

Alec wiped his forearm across his face. "Sorry, Claire, I'm afraid we got the wrong end of the stick."

"About a church crypt being an appropriate place for a dead body?" Pakenham said sarcastically. "PC Wood says you also suggested dogs, Claire. I've located a team in Newcastle, but they have more than enough to do without chasing wild geese, they tell me. So do I, for that matter."

Richard rocked back on his heels, hair once again standing at attention. The townspeople and tourists started to drift away. Derek and Trillian Nair waved cheerfully at Claire as they passed. Some other locals favored her with that particularly English look of disapproval, as though they smelled something rancid and yet were too polite to say so. Only Priscilla gave Claire a sympathetic smile as she walked into the church.

Claire made a face. "The crypt wasn't one of my brighter ideas."

"I'm the one who called in the search teams," Alec pointed out.

Another constable slogged across the green toward them, even dustier and cobwebbier than his colleagues at the church. "It's no good, Sir," he reported to Pakenham. "Those cellars are a right bit of muck and no mistake, but she's not there."

Pakenham pulled a notebook from his breast pocket and jotted something down. He didn't say, "That's all folks." Instead he nodded coolly to her and Alec and said to Richard, "Come along then, Lacey, you're the caretaker, you can give me the penny tour."

"Certainly," Richard said, and to Alec and Claire, "Later."

She watched Pakenham's broad back and Richard's tall, lean one retreat across the green. Just as they reached the alley leading to the main road, Richard stopped, turned around, and caught Claire watching him. Deadpan, he made a cavalier's extravagant bow. She could almost see the plumed hat and the sword. Whether he was acknowledging their agreement, flipping her his version of the bird, or simply making a curtain call, she couldn't tell. Men! she thought, with more appreciation than cynicism.

Alec was eyeing the church. "Melinda's not there," he said under his breath, "but Elizabeth is. In a wooden coffin beneath the altar." He turned and seemed somewhat surprised to see Claire still beside him. "I left flowers two years ago. It gave me a start to see them still there, all brown and dry."

"I would have left flowers for her, too. And for her cat. I bet they just threw him on the trash heap."

"No, he's there too. There's a small basket at the foot of the coffin, all falling to pieces. You can just make out the skull and the bones."

"One of her old sewing baskets?" Claire asked. "I think I like Walter. Fine sensibility for a man of his time."

Alec smiled. "Come to the station with me, I need a wash and a brush before my evening pint."

"You plan to protect me from the enraged populace?"

"They're less angry with you than frustrated over the entire problem. I know I'm frustrated. Not half like you are, though."

"No kidding," Claire returned. They crossed the green, giving Elizabeth's cement memorial a wide berth, and walked down the alley to Alec's cottage. Claire paused in the garden. Roses she recognized, and the iris which repeated the blue of the neon "Police" sign, and bright orange marigolds. Masses of other leafy and flowering plants she did not.

"Rue," Alec pointed out. "Thyme. Lemon balm. St. John's Wort. Mullein and rocket. Mistletoe, vervain, henbane, primrose, wolfsbane, pulsatilla, clover. The lettuces and beans are round the back."

"Don't tell me you cook," said Claire.

"I'll pinch off a bit of this and that and throw into a soup or stew. Mind your head, the lintel's a bit low." He ushered her through the front door and installed her in a small sitting room while he hurried upstairs. She looked around, half-hoping a clue would jump out at her ringing bells and blowing whistles, half-hoping one wouldn't.

Alec and Richard, she saw, were graduates of the same school of housekeeping. Above the fireplace hung a set of antlers. A couple of candles dripped wax onto saucers. Sprays of dried herbs emitted savory smells. Books on every imaginable topic overflowed a set of shelves. Newspapers spilled over the end of the couch. Claire stacked them up, straightened a lampshade, picked up two empty mugs and set them down again, not wanting to barge into the kitchen. From the closed lid of a roll top desk dangled printed forms and other papers looking as though they were trying to escape custody.

In fact, she discovered on a closer look, several already had. She bent to pick up the fugitives and traced several to beneath a chair. Below two traffic ticket carbons dutifully initialed "ASW" lay an empty envelope with a shopping list written in block letters down the back. Claire scooped them all up and turned to set them on the desk. Bells rang. Whistles squealed.

On the front of the envelope was a cancelled Scottish Parliament stamp. It was addressed to Alec in what looked like the same typeface as the letter that had been addressed to Richard. It was postmarked London, last summer.

Claire moaned, more with weariness than surprise. She dug Richard's letter out of her billfold. Yes, it was the same typeface, the same paper. So the mysterious blackmailer was after Alec, too. Unless . . .

Water was running upstairs. She had time to search the desk for the letter that'd come in the envelope, but she wasn't ready to become an out and out sneak. Instead she thrust Alec's envelope into her pocket.

She took one of the traffic tickets, found a pen, and wrote with perfect honesty, "I have a headache. See you at the pub." Propping it on the stairs, she slipped out of the house and ducked around the garden wall.

There was Elliot, parking his Jaguar in front of the house across the street. He opened the door and called, "How now, blithe spirit, whither wander you?"

Claire made brisk "in a hurry" gestures and sped on her way. Tempted as she was to challenge Elliot with his own letter, she just couldn't stomach another confrontation today. Besides, Elliot wouldn't confront. He'd slide, and she'd find herself shadow boxing.

Claire dodged into the shop and stood wheezing at the counter.

Sarita bustled out from the back. "Hello! Did you enjoy Haddon Hall?"

"Oh, oh yes," said Claire, having almost forgotten Haddon Hall. She pulled out the envelope. "Look — Alec gave me a stamp, too!"

"Yes indeed," Sarita replied. "He received two or three of those letters last year, too, but only one this year."

"Some kind of charity ad, probably. Who else got them? Do you remember?"

"Elliot. Diana Jackman. And Rob, separately. Trevor Digby — he always is receiving elegant letters."

Which were from the diocese, most likely . . . Claire muttered her thanks, backpedaled from the shop, and ran up the stairs to her flat. Tensed for anything, she opened the door. Silent tidiness. She shut the door and sat down hard on the couch.

Some detective she was. She let herself be attracted to a suspect. She hadn't asked the right questions of a helpful witness. Every time she found a clue it was by accident.

Yes, she'd been suspecting Alec on general principles — like Everest, he was there. But now? Maybe it was Alec, not Elliot, who'd sent himself a letter. Like the local vicar with his convenient prayer vigil, the local bobby was in a great position to know what the villagers swept under their rugs.

Alec had turned up the volume of the boom box to cover Melinda and Richard's argument. Maybe just to be polite. Or maybe to hide what they were saying. She only had Richard's word that they hadn't talked about the letters. Or about Alec himself, for that matter.

Now there was a thought. Who was Richard protecting? Why? Maybe you couldn't hide from your individual past in a village, but the village as a whole could hide its own past . . . Don't get carried away with conspiracy theories, Claire told herself. Inhale, exhale, no problem.

Melinda would carol "No problem" to anything from a hangnail to a hurricane. Had she known she had a problem even when someone came to kill her?

Groaning, Claire got up, inserted her favorite Mozart CD in the player, and headed toward the desk.

Chapter Eleven

*I*t was as perfect an English evening as Claire could have imagined. The air had cleared and cooled. Like a strategically placed spotlight, the sun illuminated the western faces of village and Hall and threw long dark shadows toward the east. The temper tantrum of rain earlier that day was only a memory. The two-act play of the blackmail letters was not. Surely Alec's carelessness with the envelope was a point in his favor.

Time to rejoin the program in progress. Claire locked her door, stepped down the stairway, and headed across the cobbled yard toward the pub. Alec, in civilian jeans and sweater, was standing beneath the swinging Druid's Circle sign. His level gaze scanned the rooftops and the surrounding hills as though searching for poetic inspiration.

Claire crossed the street. "Hello."

Alec lowered his eyes and considered her face just as carefully. "Well then, how's the headache?"

"Better, thank you. Sorry to run out on you."

"I know how you feel. It's been a bugger of a day. Of a year, actually, with Melinda going missing and all." After a long pause and another sweep of the countryside, Alec went on, "Do you by any chance have something of hers? A bit of jewelry, like?"

"I have her wedding ring."

"Brilliant. Could you fetch it, please?"

"Sure." Back across the street and up the stairs went Claire. What was he up to now? Fingerprints?

She retrieved the box with the ring, retraced her steps, and told Alec, "My turn to buy the drinks."

"Thank you kindly." He opened the door of the pub, releasing a thin cloud of smoke scented with sausage, beer, and cleanser.

No matter what the weather was outside, the atmosphere in the Druid's Circle was always the same hazy gloom, either snug or claustrophobic depending on Claire's mood. Fortunately there weren't too many people inside tonight.

The Digbys sipped sherry with another elderly couple, their voices clipped and cool — probably discussing the weather or the latest cricket scores, not the day's disruptions. Another table of people turned toward Claire when she walked in, then quickly turned away again.

Detective Sergeant Pakenham held down one end of the bar, a pen in his hand. A glass of wine, a cell phone, and an open notebook were arranged like trophies in front of him. Rob Jackman craned from behind the taps, trying to read what he was writing.

The other Americans sat by the back door, which stood open onto a scraggly garden. "You sure stirred things up around here," Janet told Claire. "Kind of like taking a stick to a beehive, all the police coming and going and everything. You've even dragged Pakenham out from under his rock."

Susan pointed out, "If Melinda hadn't disappeared last year Claire wouldn't even be here. You can't blame her."

"Sure you can," said Fred. "Someone would've been just as happy to let Melinda stay disappeared, if you know what I mean."

"Thanks," Claire told him. Yes, she knew exactly what he meant. She walked on toward the large round table by the fireplace where Alec was holding a chair for her. Richard and Elliot already sat there, Elliot making histrionic gestures, Richard nodding like a metronome, automatically.

"Should you be helping Pakenham with his report?" Claire asked Alec.

He replied tightly, "The sergeant doesn't want help, does he?"

Oh, Claire thought. Pakenham feels superior to the simple village bobby and the not-so-simple bobby is miffed. Alec really did have an irritation threshold. And a sense of humor — he was holding the chair next to Richard. With a half-shrug, she sat down.

"Good evening." Richard's smile was like a black bow tie, bland and formal. She returned it in kind.

"Ah," said Elliot, "our fair visitor from the west and the village gendarme as well! Please, join us in a libation. I was just telling Richard, Alec, about forensics procedures. DNA-typing, now . . ."

"Is useless without a body," Richard stated.

Alec sat down between Claire and Elliot. "Quite right."

Diana appeared at Claire's back. Claire ordered lemonade, Alec stout, Elliot another whiskey. Richard stood pat on a half-empty pint of dark ale. "And I'd like one of those tourist maps of Somerstowe," added Alec.

"Eh?" Diana returned. "Have you gone crackers?"

"A map, please."

"Right." Shaking her head, Diana walked away.

"May I have the ring?" Alec asked Claire.

She handed over the box, then exchanged a glance with Richard, asking silently, *is he teasing me?*

But Richard seemed more bemused than baffled, his brows only a bit off the horizontal. Elliot yawned. In the garden the huge dog snuffled through some odd pinkish-purple lupins like the Hound of the Baskervilles on holiday.

Alec held up the ring. In his hand it looked lilliputian. Melinda's hand had been almost too small to span an octave on the piano. Few people realized she was a small woman, her personality was so large. Large enough to last a year after her death.

Diana appeared in Claire's peripheral vision, tossed a folded piece of paper onto the table, and took up a position at Alec's shoulder.

"Unfold it, please," Alec said to Claire. He reached into his pocket.

She spread the map on the table. It was a very nice pen and ink schematic of the village, every structure from the Hall and the church down to the Jackman's garden shed precisely drawn, every place of interest neatly labeled. The word "Somerstowe" crowned the drawing, its "S" an intricate Tudor spiral. She wasn't surprised to see the initials "RCL" at the bottom.

"Nice work," she said to Richard.

"Thank you." His smile grew a little more personal.

Producing a length of fishing line, Alec tied it to the ring.

"Oh no," groaned Elliot. "Spare us the parlor tricks, there's a good chap."

Claire leaned forward. Surely Alec wasn't going to try what she thought he was going to try. Parlor tricks, indeed.

The muscle jumped in his jaw. He closed his eyes and breathed in and out. His lips moved, as though he silently repeated words. Claire found herself breathing with him. His jaw relaxed. Hers didn't.

Alec opened his eyes. Bracing his elbow on the table, he raised his hand in a gesture that on stage would have produced a rabbit from a hat. The ring, suspended from the invisible fishing line, seemed to hover weightlessly above the map. It turned in quick glints of light, and then, although Alec's hand remained rock-steady, began to swing back and forth.

Claire was reminded of the Ouija board games she and Melinda used to play. Either they'd be giggling so hard they'd get only gibberish, or one or the other of them would obviously be manipulating the planchette. But Alec wasn't giggling, and if he was making the ring move it was through muscle control subtler than Claire had ever been able to achieve. Weird, she thought. Not that she wasn't getting used to weird, here in Somerstowe.

The voices in the room murmured like the distant sound of the ocean. Behind the bar Rob wiped a mug, the faint squeak of cloth on glass oddly loud. "Use the force, Luke," Elliot jibed.

The ring's arc grew shorter and shorter. Claire half-expected Alec to intone, "You are getting sleepy." But he didn't speak. And she wasn't getting sleepy. Her nerves prickled as though she touched a low-voltage wire.

Richard was utterly still. Elliot turned away disdainfully, watching from the corners of his eyes. Diana straightened from her slouch, her mouth hanging open. And there was Pakenham, elbowing Diana aside, his already small eyes narrowed suspiciously.

Beads of sweat broke out on Alec's forehead but his hand remained steady. The ring stopped, quivering gently, then jerked. It began to sketch a circle in the air. The fishing line was a quick glimmer, extending at an angle from his fingers as though pulled by some invisible force toward the edge of the map.

Then, abruptly, the ring stopped swinging and thudded onto the paper. Alec dropped the line and bent his face into his hands, but not before Claire noticed how pale he'd gone. She laid her hand on his shoulder. Whatever he was doing — whatever he thought he was doing — she'd goaded him into it.

"Constable," Pakenham demanded, "what're you playing at?"

Alec looked up. "We have to have a body before we can move the investigation any forwarder."

"Yes?"

"I've located it."

"Get a grip, man. You can't be serious."

"I've never been more serious," Alec said.

"It's like searching for water with a forked stick," said Richard quietly. "Dowsing, water-witching, divining — whatever you call it."

"When one of our girlfriends was pregnant," Claire added, "Melinda and I dangled her wedding ring over her stomach to see whether the baby was a boy or a girl. It was right."

"You had 50-50 odds of being right," Pakenham told her. "This is nothing more than jiggery-pokery."

Warily, Richard extended a finger to the map and touched the ring. Since he didn't jump back, Claire assumed it didn't shock him. "Is it? The ring's lying on the store of old stones and the new rose garden behind the Hall. We were working on the wall and the garden when Melinda disappeared."

"So you were," said Alec, and to Pakenham, "We should turn over that pile of stones and have a shufti round the garden, Sir."

"This is not accepted procedure," Pakenham stated, loudly enough that Fred looked around.

"We've tried accepted procedure." Alec stood slowly, wearily, as though whatever gravity had pulled the ring onto the map was pulling him back into his chair. He bumped against Diana. "Sorry."

She stared at him, not reacting.

Elliot stretched. "I take it you intend to waste the evening in a macabre treasure-hunt, Alec? How entertaining. I vote we stay here. It's my shout this time roun . . ."

"I'll come with you," Richard said, getting to his feet.

"Me, too." Claire untied the ring, put it into its box and the box into her pocket. *In for a penny, in for a pound.*

"They think they know where the body is," Fred said to Susan and Janet.

Trevor overheard. "Alec, I've already closed the crypt . . ."

"Not there," Alec assured him. He moved toward the door, Richard at his back. Claire detoured to the bar so she could hand Rob a five-pound note.

First Fred, then Janet and Susan, then everyone else in the room got up and headed toward the door. So did Diana, in spite of Rob's irate, "Eh! Where do you think you're going?" Pakenham had to hustle to get to the front of the procession.

Richard muttered to Alec, "Are you sure it's worth it?"

"Melinda never liked being on her own. It's time she was found." Alec opened the door and headed purposefully up the street.

Claire looked at Richard. "You don't think it's worthwhile finding Melinda's body?"

"Of course it's worthwhile finding her body," he returned. "Alec's not doing himself any favors finding it is all."

What? Reminding herself that if no crime had been committed to begin with she wouldn't have slugged that beehive, Claire hurried to catch up.

The sun slipped coyly along the horizon, stretching the shadows longer and thinner. A faint aroma of smoke hung in the air. The baroque roofline of the Hall, gabled, turreted, and balustraded, wrote intricate script across the pale golden-blue sky. Its huge windows shone so brightly with the westering sun it looked as though the rooms behind them were on fire.

"We'll need crowbars, shovels, trowels," called Pakenham.

"This way," Fred said, and led the way toward the tool sheds.

By the time Richard had darted into the Lodge and emerged again, the small group of people from the pub had become a crowd alerted by some sort of village telegraph.

Everyone surged around the side of the Hall, Richard making sheep dog-like parries to keep them away from the scaffolding. The pile of old masonry anchored the end of the lawn exactly as it had the evening before. Beyond it the wall of the new garden gleamed like gold jewelry against the velvet green of the grass. On the opposite hillside the one standing stone strained upward, on tiptoe. Cawing crows exploded from the trees — cued, thought Claire, by the special effects crew.

Shouting commands, Pakenham organized the people with tools into several squads and ordered the watchers to stand back. Elliot, caught up in the crowd, lurked along the side of the lawn making witty if disparaging remarks. Diana stood with her arms crossed, her red lips parted. Susan kept up a commentary directed at the Digbys, who smiled politely and said nothing. Rob, having followed his customers, stood with his hand knotted in his dog's leash. The animal butted its head into Janet's stomach. Absently she tickled its ears. The adult Nairs held back Derek and Trillian as though the teenagers, too, were on leashes.

Alec, Fred, and others began shifting the small antique stones. With thunks and clacks they came tumbling down. The walls of Jericho, Claire thought, undermined not by a trumpet blast but a gold ring. . . . It'd take a whole crew of people to make a hole in those rocks big enough for a body and then cover it up again, wouldn't it? And what of — she shuddered and yet followed her thought to its end — what of the smell of a decomposing body?

Richard was standing in the gateway of the garden, flipping through a small notebook. Claire walked up to him. "You were planting roses the weekend Melinda disappeared?"

"Yes," he said, his eye flashing between the book and the lines and parabolas of rose bushes, boxwood, and other plants. His forefinger targeted one line of his own precise handwriting. "Those red ones just there, the Souvenirs de Malmaison. We spent most of June preparing the beds and working in the compost, and we'd just begun the planting when The Play opened. I had to shower off before rehearsals, I stank like a farmer's midden."

"So that entire long bed was just dirt, smelly dirt, the night she — well, the last night anyone saw her."

"Oh aye. When we came to plant the roses on the Sunday I ticked Fred off for leaving the tools out overnight, but he'd been late for the cast call . . . Jesus, we didn't miss her until the Monday and Blake didn't set up a proper search until the Thursday, and by then the roses were all planted." Richard made an about-face. "Here, Sergeant, this row of bushes needs moving."

"What? Why?" Pakenham demanded. Richard explained his reasoning. Pakenham glared at him. He glared back. Pakenham shouted, "You, Wood — you and you — into the garden. Just there."

Richard pocketed his notebook, pushed up his sleeves, and started slotting a shovel around the roots of the rose bushes. Fred or Alec picked up each one and set it aside. A couple of other men waded in with shovels of their own. The blooms bowed and swayed, raining red petals on the dark earth.

Minutes elongated like rubber bands. Some of the watching people hung back, others jostled for space along the garden walks. Pakenham stood in the gateway like Napoleon, head back, hands on hips. Claire waited just outside, her arms clasped across her chest — in spite of the glowing light the air was cold. Her mind stuttered, *I sometimes think that never blows so red the rose as where some buried Caesar bled*... Melinda wasn't Caesar. She wasn't even Cleopatra. *She was my friend.*

Then, suddenly, Richard shouted, "Stop!" Everyone stopped in a cinematic freeze-frame.

The dog's head went up. Whining, he jerked Rob several steps across the lawn. Pakenham jostled Fred aside. Alec leaned on his shovel.

Richard went down on his knees in the dirt. Picking up a trowel, he dug and scraped as delicately as an archaeologist. Then he sat back. A long scratch on his forearm welled with blood but he didn't notice. Compared to the sudden pinched pallor of his face, Alec's had been positively florid.

Pakenham produced a penlight, peered, then straightened. He pulled a cell phone from his pocket. "Right. PC Wood, set up a perimeter. Where's the Godwin woman? We need a preliminary ID."

Grimacing, Alec hurried past Claire, then doubled back. "Are you all right? Here, sit on this bench."

His sturdy hands tried to ease her down. Her knees were locked. Sparks wafted across her eyes. Her face felt as though she'd rubbed an ice cube over it. She wrenched away. "I want to see her."

"She's wrapped in dustbin liners," Alec said. "All you can see is black plastic and . . ."

"Get to it, Wood!" bellowed Pakenham, his fingers playing a series of chirps on his phone.

Richard materialized from a surrealistic swirl of shapes and colors. His eyes were tarnished, his lips thin. "I'll take care of her."

Making an apologetic gesture, Alec disappeared.

Claire's auto pilot said, "I can take care of myself."

"Of course you can," Richard said gently. "Pakenham wants you to have a look. Can you do it?"

"She's my friend. She's my sister. Of course I can look at her."

Richard's arm closed strong and reassuring around Claire's shoulders. The clumsy hole — the grave — was filled with shadow. The lump of black plastic at its bottom was bunched and brittle. A breath of cold, dank air emanated from the opening, adding a hint of something sweetish-rotten to the odors of dirt and roses already filling Claire's nose. She swallowed fiercely.

Pakenham's voice said, "I've found the body, Sir. Send a forensics team." The thin, pale beam of his flashlight moved up and down the plastic. Through a rift appeared a desiccated brown fan. A hand, Claire realized. A withered hand. With something gleaming muted and dusty on one bony finger.

She sank to her knees, Richard's arm following her down. She saw the three diamonds flashing on Melinda's finger. She saw the same diamonds dull and stained in the depths of her grave. The hand which wore them seemed to have thrust aside its wrappings — trash bags, the very idea — Melinda deserved an Aubusson tapestry at least . . . Claire blinked stupidly upward and croaked, "It's her ring. It's still on her finger."

"Yes, Sir, it's hers. PC Wood knew where she was," Pakenham said. And, "Lacey, take her somewhere and stay with her."

The firm arm around Claire's shoulders lifted her and turned her into the cool, polished, indifferent light of evening. Faces stretched and smeared around her. Voices ebbed and flowed in her ears. Trevor was praying. Tears shone on Janet's face. Sarita's face sagged with horror. Rob and Diana Jackman stood shoulder to shoulder, his face stunned, hers twitching like a rabbit's. The dog plunged at the end of his leash, barking and whining. Elliot looked faintly green. Fred stood driving his shovel into the turf, leaving ugly divots.

We're all on stage, Claire thought. *A full cast call. End of act one.*

And she couldn't help thinking, Alec may have pointed the way to Melinda's body, but it was Richard who'd planted rose bushes on her grave while she was still bleeding.

Chapter Twelve

*T*he walls of the Lodge were so thick that the sills of the windows in the sitting room were two feet wide. Claire sat on one and Richard on the other, watching the official flood flow into the Hall gardens.

The sun sank red into the west, its glow making the passing faces seem feverish. Night coagulated around the Hall. It past midnight by the time the tide of photographers, investigators, and constables ebbed. A van carried the black-wrapped bundle into the night. Reporters clustered before the gate. When Pakenham emerged he paid his passage through them with a few tidbits of information.

Richard had made Claire a stiff cup of tea laced with an even stiffer dram of whiskey, which scoured away her numbness and left her senses hyper-extended. Then Priscilla Digby popped in with a couple of tea-bags. "Alec asked me to bring you these," she explained. "Chamomile and valerian from his garden. Very calming." Richard brewed up another pot, holding off on the whiskey this time, and Claire drank the herbal tea too.

Now her jangling nerves played accompaniment to a fitfully gurgling stomach. Her glasses cut into her head. She hated to think what Richard's contact lenses felt like. Pakenham's knock on the front door seemed to jar the fillings out of her teeth.

Richard uncurled from his windowsill. The bandage on his arm didn't seem much whiter than his face. "I didn't kill Melinda."

Claire shook her head, unable to answer.

With a lingering look of frustration and pride mingled he went to answer the door.

Groaning, Claire stood up. The cold stone had sapped all feeling from her rear end. Maybe if she beat her head against the sill she'd lose all feeling there, too. But she'd done what she came to England to do. . . . No. She'd done half of what she came to do. Now she had to find a murderer.

Pakenham's silhouette filled the doorway. "Blake's wanting you, the both of you, for an interview. Now."

"I wasn't going anywhere," Claire told him.

Richard was waiting in the front hall. Together they followed close behind Pakenham, making a flying wedge through the reporters. Several guardian bobbies closed off the grounds behind them. Susan Zielinski was just leaving the portico of the Hall. "I'm so sorry," she said to Claire. "I've told them all about it, I'm such an idiot not to have realized."

Realized what? Claire asked herself.

Glowing bulbs dangled from the ceiling of the entrance hall, splashing streaks of light and shadow down the walls. A draft sneaked under Claire's collar and her arms broke out in gooseflesh. The floor echoed like a drum to her steps. An odd smell, gardenia with an afterglow of old socks, teased her nostrils.

Alec, back in uniform, stood at parade rest by the fireplace. His mouth was compressed, his clear eyes dimmed. A stray lock of his hair hung over his furrowed forehead. Claire winced. Now, too late, she understood Richard's "Are you sure it's worth it?" God only knew what sort of guff he'd been taking from his fellow officers. "Thank you for the tea," she said.

He nodded politely, not even attempting a smile.

Detective Chief Inspector Blake sat in a folding chair at one end of a long trestle table. Papers and photos drifted across the three-hundred-year-old wood. His suit jacket was draped over the back of his chair, the knot of his tie dangled half way down his shirt, and his sleeves were rolled up. With his moustache and his bifocals he seemed as innocuous as a shopkeeper doing his accounts. But his eyes looked like mirrored sunglasses, impenetrable. "Miss Godwin. Mr. Lacey. Sit down."

Richard and Claire sat down on the bench running alongside the table, Claire facing Blake, Richard behind her. Pakenham settled on the opposite side, his tie tight at this throat, his jacket properly buttoned. He pulled an assortment of pens from his pocket and arranged them in a neat row like the leveled rifles of a firing squad.

"So you did find her," Blake said to Claire.

"Yes," she replied. "Well, not me personally. I was the catalyst."

"Several people have testified that PC Wood uses his map trick to find lost items. Bits of jewelry and the like. Hardly bodies." Pakenham shot a suspicious glance over his shoulder at Alec.

"We've never had a body in Somerstowe," Alec said.

Claire tried to catch his eye again, but he was focussed on the tapestry on the opposite wall.

Blake settled his glasses on his nose. "The body is Melinda Varek's, right enough. We had her dental records on file from last year. Someone coshed her from behind — with a rock, maybe, not a sharp-edged tool — and then strangled her with a cord or strip of cloth."

"Like Elizabeth Spenser," Alec muttered.

"PC Wood," said Blake, "I'd be obliged if you'd join the other constables outside."

"Yes, Sir." Alec marched out the door, Pakenham's beady eyes raking his navy-blue back. Hercule Poirot to the contrary, Claire thought, no detective worth his badge would interview his suspects en masse. And Alec had just put himself at the top of the list.

"If he'd killed and buried Melinda," Richard said, "why in God's name would he show you where the body was?"

"He's not half looney," answered Pakenham. "He expects us to buy into this New Age woo-woo rubbish, doesn't he?"

Claire wasn't particularly into woo-woo herself, but she knew there was more to reality than met the eye — music, religion, poetry, quantum mechanics. Why not a village bobby with second sight?

Alec couldn't be the killer, she thought. Anyone else — well, not Richard, either. . . . A movement on the shadowed landing of the staircase, behind Blake and Pakenham's backs, resolved itself into the calico cat. It sat with its tail wrapped around its front paws, head cocked to the side, eyes shining like gold foil. The detectives wouldn't believe it was a ghost. No need to mention it.

Claire sensed a fluctuation in Richard's gravitational field. He saw the cat, too. Inching a bit further down the bench away from him, she asked, "Chief Inspector, Melinda was dead when she was buried, wasn't she? The way her hand was sticking through the plastic . . ."

"The bin liners grew brittle," Blake replied. "The site is well-drained and the body is quite well preserved. Or do you want to know that?"

Once again Claire tried to clear her throat of the sweet smell that neither tea had washed away. The odd odor in the room wasn't helping. "I want to know everything. That's why I'm here."

"Very well then," said Blake. "To begin, Miss Varek was still wearing her costume from the play production."

"She sent me a picture of herself wearing that dress. She said it made her feel elegant and poignant . . ." Claire's voice caught in her throat.

"This gives us, at long last, a time of death," Blake went on. "She must've been killed immediately after the cast party, before she'd had time to change. Her missing car was purposeful misdirection, to make it appear she'd gone away for the rest of the weekend as per her usual habits. What is interesting is that when Mrs. Zielinski was going to the church, just before midnight, she saw the ghost of Elizabeth Spenser walking through the portico of the Hall."

"She said she'd seen Elizabeth in full manifestation," Richard said. "She never said when, exactly. If it was that very night, then she saw Melinda."

Pakenham snorted. "Even a halfwit could make that out."

"Miss Varek might have been waiting in the portico to meet someone. Perhaps her killer." Blake shuffled his papers. "Now. The prayer vigil began at midnight, an hour after the end of the cast party. Everyone was supposed to stay until first light. I understand, though, some people slipped out earlier."

"Aha," muttered Pakenham.

"Surely you can eliminate an older person," said Claire. "It'd take work to dig a hole large and deep enough for a body. Even a small body."

Richard shifted uneasily. "The beds were prepared to a good depth. The tools were ready to hand."

"I should expect any fit person to be capable of burying the body," concluded Blake. "Sufficiently motivated as they were."

Pakenham demanded, "Why didn't you point us toward the flower beds last year, Lacey? For all I knew those bushes had been there for years!"

"And for all I knew Melinda was alive and well miles from here and days later!" Richard retorted. "We only just found out she died the night of The Play."

"Twenty-twenty hindsight," suggested Claire.

Pakenham eyed them both, a leer lurking in his tiny eyes.

No, Claire thought irritably, there's nothing going on between Richard and me . . . *Yeah, right.* She went on the offensive. "Your team didn't find that overwrought death-threat letter that was under Melinda's carpet, did you?"

"What?" exclaimed Richard. "You didn't tell me about that!"

You didn't tell me everything, either. And yet his surprise was — seemed to be — genuine. Looking over her shoulder, she told him about the snapshot and the letter.

"Oh, aye," he said, "I remember that snap. Alec posted it on the notice board just there, beside the fireplace. Anyone could have pinched it."

"The same someone who killed Miss Varek?" asked Pakenham.

"And buried her in my garden," finished Richard. "Why here? Because it was convenient? Or to fit me up?"

To frame him, Claire translated silently. The chill draft in the room pushed her toward his warm aura. Tonight was the first time his touch had been comforting . . . Don't lose it now, she warned herself.

"Any number of people would've had the opportunity to kill Miss Varek," Blake went on. "Logically, though, it was someone she knew who lured her into the garden and killed her there. Whether it was to fit you up or not, Mr. Lacey, I couldn't begin to guess. Robbery wasn't the motive, not with that ring still on her finger."

"Have you any enemies?" Pakenham asked.

Claire contemplated the empty maw of the fireplace. Was it a trick of the light or were there several paw prints in the ashes? In the silence faint echoes fluttered in the far reaches of the house, footsteps, ghosts, bats, whatever.

At last Richard answered. "It seems so, yes."

Blake nodded. Pursing his lips, Pakenham started writing. Richard spoke in short, clipped phrases, describing the letters of last year and this and why he suspected Melinda. "I tried to talk to her about it during the cast party," he finished. "We ended up rowing about — well, about how she wanted to have sex with me."

"And you refused her?" asked Blake.

"Pull the other one," Pakenham murmured.

"I'd just ended a rather intense relationship," said Richard, "and at the time had no intention of — of wading into battle again, so to speak."

Blake turned toward Claire. "Was Miss Varek given to blackmail?"

She raised her chin, folded her cold hands in her lap, and said, "I never knew her to do anything malicious. But she was a practical joker. She might've gone overboard."

"Other people in town may have been getting blackmail letters as well," Richard said. "One of them must have left the letter and the snap beneath the door. Beneath the carpet."

Blake's eyes lost Claire's image and looked through her. "If Miss Varek was sending the letters last year, she must have a confederate who is continuing her — ah — work. And judging by the carpet letter, you're not the only one who suspected her, Mr. Lacey. Although . . ." His voice trailed away into a "hmmm." "That letter was put together from newspaper cuttings — no typeface to be going on with. The blackmail letters were typed?"

"Yes," Richard said. "Not printed out, typed."

"We'll have them at the lab, then. Sergeant, vet every typewriter in town."

Pakenham wrote furiously. "Who else received letters, Lacey?"

"I think that's for them to tell you."

"We'll ask, then, won't we? And what did the blackmailer demand?"

"At first, artifacts from the Hall. I found some items in antique shops and sent them on. Then she — he — wanted money."

"And just what is it the blackmailer is threatening to reveal?" Pakenham asked. "What are you hiding?"

Richard's gravity field rippled and flared. Claire thought of Melinda leaning into that attraction only to find it repulsing her. She'd already been hurt. To be rejected by a class act like Richard must've been a blow on a bruise. Resilient Melinda would've healed in time. But she hadn't had time.

Yeah, maybe she'd decided to play a nastier-than-usual joke on him, using something she'd found out from Nigel. But she'd never actually have published it . . . Anyone could publicize a secret. Create a scandal. You didn't have to have a prior connection with a publisher. Unless, Claire thought, the issue wasn't "publish and be damned" at all. What if the secret had already been published, and it was Richard who was damned?

He'd bailed out of the Digbys' coffee-and-cookies party when Trevor said something about The Play being fictionalized history — well of course it was, Philip hadn't been there for Elizabeth's trial — history was always fictionalized, the best scholars couldn't avoid that — Richard's parents were scholars. Richard's parents had found The Play in the attic of the Hall . . .

My God, Claire thought. It wasn't just that he wanted to avoid the Trust seeing him involved in a murder investigation. It was that the secret itself had to be hidden from the Trust.

She spun around to face Richard. Their knees touched. He jerked back, startled. If it's not his secret to tell, she thought, then it sure as hell isn't mine. But for Melinda's sake, for the sake of peace and truth and all the usual ideals . . . "The Play," she mouthed, barely even whispering.

He heard. His eyes flashed. He leaped to his feet. Claire waited for him to pluck a halberd from the display beside the fireplace and take a swipe at her head. But no. He stood stiffly on the tiles and faced Blake foursquare, like an English sailor heading into Dunkirk.

"You must understand, Detective Inspector. It's not my secret. It's not, however, a particularly well hidden secret. I'm not surprised that Melinda, with her connections, winkled it out."

"Yes?" prompted Blake. Pakenham scribbled away, not bothering to conceal a smile of satisfaction.

"The Play. 'An Historie of the Apocalypse as Visit'd upon Summerstow.' It's a fake. It was written by my parents. That is, my father found several pages of it amongst Phillip Lacey's effects and completed it."

"And he passed it off as authentic?" Blake asked.

"No. He did it as a scholarly lark, never intending to publish, certainly never intending to profit by it either academically or monetarily."

"So who did want to profit by it?"

"Maud Cranbourne," Richard said. "She published The Play without my parents' knowledge. She was even clever enough to send only the original pages to the British Museum for authentication."

"A bit greedy, weren't we?" murmured Pakenham.

"The reason she asked my father to have a shufti round the attics of The Hall to begin with was to see if there was anything valuable she could pass on to her relatives." Richard's usually velvet voice was rough, brushed against the nap. "Maud Cranbourne was the last of her generation, the last Cranbourne to live at the Hall. She never married. Her nieces and nephews and their children were her family. Miss Maud, as I knew her, wanted to leave a legacy for them — especially the descendents of her favorite brother, Vincent, who'd been disinherited. She had very little cash. What she had was the Hall.

"But the Hall was falling apart. Nowadays an old building such as this one is too expensive for a private individual to maintain unless he's a rich rock star or computer tycoon — not the sort who's usually into historic preservation.

"Maud saw her chance with The Play. The income from it would provide funds to maintain and even restore the Hall. Her relatives, however, made it clear that if they inherited the Hall they'd sell up. A housing developer had already made one of the cousins, Maurice Applethorpe, an offer." A spasm contracted Richard's face. The prospect of the Hall demolished, the gardens plowed up, the village a yuppie suburb, caused him acute indigestion. It didn't sit too well with Claire, either.

"By the time Maud died, ten years ago, The Play had already been performed five times, bringing people into Somerstowe from far and wide. Elliot had built an entire industry in scripts, recordings, and sub-rights. The Play was proving more lucrative than we'd dared to hope. It made Maud's estate even more valuable. Applethorpe wanted to eat his cake and have it too, have both the profits from selling the Hall and the income from The Play. Not that he needed any cake at all, mind you, he's a wealthy man in his own right."

"But Maud left the Hall to the National Trust," said Blake. "With the income from The Play as endowment. That left your parents in a bit of a spot, didn't it?"

"Oh aye. Therefore they — we, I was at university then — made the deliberate decision that the end justifies the means. To sell our honor for the Hall and for the village." He made an abrupt about-face toward the fireplace, hiding his expression. The Lacey stag and leopard gazed benignly down at him, forgiving all. From the ramrod straightness of his back Claire knew he was not forgiving himself.

Julian and Dierdre had had good precedents for their lark. Ireland's "newly-discovered" Shakespeare plays had been laughed off the stage. The jury was still out on MacPherson's "Ossian" poetry cycle, supposedly translated from the Gaelic. The Laceys' scheme wasn't as blatant as the Hitler diary scam or the fake Howard Hughes autobiography. Their motives for concealing the truth could hardly be faulted. But what a burden for Richard! No wonder he'd been downplaying his connections to — and love for — Somerstowe. "Where's the original?" the librarian in Claire asked.

"In the publisher's safe in London. He knows, but he'll never grass. Why should he? He sells the scripts all over the world. I had a letter last winter from an ex-pat theatre group in Ghana wanting a photo of the Hall to use as a backdrop in their production."

"The truth would cause a proper scandal," said Blake. "Which might only bring The Play more publicity — hard to say. That's beside the point. The point is whether hiding the truth is a motive for murder."

"Of course it's not," Richard returned. "I doubt if the — the forgery — had anything at all to do with Melinda's death."

"Do you now? Could that be because if the forgery did have anything to do with her death, you're the one with the motive? You don't want your family shown up as liars." Pakenham smiled sweetly and drew a flourish on his page.

"No, I don't want my family shown up as liars. My father's dead, but my mother has a full professorship at a university in Canada. This is just the sort of thing that might could cost her her position. I repeat, though, it's not worth a murder."

"Lacey," Pakenham snickered, "I've seen men murdered for sixpence."

Scowling, Richard spun back around. "Here, Sergeant, I don't care for your attitude!"

"Steady on." Blake held up his hands like a traffic cop.

Richard's blazing eyes fell on Claire. She wasn't sure whether he was asking her for help or defying her to join in Pakenham's condemnation.

But the sergeant was wrong about Richard. He'd better be wrong about Richard. She didn't know what she'd hate more, finding out Richard was the murderer or hearing Pakenham crow about it.

"You said it's not a very well-hidden secret," she waded in. "I mean, if *I* could guess it — well, you gave me some clues . . . What I'm trying to say is that the secret means a lot to everyone in the village. And Elliot, whether you count him as part of the village or not. There were a lot of people with motives."

One of Richard's brows lifted slightly, his way, no doubt, of thanking her for defending him.

"So then," Pakenham asked, "who else knows about the fakery?"

"I'm quite sure the Digbys suspect my parents' contribution to The Play was greater than they implied. Elliot's in a good position to have seen the original manuscript. Melinda — well, I thought Melinda knew about it." Richard looked less like he had indigestion than like he had a knife in his heart.

He wasn't just prodigal son returning to his ancestral home, Claire thought, but the fatted calf, too. His hands were shaking and he clenched his fists. She had to almost sit on her own hands to keep herself from reaching out to comfort him.

Footsteps tapped quietly across the floor of the room above the entrance hall. "Eavesdroppers," snapped Pakenham. "Wood said the house was empty."

"It's only Elizabeth," Richard said, flat.

"The house ghost?" Blake's tone was not, oddly enough, sarcastic.

The footsteps came back the other way, light, urgent. Pakenham peered indignantly upward, red-faced.

"Do you have anything more to add tonight, Mr. Lacey?" Blake leaned back in his chair. "Miss Godwin?"

"Are you going to shop me to the fraud squad?" Richard asked.

"Not unless someone files a complaint against you."

"Someone will, if you blow the gaff about The Play."

Blake shook his head. "I'm investigating a murder. If I feel blowing the gaff would help us find the killer, then I will. Right now, though, it'd be much more useful to keep quiet and see who else knows the truth. That threatening letter, now — it was written with lines from The Play, wasn't it? Changed a bit as per last year's production?"

"Any number of people had revised scripts," Richard told him.

Once more the footsteps passed overhead. Pakenham rolled his eyes. Blake pushed his chair back from the table and stood. "We'll move a formal investigative team into Somerstowe tomorrow. Go home now. Get some sleep."

Yeah, right. Claire's nervous system was still humming a high-pitched note but her brain seemed empty, as though its gray matter had been sucked away. Dawn would find her wide-eyed, struggling to spell her own name.

She stood up and extended her hand. "You know where to find me, Chief Inspector."

"That I do." Blake's handshake was firm and dry. Pakenham's was aggressive and slightly damp. The smell in the room, she realized, was his cologne. That figured.

Side by side Richard and Claire fled the entrance hall and stopped under the portico. That tall shape in the shadows at the far end was Alec, his face turned up to the windows above. Several other man-shapes stood by the gate. Somewhere a sheep bawled.

Claire inhaled lungful after lungful of fresh air. It was only a little cheering to hear Blake telling Pakenham inside, "We're trying to collect facts here, Sergeant, not pass judgement."

"They're suspects," Pakenham retorted. "No need to treat them with kid gloves."

Richard leaned against a pillar, his face a gray mask, his eyes downcast. And she'd thought she was drained. "I wouldn't have said anything about The Play to them. It was just a lucky guess."

"You're the canny one, aren't you?" he asked, but without resentment. "No matter. The truth wants telling."

Yes, Claire thought, and he'd told it pretty darn easily, too, when yesterday he'd given her the impression wild horses wouldn't drag it out of him. She simply wasn't as intimidating as two policemen, was she? "Is there anything I can do? Or have I done enough already?"

He answered with a shake of his head. For just a second his eyes gleamed in the light reflected from inside, then dulled again. "I'm sorry."

For what might've been? she wondered. If only Julian and Dierdre hadn't fiddled with The Play, if only Melinda hadn't come to Somerstowe, if only Richard's ex hadn't left him so badly burned?

For what might've happened between us, if only we'd met some other time and place. "No, I'm the one who's sorry. Good night, Richard."

"Good night, Claire."

The grounds were pooled with shadow. The stars were like Richard's eyes, distant, blunted gleams, and shed no light on the path. A fragile crescent moon hung low in the west. Claire felt her way to the back gate in the perimeter wall and into the alley, where she tripped over a step and banged into the trash cans behind the pub. Inside the building the dog barked frantically. Rob's muffled voice shouted at him.

A police car, its fluorescent orange stripe a sickly glow, coasted down the main street. Claire waited in the shadow until it passed, then rushed across the street and up the steps to her flat.

She turned on the overhead light and slammed the door. Alone at last. Alone with her thoughts, her questions, her nightmares — she had to call home, spread the news — Melinda really was dead — Melinda, the soft darkness scented with roses, the sudden blow, the twist of the rope . . .

Propped on her desk was a letter. Even from the door Claire could see that her own name was spelled out in letters cut from a newspaper, the black and white as sharply defined as a slap in the face. In one convulsive movement she leaped across the room, seized the envelope, and ripped. "Go home now," the letter read, "or rot with Melinda."

The first thing she was thought was, *Richard didn't leave this here, I was with him all evening. He didn't kill Melinda. He didn't.*

Only then did Claire realize what else the letter meant. If she stayed in Somerstowe, the killer would be coming for her next.

Chapter Thirteen

*T*he afternoon was warm and still. The air in the long gallery seemed too turgid to breathe. But then, in the week since Melinda had at last been found, Claire hadn't exactly been breathing.

The first act may have ended with finding Melinda's body. Or it may have ended with that first interview by the police, when Richard finally told his secret. Or it may have ended with the memorial service, sensitively performed by Trevor, the small church filled from wall to wall not so much with the bereaved as with the curious.

This last week, Claire thought, had been the Intermission, when you cleared your mental palate for the next act and at the same time started anticipating the climax. The quiet of this intermission, though, was more intimidating than her own personal threatening letter. She envisioned plots thickening, schemes coming to fruition, and secret forces marshalling their strengths. She imagined no second act at all, the drama of Melinda's murder trailing off into inconsequence.

With a sigh, Claire polished her magnifying glass and bent over the embroidered cloth panel from the attic room. Through the lens the mysterious fibers she'd wondered about resolved themselves into strands of fine blond hair. Now that was interesting.

She agreed with Richard that the cloth had probably been stitched by Elizabeth Spenser. Elizabeth had embroidered the panel in the church to Lettice Lacey's commission. Maybe Elizabeth did this one as her own offering. But she'd sewn nature and astrological motifs instead of Christian symbols. And she'd included hair in the design, as though she meant the cloth to work magic . . .

Slowly Claire stood upright. *Good grief.* Was it this cloth — or the beliefs this cloth seemed to symbolize — which had condemned Elizabeth? The witch-finders made no distinction between devil worshippers, who were almost always figments of their own tormented imaginations, and village wise women who clung to the more benign aspects of the ancient nature religions. That was the flip side of the Age of Faith — the Age of Fear.

She'd have to ask Alec's opinion of Elizabeth's belief system, whether she may actually have been, more or less, a witch. Rolling the cloth, Claire wrapped it in acid-free tissue paper and tucked it away in a cardboard box. Just as she fitted the lid on the box and set it aside she heard footsteps tapping briskly across the upper great chamber. Elizabeth herself? What would happen if Claire tried to talk to her — would she answer?

Or was it Elizabeth? Claire couldn't tense any further. Her neck already hurt from constantly looking over her shoulder . . . Kate Shelton walked through the door. "Ah — here you are. In the future you'd better be collecting me on your way, not coming up here alone."

"Yeah," Claire said with a grimace. "I guess so. I will."

Kate had the delicate features, pink cheeks, and carefully bound hair of a Dresden doll, but her solid jeans-clad body owed more to her black belt in karate than to any porcelain mold. She'd joined the volunteers pretending to be a secondary needleworker when in reality she was one of Blake's people, detailed to hover at Claire's elbow and protect the rest of her body as well.

With a searching look up and down the gallery, as though expecting an assassin to pop out of a trapdoor, Kate sat down in her chair at the tapestry frame. For someone who admitted she didn't know which end of a needle to thread, she was doing a nice job mending the linen border of the Venus-and-Adonis canvas, her stitches uneven but unobtrusive. "You've had your lunch, then?" she asked.

"And survived to tell the tale. Richard didn't put rat poison in my sandwich, or bean me with the teapot, and if he has a dungeon at the Lodge, he's using it to store books and drawings . . . Sorry. Attempt at humor."

"No need to go about po-faced," Kate said with a smile. "Richard's the only person in town who couldn't have left you that letter. Alibi'd by Pakenham himself. That's rich."

Allowing herself a smile of her own, Claire sat down and turned on the light. She reached for the needle she was using to baste a fresh piece of canvas to the back of a tear. There. Two corners secure. She started making microscopic stitches between them.

The one good thing about her own personal threatening letter was how it had re-opened her dialog with Richard. In the past week they'd eased their way from allies to friends. She tidied up the Lodge while he watched in bemusement. He teased her that she was only hanging around so she could use his computer. They sat side by side watching videos, pretending they weren't breathing heavily during the sex scenes in *Shakespeare in Love.*

But every time the friendship — promised? threatened? — to catch fire, a chill draft of the unresolved past, the mysterious present, the doubtful future, damped it down. The last week or so might be a prologue. Eventually she and Richard might be able to write a play of their own. And yet it could just as easily turn out to be tragedy or farce as romance.

As for the rest of the cast and crew, the townspeople and those volunteers who'd been in Somerstowe last year had gone one by one to the empty shop where Blake now had his command post. They'd emerged looking like students released from detention, and hurried to the pub for liquid reassurance and spin control — it being better to volunteer some sort of explanation for getting blackmail letters than to let the village grapevine invent one.

After his interview Alec had methodically downed a pint of beer. Only then had he insisted that his letter "was only a bit of mischief, like knocking off the bobby's hat and legging it down the street." This said to his glass, followed by, "Of course you had to be giving the envelope to Blake, Claire. You thought it was a clue, didn't you?" Which had only made her feel worse about ratting on him.

She could see the scene in the interview room, Pakenham sneering, Blake stern, Alec sitting there if not with blood on his hands at least with egg on his face. Richard had confessed his secret, she told herself. Why not Alec? Claire couldn't see him killing the deer whose antlers hung above his mantel, let alone Melinda, and yet he was hiding something that must give him a good motive. Could even Alec be driven to murder, if threatened?

Rob had glared belligerently at everyone. "Think I've been cooking the books, do they? I told them get on with it, bring in the Inland Revenue, everything's shipshape and Bristol fashion, it is, down to the last penny. Alec, are you needing a receipt for that beer? Elliot, are you wanting an accounting for each sandwich I send up to rehearsal? It's getting so's a man can't run his business without some ponce of a government official asking who paid what to who and when and for what."

The blackmailer must've been accusing Rob of skimping on his taxes or selling duty-free liquor. She wasn't about to ask. Elliot might shadow box, but Rob came out throwing hard punches straight to the stomach.

Diana had flounced in after her interview. "Bloody rozzers, always digging dirt, aren't they? They make it out to be me own fault I had a bit of an intrigue when I was a lass. Well what pretty girl didn't? Had the boys round me like paparazzi round a princess, I did. So what if one of them had a rich father, filthy rich and a title too." She tapped her finger against her nose, hinting that everyone would recognize the name. "So he gave me a bit of a consideration, like, to bugger off and forget the lad so's he could have himself a posh wedding to some kiss-me-hand society bird."

She was more irritated with the police than with the anonymous letter-writer, thought Claire. Diana's secret wouldn't cause much of a scandal, not in this day and time. Although if she'd signed some sort of formal agreement, publicizing the story could get her into legal hot water — and that would hardly sit well with Rob.

Elliot had been eager to talk, explaining that he was being black-mailed for an indiscretion with a famous rock star's wife. "She craved a gentleman, don't you know. That great hairy baboon of a husband just wasn't adequate. Unfortunately the baboon's entourage includes several yobbos with spiky hair and hobnailed boots. I preferred his not sending them to belabor the point, if you know what I mean, so I dutifully paid out."

His story was plausible. Just. So was Richard's own story about some academic scandal in his parents' past, which was true up to a point. Was anyone else being any more candid — to each other, at least — than he was? She stabbed her finger. "Ouch!"

Kate jumped.

"Stuck myself," Claire told her. "No problem, it's not even bleeding."

Since Susan's realization she'd seen Melinda instead of Elizabeth the night of the murder, she'd inundated anyone who'd listen with detail after detail, trying to find something else helpful. She seemed miffed she hadn't gotten any blackmail letters.

Fred and Janet, though, had both had letters last year. After her interview Janet had demanded lemonade with ice and muttered, "Hey, I came clean about it, okay? So my brother got into trouble with the law back home. It's nobody's business except mine and Fred's. He served his time, he's out now, in a rehab program, everything's okay. I swear, the cops get hung up on totally insignificant details when they could be out catching murderers."

Fred had eyed Janet, his jowls drooping as though contemplating the horrors of crime without punishment. "That's what they're trying to do, catch a murderer. Not that I have anything to do with that or blackmail or anything. So some jerk decides to accuse me taking stuff from the Hall. I wasn't even inside the Hall, most days, to take anything. What'd they think I was doing, selling wheelbarrows and trowels on the tool black market? Sheesh."

Even Trevor Digby had received a letter. "Suggesting that several members of my flock are laboring beneath the burden of sin," he'd explained. "Which is the equivalent of telling me the sun rises in the east. I'd have no work at all if everyone were a saint, now would I? I assumed the letter was meant to stir up trouble and threw it away, never thought for a moment of paying up."

Claire had never thought the Digbys were serious suspects. They always had a prayer vigil on one of the shortest nights of the year, it turned out. And after The Play, with its tragedy of sexual and religious prejudice, a little positive prayer probably went a long way.

She worked her needle behind the stitches she'd already done, securing the end of the thread. There. The stitches were nice and neat. Like her notes on the case, which were starting to look like the old card file in the library. She'd done everything but assign accession numbers to the suspects. Any conclusions she'd reached, though, had been about herself.

Until now her life had been pretty much organized, alphabetized, and properly spelled. Richard had described his prior relationship as "intense." Claire's had been bland and bloodless. Steve had wanted things to stay that way. No wonder he'd never been comfortable around Melinda, Claire's alter ego. No wonder Melinda's death had turned Claire's temblor of discontent into an earthquake.

Melinda's life had been measured on the Richter scale. Everyone in Somerstowe had been rocked by her seismic wave. She hadn't intended to bring down someone's house, but she had. That someone had struck back. And now that same someone was out to get Claire. For revenge for re-opening the case? Or did someone else besides Richard think she knew what Melinda had known?

Claire mopped at her forehead. Her brain was leaking. She was drowning in the scent of mothballs, which overwhelmed the not unpleasant odors of potpourri and rush. The Hall was even more silent than usual, the thick walls absorbing noise. The punk-punk-punk of her needle punching through canvas sounded like distant cannon. Across the canvas Kate moved like a robot, hardly blinking.

Claire cut the basting thread and reached for some fine green wool. Adjusting the lamp, she carefully repeated two stitches in the leaf at the edge of the tear and then stitched in the same style across the new piece of canvas. If it weren't for the chart she was filling in, no one would notice where the original stitches ended and hers began. Just as no one noticed where Phillip Lacey's text stopped and Julian and Dierdre's began.

The Play might be Richard's secret, but unless everyone in Somerstowe was lying it wasn't anyone else's. And she sure hoped everyone wasn't lying. Things were complicated enough.

Kate looked around. Blake, shadowed by Pakenham, walked in the door. "How are you getting on?" Blake asked.

"No one's gotten me yet, thanks to PC Shelton," Claire replied.

"That's WPC. Woman police constable. No women's lib here," corrected Pakenham, with a gesture dismissive of uppity women from Margaret Sanger to Margaret Thatcher.

Kate swept a box of pins onto Pakenham's feet. "Oops. Sorry, Sir."

Cursing, he bent over and started fishing pins out of his cuffs.

Blake's moustache crimped a bit. "My lads have located the typewriter that did the blackmail notes. An old manual in the vestry of the church. Digby's not used it since he bought a word processor. It had a new ribbon in it. The paper and envelopes came from supplies stored in a cupboard there."

"In the church," Claire repeated. "Where anyone could get it."

"Lacey had three letters last year and the two this year," said Pakenham, his voice muffled by his crouch. "No one else had more than two last year and none at all this — ow, sod it! Lacey's the only one saved his letters, more's the pity. Miss Varek's fingerprints were on the first one, but on none of the others or their envelopes. We couldn't test that first envelope, he says he lost it."

Melinda's fingerprints. No surprise there. Claire sewed another stitch. "And Alec's envelope?"

"None of the other letters had good enough prints to be going on with," Blake said. "So far as we can tell, Lacey's first letter is the only one of the lot that didn't demand a pay-off."

Claire had at last seen a copy of the famous letter. She'd memorized it the way she'd memorized lines from The Play — and the letter had a much better chance of producing a clue. "Mr. Lacey, you think you have everything under control. Are you sure? Are you entirely confident in your own willpower, to paraphrase a line in The Play? But then, there's a secret behind The Play, isn't there? What would happen to you, Mr. Stone, if it got out?"

So far Claire had avoided discussing the letter with Richard — that would've come a little too close to picking at a scab. Not that she needed his help to read between the lines.

"Willpower" referred to a scene in Act One when Cecil, speaking bitterly about the woman he had, Lettice, and the woman he wanted, Elizabeth, quoted the Roman poet Terence. "I know the disposition of women: when you will, they won't; when you won't, they set their hearts upon you of their own inclination." Which pretty well summed up Melinda's feelings toward Richard.

"Mr. Stone," wasn't much of a puzzle either. Claire had the answer beneath her hands at this very moment — the story of Venus and Adonis, the hopeless pursuit of a handsome, self-centered man by a beautiful woman. As Shakespeare had Venus say scathingly to her quarry, "Art thou obdurate, flinty, hard as steel, nay more than flint, for stone at rain relenteth . . ." Heck, Claire herself had used the rain-on-stone image about Richard that afternoon at the Digby's house.

Melinda had picked up a taste for word games and literary quotes from Claire, using them to prove she didn't come from the wrong side of the tracks. Maybe the police had had to find her actual fingerprints, but Claire knew who'd sent that letter the moment she read it. The other ones, though, weren't written in the same style.

She stuck the needle into her pincushion. "Richard's first letter was the only one Melinda sent. As a joke. She didn't need an accomplice to tease Richard about their, well, lack of a relationship. It was someone else, some opportunist, who read that first letter, took the envelope as a sample, and sent the rest."

"Which means her murder wasn't a falling-out among thieves. So to speak," Kate added, with an apologetic glance at Claire.

"I expect you're right," Blake went on. "When you arrived in Somerstowe that same opportunist started up again, with Lacey at the least."

Pakenham stood up and set the box of pins on the windowsill, out of Kate's reach. "Pity everyone was too timid to hand in their letters last year."

"Pity you didn't find the letter beneath the carpet of the flat last year," Blake commented.

"Needed our village bobby with his ESP fiddle, didn't I?" retorted Pakenham. "Your letter last week, Claire, was very like that one, done quickly just after I found the body. Both had the same motive: to send off a tiresome outsider."

"I don't know what Melinda knew," insisted Claire. "If anything."

"Perception can be more important than fact," Blake said. "Like Lacey, the murderer thought Miss Varek was the blackmailer. The murder was a case of mistaken identity. The threat to you, however, is not at all mistaken."

Was it better for Melinda to have died by mistake? Claire picked up a loose pin and thought of the punctured snapshot. *No, it wasn't.* "So there are two people writing anonymous letters?"

"The murderer got the idea from the blackmailer. Plain as a pikestaff," said Pakenham.

Blake went on, "Mrs. Nair says that the lock to her — your — flat's not been changed for donkey's years. Anyone could have copied the key."

"Someone knows something," Pakenham said. "Everyone in a small town knows everyone else's business. If I keep at them long enough, they'll talk."

"Not necessarily. It was an outsider who died here," Blake told him. "It was an outsider who brought the matter to a head. The villagers may well have closed ranks. As for The Play, well — you can't ask right out, 'Do you know The Play is a fake?' You can't lead your witness."

"Supposedly none of the other letters referenced The Play, just an assortment of grotty little secrets," Pakenham said. "Think — the shop-keepers are outsiders. They've not received any letters and yet the post goes through their hands. Have they been opening letters, reading them, re-sealing them, and using what they learned to run a tidy little blackmail ring?"

"Re-sealing a letter's not easy," said Kate.

Claire said, "The Nairs are no more outsiders than Richard or even Elliot."

"And since they hardly speak English," concluded Pakenham, "it would be stretching a bit to think them capable of blackmail, wouldn't it?"

Blake eyed his sergeant, face inscrutable. "Mrs. Nair helped us pin-point who had had letters. Lacey saw Moncrief with one, and he and Wood each knew the other had gotten something a bit awkward, but most everyone else assumed their letters were unique."

So Richard hadn't told even Alec what was up? Claire asked herself. Alec could've guessed about The Play. He could hardly tell Blake he'd known about it all along. Was that why he was being so evasive?

"I asked each person who they thought was the blackmailer. Some of them thought it was Melinda, right enough. But then," Pakenham concluded cheerfully, "every man jack of them might could be lying."

Feeling Shakespearean, Claire added, aye, there's the rub.

Blake glanced at his watch. "The cast party began about ten pm, with everyone scoffing down sandwiches, crisps, and champagne. It ended about eleven. Miss Varek was last seen alive at midnight. We've had the post-mortem report — judging by how well she'd digested the sand-wiches, she probably died no later than half-past twelve. And further excavation of the grave turned up her camera, broken. Couldn't retrieve any data from it at all."

Claire tried not to think about Melinda's poor withered husk, a mockery of her beauty and vitality, turned into an exercise in biological necromancy. Just another source of data. "So who was out and about around midnight?"

"Most everyone," answered Pakenham. "The Digbys and their prayer service, remember? I thought I had something when Heather Little told me Diana Jackman left around one am, said she was ill. Diana — she's a piece of work, isn't she? — told us she'd gone to Elliot's cottage for sex. He confirmed her story, said she'd arrived there just past one and stayed until first light. They've been having it off for years."

Claire shook her head, unsurprised. So Melinda hadn't broken her date with Richard to see Elliot. Not if he'd been with Diana.

If Elliot had offered Melinda cheap amusement, he offered Diana the glitter she yearned for. That it was glitter without the gold was something she seemed to have noticed only recently. What had happened to break them up? Claire's own arrival in Somerstowe, reminding Diana of how Elliot had acted over Melinda? And yet if Diana was still having sex with him the night Melinda died, she mustn't have been as big an issue between them as Claire had thought.

Kate said, "That doesn't clear Moncrief for the hour between twelve and one."

"He could hardly have killed Miss Varek," replied Blake, "buried her, driven her car to the reservoir, and returned here in the space of an hour."

Even if he did drive like he was trying out for the NASCAR circuit, Claire thought. . . . "Wait a minute. Who says he drove the car to the reservoir right then? Maybe he waited until the next morning."

"Very good!" Pakenham told her. "But Roshan Nair noticed Melinda's car missing from the car park beside the shop when he gave the prayer service up at a quarter to two. Didn't think a thing of it, though. Not then."

"Oh," Claire said. Just because she didn't like Elliot didn't mean he was the killer, she reminded herself.

"As for Rob Jackman," said Blake, "he never went to the vigil to begin with. Has little use for Digby and his ilk, I gather. Says he went home and went to bed. Never missed his wife, though. Separate bedrooms. Jackman knew about her and Moncrief, called her a whore and Moncrief her ponce."

"Jackman has form," added Pakenham. "He was inside for several months in his early twenties, convicted of assault and battery. And word on the high street is he knocks his wife about regularly. Since he has no alibi for the time of the murder, just now he's our prime suspect."

"Motive?" Kate asked.

Pakenham shrugged. "He didn't want the blackmailer to let the village know he can't keep his wife in line."

"Some of the volunteers aren't accounted for," concluded Blake. "Fred Siebold and Janet Harlow had a row on their way to the church and he went back to the B&B alone. No alibi for him, either. And then there's PC Wood. He says he was at home, but since he lives alone . . ."

"No alibi," Pakenham said with obvious relish. "I don't care for his looks at all. We should have the Chief Constable relieve him of duty."

"I'm afraid so," agreed Blake.

Claire picked up her needle, compressing her lips to keep herself from wading in in Alec's defense. So had everything in Somerstowe been going along smoothly and happily until first Melinda and then she herself came along? Or would all those fault lines have slipped no matter what? If people didn't hide secrets, she thought irritably, then no one would get hurt.

Pakenham reached into his jacket and pulled out his cell phone. Blake gazed out through the leaded glass lights of the window. The panes were warped with age and no doubt gave him a view of the world as distorted as the reflection in a fun house mirror.

Turning back to the canvas, Claire told herself she was ready, willing, and eager for Act Two to get under way. Was anyone else?

Chapter Fourteen

*B*y the time the workday was over Claire had finished her patch. It looked good, she told herself. Any triumph in a storm, or however the adage went. She turned off the light and headed downstairs, Kate at her heels. Susan was posting an article on preservation theory on the bulletin board in the entrance hall. "Richard's gone on to the Lodge, Claire. If you hurry you can catch up with him. You have a couple of hours before rehearsal."

Great, Claire thought. Was it that obvious she and Richard were very tentatively considering a relationship? She should put a notice on the board herself: *Hear ye, hear ye, we have barely held hands.*

"My granny's like that," Kate commented. "Always match-making."

Claire walked right on past the Lodge instead of stopping in for afternoon tea and meaningful if cautious eye contact. She parted from Kate at the Nair's back door — Kate was renting their extra bedroom — and fixed her own mug of tea in her flat.

She tried playing one of Melinda's jazz CDs. The aimless wailings of a saxophone layered onto the repetitive shuffle of a brush-stroked drum was more maddening than inspiring. They'd never agreed on jazz. They'd never agreed on bagpipes, either.

Turning off the CD player, Claire skimmed the day's newspaper — war, pestilence, corruption, celebrities — been there, done that. Then she doggedly updated her night-of-the-murder timetable. But there seemed little point to her note taking. Been there, done that, too.

When Claire emerged, the evening sky was bruised with clouds. Fine, let it rain tonight, if only it would be clear for the first performance Friday. Reckless, to perform The Play in the forecourt of the Hall, in whatever weather the English summer dispensed, but it certainly added authenticity.

She said as much to Sarita, who bustled from the shop carrying several long cardboard boxes and her sewing basket. "It has never rained on The Play," Sarita replied. "Not so much as once, I am told."

"Elizabeth's dead hand from beyond the grave?" Kate followed Sarita out the door, her arms draped with fabric.

"Alec would say it was a sign of her innocence. Here, let me . . ." Claire hoisted the basket.

"Two days only remaining until opening night," Sarita went on. "The weather I cannot control. What is concerning me is the wardrobe."

"I'm sure everything will be ready in plenty of time."

"For the second year in a row I am making a new costume for Elizabeth. Last year Melinda was much smaller than Diana. This year we cannot use Melinda's dress for Trillian. . . ." Sarita's lustrous dark eyes flicked to Claire's face. "Of course we are not using Melinda's dress. I am sorry to be speaking so thoughtlessly."

"You're not speaking thoughtlessly," Claire assured her, "you're focussed on your work. It's good to have work to focus on."

"Quite right," said Kate behind her back.

Past the main gate of the Hall they went, and through the door off the courtyard into the old kitchen. The huge fireplace, big enough to garage a car, emitted a chill draft and the furtive scurryings of squirrels and starlings. Claire set the basket down on the long trestle table and helped Kate spread out the dresses with their billowing skirts.

Everyone in town seemed to be milling around the room, their voices echoing from the vaulted ceiling. Priscilla Digby applied a match to the mysterious recesses of the AGA cooker and filled two kettles at the trough of a sink. Rob arranged sandwiches, crisps, and biscuits beside a row of teacups. Alec, in jeans and sweater, coached Fred in his three lines. Blake, his moustache looking distinctly wilted, and a uniformed constable waited in a corner. Their eyes focussed mostly on Rob Jackman, although everyone else came in for the occasional sweep, like searchlights across a prison yard.

"View halloo!" caroled Elliot from the outer door. "Is everyone ready? The play must go on!"

The human surge toward the door snagged on the imposing figure of Roshan Nair. His moustache looked freshly starched. When Elliot reached for Trillian's hand Roshan favored him with a shining white smile as sharp and bright as a scimitar. Elliot backed off. This was one Elizabeth he wouldn't be road-testing.

Richard materialized from the main house, exchanged a carefully gauged smile with Claire, and followed everyone else outside. Blake and his constable brought up the rear.

Sarita started checking the costumes for securely attached buttons and functioning, if concealed, zippers. Kate and Claire waded in where they could, shaking out jackets and testing hooks and eyes. Through the open door came currents and cross-currents of voices, suddenly quelled by Elliot's peremptory, "Places, everyone. A quick run-through and then costume call. Full dress rehearsal tomorrow night. If it doesn't fit, now is the time to call our lovely multiple wardrobe mistresses' attention to it. Richard — Phillip — the prologue, if you would be so kind."

Claire unfolded a lace collar and pricked up her ears. Even issuing bald architectural directives Richard's voice was a delight. Now, tuned and strummed, it sent shivers down her back.

"Look down, O Muse, and smile upon this unaccustomed hand. Here do I, a man of uncouth and idle pleasures, bend his meager talents toward that year long past, wherein Summerstow was assailed by plague and fear as though the four eternal horsemen did ride about its narrow streets and harvest souls like corn. Save the soul of a maiden, snatched untimely not by immortal terror but by mortal calumny, by her very neighbors who so forsook the duties of humanity. All but one, and he, amid his toils and care, could not deliver her.

"On yonder green, beneath St. Thomas's o'ertipping tower, stands the place of infamy where the pitiful story was played out. O man! both loyal and perverse! O woman! gentle and spiteful in equal measure . . ."

Elliot's affected voice was a bucket of cold water. "Richard, this a tragedy. Could you find a little emotion in the lines, please?"

"I'm quite familiar with the tragic nature of the play, thank you, Elliot," Richard retorted.

You can say that again, Claire thought. The quiet conviction of his delivery suggested unfathomable depths of emotion, underscoring the tragedy better than any amount of "thud and blunder," as Melinda would have put it.

Sarita stitched the mile-and-a-half long hem of Trillian's costume, a modest teal-blue gown. Kate polished the buckles on several pairs of shoes. Claire sewed button after button down the back of her own costume — since she was turning pages for Priscilla, the pianist, it was her back that would be to the audience — and listened.

Even though Trillian hadn't the experience to plumb her dialog for Elizabeth's innate dignity, her youth emphasized the woman's plight. She was still a bit shaky on her lines, earning more than one elaborate sigh from Elliot. Alec's Walter was stiff. Claire suspected he was pointing up that the young clergyman's inability to save Elizabeth stemmed as much from the flaws in his own character as from the lynch mob mentality of the townsfolk.

Diana played even Lettice's minor lines as though she was doing Lady MacBeth's sleepwalking scene. The normally taciturn Rob ranted and raved, overshooting Cecil's motivation, doubt and disillusionment, to target a malicious rage. Claire shuddered. Rob could've broken Melinda in half with his bare hands.

The secondary characters spoke their lines with skill mingled with boredom, depending on how many years they'd been playing the same parts. Richard's voice came and went, providing a base line to the orchestrations of the others.

Phillip had written — well, had begun — a play about the tragedy of witch-baiting while he and his cronies in the Hell-Fire Club amused themselves with occult mumbo-jumbo exponentially more offensive than anything Elizabeth had stitched into her cloth. But if Phillip had been caught the repercussions would've been social, maybe political, not legal and certainly not lethal.

In real life, Phillip had taken the occult too lightly. The truly tragic aspects of The Play probably had been Julian and Dierdre's work. It was Cecil who'd taken the occult much too seriously.

Both men, passionate in their own ways, were Richard's ancestors. Did their personalities linger in his? How much of the Celtic warrior poet from his mother's ancestry was concealed behind that crisp Norman exterior like nuclear fuel rods concealed behind lead shielding? If Richard ever went critical Claire wanted to be miles away. Or else with him, in the upstairs bedroom at the Lodge . . . It was way too soon to be thinking about sex.

"Lovely!" Elliot shouted. "Tea time! Cue-to-cue afterwards, with music!"

People flooded into the kitchen, seizing sandwiches and rattling teacups. Sarita, Claire, and Kate scrambled among the drifts of material matching costume to body.

Janet, playing a shopkeeper, was swathed in yards of gray cotton with the obligatory white collar. Both Rob and Alec were in strict black and white, although Rob, as Cecil, was permitted a bit of lace. Claire checked inside the first black coat. "ASW" read the printed initials. Since Alec was still outside, she put that coat down, handed Rob the one labeled RPJ, and tried not to shrink back as he tried it on. No alterations required. No conversation, either.

Claire picked up a pile of pink cotton, glanced at the "DCJ" marked inside, and called, "Diana?"

Diana laid down her cup and reported to the table, where Claire and Sarita lifted the yards of fabric over her head and settled them around her. "A bit snug," said Sarita.

"I have me other clothes on beneath," Diana pointed out. "It'll fit a treat, just as it did when I first wore it."

"This was Diana's costume as Elizabeth," Sarita explained as they levered the material back over Diana's helmet of blond hair. "I added fancy buttons and lace, as befitting the lady of the manor."

Judging by the minuscule rows of stitch punctures paralleling the seams of the dress, Claire suspected that Sarita had also let it out — without consulting Diana. Technically the pink dress, like Trillian's teal and Melinda's blue, wasn't historically accurate garb for a servant, but the drama demanded that Elizabeth be set off by color.

Elliot walked Trillian in the kitchen door, bending condescendingly over her dark head. "Do try to remember your lines, there's a good girl."

Roshan loomed up behind them, disengaged his daughter, and led her to the tea table, where Alec plied her with cookies and reassurances until her red lips lost their pout and smiled. Now, Claire thought, someone needed to erase the worry that not only thinned Alec's lips but stiffened his entire face, as though he'd been taking tension lessons from Richard.

If he hadn't had The Play to occupy his time the last two weeks he might just as well have left town — although suspects weren't allowed to do that, were they? Blake and Pakenham had made the young constable as welcome as a wizard at a Puritan revival even before he became a suspect. Now they were going to relieve him of duty. For having been so congenial when Claire first arrived, Alec now seemed ill at ease around her. She couldn't turn back time and tell him not to find Melinda, though. She'd come here to find Melinda . . .

"Lacey, Richard Callander," Richard's voice said in Claire's ear. "That's initials RCL."

. . . and she'd found Richard, too. "An eighteenth century costume kind of stands out from the rest, you know. Here you go. Frock coat, knee breeches, stockings, gold buckles. Even your ponytail and ribbon, unless you can grow your hair out before Friday."

"I think not. Sorry." He grinned. The strain still lurked at the corners of his eyes and mouth, but tonight his hair was a bit more relaxed, the kitchen lights striking auburn gleams from its soft dark bristles.

She grinned back. "Good. I like the mood hair just as it is."

"Eh?" Richard asked.

"Oh dear," said Sarita. "I have no more pins. Where is Roshan, he must run to the shop."

Claire tore herself away from the vision of Richard. "There's a box of pins upstairs. I'll get them."

Blake and the constable were still outside. Kate was smoothing a farmer's smock over Fred's narrow shoulders. Claire started to signal to her, then paused. They could hardly go around joined at the hip.

"I'll fend off the bogles," Richard said under his breath. "Come along." A swift touch of his hand to her back urged her into the corridor.

In the sudden darkness it seemed as though the dusty lamps in the kitchen had been bright as limelight. Claire blinked and stumbled. Richard slipped his arm around her waist. "I know the place like the back of my hand."

"I'm sure you do." She draped her own arm over his shoulder and leaned into him, captured in the warm gravity of his body even though her eyes quickly cleared. It felt good to touch him. There was nothing wrong in touching him. She could trust him. Blake trusted him. He'd even told Richard who Kate was, since she had to be slipped into the volunteer program.

True to his word, Richard needed to switch on only two lights on their way upstairs. The bare bulbs hanging from elegant plaster moldings grudged out a few watts. The voices in the kitchen faded and died. Except for the gentle creak of the floors the house was so silent Claire found herself tiptoeing in complement to Richard's discreet tread.

The chill, musty, darkness parted before them and closed behind them. In the long gallery the windows were networks of pale light. Claire picked up the box of pins, put the top on it, and tucked it into her pocket.

Footsteps moved along the corridor at the far end of the gallery. She spun around. "It's Elizabeth," Richard whispered.

"I think it was Diana said something about her being more active or more substantial the last couple of years."

"She has been that."

"It's all about her, isn't it? The Play and everything. And Melinda teasing you about 'the truth behind' it." Claire looked over at him. "I was checking out Elizabeth's embroidered cloth today, thinking about the significance of the designs. Do you think maybe Melinda didn't mean the truth about your parents writing The Play but the truth about Elizabeth, that she may really have been — well, a wise woman, you know what I mean?"

Against the spectral gleam of the marble fireplace Richard's profile listed into a wry smile. "You're still the canny one, aren't you? Yes, I imagine Elizabeth was after making healing and weather magic. Which was enough to condemn her. But we'll never know what Melinda . . ."

The footsteps came back the other way. A skein of yarn fell with a plump off the tapestry frame. In spite of herself Claire jumped. No surprise that she'd jump toward Richard and find herself pressed against his chest. His arms tightened around her. Her nostrils filled with his scent, clean wool, shampoo, and a hint of wood smoke. She didn't wrench away.

There was the calico cat. For several long seconds it batted the yarn across the floor, its paws making a faint rustle. Then it vanished, leaving the yarn in a tangled heap against the wooden planks.

After a long count of ten, Claire whispered, "How did the Cranbournes like living in a haunted house?"

"There's not a word about either ghost in their letters and diaries. A classic case of denial, I should think."

"Surely your father had a close encounter or two when he was looking over the hidden room. Or was he of the stiff-upper-lip school?"

Richard shook his head. "He wasn't, no. But he didn't know about the room, not until Alec and I found it."

"Really?" Claire tilted her head so she could see his face.

Its angles were softened by shadow. A spark flared in his eyes. His voice was so soft she could hardly hear it, and leaned in even closer. "I was perhaps twelve, Alec ten. And yet he was the bold one, keen on following the ghost up the stairs. I went along because I wouldn't let a younger and smaller lad — and he was smaller then — show me up."

"Cool," Claire said, but she wasn't at all cool. Richard's breath stirred the fine hairs around her ears. His body was firm and steady against hers. His hands moved slowly down her back and circled her flanks. His voice had sent a shiver down her spine. His caress drew a shudder of delight from her entire body.

She traced the musculature over his shoulders to his back, the wool of his sweater tickling her fingertips. His heart beat against her breast like a snare drum setting the cadence of a reel. His face was inches away from hers, his eyes bright glints, for once easy to read. Oh yes, she thought.

The kiss wasn't at all tentative. They went lip to lip, mouth to mouth, tongue to tongue so fiercely Claire's breath caught in a muffled gasp. *Yes!*

Of course Richard was focussed, thorough, meticulous. Of course she went at him with banners flying from every nerve ending. No more secrets. No more hidden emotions. All that he was, all that she was, not only revealed at last but flaunted and savored. Every fiber of her body vibrated like a strummed harp string. Lightning flashed . . . *Oh.*

Kate stood with her hand still on the light switch and her face set in a sheepish smile. "Sorry, sorry — Sarita said you were after fetching the pins — Blake'd have my guts for garters if anyone got at you — if you'd told me you were off with Richard — sorry."

In one simultaneous movement they stepped apart. "No problem," Richard said. His mouth was set so tightly Claire couldn't believe that just a moment earlier it'd been so flexible. She cleared her throat and shook herself. *Whoa.* They'd leaped several stages of relationship there. Suddenly that bedroom seemed like a real possibility. Or the living room couch. Her own hide-a-bed. The back seat of the Rover . . . Well, no, they could do better than that.

Together the three of them walked down to the kitchen, Kate in the lead, Richard and Claire sharing quick, curious, cautious looks behind her back.

Everyone was filing back outside. "Claire!" Elliot called. "Musicians on-stage!"

Her knees shaking, her hands for once trembling with pleasure instead of fear, Claire walked outside and took her place at the beginning of the next act.

Chapter Fifteen

*T*he view from the back window of Claire's flat was of an alley and the rear of a row of shops. Beyond their lichen-freckled roofs green fields stitched with silver stone fences billowed toward a closed and shadowed horizon. Birds sang arias in the uncertain sky.

Close by a nasal voice was ranting, anything but uncertain. Who was Pakenham hectoring at eight o'clock in the morning? Claire opened the window and leaned out into the chill.

The shop directly behind her was Blake's command post. Through one window she could see a constable staring at a teakettle, apparently not believing that a watched pot never boils. Through the other window she saw Pakenham, three-piece suit immaculate, mouse-colored hair slicked back, standing beside a table littered with papers. A shirt-sleeved forearm resting on the table was Blake's. Across from him two female hands picked at a tissue. Each one glinted with a fleck or two of gold. So what's up with Janet? Claire asked herself. But she'd probably be hearing all about it.

She drained her cup of tea, washed her dishes, and brushed her teeth. A knock on her door was Kate coming to put her on her leash for the rest of the day. Dutifully Claire called, "Who is it?"

"Kate here."

"I'm ready." Picking up Trevor's umbrella and opening the brand-new dead bolt, Claire went outside and locked the brand-new lock. She followed Kate down the steps, telling herself not to be irritated — the WPC was only doing her job.

In fact, she might be doing too good a job. Claire had the queasy feeling she was playing the part of the goat, staked out to attract the village predator. Not that any woman-eating beasts would attack bait so closely guarded. If Kate abandoned her post, though, she, Blake, and Pakenham would be blamed for every tooth-mark on Claire's body. Not that Claire herself would be too thrilled. Catch-22. Damned if you do, damned if you don't.

She didn't like being frightened. She didn't like being manipulated, by the murderer or by the police. She didn't like feeling helpless. . . . At the end of the street Richard emerged from the Lodge and strode toward the Hall, his lean, lithe body moving with the ease of a hunting cat. And she didn't like being chaperoned, she concluded.

Blake and Pakenham appeared from the side street. "Good morning," said Blake. He looked so tousled and woebegone, in contrast to the dapper Pakenham, that Claire expected him to add, "not that there's anything good about it." He fell into step beside her, leaving Pakenham and Kate to elbow each other on the narrow sidewalk behind.

"I had a profitable interview this morning," Pakenham announced.

Kate, obviously not wanting to encourage him, said nothing. But Claire figured she might as well get it over with. "Yes?"

"Janet Harlow admitted she had a one-night stand with Rob Jackman last year."

Aha — that explained a few looks and gestures across the bar. Unfortunately that wasn't all it explained. "Which happened to be the night Melinda was killed," Claire stated.

"Got it in one," Pakenham told her.

Blake stepped off into the street to avoid a car parked over the curb. A couple of volunteers veered in another direction, avoiding him. "Miss Harlow rowed with Mr. Siebold over him spending an afternoon with Miss Varek. He went back to their B&B. She went on to the church, arriving there at a quarter past twelve or so, as Mrs. Digby already told us. What Mrs. Digby didn't notice, though, is that Miss Harlow slipped out again at a quarter to one, meaning to return to the B&B. She met Rob Jackman walking his dog in the high street and stopped for a chat. When she told him about the row, he told her Fred was probably — er

— with Miss Varek at that very moment."

"So she thought she'd have herself a bit of a giggle and get her own back, all at once." Claire could hear the nudge-nudge, wink-wink in Pakenham's voice. "She finally came forward, she says, because she was afraid my asking questions would have her precious Fred putting two and two together."

Claire didn't even try to imagine what it would be like having sex with Rob. It wouldn't be making love, that was for sure. "Sounds as though that'd give Fred a motive to murder Rob or Janet, not Melinda. You never can tell how people's minds are going to work, though."

"Janet Harlot — get that, Harlow, Harlot?" Pakenham snickered. "She says Fred wouldn't kill a fly. He's a bit wet, right enough. But then some murderers are mild-mannered little sods pushed just a bit too far."

"Money, jealousy," murmured Kate, "when it comes to motive we're spoilt for choice."

"As for PC Wood," Blake went on, "Miss Harlow says she saw him and Miss Varek in what she described as a passionate clinch right after dress rehearsal, a couple of days before she died."

Claire nodded glumly. At least that didn't take her by surprise. *Damn Alec.* She was prepared to believe anything he said, if only he'd say something about his letter more substantial than "just a bit of mischief."

"Village is a bleeding knocking-shop," stated Pakenham, who always had something to say. "Not surprising the nosy Miss Melinda knew something she shouldn't have known. Of course, if she'd just kept her mouth shut, hadn't gone about making trouble for people . . ."

Claire stopped so abruptly Kate bumped into her back. She spun around and fixed Pakenham with her hottest glare. "How about looking for the killer instead of passing judgement on the victim? Or on anyone else, for that matter. Or don't y'all believe in innocent until proven guilty, let alone common courtesy?"

Pakenham went red in the face. Blake's moustache quivered. Clutching the umbrella, Claire stamped past a couple of flatbed trucks loaded with pipe and wooden planks and burst into the Hall.

Kate was just behind her, laughing. "Well done. That'll teach Pakenham to keep a civil tongue in his head."

"I hadn't realized I had such a rude tongue in mine," Claire returned.

Richard was standing on the staircase looking very much at home, more like the laird of the castle than its chief steward. But he was an aristocrat. Blake was a sturdy yeoman. Pakenham was a toad.

"Kate, if you'll excuse us. Claire, please." Richard started up the stairs, his mouth crumpled in a wry smile.

She wasn't exactly up to dealing with his mouth, her tongue, or any juxtaposition of the two this morning. However, you never put off a man who wanted to talk. Handing Kate the umbrella, Claire went after him.

She found Richard in the library standing on the hearthrug, his hands braced on his hips. Behind him gleamed the marble mantelpiece carved with partially draped figures. At his feet sat a Victorian picnic basket filled with tools — brushes, files, screwdrivers. Against it leaned the clipboard and a copy of *Architectural Graphic Standards.* "What happened to the pheasant, strawberries, and champagne that basket used to hold?" Claire asked.

"The same thing happened to the long gowns and starched collars of the people who ate them," Richard answered. "The world moved on and left style behind. It probably gained honesty, though."

"Or crude tactlessness, take your pick."

"It can be a right juggling act, can't it?"

"Yes," Claire agreed. She looked up at the family portraits lined up like mug shots at the post office.

Various Cranbournes inspected their property with lead-lined eyes that suggested less hidden passion than constipation. But the painting on the far wall, between the windows, was of a man in eighteenth century coat and throat-concealing stock. His face was puffy although the bones beneath the overused skin were fine and strong. The brow was clear, conscience concentrated in the sagging jowls and weary eyes — eyes that even in yellowed oil paint were bright with a self-aware intelligence. "Is that Phillip?"

"So it is," said Richard. "By Joseph Wright of Derby. Rather contradictory features, I'm thinking."

"Take away that air of dissipation and he could be you."

"Dissipation not being all it's cracked up to be."

"No, it's not." Not that Claire had an intimate knowledge of dissipation. What she'd tasted — or tested — was enough. What was in Richard's past she could only guess, but she doubted he'd ever been much of a rake. Like her, he looked before he leaped.

The room smelled of musty books. Her librarian's instinct kicking in, Claire traced the odor to a shelf beside the door and pulled out several volumes. Bits of leather peeled off and stuck to her fingertips. The pages were mottled with damp. "Scott, Tennyson, Dumas — what a crime, to let these beautiful books rot."

"The Cranbournes were proper Philistines," Richard agreed. "We might could get the classics restored. Those others, the cheap romances, they're beyond redemption."

Claire checked over a couple of other books, these with cardboard bindings that fell apart in her hands. "Inexpensive, maybe, but valid reflections of their time. What's the name on the flyleaves — Vincent Cranbourne? Wasn't he the black sheep of the family?"

"By our standards only gray. He was Maud's only brother, a proper

Roaring Twenties playboy. Impregnated one of the servant girls. The elder Cranbournes wanted him to give her the elbow — she wasn't their sort, was she? When he married her instead, they disowned him." Richard shrugged. "There you are, try to do the right thing and you're disowned for making an unsuitable marriage. Mind you, nowadays there's no such thing as an unsuitable marriage."

"Sure there is. You and I both escaped making one. Melinda didn't." Claire put the books back and wiped her hands on her jeans. "Richard, you didn't ask me in here to discuss changing manners and morals."

"No. I thought we should be saying something about Melinda."

"Yes, we probably should."

He drew himself to attention. "I hurt her. She teased me in return. She never meant to hurt me. That first letter wasn't even blackmail. More of a flirtatious, 'I know something about you.' She didn't even say what it was she knew, did she? My guilty conscience filled in the blank spot."

"As well as the name of the sender?" Claire asked.

"That was no secret. She gave herself away by quoting, 'when you will, they won't; when you won't, they set their hearts upon you of their own inclination.' Which is part of Phillip's original text, by the by."

"When I first read The Play I attributed that quote to Jonathan Swift and thought it was an anachronism," Claire told him. "But when I looked it up I saw it was an old Roman, Terence, the sort of classical reference everyone made in Phillip's day. History's full of misogynists."

"And Melinda was after doing battle with every one of them."

"If she hadn't liked men so much she'd never have bothered." Claire walked back to the fireplace and looked as closely at Richard as he was looking at her. She detected fatigue in the skin beneath his eyes, worry in the V of his eyebrows, stress in the line etching itself into his right cheek perpendicular to his mouth. What she didn't detect any more was challenge. Last night he'd called off his guards and opened his gates. So, for that matter, had she. "Melinda would've apologized to you."

"I daresay she would've done. I owed her an apology as well, I suppose. As for you, I don't know whether I'm owing you an apology . . ." He shook his head. "I'm not usually this inarticulate. Sorry."

Claire smiled at him. "What you're trying to ask is whether we can go on with what we started last night when Melinda's ghost is walking around in the next room."

"Just that, yes. Not that Melinda and I could ever have had anything," he added quickly.

"No, you couldn't. You're too much alike."

His brows tilted upwards. "Alike?"

"Intense. Intelligent. Focussed. With something to hide. And a great sense of humor, although yours is more subtle than hers. I bet she's laughing at the way we're tap dancing around each other when she went to so much trouble to bring us together . . ." Claire's voice died away. Put into words that sounded unbelievably lame. What else was she about to say? *Because I loved Melinda maybe someday I'll be able to love you?*

Richard's eyes flickered, telling her that words only went so far.

Claire felt dizzy — she was standing on the brink of a chasm, toes hanging over the edge, the updraft ruffling her hair — if she reached far enough from her side and he reached far enough from his . . . Richard blinked and stepped back from brink.

He didn't think emotional cliff diving was any more of an option than she did, not now. That was why neither one of them was like Melinda at all. "Well," Claire said, her voice not quite steady, "we'll just have to give it a go and see how we get on."

"Oh yes. That." With something between a smile and a grimace Richard touched her lips with his own and turned away.

Tingling gently, Claire walked back toward the staircase. Kate was looking out the window. Making a vague gesture toward the gallery, Claire headed off to work. And to what should've been some serious thinking, except she couldn't think much more seriously than she already was without blowing a gasket.

Kate sat down at the canvas without comment. Claire took up her needle and focused on a problem she could solve.

Rain began to fall outside. From somewhere in the house came a penetrating chemical odor. A variety of clinks and clunks, sounding like a preliminary exercise for *The Anvil Chorus,* reverberated in the high great chamber next door. After a time Claire and Kate went to look.

Susan was cleaning the marble fireplace with poultices of kaolin and benzene. She waved a rubber-gloved hand toward the tall windows overlooking the forecourt. "They're setting up the bleachers for The Play."

Of course. That's what the trucks with the pipes and planks were for. Claire looked outside to see Alec's and Fred's familiar faces among the strange ones of the workmen. No wonder she hadn't heard the plink plink of masonry and trowel that morning — Fred had been drafted. And apparently Alec had nothing better to do than help. She lifted her hand to wave at him, but he never glanced up from beneath the hood of his yellow slicker.

Claire and Kate went back to work. Raindrops pattered against the gallery windows. The workmen worked on. More than once a wet piece of metal tubing slipped from someone's grasp and amid cries of warning crashed to the ground. A variety of voices rose and fell in the entrance hall and faded toward the kitchen where Sarita was sewing last-minute alterations.

Claire was wondering if it was lunchtime yet when Kate looked abruptly around. "Who's there?"

Claire glanced toward the far door. The footsteps in the corridor outside were quick and light. "It's the ghost."

"Ghost?" Kate repeated dubiously.

"Sure. Any self-respecting old house has to have a ghost. This one has two, Elizabeth Spenser and her cat. I'll show you."

"Right," Kate said. She tucked her needle into the pincushion and stood up.

Claire led the way out the door and up the stairs, thinking not of the time she'd followed Elizabeth but of Richard and Alec as boys. Richard had probably felt protective and irritated in turn, like an older brother. He probably still felt that way. And vice versa. That was part of friendship.

Claire opened first the closet door, then the sliding panel, and stood back so Kate could step into the secret room between the chimneys. "We assume this was originally a priest's hole," she said, and wondered where that "we" had come from, like the flip side of Pakenham's incessant "I."

"Well, well." Kate inspected the rafters, the bench, the table.

The rain on the roof sounded like slow, aching tears. The smell of decay was milder than Claire would've thought. She listened but heard no footsteps. "This might have been Elizabeth's private room. You know that embroidered cloth in the cardboard box? It was on that table. She probably stitched it. Richard says the Laceys kept it all these years, unlikely as that seems when you consider what they did to Elizabeth to begin with. Why Richard would leave the cloth in here I don't know. At least he gave me the go-ahead to do some conserva . . ."

"What's all this in aid of?"

Kate and Claire spun around so fast they collided. Claire gulped. "Oh hi, Alec. I was just showing Kate Elizabeth's room."

No wonder she hadn't heard him coming. He was wearing thick wool socks, probably having left his wellie boots in the entrance hall. His jeans were wet to the knees, his brown hair, usually a russet-gold, was a damp burnt umber, and his cheeks were pink. When he stepped through the door he exuded a cold, fresh scent. One more person, Claire thought, and they'd be wedged so tightly in the tiny room they'd have to pried out with a crowbar.

"Elizabeth," said Alec. Or perhaps he asked, talking to some memory of the betrayed girl. "She'd sit here and. . . . Where's the shroud?"

"Shroud?" Kate asked. "You mean the embroidered cloth?"

Shroud? Well, that answered that question, Claire told herself. Richard had let Alec put the cloth in here, as Exhibit A in the Museum of Elizabeth. "I have it. It's in the gallery."

Alec's head swiveled so fast she felt sympathetic whiplash. But his green eyes were closed and locked just as tightly as they'd been all this week. "Melinda told you, did she?"

"No, I followed Elizabeth up here one afternoon and then I asked Richard. He said it was all right to take the cloth. I was going to clean and mend it and surprise you with it — ah — I should've let you know I had it. I'm sorry."

"Oh. Well then, no need to apologize." Alec looked down at his feet. "Would you like to see it?"

"Yes, if you don't mind."

Exchanging a nonplussed glance, Kate and Claire strolled into the outer room and waited while Alec carefully closed the doors behind them.

Chapter Sixteen

*A*s they started back downstairs Claire asked, "Shroud?"

"So I'm thinking," Alec answered. "But she wasn't laid out in it properly, being taken untimely and all."

"Isn't that the truth." *His heart belongs to another,* Claire repeated silently. Alec had a crush on Elizabeth. He was in love with a woman who'd been dead over three hundred years. Now there was an unrequited romance. If Melinda had trusted him enough to tell him about her past, then he must've trusted her enough to tell her about Elizabeth. Claire tried, "Melinda's novel, about Elizabeth's trial and everything."

"Yes?" returned Alec, waving Kate through the gallery door.

"She would've done it right, you know, treating Elizabeth with the respect she deserved."

"I know." Alec paced down the creaking floorboards.

She wouldn't have exploited your feelings, either, Claire added to herself. But Alec might not believe that, especially if he was remembering the way Melinda jumped out at him and Richard right before the cast party . . .

Oh my, Claire thought, darting a sharp glance at Alec's sober face. Janet had seen Alec and Melinda kissing right after dress rehearsal.

Which meant Melinda had probably been wearing Elizabeth's dress. Over and beyond playing the part, she might have been playing the part for him specifically — trying to get into Elizabeth's head, maybe, or trying to seduce him. And then what? Had he rebuffed her, too, not because he didn't want a relationship but because she wasn't the relationship he wanted? She'd jumped out at him for the same reason she'd sent Richard that letter, as a joke gone overboard.

Maybe his blackmail letter threatened to reveal his infatuation with Elizabeth to — whom? Was it Diana or Elliot who'd been twitting him about "his Elizabeth?" His crush was hardly a secret. Admitting it might be embarrassing, but it wouldn't get him into any sort of legal and ethical tangle. Claire tried again. "Blake's decided Melinda only sent the first letter, the one teasing Richard, and someone else sent the others."

"So I hear," Alec said. "Is this the box?"

Kate sat down and started sewing, her face downcast, her ears pricked forward.

Claire put the box on the windowsill and opened it. In the dim light the linen cloth looked fragile as gauze and the embroidery seemed colorless. The mildew odor wasn't nearly as bad as that of the much younger books downstairs. It just went to show you how much influence Alec had over Richard, talking him into leaving the cloth in the damp little garret instead of in the storeroom with the dehumidifier. "A bath in distilled water would help preserve it," she suggested.

Alec reached toward the cloth. "There's an herb, *saponaria officianalis,* also called 'Bouncing Bet,' which foams up in water and makes a lovely soap for old needlework."

"Really? You'll have to give me the recipe." Claire pointed. "There're some holes in the stitching, moths eating the wool threads, probably. I'll try some unobtrusive repairs, assuming I can match the colors. Sometimes the modern dyes are too vivid."

"Vegetable dyes duplicate the old colors."

So he didn't mind her working on the cloth, then. "These colors are vegetable dyes, aren't they? Loden green, chestnut brown, madder red, yellow — yellow's made from onion skins, right?"

"Right"

"Did you ever notice the hair stitched into the patterns?"

"Yes." Alec traced the intricate embroidery with his forefinger, lightly, barely touching the cloth, as though it was singing a distant song that he could hear through his fingertips.

"Do you think maybe Elizabeth really was a witch?"

His fingers curled defensively back into a fist. "And if she was?"

"Well, then she was. I mean, everyone takes The Play as gospel, that Elizabeth was innocent. . . ." Claire realized she was mixing metaphors. Hard to believe it'd once been so easy to talk to Alec when now he was standing with the breadth of his shoulder turned toward her, shutting her out. Like Richard with her, it wasn't that she was particularly inarticulate, it was that she didn't want to violate Alec's boundaries. Except unlike Richard with her, she had no idea where Alec's boundaries were.

"They accused Elizabeth of poisoning the well and of devil worship," Alec said, his voice so low it was almost hoarse. "She *was* innocent."

"Oh yes, she was. So what if she really was the village wise woman or Wiccan or whatever. That was all a long time ago. It's not an issue any more. We know better now."

His hand opened and flattened against the cloth.

Claire imagined a man lying on his lover's breast. She blundered on, "Is that what Melinda meant in Richard's letter about 'the truth behind The Play'? Is that what you were asking if Melinda told me, not that the room exists but that Elizabeth's story is a lot more complex than The Play lets on? I'd like that. I'd like to think she was more than just a victim."

Kate stitched calmly on. The odor of benzene sharpened the cool draft from the room next door.

"Thank you," Alec said. Gently he fitted the lid on the box. "Now if you'll excuse me, Claire, Kate, dress rehearsal is tonight and it's still raining." He turned toward the door.

Claire was right behind him. She took his arm and pulled him around to face her. His face was keener than it had been a week ago, its composure eroded. She'd already violated his boundaries today, for whatever reason. She might as well add assault and battery to the trespassing charges. "I'm sorry, Alec, but I have to know. Were you and Melinda having sex?"

"No. That wasn't right, not for us. We were friends is all." Politely Alec pulled his arm away and walked off, his steps booming, leaving Claire to swallow her next invasive question: *Why were you being black-mailed?* And yet he wouldn't have answered that if she had asked it.

Kate waited until he'd disappeared out the door. "Good go, but no joy."

"All I did was step on his toes. I've been stepping on his toes ever since I got here. Melinda stepped on his toes and I don't know why."

"Pakenham's a gormless git. That doesn't mean he's wrong about Alec. He's a bit peculiar, isn't he? And he did find the body."

"That's a point in his favor. Melinda's body could've stayed in the garden forever and no one would have known."

"True," said Kate, an equal opportunity cop. "A lot of things could've gone on here forever and no one would've known. But now . . ."

"Now?"

"It's like the curtain's gone up, the show has started, and everyone in

Somerstowe is playing a role."

"Everyone in Somerstowe except Richard is playing a role," Claire corrected.

Kate squinted down at her needle and didn't answer.

Claire dropped heavily into her chair and considered the needlework. A few continental stitches at the edge of Venus's artfully draped gown to steady the spliced-in bit of canvas and then a trame stitch across the hole so that the new stitching would be as thick as the old. Tentatively she pressed her needle into the pre-existing stitches, wondering whose hand had made them. Alec may have sensed something in the old cloth but all Claire's fingertips sensed in it or in any of the old needlework was dusty thread. She'd take Alec's kind of peculiar any day, though, considering what some nut cases got up to.

Great — the rosy pink cotton thread was shinier than the antique wool, the modern wool thread was too thin, and neither of them was quite the right color. Richard would spot the patch from across the room. Yes, you needed to mark where you'd made the restoration, just not with a flashing neon sign.

She could unravel several strands of cotton and several of wool and twist them together. After checking with Richard, of course. She stabbed her needle into the pincushion. "Let's go get lunch," she said to Kate.

"Good idea."

Huddling beneath the umbrella, they bought sandwiches from Roshan and took them back to the Hall kitchen. There they sat chatting about herbal dyes and old needlework with Sarita, Priscilla, and Janet, who answered in words of one syllable and stared off into space. Embarrassed, Claire guessed. Hoping she's somehow made it all go away. Claire had always thought confession was good for the soul, but then it hadn't done much for Richard, either.

Elliot sat in lonely splendor in the cooker's aura of warmth, making notes in his copy of the script. Occasionally he tilted the contents of a silver flask into his mug of tea and threw a comment toward the women, sharing his extensive knowledge of Hollywood costume design and the idiosyncrasies of Americans. Some of his remarks were more than a little barbed — his tirade on how awkward American money was, for example, all the same size and color — but Claire refused to rise to the bait and agreed sweetly with every bit of blarney he emitted.

Diana popped in with a box of utensils and crockery. She and Elliot ignored each other. Fred wandered through and Janet rushed to make him a cuppa. Rob appeared with a box of sandwiches. Richard walked in one door and out the other, face set in deep thought, oblivious to the multiple eyes that followed him across the room let alone Claire's "Yo! Over here!" gesture. Alec never showed up at all.

Well, she reflected as she rinsed out her mug, in any play there was more going on behind the scenes than on the stage. "I need to ask Richard about that thread," she said to Kate. "He went thataway, didn't he?"

The entrance hall was gray and damp, the brave tile floor filthy with footprints. A couple of pairs of boots, each in its own puddle, stood in front of the cold and empty hearth. Richard wasn't in the needlework storage room, although the bare bulb hanging from the cobwebbed ceiling was glaring away. Claire turned it off, then turned it back on.

Were the tidy rolls of needlework disarranged? Hard to tell. Richard might carry an inventory in his head, but she certainly didn't. Probably he'd had some organizational inspiration and changed a few things around. Focussing on your work being therapeutic and everything.

He wasn't in the library, although his clipboard leaned against the fireplace. When Claire and Kate circled back into the kitchen Sarita said she thought she'd glimpsed him outside. Claire stepped out into the forecourt.

Several men were bolting the wooden seating to the jungle gym of tubing. Others raised light standards, running various cords and cables from them to the antique fuse box by the kitchen door. Fred leaned against the wall beside it, huddled into his yellow slicker. He wasn't goldbricking — he was making sure no one turned on the electricity to the forecourt outlets until the wires were properly insulated and secured in their conduits beneath the bleachers.

"Fred!" Claire called. "Have you seen Richard?"

"He said he'd be in the library," returned Fred.

"I was just . . ." She turned back into the house. Fine. She'd wait by the waterhole for a few minutes. Maybe he'd run down to the Lodge.

With the faithful Kate still tagging along — well, her job was tagging along, wasn't it? — Claire went back into the library and walked down the room to the portrait between the windows. "This is Phillip Lacey. Looks a bit like Richard, doesn't he?"

Kate considered. "In the forehead, maybe . . ."

Speak of the devil, or the household god, whatever — just outside the library door Richard's vibrant voice said, "I thought you'd be out organizing the animals two by two."

"The rain'll clear this evening, no fear," Alec's cooler tones returned. Stiff fabric rustled and creaked — he was either putting on or taking off his slicker. "Richard, you let Claire take Elizabeth's shroud."

"I had no reason to stop her. She's good, she won't damage it. She won't, will she, by cleaning and mending it?"

"I don't think so, no. It's not that. I'm wondering how much she knows."

"Here we are again," Richard said, his voice dropping almost into a whisper. "Last year this time we were asking ourselves how much

Melinda knew."

The long room funneled his words directly to Claire's ears. Which seemed to be ringing — oh, the blood was draining from her face. She lurched forward — *don't say any more, please don't say any more . . .* Kate's hand closed firm and uncompromising on her upper arm and pulled her back.

Alec's whisper was hoarse. "Maybe if you and I had told the truth, the whole truth, Melinda might still be alive."

"Then Claire would never have come here."

"So that's the way of it, eh?"

"Oh aye, I'm afraid it is. She's here, and because she's here she's in danger. I'm caught between a rock and a hard place, Alec. I don't want to hide anything, but none of the — the secrets, the privacies — are mine to reveal, are they?"

"It's our own choice whether to remember or to forget the past. Whether to take up the memories or reject them."

"The sins of the fathers? Or their blessings?"

"Both. I know which I've chosen, for good and for ill. Let me bear my own sins, Richard. You have your own."

"They're not my own, are they? That's just the point."

"No, the point is that all this is part of — well, you can call it a divine plan or pattern, I'm thinking."

"Alec, I . . ." Richard's voice suddenly boomed. "Yes, Rob? A leak in the pantry? I'll be there straightaway."

"Choose what you've found with Claire," Alec said, and his steps, each a tiny squeak of a boot, receded down the hall and were gone.

Oh God, Claire thought. She almost fell over as Kate jerked her back behind the bookcase. Richard's footsteps came into the room. The clipboard clicked against the marble. His steps retreated out the door and faded away.

"Sorry." Kate let go of Claire's arm.

Claire sagged against the books. "You have to tell Blake what they said, don't you?"

"Yes, I do. Although tonight will be soon enough." Frowning, she added, "It's all hearsay, Claire. Inference. Not necessarily anything he can use."

"Oh, he'll be able to use it, all right." Claire felt sick, stunned, crazy-mad and angry-mad both. At Richard. At Alec. At Melinda. At herself. Hadn't she told herself recently that if people weren't hiding secrets then no one would get hurt? That might not be the most asinine thing she'd ever thought — thinking Richard had revealed everything was right up there too — but it sure came close.

Richard, of course, had nailed it. Everyone had privacies. Melinda, for example. She wanted to keep her past hidden. She hadn't hurt anyone by keeping it hidden. It wasn't the hiding that would've hurt, it was the revelation.

Claire had never revealed what she knew about Melinda's past. And yet that had been only Melinda's past. Alec and Richard weren't talking about only The Play, were they? There was more. The whole truth and nothing but, so help — what? Alec's divine pattern?

And had she ever learned something else — how easy it was to assume your conversations were secret. In the future she'd guard her tongue. Literally, when it came to Richard, if that was her only choice — Alec's comment to the contrary. But she didn't know what to choose right now, which truth took precedence. Alec? Richard? Melinda? Somerstowe with its long memory?

Claire led Kate back up to the gallery. She separated the strands of wool and cotton thread and took three threads from each. As she twisted them loosely together she visualized a seventeenth-century rope maker twisting a noose small enough for a young girl's neck.

She went to work. Rote work. Dumb, numb work. The silver needle lanced in and out of the soft pink of Venus's gown. Claire thought of Richard's bedroom and shook her head. She couldn't mourn a relationship she'd never had.

Kate stitched away silently, her brows cramped. She had no choice, had she? For her there was only one truth.

Just before quitting time Claire finished her patch and pronounced it good. As she looked up she thought she saw movement in the shadows at the end of the room. Her overworked eyes, she rationalized. She turned off the lamp and the movement was no longer there. If she detected a faint scent of pomander or the patter of paws, she ignored them.

In the high great chamber Susan was just peeling off her rubber gloves. "Dress rehearsal tonight," she called. "How are the costumes coming?"

"Sarita says they'll be ready," Kate returned politely. "Everyone's been for a fitting today."

From the window Claire saw the workmen piling into their trucks and heading down the drive. Richard was coming up the drive. He had to leap aside to avoid the spray sent up by the trucks' wheels. She'd better tell him what she'd done about the thread. If he made her pick it out, fine — she might as well backtrack on that, too. Then she could slink away to her room and bang her head against the wall or something similarly productive.

What she really wanted to do was grab a double handful of Richard's sweater and demand, "Why are you doing this to me? Why?" But she wasn't the issue. And that in itself was an issue.

Claire hurried on downstairs and out the front door. The roofs of the village hid coyly behind a Scotch mist that was too light to fall as rain. The water droplets hung in the air, gathering on her glasses and turning her view into a pointillist painting. Even so, she saw the bolt of material folded over a horizontal bar at one end of the bleachers. That was the Morris Strawberry Thief canvas she'd finished stitching last week, she was sure of it. What was it doing out here?

The flagstones of the forecourt flowed with water. She glanced around. No Fred, no Alec, no one with wellies who could rescue the fabric. Well, her athletic shoes would dry soon enough in front of an electric fire.

She waded through the puddles and stepped over a cable. The cloth was on a bar inside the network of tubing. She reached for the outside bar, to steady herself as she leaned between two others . . .

"Claire, don't move!" shouted Kate. "Don't bloody move!"

Claire froze in mid-reach, Kate's urgent command jamming her motor nerves. *What the. . . ?* Her shoes were tingling, sending pins and needles up her legs. Water. Electricity. The electricity was on. Her body was bent forward at the waist, surrounded by a metal web. She was inches away from grounding herself. She was inches away from death.

Footsteps splashed in agonizing slow motion. "Where the hell is — Fred, move your bum, where's the fuse box? The power's on? Well switch off, sod it all, switch off now!" Kate's serrated voice would have cut stone. Judging by the scramble Claire heard behind her, it motivated Fred to speed. A distant thunk, and the sizzle beneath her feet disappeared.

Hands seized her shoulders and pulled her from the trap. Kate's hands. Kate's face, eyes blazing, stared at her. Claire stared back. The only muscle in her body that worked was her heart, which was doing a syncopated somersault from her throat to her stomach and back again.

Richard pelted into her peripheral vision and skidded to a stop, sending up a bow wave. "The electricity was switched on? How did you know?"

"I didn't," Kate said. "They pay me to be paranoid is all."

"I just went inside to get a cup of tea," Fred called from several miles away. "Really, I was only gone for a minute."

Richard took Claire's other arm. "Claire, are you all right?"

"Accidents happen on construction jobs," said Fred plaintively.

"This was no accident," Kate hissed beneath her breath. "That bit of cloth was bait. She was meant to electrocute herself. Thank God she was wearing trainers."

Stupid, stupid, stupid . . . Suddenly Claire's knees crumbled. Richard and Kate buoyed her up and carried her toward the Lodge.

Chapter Seventeen

*D*etective Chief Inspector Blake walked back and forth in front of the fireplace. He glared at the gargoyle on the mantel, at the papers on the floor, out the windows that overlooked the drive. He seized the poker and stabbed at the fire like a fencer trying to impale an evasive opponent. Kate dodged away from the hearth and sat down on the desk chair.

Richard emerged from the kitchen juggling the tea tray, which he clattered onto the table in front of Claire. "Here you are," he said, handing her a squat glass filled with amber liquid. "Good for what ails you."

She doubted that, but this was no time for debate. "Thank you." Her first sip of the sharp, smoky whiskey drew moisture back into her dry mouth and steamed into her sinuses, clearing her head. Her second sent rivulets of warmth into her shivering limbs.

Setting the glass down, she peeled off her sodden shoes and socks and extended her icy feet toward the fire. Her face was wet, too, with rain, tears, or blood she wasn't sure. She mopped at it with the sleeve of her sweatshirt and looked blearily around for her glasses. There they were, perched on a drawing pad. She didn't put them on. She could see herself well enough, a tiny, almost comical figure lost in a landscape of skewed realities.

Richard poured tea for Blake and Kate and sat down on the couch beside Claire. Surreptitiously, concealed in the folds of her jacket, he took her hand and squeezed so hard it hurt. His body was humming with tension. Hers was the consistency of oatmeal. She tried another swallow of whiskey.

"All right, then?" Richard asked.

"Yes, thanks. Kate, I owe you."

Kate cradled her warm cup in both hands. "Just doing my job. Hard as it is, with you popping off like that. I had to walk away whilst Susan was still talking to catch you up."

"Sorry," Claire told her. "I guess I never really believed I was in danger.

The letter — the letters — were so melodramatic, you know?"

"The Play's a melodrama," Kate returned.

"The killer took a hell of a chance with that tapestry," said Blake to the gargoyle. "Anyone could've seen him. He's a bold one."

"Bold?" Richard murmured. "Desperate? Stupid? Lucky?"

From outside came Pakenham's bray, cut with an indignant Liverpool accent belonging to the foreman of the workers, who, Claire deduced, had been tracked down to and dragged from the pub. "I don't know a bleeding soul in this town, do I? I was hired to put up the seating, wasn't I? Why should I do a bird I've never even heard of? And with a bit of rug?"

"Tapestry," Pakenham corrected wrongly. "Was it on the metal bar when you left the forecourt?"

"Haven't the foggiest. Me and my lads was at the other end of the lash-up, weren't we?"

"And the electricity was switched off when you left?"

"When we stopped work it was, right enough. The American bloke, the one with a face like a basset hound, the switch was his look-out."

"Fred was detailed to watch the fuse box," said Kate. "Means, motive, opportunity. No one saw him fetch the tapestry, true, but . . ."

"But," Blake said, "this afternoon Pakenham turned up an American chap, name of Wilson, who was here last year. Stayed at the same B&B as Siebold and Miss Harlow. They passed him on the staircase on their way to the church service. Siebold came back a few minutes later, slamming the front door. Wilson looked out at the noise, had a good view of Siebold going into the next room. Wilson heard him walking up and down, heard the loo flush, heard him snoring. Water-tight alibi for the time of Miss Varek's murder. Which seems to take away his motive for doing Miss Godwin."

"Shit," Kate said.

Claire didn't have even that much of a response. She seemed to be miles away from her own body. Richard's steady hand would've helped, if she hadn't been feeling miles away from him, too.

Footsteps raced outside. "Is Claire all right?" Alec's voice exclaimed.

"She's all right," replied Pakenham, with little enthusiasm. "Would you step inside for a moment, Wood?"

The door opened. Alec loomed out of the dim hallway. When he spotted Claire he exhaled in relief. "I'm sorry. You're not hurt, then?"

Claire pondered whether he was sorry she was all right or whether he was expressing some broader, if undefined, regret. "I'm fine, thank you, if kind of in shock. No pun intended."

Alec's out-of-focus face looked blank, puns beyond him. Richard's face was close enough to be in focus but was just as blank. Blake clanged the poker into its rack. His moustache drooped under the strain of suspecting one of his own. "What were you about this afternoon, PC Wood?"

"I helped assemble the seating until three or three-thirty," Alec replied, "then I went home to sort my paperwork. Elliot just stopped in and told me what happened. No needlework was hanging on the pole when I left. Everyone in the village has been at the Hall today, though."

"That's what Mrs. Nair told us," Kate said.

Alec turned to her. "Here, I reckon you're police as well."

Kate's sudden interest in her teacup admitted everything.

"This village is my patch," Alec said to Blake.

"The only reason this dump has a police presence at all," said Pakenham's voice from behind Alec's back, "is because of the tourists. You've been relieved of duty, Wood. Give it a rest."

Alec bit off his words rather than Pakenham's head. "If you'll excuse me, Claire. Richard." Like an unusually graceful bull escaping a china shop he vanished out the door. Pakenham followed.

Claire imagined a SWAT team chasing Alec to his cottage, trampling his garden, shooting out the blue light above his door. It wouldn't be long now. She drained her glass.

"Another wee dram?" Richard asked, flat.

It wouldn't be long until his solicitousness evaporated, too. "No, thank you."

"Well then," Blake said. "Everyone knows the lumber room where the tapestries are kept. It's usually unlocked. Siebold says the fuse box was switched off, but Mrs. Nair says he was in the kitchen with his cuppa for at least half an hour. Anyone — including Siebold himself, mind you — could've baited the trap for you."

"There is one thing," said Kate.

Claire squeezed Richard's hand and let it go, so he wouldn't have to let go of hers. She reached for her glasses, put them on, and looked over at Kate. *Get it over with.*

"Wood's been around and about the Hall today, as he said. Claire was showing me a little room in the attics that belonged to Elizabeth Spenser and he came on us sudden-like, seemed a bit narked to find us there."

"The Elizabeth Spenser in The Play?" Blake asked.

"Miss Varek was writing a novel about her. Wood has some strong opinions on the subject. Could be they rowed about it. He still says they were never lovers, by the way, just chums."

"Why should Elizabeth Spenser matter after all these years?"

"I don't know, sir. You'll have to ask Wood. Or maybe . . ." Kate's eye turned to Richard. "I overheard you and Alec talking just outside the library."

"We overheard you," amended Claire. "Accidentally. I was looking for you to ask about the yarn for the Venus and Adonis canvas."

Richard's eyes widened in comprehension. Then he closed them and set his jaw. No, he wouldn't request a blindfold, would he?

Blake straightened. "Yes?"

"They started off talking about an embroidered cloth from the secret room and went on asking each other how much Claire knows, and how much Melinda knew last year. And Alec said, 'if we'd told the truth, the whole truth, Melinda might still be alive.'"

Galvanic shudders ran down Richard's body.

"Then they went on about hiding secrets and choosing whether to remember or forget the past and the sins of the fathers or some such. And Alec said, 'Let me bear my own sins, you have your own.'"

Richard opened his eyes and fixed them on the pictures on the desk. One was a studio portrait of his parents, a dignified silver-haired man and a slender smiling woman with glints of red in her dark tresses. The other was Claire's favorite, a little boy with Richard's sculpted features still a work in progress, grinning and making a "ta da!" gesture at his kilt and knee socks.

Ta da was the last thing he was thinking now. His voice was icy. "The point is that the sins, the secrets, are not my own."

"No," Blake growled, "the point is that there's been a murder and an attempted murder, and you've been playing silly beggars with us."

Richard catapulted to his feet and ran his hands through his hair, which was already in full anxiety mode. His eyes flashed like a drawn sword.

But Blake stood his ground. "What do you have to say for yourself?"

"Oh, I could say quite a bit, Chief Inspector. Most of it would be pointless speculation about what's relevant and what's not, and how the blackmailer found out what they found out."

"Did they actually know anything?" Kate asked. "Or did they just throw a rock into the dark and hit your guilty conscience?"

"The question," retorted Richard, "is whether my guilty conscience killed Melinda. Not only who killed her, in other words, but why."

Blake crossed his arms. "We're asking the questions here, Lacey."

Claire slumped into the couch. Every time Richard turned around he fell over first Melinda's and then her own curiosity. Every time she turned around she fell over his damnable secrets or privacies or whatever he wanted to call them. So what was the point, anyway? That Melinda died to bring Claire and Richard together? How arrogant, how off-base, how out-of-focus was that? No wonder Melinda's irrepressible ghost kept coming between them. They didn't deserve a relationship.

Richard braced both hands on the mantel and gazed into the fire. The angle of his shoulder was turned toward Claire like Alec's shoulder had been turned toward her this morning. "It was almost twenty years ago when my parents faked The Play. Most of it, at the least. Mind you, they never intended to publish it, but when Maud did do, they kept silent for the Hall and the village."

"Yes, yes," said Blake impatiently. "Maud left the Hall to the Trust, The Play provided an endowment, and everyone except the Cranbourne heirs lived happily ever after — until Miss Varek started asking questions. You told us this already."

"What I told you was the tip of the iceberg," Richard said. "My parents and I sold our honor not once but twice. The first time by never telling the truth about The Play, even after Maud died. The second — well, Maud's death is the crux of the matter."

Blake leaned forward. Kate set her cup and saucer down on the desk and glanced from Richard to Claire and back.

Oh no, Claire thought. *Willpower.* It was the word "will" that'd landed in Richard's scruples like a rock in a pool of water.

No surprise his accent was taking the high road again. "Maud died ten years ago, as unexpectedly as one can at the age of ninety-six, just after the fifth production of 'An Historie.'"

"Any suspicion of foul play?" Kate asked.

"No. She caught a chill, it became pneumonia, and it carried her away."

"And?" prodded Blake.

"She'd originally intended to leave her entire estate to her great-nieces and nephews, her only family. She'd made a will to that effect in the fifties, long before some of those same nieces and nephews became wealthy. Long before she met my father and began to appreciate just what she had here in the Hall. What she chose to do with The Play shows you that she did begin to appreciate the Hall."

"And then she died without changing her will," Claire stated.

Richard stood still as a statue. A very good statue, by Michelangelo or Donatello, but cold and hard even so. "It's human nature to think we can cheat death by ignoring its certainty. By not considering what might happen after we die. Yes, she died without changing her will. Her estate, the Hall and the income from The Play, went to her relatives. So my father wrote up a new will, dated a week before she died. He and my mother signed it as witnesses, put the will in Maud's desk, and waited for it to be found. I leave to your imagination the gnashing of teeth when it was found."

"But her relatives were honest," said Blake. "Instead of burning the will, they gave it to the lawyer. What's his name?"

"Nigel Killigrew. Eight years later he married Melinda Varek and, in a way, sent her here."

"Poetic justice? Or a cruel twist of fate?" asked Kate.

"Both," Richard said, with a quick glance toward Claire. "One particularly stroppy cousin, Maurice Applethorpe — the wealthiest of the lot, mind you — sent his solicitor to challenge the will. He claimed my father had hounded Maud into depriving her relatives of their rightful inheritance or some such rubbish. But the will passed inspection by the court, Applethorpe was handed a trusteeship as a sop, and the rest, as they say, is history."

An Historie, Claire said to herself.

"You can shop me to the National Trust if you like," Richard told Blake. "I doubt it'd be best pleased."

"The Trust would be angry at you," Blake said, "not at us."

Richard stood immobile. Claire thought of him walking through the darkness of the Hall without needing to turn on a light. Of his mouth moving gently but insistently against hers. Nervous tension, she decided, was like centrifugal force. It was the only thing keeping her from flying to pieces.

Blake thrust his hands deep into his pockets and squared his shoulders. His moustache twitched. "Now then, Lacey, I think you just provided us with another motive for Miss Varek's murder."

"Did I?" Richard returned. "Did her letter have anything at all to do with the will? The bit about willpower — she was referring to the lines in The Play about 'a woman's will,' in reference to my — ah — rejecting her. That ties in with the bit about 'Mr. Stone.'"

"Are you saying her use of that word is nothing more than coincidence? With her married to the lawyer and all?"

"That angle was a bit worrisome, yes. As for the berk who sent the other letters — I don't know whether he actually knows anything or not. I couldn't afford to call his bluff, could I now?"

"Wasn't Killigrew suspicious at all?" asked Kate. "A will not drawn up by a lawyer is a bit dodgy."

"If Killigrew suspected the will was queer he'd have called the court's attention to it," said Richard. "I've no doubt Applethorpe would've made it worth his while. No. My father was a superb forger. No one doubted the will was in Maud's own hand."

"We'll talk to Killigrew, even so," Blake told him. "As for you . . ."

Richard shook himself, as though trying to shrug Blake away. "I couldn't have bunged that letter onto Claire's desk the night we turned up Melinda's body, you said so yourself."

"I don't mean a motive for you personally to have murdered Miss Varek. The entire village benefits from the status quo, doesn't it? PC Wood amongst them. Pakenham is right, his job depends on the tourists. No Hall, possibly no Play, and no more tourists."

"Does Alec know about the fake will?" asked Kate. "Is that what you were talking about this afternoon, the sins and the blessings of the fathers?"

"He knows about the fake will," Richard answered. "I told him soon after my — after it happened."

"So if the will is your sin," persisted Kate, "then what's his? Murder?"

"No!"

"How do you know?" Blake demanded.

"He's my friend."

He ain't heavy, Claire added silently, he's my brother.

"You said last week you don't think the Hall is worth killing for. Well, maybe you don't, but someone bloody well does." Blake turned away.

A faint gleam of sunlight illuminated the western windows. The door opened and Pakenham strode down the corridor rubbing his hands together. "One hour 'til rehearsal. I told Moncrief you'd be there, Lacey. And you, Claire, if you're up to it."

Richard stared at him. Oh, Claire thought, rehearsal. Once more into the breach, brandishing costumes and masks.

"Make up a timetable for this afternoon," Blake told his sergeant.

"Yes, sir," replied Pakenham.

"I'll be interviewing Wood again after the rehearsal."

"Wood? Something wrong with him, right enough."

"He can't tell you any more than I've told you," insisted Richard.

"We'll see about that," said Blake. "Don't let those workmen leave town until I've had a go at them."

"They're in the pub," returned Pakenham. "They'll keep."

Blake asked, "What was that cousin's name, Lacey?"

"Maurice Applethorpe," Richard said dully. "He manufactures dog food in Leeds."

"Find him," Blake ordered Pakenham.

"What? What the hell for? I've quite enough to do here without heading out on a wild goose chase."

"He's a trustee of the Hall, was involved in a court case over Maud Cranbourne's will. I'll explain." Blake glanced at Richard, chewing his moustache thoughtfully. "Is there anything else?"

Surely, Claire thought, Richard was going to protest — sending Pakenham to interview Applethorpe was like throwing gasoline on a fire. All he said was, "No. I've told you my truth, every last bit of it."

"Right." Blake started toward the door, pushing Pakenham in front of him. "Now Arnold. This chap Applethorpe wants special handling . . ."

Kate brought up the rear. "Ah — I'll be outside, Claire."

"You may hear screams," Claire told her, "but you can ignore them."

Kate offered her a quick, cramped smile and vanished.

A log collapsed in the fire and sprayed Richard's feet with sparks that quickly faded to ashes. He contemplated them, took the long-handled brush from the stand on the hearth, and swept them back into the fireplace.

Stupid, Claire told herself, to think Richard was a steady hand in the midst of confusion and deceit. He was as confused as she was. If more — dishonest was a strong word, wasn't it? She reached for her shoes and socks. They were clammy-cold, making her flesh crawl. "Were you there when your parents made the fake will?"

"No. I was up at Cambridge when Maud died. My father never told me. My mother did, after his death."

"Please tell me he didn't die of a broken heart or fall on his sword or anything like that."

"No, he'd made his decision, he accepted it. It was a heart attack that took him, yes, but then he was in his seventies. Twenty years older than my mother."

"And how does she feel?"

"I'm thinking one reason she emigrated to Canada was to put it all behind her."

"And you came here. Like a moth to the flame."

"Oh aye," he said softly.

"So why didn't you tell Blake you had nothing to do with the will?"

"Would it matter?"

"No." Claire tied her shoes into nice, uncomplicated knots.

Richard turned to face her. He tried to smooth down his hair but it popped right back up again, like spikes on an EKG. His eyes seemed as gray as the ashes he'd swept up.

"You've told them your truth, all right," Claire went on. "Just not the whole truth. What about Alec? What's this choice of his?"

"I can't tell you."

"Can't?"

"All right, I shan't tell you. Try to appreciate my position."

"Between a rock and a hard place? I've noticed, okay? I've got a damned heavy rock and a damned solid hard place of my own. Someone I've just begun to care for, someone I've just learned to trust, uses the word 'honesty' at lunch and by supper admits he's been — oh hell, you were lying, yes, and no, it isn't necessarily any of my business, let alone Melinda's. And you know what the really horrible part of all this is? She may never have known anything about anybody, period."

"She didn't tell you a bloody thing, did she?"

"I got the impression she was saving up some good stories to tell me, but no, she didn't tell me anything except the names of the characters."

"Do you think if I'd aired my family's dishonor, then, Melinda would still be alive? Do you think if I'd — I'd prostituted myself she'd still be alive?"

"Do you?"

"I don't know what the hell to think." Richard scowled, giving Claire a glimpse of his long teeth. "Kate edited out what I said to Alec about you."

"Yeah. She did." Claire pried herself from the couch and discovered she was capable of standing up, even though the floor seemed to ripple gently beneath her feet. Richard, she thought. The prodigal son. The fatted calf. Once the truth came out about the will he'd be carved into cutlets — and Alec with him.

Her own voice sounded thready. "I'm flattered he'd tell you to choose me, I just don't know what choices are even possible right now."

"Nor I, Claire. Nor I."

She turned toward the door. Neither of them had screamed. Neither of them was angry. They didn't have a relationship, that kiss hadn't meant anything, she hadn't even taken off her glasses — yeah, right. Her jaw felt ice-brittle. Even if she'd had anything else to say she couldn't have spoken.

Maybe he'd call her back. They'd embrace and tell each other everything would be all right. But everything wasn't all right. Only silence followed her down the hall. He was too proud, she thought. Too — all right, too honest. Just her luck she'd fall for the last man on Earth who said "honor" with a straight face. And yet, whom else would she fall for?

Claire went out the door and pulled it shut behind her.

Chapter Eighteen

Outside a cold wind was bundling the clouds into the eastern sky. To the west the sky was clear and clean, etched deeply by the blue-gray hills of the horizon. Crows complained in the gardens of the Hall. Kate was leaning against Richard's Rover holding the umbrella. When Claire walked past her she heaved herself up and followed.

Kate was something else again, Claire thought. She not only knew when to keep her mouth shut, she could keep track of an umbrella.

Kate saw Claire to her door, checked out the interior of the flat, and melted away to her own room. Claire changed into dry clothes and made herself a hearty sandwich and a mug of tea. The sandwich tasted like its name, sand, and lay on her stomach as though it was shoring up a broken dam. But the tea was good. She made a second mug and sat down at the desk.

She read through Melinda's letters one more time and stacked them up again feeling vaguely foolish. Her friend had never said in so many words that she had a new lover in the village, just that she had a candidate. Knowing Melinda's tendency to cut to the chase, Claire had assumed the consummation was a done deal. But it'd never happened.

Sure, Richard had been on Melinda's short list. While they were too much alike, though, they were also too different. Melinda's life was constant re-invention. Richard's was constant re-investment. She'd been a clambering, far-ranging, vine. He was a rosebush, his roots sunk deep . . . That wasn't the image it should've been, thought Claire, not any more.

By the time Melinda came to Somerstowe she'd already tried investing in roots. She'd married Nigel. And what she'd found were weak, pale, overbred tendrils. Nigel, while smug he'd transplanted an exotic passionflower, found Melinda's refusal to grow correctly up his private garden wall at first perplexing and then offensive. Why, she wouldn't even take his name but remained stubbornly Melinda Varek.

Priscilla Digby had called Richard's mother "Dierdre Callander that was." Chances were Dierdre hadn't been nearly as given to political statements as Melinda. Or to practical jokes, for that matter.

Then there was Alec. His roots were as deep as Richard's. He was committed to another woman, in an obsessive sort of way . . . Claire frowned. Richard was an open book compared to Alec.

That left Elliot as a remote possibility. Melinda had always had a stronger stomach than Claire when it came to men. It was time to find out whether the sleek and sly director had really played a role in Melinda's private production.

Claire tucked the letters away in the bottom drawer, stood up, and stretched. Melinda should've written another play titled, "The Curse of Somerstowe Hall." Not that the Hall was cursed. It was simply the focus of people and passions past and present — Cecil, Lettice and Elizabeth, Phillip, Julian, and Dierdre, Alec, Melinda, Richard, and all the villagers. With a cameo appearance by Maud Cranbourne.

But all you had to do at a play was keep watching until the final curtain. This tangle was more like a game. And not a logical game like chess, either. A poker game played with tarot cards, where hidden meanings counted for more than either chance or skill and calling another player's bluff could prove fatal. She'd sat down and demanded to be dealt in, Claire told herself. Folding wasn't an option. Getting out without losing her emotional shirt — or her life — might be all she could hope for.

She glanced at the clock. It was almost seven. She ran a comb through her hair, put on fresh lipstick, and headed toward the Hall with Kate.

Gold-edged clouds receded over the eastern horizon. The sun settled gently toward the west, polishing the blue sky to a rosy glow. Alec had promised the weather would clear, hadn't he?

The forecourt had drained nicely and was almost dry. Two constables coiled the last of the cables beneath the bleachers — the ordinary floodlights beneath the eaves gave enough light for rehearsal. The prop manager arranged several chairs and tables at one end of the portico while his assistant placed a piano and a harp at the other. The cover of the fuse box was closed and fixed with a shiny new lock. Inside the kitchen was a crowd scene out of a Spielberg epic.

People ran in and out with bits of costume. An occasional shriek echoed from the storeroom that was the women's dressing room, a sporadic bellow resounded from the men's. Sarita looked as though she was trying to conduct a Beethoven symphony and eat a plate of spaghetti at the same time. Hems ripped out, buttons flew off, stockings slithered away from their mates. Kate beside her, Claire plunged into the fray, and for a few moments managed to forget she was looking for one — well, two — particular faces.

She brushed Rob's jacket, pinned Susan's hair beneath her cap, and helped Janet button her dress. "Fred told me about the so-called accident," she said darkly. "I'd be on the first plane home if I was you. They don't like foreigners here."

Claire voiced reassuring noises she didn't really feel and collected discarded scripts into a cardboard box. If anyone still didn't know his or her lines, Elliot announced from the doorway, there would be hell to pay. Trillian squeaked nervously. Her brother Derek, the prompter, waved Elliot's master script at her. "Don't worry, I'll slide you the words."

Sarita had managed to separate her daughter from her hairspray and black eyeliner, and Trillian and her broad white "Puritan" collar looked appropriately demure. Some of the other actors were less fortunate. "Those collars," Claire whispered to Kate, "have a kind of a John the Baptist effect, don't they?"

"Eh?" Kate replied.

"They make you look as though you're carrying your head on a tray."

Kate smiled politely and turned to tie Heather Little's sash.

Richard would've gotten the joke, Claire told herself . . . There he was, standing with Alec just outside the door into the main part of the house, half concealed by shadow. Alec's face was tilted down, Richard's up as he spoke quickly and urgently. What he was saying, Claire thought, was the British version of, "The shit's hit the fan."

Alec's brows tightened. He said something.

Richard shook his head and grasped Alec's arm, his mouth making an "O" shape. *No.*

Alec nodded. His hands smoothed the air, palms down. *It's okay. Don't worry about me.*

Richard's lips thinned into a slit, unconvinced. His hand on Alec's arm tightened. He leaned closer.

Elliot swanned toward them. "Gentlemen, we'd be honored by your participation in the evening's festivities."

Both faces were instantly wiped blank of all expression except mild resentment.

"Come, come, the show must go on and all the appropriate bromides." Elliot made shooing gestures.

Alec and Richard darted quick, meaningful looks at each other and allowed Elliot to usher them toward the men's dressing room.

Yeah, Claire thought, I would've warned Melinda someone was out to get her, no matter how badly she set herself up. . . . "Oh, sorry, Sarita. Here's the card with the extra snaps, no problem."

Soon there was a general movement out the door and across the forecourt to the entrance hall, which served as backstage and wings both. Claire, Kate in tow, seized her own costume and darted down the hall to the storeroom by the public toilets.

Diana was posing before a mirror leaned against the wall, which made her reflected image taller and thinner. Except for its rosy pink color, her gown was in 1660's high fashion. Several yards of material shaped a loose bodice, voluminous sleeves, and a flowing skirt. A sash that was no more than a ribbon cinched the extravagance of cloth. "You look very nice," said Claire, not adding, "A smaller woman would be lost in so much fabric." What a shame Diana felt inadequate by today's standards. But even the appropriately curved Melinda had fretted over the shape of her hips and started muttering darkly of liposuction.

"Do you need any help?" asked Kate.

"I can manage, ta." Diana swept out.

Claire turned with misgivings to her own garment, a wasp-waisted gown from 1776, the year The Play was supposedly written. Staging the drama as a play-within-a-play narrated by the author worked well, although a pair of jeans and a T-shirt from The Play's actual origins in the eighties would have been much more comfortable.

The gown was an authentically snug fit, requiring Kate to heave on the strings of an Inquisition-inspired corset while Claire's eyes bugged out. By the time they poured her into the petticoats and dress, Claire felt like a mythically proportioned Barbie doll. She settled her cap with its dangling fake curls and inspected herself in the mirror. The gown was attractive, she had to confess. Not only did its jade-green flatter her red hair and the suffused pink of her complexion, but the corset beneath had squashed her torso into an actual bust line, displayed by the gown's neckline like sweets on a tray. Her wire-rimmed glasses didn't clash too badly with the satin and flesh ensemble. She was, after all, a scholar and a woman both.

She walked gingerly into the hall and came face to face with Richard. Of course he was gorgeous. His long coat, lace cravat, and knee breeches, as well as his fake ponytail nestled into his dark hair, made him look partly like a member of Parliament railing about the iniquities of the Boston Tea Party and partly like the hero of a swashbuckler.

He looked gravely at her. She looked soberly at him. Her head spun. Damned dress, she thought, and forced a breath into her lungs. *Damned Richard.* They were just going to have to see it through to the end, whatever the end was. Offering an olive branch across their metaphorical chasm would be enough for now. Such courtesy might be enough for ever. She curtsied.

Richard extended an arm and a leg and made a deep formal bow.

Claire dipped even further — and found herself stuck in a crouching position. Richard took her hand and pulled her back up, taking the opportunity to check out her neckline. For just a moment his cool, remote gaze warmed up. She leaned forward . . .

From somewhere behind Claire's back Kate cleared her throat. From the kitchen came Elliot's plummy voice, "Richard, if you please!"

Claire and Richard broke and hurried into the forecourt. He continued on into the entrance hall. She collapsed wheezing at the piano beside Priscilla. Another villager, a tiny woman with silver hair, sat before the harp.

Blake lurked along the portico, Pakenham perched on the bleachers beside Derek and his parents, two or three constables drifted along the drive. Kate took up a position behind Claire, from where a flying tackle would bring down an attacker. Barring Priscilla drawing a dagger, Claire decided she'd be safe for the next couple of hours.

Elliot, looking out of place in his turtleneck sweater and canvas slacks, took center stage. "Speak the speech, I pray you," he declaimed, "as I pronounced it to you, trippingly on the tongue."

"Get on with it," said Richard.

Elliot gave way, his sweeping gesture gracious and mocking at once.

Richard stepped forward and raised a sheet of parchment that was supposedly his manuscript. "Look down, O Muse, and smile . . ."

Richard's diction, Claire thought, made her own accent seem mush-mouthed. Maybe when she got back home — as strange a concept as "home" was at the moment — she would take elocution lessons. She leaned forward, her eyes on the musical score.

". . . so let it begin." Richard stepped aside.

Priscilla and the harpist launched into "The Crystal Spring" while the various spear-carriers, including Susan, Janet, and Fred, filed from the hall and pretended to be drawing water from the well. Casually they parted and Trillian appeared carrying a plastic bucket.

"Cut!" shouted Elliot.

"I'll have her a wooden one tomorrow," called a voice, presumably the prop manager's.

"Action!" Elliot shouted, and mimed, "I am surrounded by idiots!"

This was the first time Claire had actually seen The Play. The sun-gilded façade of the Hall loomed over the actors' shoulders. Its stones had soaked in centuries of passion. Emote as they would, the· puny humans below its windows were only single notes against the chords of its memories.

Richard appeared at intervals, commenting on the action. Trevor did his turn as an old man dying of the plague who nonetheless delivers himself of a lengthy soliloquy on God, faith, and clean water. Rob and Diana stamped and ranted. With heartbreaking tenderness, Alec parted from Trillian. Elliot darted in and out like a piranha, cajoling here, browbeating there.

Priscilla and the harpist played "Bedlam," "Hares on the Mountain," "The Briery Bush," and concluded — as Trillian died discreetly offstage — with "Death and the Lady." Claire mouthed the words, "My name is Death, hast heard of me? All kings and princes bow down unto me, and you, fair maid, must come along with me." She shivered. That was a hazard of knowing the words. Probably three-quarters of the audience would think, *Nice old tunes, there,* without catching the significance.

The Play ended with the main characters piously singing the hymn Claire had always associated with Pilgrims and Thanksgiving — but then, where had the Pilgrims come from but English Puritan stock? "We gather together to ask the Lord's blessing, he chastens and hastens his will to make known; The wicked oppressing now cease from distressing: Sing praises to his Name, he forgets not his own."

Odd, how the words took on new meaning after Elizabeth's tragedy. They suggested the pitfalls in reading God's will as your own and implied that God was inclusive enough not to forget poor Elizabeth, who was "his own" as much — or more than — the fear-mongering villagers. The song must've been Julian and Dierdre's addition, Claire decided. In spite of his occult games, Phillip had been a son of the eighteenth century. Post-modern ironic subtexts were a fashion of the twentieth.

Then Richard was standing alone, head bowed, manuscript rolled. The Nairs and the watching policemen applauded, although Pakenham had to be goaded with Sarita's elbow.

"All right, all right," shouted Elliot. "That was much too uneven, it has to run more smoothly."

"Perhaps if you didn't interrupt as often," Alec suggested.

"I shan't be interrupting you tomorrow night, will I? Dashed awkward, I should think, for you to be standing before the audience without a clue."

Richard and Alec exchanged smiles, clearly agreeing on who it was who hadn't a clue.

"Trillian, my dear," Elliot continued, "you knew your lines! Brilliant!" He opened his arms as though to embrace her.

Roshan interposed himself between them. "Thank you kindly."

Elliot turned on Diana. "And you! You're playing Lettice, not Elizabeth. Stop the simpering. Move as though you have some wit about you."

Diana snapped her head back like a flamenco dancer at the first beat of music. "Get stuffed, Elliot."

"Stupid cow," Elliot muttered.

Claire wondered again whether it was Melinda's disappearance last year or her own appearance this year that had helped end their relationship. Although the odds were it'd simply died from lack of fuel.

She helped Priscilla carry the music books inside and stow them in the box with the scripts. Some of last year's programs were in there too. Claire picked one up and opened it to the cast list, reading, "Elizabeth Spenser . . . Melinda Varek" With an attempt at a sigh, she put the program back in the box. Melinda had hardly bowed down to death. It had sneaked up on her.

By the time Claire shed the chrysalis of her dress and helped put away everyone else's costumes it was almost dark. She and Kate walked out into the twilight to find the forecourt deserted except for the small cat-shape sitting beneath the portico. It turned its head to watch them, eyes catching and then spilling the light.

"I wonder who feeds the moggie," asked Kate. "Richard? He keeps it to clear the place of mice, I reckon."

Claire imagined ghost mice, or angels bending low with saucers of milk, and shook her head. "You know cats. Very resourceful."

A light glowed in the sitting room of the Lodge. The village was quiet. Blake and Pakenham had whisked Alec away as soon as he'd changed his clothes so that he could help them with their inquiries, as the euphemism went. It didn't seem fair, though, for them to apply the verbal thumbscrews in his own office.

Not that any of this was fair, Claire told herself. Least of all Elliot, who was lingering outside the pub. "Claire, my dear, would you do me the honor of sharing a nightcap with me?"

All she wanted to do was crawl into her bed and pull the covers over her head. But here was her chance — maybe she could get the truth out of the man at last. "Yes, thank you."

Elliot opened the door for Claire and then stepped in behind her, cutting Kate off at the pass. Kate strolled casually away, sat down, and pretended to be watching the TV, which was showing one of those baffling British game shows — in this one, the contestants were dressed like vegetables. What she was really watching, Claire saw, was Fred. He sat nursing a beer at the end of the bar next to the phone, as though he was waiting for the governor to call with a reprieve.

Behind the bar stood a weedy young man wearing a deer-in-the-headlights expression and a nametag reading, HELLO! MY NAME IS GILES. Temporary help for Play season, no doubt. Claire let Elliot seat her at a table in the corner and tried to look enthusiastic when he called, "Two Bristol creams, there's a good lad."

My Name Is Giles started searching up and down the rows of bottles and finally pushed through the swinging door into the kitchen. Rob emerged like a grumpy bear from his den. Snorting irritation, he pointed out bottle and glasses and stood menacingly over the youth while he poured. Then Rob snatched the glasses away, stalked out from behind the bar, and plunked the glasses onto the table so hard they slopped over. Ignoring Rob — he was used to ignoring Rob — Elliot captured Claire's hands and pressed them in his own cold and dry ones. "I was simply aghast at your accident today. Although I assume it was no accident."

"Hard to say." Claire rescued her hands and took a tiny sip of the sherry. It tasted like cough syrup. She thought wistfully of Richard's whiskey. Not to mention Richard's scent. Elliot's after shave wasn't quite as noxious as Pakenham's, but there was still way too much of it.

"How terrible it must be for you," Elliot went on, "to be beset with danger so far away from home."

"It's no fun being beset with danger *at* home."

"Don't you feel that a comforting human touch is helpful in such moments of loneliness and fear?"

Don't be obvious or anything, Claire groaned silently. She asked, "I suppose Melinda wanted a comforting human touch, after her divorce and all?"

"Ah . . ." he waffled.

He was trying to figure out which ploy was most likely to work, Claire told herself. She tried dangling some bait. Or an outright lie, take your pick. "Melinda cut quite a figure, didn't she? I always felt I was second best to her. The ragpicker's daughter getting the leftovers."

"Ah yes, quite. Melinda was a beautiful girl, mind you, but I can't say — well, not to speak ill of the dead . . ."

His knee was pressing hers beneath the table. Claire inched away. She sipped again. Her fingertips were sticky from the spilled sherry. She didn't dare lick them, not with Elliot undressing her with his eyes. Although so far he hadn't gotten past her sweater.

"Actually, Claire, Melinda and I were only friends. Nothing physical. She was well and truly a brilliant girl, very smart, no doubt about it. But every now and then a man is fortunate enough to meet someone special, someone who eclipses everyone else. Whilst Melinda and I had a jolly time, I've only truly fancied scholarly ladies like you."

Yeah, Claire said to herself, and right after I fall for that line I'm going to buy a bridge in Brooklyn. Cut to the chase, already. "You told me you and Melinda had an affair."

A smile chased a shrug across Elliot's face. "Well, I shouldn't want her no doubt lovely ghost to think I found her physical shell unattractive."

So Richard turned down Melinda, Melinda turned down Elliot, Elliot broke up with Diana — it would've been a French sex farce if it wasn't ultimately a tragedy. The nape of Claire's neck contracted. She glanced around to see Diana, her elbows propped on the bar, staring at her. Resentfully? No, Diana was smiling acidly, as though watching Elliot at work on someone else was the joke of the day.

Claire shoved her glass away. Another drink, another question of motive, another hidden emotion and she'd gag. "Thank you, Elliot, but it's been a long day and I'm exhausted."

Funny, she'd never noticed how hard Elliot's watery blue eyes were. They looked beady as a snake's. Was he going to slither away now or strike? "Going back to your cold and lonely bed?" he asked.

"Yes."

"Wouldn't you rather stop at my cottage? I have some lovely antiques, including a bedroom suite that once belonged to Lord Byron. Surely, as a lover of literature . . ."

"No, thank you."

"Then I'll walk you to you flat, shall I?"

"I can get there, thanks anyway," Claire said. She shoved back her chair.

Elliot tried out several different expressions, probably debating whether to switch from the world-weary sophisticate routine to a pathetic little boy number. Even when he settled on a brave smile he couldn't keep that malicious humor — if you could call it humor — out of his face. No, Claire told herself, he wasn't the comic relief in this production any more than he was the village idiot.

Did he have an ulterior motive for trying to get her alone? It would be almost as easy to underestimate Elliot as to underestimate Fred, although for very different reasons. Even though, like Fred — like Rob or Diana, for that matter — Elliot had an alibi for Melinda's murder, that didn't mean he couldn't be playing the pivotal role of blackmailer.

With a shudder of revulsion that came close to fear, Claire stood up. "Good night, Elliot. Thank you for the sherry."

Kate swallowed her lemonade and sidled out the door. Claire waved at Giles, who stared blankly at her, and spurted onto the street before anyone, suspect or otherwise, could follow her.

Wishing Kate a good night, Claire went back to her cold and lonely bed.

Chapter Nineteen

Claire inspected the old needlework canvas thoroughly, first with her eyes and then with her magnifying glass. She turned it over on its frame and examined its backside, stitch by stitch. Very professional job, if she did say so herself. Even the linen border was now sturdy enough to hold the weight of the canvas. At least she could do one thing right.

She signed and dated the chart and turned to Kate. "Well done."

"Thank you," Kate replied. "Didn't know I had it in me."

Together they pried out the staples holding the canvas to the frame, rolled it up, and carried it downstairs to the storeroom. Kate insisted on stepping inside first — just in case, Claire assumed, the killer had left a boa constrictor draped over the doorway.

But the room was empty, faintly musty, and cold. The Morris canvas that had lured Claire into the electrified bleachers yesterday afternoon now lay rolled guilelessly on its shelf. She and Kate boosted the Venus and Adonis canvas up beside it. "I guess I'd better find Richard and tell him another mission is accomplished," Claire said, not sure whether she wanted to find Richard or not. When he'd come to inspect the canvas his "Good morning" had been cool and correct, with an aftertaste of ashes. Not that Claire's had been any less wary.

"Right." Kate closed the door of the storeroom.

They found Richard in the chapel scrutinizing a gilded cherub. Janet and Susan stood nearby holding cans of varnish and glue like nurses ready to hand a surgeon his scalpels. Claire smiled at her fellow Americans. Susan, all sturdy no-nonsense as usual, smiled back. Janet's mouth was pursed as though she'd been sucking on a lemon, and managed a grimace.

"Brilliant," Richard pronounced. "Very nicely done indeed. Did you know that before 1770 artisans would mix gold dust with honey to make it stick?"

"You don't have very aggressive ants here, do you?" returned Susan.

"No work this afternoon," Richard went on with a ghost of a smile. "The Play opens tonight. Have a rest, the both of you."

"Come on," Susan said to the younger woman, "let's have some of that curried tomato soup at the tearoom."

With a tight shrug, Janet fell into step with her.

Richard turned to Claire. "You've finished the canvaswork, then?"

"Yes. We put it in the storeroom. If you'd like to look it over . . ."

"No need."

They stood awkwardly on either side of the cherub's plump nudity. A chill draft eddied through the chapel. Kate looked at her watch. "Don't forget, DCI Blake's after having a word in the garden."

Side by side Richard and Claire followed Kate from the chapel through the entrance hall, carefully not making contact in the doorways. Outside the sun was shining so brightly Claire blinked. The sky was a deep cerulean blue, the lawn and the trees a rich green, the stone of the Hall a warm dark gold. The scents of both growth and decay hung on the warm air. There must be a dome of high pressure parked right over Somerstowe. Once again The Play was having beautiful weather.

Kate led her charges past the forecourt, where the workmen were putting the finishing touches on the bleachers and the lights — and where today a uniformed constable guarded the fuse box — to a low wall edging a gravel walk.

Blake sat on the wall, his jacket and tie draped over the stone beside him, his shirtsleeves rolled up, wiping his glasses with a tissue. His scalp reflected the sunshine like a lighthouse warning ships off a rocky coast. Claire suppressed a smile. He was acting like it was hot when it was barely over eighty.

"Good morning," Blake said. "Or afternoon, as the case may be. This should take only a few minutes, you'll still have your lunch."

"No problem." Claire sat down beside him. Richard took his other side. Kate kept on walking — police? me? — and settled in the shade of a tree.

A rotund figure strutted toward them from the gate. Pakenham, Claire noted, was well on his way to a sunburn. Another couple of hours outside and he'd be roasted to a turn, ready for an apple in his mouth and a garnished platter. "We can start now," he said, propping one polished shoe on the wall so he could address them all from above.

Expressionlessly, Blake handed Claire a printed sheet of paper. "This is the timetable for yesterday afternoon. Is it accurate?"

She scanned it. Four o'clock, four-thirty, five — it was all neatly organized, with the names of a dozen villagers and volunteers spotted at intervals down the page. "If this is accurate, the Morris canvas rolled out of the storeroom and climbed up on the bleachers all by itself."

"In other words, someone is lying," said Pakenham. "I'm not going to faint in amazement at that."

Richard leaned over to read the paper himself. "The usual suspects, I see. Uncle Tom Cobleigh and all."

"We're taking some possibilities more seriously than others," said Blake.

"Namely," Pakenham said, "the two remaining suspects who have no alibi for the time of Melinda's murder. Who were both in and out of the Hall all yesterday afternoon. Lacey and Wood."

Richard looked up at him with a glance like a spear-thrust. "What're you on about now?"

"A bit of a coincidence, isn't it, that someone lures Claire into a trap the very same day she tells Wood she's mending that bit of cloth from the attic room. The very same day she and Shelton overhear a positively damning conversation. Maybe the trap was set for Shelton as well, eh?"

Blake didn't say anything. Richard rolled his eyes. "Get a grip, man."

Claire opened her mouth to say, "Richard's not a suspect," and closed it without speaking. An ice cube seemed to slide down her esophagus and plop into her stomach. As far as Pakenham was concerned, Richard *was* a suspect. So he hadn't left the threatening letter on Claire's desk. Alec could have. No one would faint in amazement if they turned out be working together.

And yet why would they be working against her? She'd insisted over and over again that Melinda hadn't told her anything. While revenge for stirring it all up would make a motive, it was Alec who found Melinda's body, and Richard had sure put himself in harm's way with his confessions. . . .

The ice cube melted. As usual, Pakenham was building a house out of straw and parking his ego inside. If he wanted to indulge in conspiracy theories, there were better candidates than Alec and Richard — Elliot, Diana, Rob, Janet, in whatever unholy combination.

Richard was innocent. Period. As for Alec — well, Richard admitted he was covering for him, but he wouldn't cover for a murder. If Melinda had murdered someone, Claire would've been devastated, but she wouldn't have covered for her.

If I'm going to trust Richard, she thought, then I'm going to trust him. She looked around at him and saw he was looking at her, frowning slightly, probably thinking the same thing she was — what a fine mess they'd gotten each other into.

Whether Blake put much faith in Pakenham's house of straw Claire couldn't say. Whatever, he changed the subject. "How did you get on with Applethorpe?"

"It was Applethorpe's morning for golf. Had to follow him about the course — surprised he didn't have me caddying for him, pompous twit."

Takes one to know one, thought Claire.

"I got him talking about the dispute over the will," Pakenham continued.

"How much did you tell him?" demanded Richard.

"I handed him some flannel about covering all the Hall's financial angles. Did you think I'd blurt out your tatty little secret? You don't broadcast one of your best clues, do you now?"

Richard glared up at Pakenham from under his brows, unblinking. Claire hoped the sergeant would shrivel into a pork rind on the spot. He did take his foot off the wall and retreat a step or two. Blake shook his head, very subtly, as though reminding himself that the sergeant was his cross to bear.

Pakenham stuck out his chin and his chest. "Applethorpe said he was simply following accepted procedure when he challenged the will. He had no specific reason to suspect anything wrong. He thinks the Laceys more or less brainwashed old Maud, his great-aunt, into leaving the Hall to the Trust. He resents it, but he realizes he can do eff-all about it."

Richard dropped his eyes to his clasped hands.

"Applethorpe admits to having been in Somerstowe on numerous occasions. Maud's funeral. One of Trevor Digby's genealogical lectures. The Play twice — to see if he wanted to back one of Moncrief's West End shows. He wasn't here on the night of the murder though. He was at an International Pet Food Producers function in Brighton. I didn't see any reason to question his mates about it and establish an alibi."

"No," agreed Blake. "If Applethorpe — or any of the Cranbournes, for that matter — thought Miss Varek had proof the will was a forgery, he'd throw himself in front of a lorry to keep her alive, wouldn't he? He wouldn't murder her."

"So our murderer is someone who didn't want any such proof to come out. QED." Pakenham looked down at Richard's bowed head, his lip curled in a self-satisfied sneer. "I suggest we have another go at the local plod."

At Alec, Claire translated.

"He claims he never laid a hand on Melinda, certainly never kissed her. That means either he or Harlow is lying. Isn't it obvious which one?"

"Not a bit of it," said Richard. "It'd be a hell of a lot easier for Alec to tell you he did kiss her. Just as it'd be easier to tell you his blackmail letter was about The Play. He gave you an honest answer."

Pakenham laughed. Blake's brows tightened, some skein of thought apparently raveling and knitting itself together again.

All of Alec's answers were probably honest, Claire told herself. They just didn't go far enough. A good thing the police weren't allowed to use torture any more — not that that guaranteed honesty. The authorities of 1666, under Cecil's supervision, had tortured Elizabeth. Unlike other judicial victims, though, she'd never "confessed" to making a pact with the devil but had maintained her innocence to the end.

The windows of the Hall glittered, catching the light like laughing eyes. Claire thought of Elizabeth I, who though raddled with age still commanded the hearts of young gallants — and who still sent them to die for her . . . There was Alec himself, opening a window in the upper great chamber and leaning pensively on the sill.

"Blowing the gaff about The Play might have earned Miss Varek a few pounds from a newspaper," said Blake. "Blowing it about the will might have earned her a reward from the Cranbournes."

"She could have creamed off a tidy commission," Pakenham agreed.

"If she knew anything," Blake reminded him. "By the way, her former husband, the lawyer, was planning to stop by Somerstowe this weekend in any event, being a trustee of the Hall and all. Agreed to an interview right off."

Good old Nige, thought Claire.

"Any chance you'll be handing him the same flannel?" Richard inquired.

"No one knows about the fake will except us. And him. He did admit to that." Blake pointed toward Alec.

Pakenham inspected his nails. "I should charge Wood with concealing a crime. You, too, Lacey . . ."

"Not worth the effort," said Blake. "At least, not yet. Miss Godwin, WPC Shelton says you had a chat with Moncrief last night."

"If you can call it that," Claire said. "He admitted he'd never had an affair with Melinda after all, if that's any help."

Richard snorted. "Elliot? Melinda had too much taste to fancy him."

Especially since she fancied you? Claire wanted to ask.

Pakenham snickered. "So no one in town wanted to put a leg over the lovely Melinda? There's a turn-up for you."

"Arnold," Blake said reprovingly.

Pakenham shrugged. "You'd think Melinda would have a string of lovers, is all. But no, that harpy Diana Jackman is having it off with Moncrief, and Janet Harlow . . . Ah, yes, I had Rob in again, he corroborates Janet's story. Said she was a proper little tart and no mistake, leaving it lying about in the street like that."

"So what does that make Rob?" Claire demanded. "What's the male version of a tart?"

"Eh?" asked Pakenham.

Richard chuckled beneath his breath. "Rob's no better than he should be, is he? And Janet — well, she's in a state. Probably feels if she was going to have herself an adventure she should've picked someone worth the risk."

Amen, thought Claire, glancing gratefully at Richard. Yes, Janet was in a state. And yet she wasn't the one who'd opened Somerstowe's Pandora's box. Melinda had done that.

"That's how it stands at present," Blake concluded. "Anything else? No? Come along, then, sergeant." He stood up, rescued his coat and tie, and strolled off toward the Hall. Pakenham followed. Kate got casually to her feet.

Richard's head was bowed over his hands dangling clasped between his knees. Melinda had wanted him. He'd repulsed her. He could never have been to her what she wanted him to be. If he had, then he wouldn't be so tantalizing to Claire.

The sun brought out the reddish highlights in his hair, which was rippling entrancingly in the breeze. She touched his arm, meaning to ask, "Are you okay?" But it wasn't as though Melinda was a disease. She tried, "Lunch?"

He looked up, his lips curled on a rueful smile. "I'd better be organizing a new needlework canvas and chart for you, before I get carried away by The Play."

And you have some thinking to do, Claire added silently. "See you later, then."

"Later," he said, and with a cordial nod to the approaching Kate walked purposefully off toward the Hall.

Kate watched him go, then turned to Claire. "Off to your flat?"

"Yes. I have a couple of newspapers to catch up on and some postcards to write. You know, 'having a very stressful time, glad you're not here.'"

Kate laughed. Together they strolled out of the Hall grounds and into the village.

Several shops now had hard and paperback copies of "An Historie" propped up in their windows, along with costumed dolls, posters, needlework kits, and various quaint olde artifacts. Reporters, identifiable by their cameras and tape recorders, cruised the sidewalks asking questions about last year's murder and no doubt hoping for a reprise this weekend.

Kate conducted Claire through the gauntlet and made her standard inspection tour of the flat. "Thanks," Claire told her. "The curtain goes up at eight. Costume crunch starts at six-thirty. Meet you here at six.

"Right." Kate hesitated. "Blake's still watching Richard, you've twigged to that. But I don't think he's guilty of anything more than loyalty. Than love, if you want to go that far." She turned and went down the steps.

Claire went inside, thinking, yeah, I'd like to go that far. Over the top, all the way . . . Kate could only protect physical vulnerability, couldn't she?

*K*ate was ready at six. "It's a proper tailback out here," she announced.

Huge tour buses looked like pigs moving through the python of the narrow street. Their belching exhausts filled the air with diesel fumes. Cars wove in and out to the accompaniment of screeching brakes and the occasional shouted epithet, while constables gestured emphatically toward designated parking areas. Customers overflowed the pub and stood on the sidewalk clutching sandwiches and beer, while Giles and a couple of other temporary workers ran back and forth jangling coins and clashing mugs. Down the street at the tearoom a line waited to get in the door.

Claire and Kate evaded the journalistic stakeout at the gates of the Hall and whisked inside behind the police barriers. A couple of workmen sat atop the bleachers, eating fish and chips from a newspaper. Here in the land of real ale they were drinking, Claire saw with a shudder, Budweiser. All the cables were either tucked away or taped to the pavement. The fuse box was closed, but the outlets were presumably live.

An experiment in chaos theory was underway inside the kitchen. Kate and Claire helped Sarita dole out clothing, cosmetics, and soothing noises, and intervened when Janet confused her costume and its "JLH" with Heather Little's costume initialed "HJL." Fred sat in a corner mumbling his lines to Derek while Trillian gyrated toward the storeroom, earphones clamped to her head.

The dressing room smelled like powder. Claire put on her own costume and applied make-up, starting with the greasy stage base which made her feel as though she'd dipped her face in Crisco. Then the eyeliner, the lipstick, and the blush — her artistically enhanced features in the mirror were much too glamorous to be her own. She thought again of Melinda. One year ago this weekend, Melinda had died.

Claire leaped up and walked so briskly through the dressing room she had to clutch the doorframe and catch her breath. Women had worn stays or corsets to support their weakness, she thought. And yet it was the corset that made them weak. Which was cause and which effect? It was all in the perception.

At a more sedate pace, Kate at her side, she wended her way through the back corridors of the house to the entrance hall. The cast stood in clumps on the tiled floor, their voices echoing, Elliot cruising the perimeter like a shark. Rob moved from group to group snapping photos with his digital camera, the one just like Melinda's.

The sunlight shone almost horizontally through the great windows beside the staircase. Squares of light bleached the paneling, except for one just above the landing. A small dark shape broke the bottom line of the square even though there was nothing there to cast a shadow. "Good God," said Kate.

It was the shadow of a cat, Claire saw. Which was levitating — no. A lighter, thinner, shadow wavered in the block of light. Elizabeth had picked up the cat and was cradling it against her bodice. If the room had been quieter Claire might have been able to hear it purring. An eerie thought, that the subject of The Play had a front row seat at its performance. Claire closed her eyes. When she opened them again the shadows were gone.

Susan appeared between her and Kate. "Is she up there?"

"Elizabeth? I thought so."

"Have you ever actually seen her," Kate asked, "or have you just heard her steps?"

"I've heard the steps many times, and more than once I've caught just that bit of glimmer in the air, you know. I'm so disappointed that the figure I saw so clearly last year turned out not to be her."

"I guess you were the last person to see Melinda alive," said Claire.

"If I'd only known. Of course if I'd known, I could have warned her or something. As it was I rushed off to the church, more thrilled than scared I'd seen the ghost. What startled me was that huge dog running along the street. It's such a softie, though, if you broke into the pub it would lick you to death."

Claire smiled. Speaking of the pub, there was Diana eyeing the tapestry hanging above the fireplace. She'd dipped very heavily into the cosmetics tray. But then, everyone's face looked artificial in this light. And Lettice in particular had to wear war paint on the stage, even though in real life she might well have been plain as unbuttered toast.

Alec moved in a holding pattern by the fireplace, his solemn expression matching his no-frills clothing. Fred and Janet stood near the door, he looking outside, she looking back at Rob. Claire wondered what on earth had prompted her to have sex with him. Admittedly he was more vital than Fred. Maybe there was something to that cliche about the woman choosing the outlaw. Even Richard had his outlaw moments . . .

Here he came across the entrance hall. His usual lord of the manor posture fitted perfectly with the frock coat and breeches, even if his hair was stubbornly contemporary. He offered Claire a smile that was on the warm side of polite. His teeth didn't look quite so carnivorous when he smiled.

"Here," Rob ordered. "By the fireplace."

Kate stepped aside. Richard offered Claire his arm. She rested her hand on it — the muscle was set like a steel bar — and turned toward the camera. She didn't have to stand up straighter. She couldn't have slumped if she'd wanted to. *Click*. They were immortalized.

"Are we ready? All for one and one for all?" Elliot wrapped his arm around Claire's shoulders. His smile looked like the wolf's grin at Little Red Riding Hood. His arm felt like rubber. "My dear, I have to tell you what a lovely time I had last night."

"I'm glad you had a good time," replied Claire, shaking Elliot's arm away. "Solitary pursuits can be quite rewarding."

Richard grinned down at the buckles on his shoes. Diana said, "Oh, good one."

Roshan escorted a giggling Trillian around the corner. Elliot turned to prey on them. The last flashbulb went off, catching three bit players in their severe Puritan outfits. Their grim faces made them look like they were about to behead a turkey. Or hang a teenage girl.

Alec peered out the front door. "We have standing room only tonight."

What Claire had thought was the wind in the chimneys she now realized was the sound of voices, lots of voices. Thank goodness all she had to do was turn her back on the audience and read music.

"Excelsior!" said Elliot, and waved the musicians out the door.

Applause hit Claire in the face. Wearing a manic grin, she scuttled behind Priscilla and the harpist to her post. Long shadows, thinned by the artificial lights, lay across the forecourt. Priscilla turned on the small lamp over the music rack.

The chatter rose again, only to stop abruptly when Richard stepped onto center stage. His voice had an even deeper timbre tonight, his crystalline vowels ringing like vesper bells in the cool evening air.

Once more the bittersweet music rose and died. The words of The Play spilled across the watching façade of the Hall, some sharp, like projectiles, others soft as milkweed. Words, Claire thought. She hid behind them. Richard found himself sabotaged by them. Melinda came here armed with them, only to find her weapons turned against her.

Literary critics wondered why The Play had never been performed in the eighteenth century. Even knowing how The Play had really been written in two separate eras, Claire couldn't tell where Phillip's lines ended and Julian and Dierdre's began. But it was Phillip who had graphed the story as an intersection between the Age of Reason and the Age of Romance. From the doomed alliance between Walter and Elizabeth sprang two different, although not necessarily opposing, trajectories of faith. Claire wondered if Alec had played the romance as tenderly with sophisticated Melinda as he did with innocent Trillian.

She turned to the next page of music, only to discover that it was missing. Rats — it must still be in the box — the pages were only loose sheaves photocopied from various music books . . . Claire shot a wild glance at Priscilla. Her hands never faltered. She soldiered on and without too many discords gained the succeeding page.

The now familiar lines and gestures spun into fast-forward. The sun set. The hymn was sung and the Play ended. The audience clapped and cheered. The cast reappeared, linked hands, and bowed. Elliot walked to center stage and graciously waved at his public. "The play's the thing," he declaimed.

Claire completed the quote: "The play's the thing, to catch the conscience of the king." Or the murderer? Someone on stage now, she thought, killed Melinda. One of them wants to kill me.

She held the sheets of music to her chest like a shield and stood up.

People clambered from the bleachers and mixed with the cast members. Some asked the performers to sign programs. Others unlimbered their cameras. Reporters and civilians alike surrounded Richard, establishing that yes, he was indeed descended from the character he was playing. The name of Melinda Varek bubbled more than once to the top of the brew of voices.

Released from good manners, children raced across the forecourt and into the gardens. Beyond the glare of the lights the sky glowed a burnished gold, as though reflecting the glow of the Hall rather than the other way around. The evening was fading like lover reluctantly parting from lover, Claire thought, unable to resist one last caress. Tomorrow was June 21, the summer solstice, the longest day of the year.

Where was Kate? Had she found a seat or was she still in the entrance hall? Standing on tiptoe, Claire peered over the heads of the crowd.

Beneath the portico Blake looked around like a secret service agent at a campaign rally. Pakenham leaned against a pillar chatting up one of the female volunteers. Roshan, Sarita, and Derek formed a protective phalanx around Trillian and carried her into the entrance hall. That blond head, that must be Kate. It'd be easier to go in by the kitchen door, take the back corridor, and meet up with her in the entrance hall. Claire had to put the music away anyway.

She elbowed her way through the throng, coming in for more than one autograph herself. Flashbulbs popped. When she stepped into the shadowed kitchen she was momentarily blinded and blundered against the cardboard box filled with programs and music. It fell off the table. With an aggravated snort she folded herself into a kneeling position. No one else was in the room, she noted as her eyes cleared. Not having Kate underfoot was like walking around with only one shoe.

There was the missing page of music. There were the scripts. There were last year's playbills. Again Claire picked one up and as though prodding a bruise opened it. Inside was written in Melinda's firm, black handwriting, "Alec. Saturday. Midnight. Garden."

Claire started to gasp and found herself hyperventilating. She clutched at the table until her head cleared. *No!* But Richard had said Melinda broke her date with him to see someone else. And that Alec was irritable. Because he'd thought they were going to have a cozy evening and then she'd teased him? *Alec, no!*

Kate. Blake. Even Pakenham. They were at the front of the house. She had to get there and — and what? Turn Alec in? Torpedo any last hope for a relationship with Richard? Do what she came to Somerstowe to do?

There was an explanation. There had to be. And the sooner she found out what it was the better. Clutching the program, she hurried as quickly out the back door of the kitchen as she could and still breathe. The mutter of the crowd sounded like distant waves on a shore, a rising and falling hum almost absorbed by the stone-silence of the house. The corridor was dark, and she didn't know where the light switches were.

She stopped, hearing footsteps and a rustle of fabric. Behind her? In front of her? It was never easy to tell where Elizabeth's steps came from, other than from another dimension. Her skin crawled.

There, in the shadows just inside the door at the far end of the corridor, silhouetted against the light leaking from the entrance hall . . . No, that was a perfectly substantial human being. Trillian, judging by the costume. How'd she get away from her family?

A tall man stepped through the door into the corridor. Alec. He swept the woman into his arms. Literally off her feet, she was so small. She wrapped her arms around his chest and lifted her face to his. They kissed, so passionately that by comparison Claire and Richard's kiss looked like a formal handshake.

Claire dodged into an alcove filled with deep shadow. Alec? Trillian? He wasn't a murderer. He wasn't a child molester either. And yet . . .

Wait a minute. Janet had seen Alec and Melinda embracing exactly the same way. What if it wasn't Trillian at all? If Susan had seen Melinda and thought she was Elizabeth, maybe Janet had seen Elizabeth and thought she was Melinda.

Down the corridor echoed a woman's sigh, caught between delight and despair. Claire dared another glance. In the dim light she couldn't make out their faces — they might both be ghosts — but yes, the woman in Alec's arms was blond. It wasn't Trillian at all. And since it wasn't Melinda, it had to be Elizabeth. She was saying something to him, her hand set on his cheek as though trying to keep him from looking away. He answered. Yeah, Claire thought, ducking back into the darkness, the ghost can see you back again.

So much for her assumption that Alec was worshipping Elizabeth from afar. That he had a hopeless crush on a tragic historical figure. Claire remembered the secret room in the attics and the long bench, polished clean. Long enough to be a love seat, wasn't it?

Melinda was going to write a novel about Elizabeth. Alec wanted her to get it right. Alec was going to — what had Alec intended, meeting Melinda secretly in the middle of the night?

More footsteps, coming from the kitchen. A shape moved in the corner of Claire's eye, a shadow denser than the surrounding darkness. She spun around. A motion, a breath of air, skimmed her face. Her nostrils filled with the scent of makeup and sweat. Something closed around her throat and tightened. Her mind chirped faintly, that's not Elizabeth . . .

She heard her own voice expelled in a wordless cry. She groped upward. Her fingertips closed on cloth, taut cloth, implacably squeezing her neck. Her lungs writhed inside the cage of her chest. Her head exploded so that the blackness around her flashed with stars. The world heaved and threw her down.

Somewhere in the distance a female voice called, "Claire! Where are you?" *Melinda, it was Melinda.* . . . The stars rained down on her face like cold kisses, and she fell into nothingness.

Chapter Twenty

*R*ing *down the curtain,* Claire told herself. *Fade to black. Roll the credits.*

It wasn't so much that death was frightening as that it was sad. She was leaving so many landscapes unappreciated and so many books unread. She'd never know whether her and Richard's bud of romance would have blossomed . . . Wait a minute. If she was moaning soppily about dying she probably wasn't dead.

Dank darkness surrounded her. She could hardly tell whether her eyes were open or not. The floor beneath her was cold and gritty. Her head was splitting, her chest was crushed in a vise, and her throat felt as though she'd tried to swallow a Brillo pad. If a band of angels was coming for her, they were taking their own sweet time about it.

Gingerly, Claire sat up. Yes, her eyes were open. Her glasses were still on her head, not that they were doing much good in this nothingness. Except for a distant drip of water the silence was absolute. The floor beneath her hands was dressed stone covered with dirt. The cloth billowing around her was her dress — she was still wearing the infernal Barbie-gown. With a hoarse curse she reached around, yanked open the buttons and loosened the corset. So what if the lights suddenly went up and she found herself in front of an audience, she was going to be able to breathe.

Wherever she was remained dark. Its cold chill seeped through her open dress and along her ribs. She tried a deep breath and winced with pain. Her entire body was sore. Surely she'd have noticed being beaten. . . .

Suddenly Claire remembered the dark hallway, the steps, Alec and Elizabeth, and strong hands tightening the garrote around her neck. Someone, Kate, probably, had been calling her name — maybe that had scared the killer away before he finished the job.

But this wasn't the back corridor of the Hall. If it were, Kate would've found her by now. Claire would be propped up on the couch at the Lodge, Richard handing her another glass of whiskey, his brow furrowed with concern and exasperation . . . Forget that, she told herself.

Groaning, she stood up. Maybe the blackness around her had thinned just a little, maybe her pupils had opened all the way, but the gloom seemed a bit thicker to her left than to her right. She turned toward the hint of light, slid her foot tentatively forward, and found her shoe hanging in mid-air.

With a gulp of vertigo and terror mingled, Claire sat down again. After a moment or two remembering Edgar Allan Poe's stories of concealed pits and walled-up crypts, she lay down on her stomach and groped. She found stone steps hollowed with age extending downward as far as she could reach. At her left was a wall, at her right, where the gloom was a bit lighter, an apparently sheer drop.

She fumbled around and found a bit of metal, a hinge or something — Richard would identify it instantly. Over the side it went. Claire held her breath, listening. The metal piece thudded somewhere below, a long way below. In the silence her heart pounded more loudly than a rain of scrap metal.

That was it. The killer had dragged her into the cellars of the Hall. Or at least to the top of the steps leading to the cellars. Richard had never said whether this part of the house was wired for electricity. He'd only warned the volunteers not to go into it.

Claire rose to her knees and felt along the wall behind her. Sure enough, there was a wooden door, but no light switch anywhere near it. The rusty doorknob turned only a fraction. The door was locked. She tried to peer through the keyhole. Either the corridor on the other side was dark, too, or the hole was blocked by the key. Richard had a key. Richard would let her out.

Richard didn't know where she was. It was Alec who . . . Claire tried to swallow. Her mouth was filled with slime rather than saliva. The program. Melinda's handwriting. Her appointment with Alec after the cast party. And yet Claire had been watching Alec with Elizabeth when she'd been attacked. He couldn't have attacked her. He couldn't have killed Melinda. Right?

Those huge hands of his had been holding Elizabeth's fragile body — very fragile body — as tenderly as though she was spun glass. He'd been listening to her voice. Claire probably hadn't made much noise, just a gasp or a wheeze. He'd never realized she was in trouble.

Claire wondered just what Elizabeth's three-hundred year old voice sounded like, and what she'd told Alec about those everyday things historians would kill to know, and whether she remembered dying . . . *Enough of that.*

Claire knocked on the door, tentatively at first, then loudly. The door was thick and solid and from the other side her knocking probably sounded like a pillow fight.

They had to be looking for her. Surely no one would think she'd just run off somewhere like they thought Melinda had run off somewhere. But the killer could have misdirected the search, saying he'd last seen Claire outside.

Did he think Claire was dead? Or was he hoping she'd revive and fall off the landing? Maybe he wasn't taking any chances and intended to come back to the cellars to finish what he'd begun. Claire had no idea how long she'd been unconscious. It seemed like she'd spent days just taking inventory of herself and her surroundings.

Slowly, carefully, her skirts gathered in one hand and her other hand splayed on the wall, Claire felt her way down a staircase as long as that proverbial one into heaven — except this one was going the other way. When a sweep of her foot detected dirty flagstones rather than steps she took a deep breath and peered into the darkness. Somewhere the water dripped on. What she didn't hear was the sound of a key in the lock at the top of the stairs.

She visualized a human form coming down the stairs with a flashlight. Its beam would probe the dark, hiding whoever was holding it. Someone could hold out the hand of a savior and then kill her with it. No, she wasn't enthused about waiting around here. But where could she go?

The shadows seemed a little lighter on the far side of the room, assuming it was a room she was in. Taking one cautious sliding step at a time she moved toward the suggestion of light. The cellars were dangerous, Richard had said. He'd also said there was an exit to the outside.

The caves had been expanded from the dungeon of the original castle, made into grottos for Phillip's Brotherhood and their ersatz occult ceremonies. Claire didn't have much hope, though, of finding an elegant candlelit eighteenth-century drawing room just ahead.

Her outstretched hand met a wall. Rough-cut stone and a wooden lintel . . . Yes! It was a doorway, the door itself hanging askew, the corridor beyond defined by a tenuous light. Strain her eyes as she might, though, she could see nothing but four walls diminishing into darkness.

She stepped through the door and stopped. Here she was, about to enter the labyrinth, without a ball of twine to her name. Muttering an apology to Sarita, she flipped up her skirt, felt along the hem of her petticoat until she found a seam, and ripped. The sound of tearing cloth made her flinch. Thank goodness nothing came charging out of the dimness at her.

Down one curving passage she went and up the next, paying out strips of petticoat behind her. In more than one place she stumbled over rocks fallen from the ceiling. Once she put her hand on a wall only to have the masonry collapse in a small dusty avalanche. Richard, of course, had been right to warn of the dangers here. He knew these cellars. Some knight errant he was, letting her struggle through them alone.

Whenever Claire encountered a doorway she went through it and groped along the walls and floor, shrinking from what she might, but never did, touch, until she either returned to her cotton lifeline or found another door. Someone, Richard probably, had cleaned Phillip's grottoes of whatever rubbish they'd accumulated over the years. She made a mental note to tell him about the lingering smell of sewage in the air and the constant dripping noise, like Chinese water torture.

Something scuttled away in the darkness. Mice? Rats? Kobolds? As long as whatever it was didn't get friendly, Claire was willing to co-exist.

Her mouth was filled with foul-tasting grit and her throat burned. Her eyes burned, too, from straining to see. Hours might be passing — she couldn't tell. Her own breath sounded like a threshing machine. Dully she fumbled on. She was probably going in circles, her cloth lifeline stitching a spider's web pattern through the catacombs.

Her limbs crawled with cold and a slow, leaden despair. The skin on her naked back was numb. Her senses were failing — she was seeing dancing glints of light in the darkness, and a faint breeze carried an almost subliminal sound of singing. Probably the cellars were haunted with memories of Phillip's occult games. What she most dreaded hearing, though, were footsteps behind her. Maybe she did, some sense other than her ears registering a subtle resonance in the stone beneath her feet . . .

Wait. That really was a breeze tickling her cheeks. There was a door somewhere ahead. And surely she was hallucinating, but the gloom seemed to be a little thinner. Solstice night in Britain was a very short night indeed. Dawn was rising outside. Heartened, Claire staggered on.

Something swooped above her head. She squeaked and crouched. Another shape swooped, fluttered, and came to rest high overhead. Slowly she straightened, barely making out the outlines of a domed room like an antechamber. Several tiny points of light shifted along the ceiling, the eyes of bats returning from their nightly foray outside.

Outside. Claire looked carefully around. She didn't see Count Dracula ready to spring out at her. She was alone except for the cold breeze and the bats and that distant baritone voice. Come on, she urged herself, a few more steps. A few more minutes.

A few minutes later she saw real light gleaming through a doorway. Beyond it an arched stone passage ended in an ornate grille, curlicues black against what seemed like a spotlight-bright glow. She didn't know whether to rush forward and throw herself against the gate or to prostrate herself on the ground with gratitude. Since the ground was littered with bat droppings she chose the former, first ripping off her cotton umbilical.

Inhaling eagerly of the fresh air and its scents of grass and green, Claire grasped the grille and pushed. It didn't move. It, too, was locked. Exhaling with frustration, she leaned her forehead against the cold, damp metal. Still she could hear the voice. It was coming not from the caves behind her but from the open countryside.

The sky was the color and texture of cotton candy. Mist softened the green edges of the land. A chill breeze stirred the leaves of the bushes surrounding the doorway. In the distance a lamb was bleating. Right in front of Claire's face lay the ancient stone circle, each rock a smooth, solid, sand-colored mass rising from the green grass.

She blinked. Her optic nerve must have gone into spasms after its hours of idleness in the dark. She was seeing an unearthly shape weaving its way through the stones, its antlered head bowing and rising again. The strange figure was singing. Or chanting, rather, repeating variations on the same note. Claire couldn't make out any words. The hair rose on the back of her neck and yet not with fear.

She took off her smudged and dusty glasses and looked. She put them back on. The apparition didn't change. She hadn't gone down a cellar or even down a rabbit-hole. She was in a never-never land where time turned back on itself, where fiction and reality knotted themselves incomprehensibly together. Elizabeth Spenser had been accused of consorting with the devil in the stone circle below the Hall — she had died, but the devil hadn't — there he was, all alone now that no one really believed in him any more.

No. The figure in the circle was a man wrapped in a deerskin robe. The antlers were attached to a headdress that was part hood, part cap. Maybe, thought Claire, the figure wasn't a man at all. Maybe it was the horned god of myth older than time. . . . She'd seen those antlers before, above Alec's fireplace.

The song stopped. The man pulled the hood away from his head and set it on top of the one standing stone, which was just a bit taller than he was himself. Then he wrapped his robe around the stone as well — it had protuberances that, if Claire squinted a bit, might be shoulders.

Yes, it was Alec, wearing a perfectly ordinary Aran sweater, blue jeans, and wellies. He genuflected, then reached into a bag resting at the foot of the stone. From it he took a small metal cup and a thermos bottle, which he opened. He poured something into the cup.

Claire sagged against the chill metal of the grille. Like most puzzles, the solution was obvious once she'd seen it for herself.

She hated to interrupt his ritual, but he needed to know he had an audience. And enough of these damned caves was enough. She kicked at the grille, making the metal chime dully, and shouted. What came out was a croak, "Alec! Help!"

He spun toward her and stared as though she was the one who was disconnected from reality. For a long moment she expected him to dematerialize into the haze. Then a ray of sunlight pierced the cloud, dew glistened on grass and tree, and the stones flushed the same warm gold as the Hall.

Alec grinned in relief. He made a "just a minute" gesture, turned toward the rising sun, and lifted the cup. Saying something that had the cadence of poetry, he genuflected again, and with a sweeping motion threw several drops of golden liquid — ale? — onto the grass. The drops seemed to strike the earth and then flame upward, spreading a reddish gold radiance into the mottled sky. Trailing flags of scarlet, the brilliant circle of the sun crested the horizon. Alec opened his arms to the light. It poured down over his body, brought a blush to his fair complexion, and polished the curls of his hair into the finest carved oak.

Earth, air, fire, liquid — each elemental power was recognized. In the ecumenical spirit, Claire bobbed a curtsey.

Alec drank off the remaining ale, turned to the bag, and pulled out a couple of small brown lumps. He walked toward Claire, his grin contracting into a rueful half smile. And yet his hazel eyes were lit like the land itself, reminding her that no matter how dark the night the sun would always rise. He extended his hand. "Have a cake. The blessings of the solstice upon you."

"Thanks," she rasped, and reached through the metalwork. What she wanted right now was a drink of water, but the cake was part of the ceremony. She nibbled. The morsel was sweet and spicy and melted on her tongue instead of gumming her mouth. She managed to say, "Blessings and everything to you, too," in a slightly stronger voice.

A shadow passed over the glow in Alec's eyes. "What a fool I was, never to have had a shufti round the cellars. Elliot said he saw you going into the Lodge, so I never thought . . . I'll fetch the key from Richard, shall I?"

"Yes, please."

Alec collected the antlers, the robe, and the bag and shoved the robe in through the grille. "Here you are. Wrap yourself up, there's a bit of a chill. The antlers may be over three hundred years old. Elizabeth probably knew them. I'll be back soon as may be." He disappeared from Claire's sight line. His steps reverberated in the earth. Then she heard only the wind rustling the leaves, like someone laughing just below his breath. Yeah, it was funny, in a way.

The stones glowed in the sunlight as though lit from within. By magic? Or simply by faith? Claire wondered. Or were faith and magic two words for the same thing?

With only a vestige of her petticoats left, the skirt of her gown seemed like gauze. Her head hurt, her throat was raw, and her skin shrink-wrapped itself to her bones with cold. She cocooned herself in the robe. It was warm and soft and smelled faintly of herbs. Alec's herb garden. She should've guessed then. Certainly she should've guessed when he used Melinda's gold ring to find her body. But you didn't meet too many cops who were witches.

She ate the rest of the cake. It slipped soothingly down her throat and warmed her stomach. She was half-dozing, imagining hot scones with jam and cream, pizza and chicken vindaloo and gallons of hot tea, when she heard voices shouting her name.

Richard came running down the slope from the Hall gardens above and behind her so fast Claire thought he was going to catapult himself over one of the ancient stones. He skidded around and crashed instead into the grille. His unshaven face was creased with worry, his hair stood straight up like multiple antennae, and his eyes were bloodshot behind a pair of glasses. He'd been up all night, hadn't he? Claire was touched. She'd have been touched even if she wasn't in a weakened condition.

Richard produced a large iron key and stabbed at the lock, ringing it like a gong. "Claire! Have you been in the cellars all this time, then? Blake's lads are searching them now, but they made a late start — Diana said she saw you outside the shop."

Kate shot down the hillside almost as fast. "Are you all right? I was dead certain you'd gone into the kitchen . . . Your throat. Someone tried to strangle you."

"They sure did." Funny, the outside of her throat was probably five shades of purple, but inside it wasn't even sore, not any more. She could talk without croaking. "It was you shouting my name that scared them away, I think. I must've fainted, with the corset and everything, and whoever it was just heaved me inside the cellar door. It was handy."

"It was also locked." Richard threw open the grille. Its rusty squeal frightened the crows. They winged across the sky like a row of exclamation points. Kate pulled Claire from the opening and patted her down with a maternal glare balancing between *I'm glad you're safe* and *Are you going to catch it now.*

"It wasn't Alec," Claire insisted. "I don't know who attacked me, but it wasn't him. And he's had a damn good reason for stonewalling."

"Oh aye, that he has." Richard's arm closed around her shoulders and shook her a little. *So now you know.*

Between them, he and Kate got Claire's legs moving and supported her up the hill. Alec and Pakenham waited above, Pakenham gloating, Alec's face sober. She'd feel bad about ruining his moment of peaceful ritual, but Somerstowe's peace was already long gone. "Is the 'S' of your middle name for 'Spenser'?" she asked.

"Got it in one," he replied without either hostility or sarcasm.

"What?" Pakenham demanded.

"Alec's middle initial is *S,*" explained Claire. "Lots of times a man will use his mother's maiden name as his middle name. Like a woman will drop her original middle name for her maiden name after she's married."

Pakenham looked skeptical. "Spenser? Like the woman in The Play?"

"Yes." Alec turned toward the village. "Let's get on with it."

Richard's arm urged Claire forward. Kate fell in behind them. Pakenham trotted along beside Alec, rubbing his hands together. "Got you, Sunshine. Caught you out at last. I must caution you that anything you say . . ."

Claire stumbled. Oh God, Pakenham was reading Alec his rights. Richard's strong arm snugged her a little more closely against his side, probably reassuring himself as much as her.

When they came to the street Pakenham steered Alec toward Blake's storefront office. Kate started to follow. Pakenham's gesticulation sent her into an abrupt left face and back to Claire's unoccupied side. "Pompous git," she muttered. "You're safe as houses with Richard, Claire."

"He may not be safe with me," she said. "All this time, if you'd just — if I'd just. . . ."

"A bit late for 'if.'" Richard stopped at the foot of the stairs leading to her flat. "Have a wash. I'll ask Sarita to cook you a breakfast." With another gentle shake he released her and trudged off across the yard.

Inside the flat, Kate hovered while Claire stripped off the torn and dirty dress and dived into the blessedly hot water of the shower. It almost took sandpaper to get the grime-laden grease off her face. By the time she surfaced Richard and Sarita had appeared with a tray laden with all the glorious excess of an English breakfast: eggs, sausage, bacon, grilled tomato, and a mountain of toast with lashings of butter and marmalade. And the gallon of strong black tea Claire had been fantasizing about. She began ladling it all in.

"I'm so sorry about the dress," she told Sarita between mouthfuls. "And I tore up the petticoat to mark my path through the caves. I don't know what happened to the cap and the fake curl."

"The dress is not important," Sarita assured her.

"We found the cap at the top of the stairs to the cellars," Richard said. "When it finally occurred to us to look there."

"Rob was saying he saw you in the garden," added Sarita.

Kate looked up from her own cuppa. "That was Janet, wasn't it?"

"The rumors were thick upon the ground." Richard filched a piece of Claire's toast. The vertical lines cutting his cheeks eased only a bit as he munched. "We had a recce round the house, but the cellar door was locked as usual. Since I have the only key we didn't look inside."

"Obviously," said Claire, "you don't have the only key. I bet keys to the Hall aren't that hard to come by, though."

"Not a bit of it," Richard agreed. "Pakenham was havering about my knowing the cellars, so at last we looked in. And there was your cap. Several constables went mucking about the place until Blake sent word Alec found you."

"Actually I found him." So the steps she'd sensed behind her had been those of rescuers. That figured. "I found a program in that box of scripts and sheet music with a message in Melinda's handwriting about meeting Alec after the cast party. That's why I was in that corridor, trying to make an end run around the crowd and get to Blake."

"We found the playbill on the floor. Blake compared it with our file sample of Melinda's handwriting." Kate's pink mouth tightened. "He's expecting us. Thank you for the breakfast, Mrs. Nair. Let me carry that tray for you."

"Certainly, WPC Shelton," said Sarita with a smile, adding, "I am very much afraid your cover was blown up to the skies last night."

"Can't keep any secrets in a village," groaned Kate, and with a glance at Richard and Claire, "I'll be back straightaway."

Crockery rattling, Sarita and Kate vanished down the steps.

Claire burped quietly. She'd never appreciated the virtues of fat as a mood enhancer quite so much. She might survive the day, after all.

Richard picked up her glasses from the kitchen counter. He wiped them with a dishtowel, sighted through them critically, then set them on her face. His hands lingered on either side of her neck, caressing the angry red stripe she'd not been surprised to see in her mirror.

His eyes flickered like embers stirred. "I thought I'd lost you."

"You sure you want to find me?" She spread her hands on his chest. The wool of his sweater tickled her palms.

"Yes."

Any other time the slow movement of his fingertips on her throat would turn her on. Now she could only smile wistfully. "I'd like to find you, too, sometime. Soon, I hope, but. . . ."

"I know." The flame in his eyes banked itself and his hands retreated.

"There's Alec's deerskin," she went on, "Kate folded it up, I need to give it back to him — that cake thingie he gave me to eat, my throat doesn't even hurt any more — Richard, he's innocent, I saw him . . ."

"I know." Richard bent forward, lips parted. Claire tilted her chin and parted her lips. Their glasses met with an emphatic click of metal and glass. From outside Kate called, "Let's be off!"

They compromised by touching foreheads. Richard offered Claire his arm and together they met Kate at the bottom of the stairs.

Maybe the police were finally getting somewhere, Claire told herself. The problem was, they weren't getting where she wanted them to go.

Chapter Twenty-one

*T*he morning haze had resolved itself into a sunny day. Each shade of green, blue, gold and gray seemed to be of stained-glass intensity. The red phone booth and Elliot's red car added their usual accents. The streets were starting to fill with traffic — it was Saturday, there'd be even more people here today than yesterday.

A constable in the front room of Blake's command post waved Claire, Richard, and Kate past two glowing computer screens into a back room furnished with a table, chairs, and the empty racks and bins of a failed boutique. The smell of Pakenham's cologne hung in the still air.

Alec sat at the focal point at the end of the table, a mug of tea resting between his hands. He sent the newcomers not a lowered-head look of resentment or shame but a raised-chin look of stubborn pride.

Blake and Pakenham were seated on either side of him. Blake was pale and worn, his moustache limp. Pakenham was red in the face, his lower lip out-thrust belligerently. He was holding the program with Melinda's note on it down with his pen, as though afraid it was going to make a break for it.

Kate perched on the windowsill. Blake motioned Claire and Richard to empty chairs and said to a tape recorder whirring away on the table, "Claire Godwin, Richard Lacey, WPC Shelton. Please give us your version of last night's events, Miss Godwin."

"I found that program," Claire began. "I started through the house to meet up with y'all in the entrance hall. I was walking along the back corridor in the dark — I didn't know where the light switch was — and I saw Alec just inside the far door."

Alec's eyes widened, catching her full meaning.

That was another stupid thing she'd said, Claire thought, telling Richard she understood the position he was in. Here she was herself, now, between the rock of telling the truth and the hard place of not betraying a friend. Between the rock of finding Melinda's murderer and the hard place of not making even more trouble for a bystander who was definitely innocent.

"Then I heard footsteps coming from the kitchen, from behind me," she went on. "Someone threw a cord around my neck and tried to strangle me. Right before I passed out I heard Kate calling for me. I guess that scared the killer away. Whatever, I woke up in the cellars."

"You mean I was standing just there when you were . . ." Alec blinked. "Claire, I'm sorry. I heard Kate giving a shout and went toward her instead."

Why should you have seen me? You were focussed on something — someone — else right then. Beside her Richard coiled like a tiger slipping undetected through the underbrush. Wishing she could slip away undetected, Claire concluded, "I was afraid if I stayed by the cellar door whoever attacked me would come back to make sure I was dead. So I made my way to the outer gate. Alec was there. He went to get Richard and the key."

Pakenham's pen hit his notebook with an emphatic tic.

"The killer," Blake said, "saw you go into the corridor alone and took the main chance on catching you up. Very clever. With several hundred people milling about we've not been able to establish who was in the forecourt and the entrance hall and who wasn't."

"Good job the killer didn't cosh you as he did Melinda. Bad luck neither Wood nor Kate caught him. Or her. Could be a her, what with equal opportunity and women's lib." Pakenham snickered.

Kate rolled her eyes at Pakenham's back. "It's just as well you were wearing that corset, Claire, and fainted. If you'd put up more of a fight the killer might have finished the job. Which might have delayed him — most murderers being men — long enough for us to catch him out, but . . ."

"As it was," said Claire, "my fainting gave him, her, or it a chance to get away. Catch 22."

"Well done, to find your way through the caverns," Richard said.

"Well done twice over," said Pakenham, "to catch Wood out for us. Because for once, Kate, you're right. The murderer is a man. And he's sitting at the table with us." He bowed mockingly toward Alec.

Blake said, "PC Wood has explained . . ."

"He's handed us a pack of lies is what he's done," interrupted Pakenham. "I say we keep at him until he tells us the truth."

"Damned if you do, damned if you don't, is that it?" Alec asked. "Keep at the witness until he tells you what you want to hear. Until he names names — any names will do. You'd have made a grand witch-hunter and no mistake."

"PC Wood," Blake said, biting the words off, "I'm in charge here, if you please."

Alec looked down at his mug, his knuckles whitening. Claire expected it to explode into fragments, but it — and he — were made of sterner stuff.

The door opened. A uniformed constable thrust his head inside and announced, "I have the parcel, sir."

"Bring it here," directed Blake.

The constable set a cardboard box on the table and left the room. Claire recognized the box holding the embroidered linen panel. "That," Richard began, "belongs to the National Trust. You don't have per-mis . . ."

"I'd suggest you cooperate, Lacey," Pakenham interrupted. "You're in deep enough shit as it is."

With low growl deep in his throat, Richard desisted.

Blake opened the box, spread the leaves of tissue paper, and tilted it toward Alec. "You said this was important, PC Wood?"

The cloth and its softly colored stitches glowed as though reflecting the sunlight outside and not the sallow fluorescent light inside the room. Its faint mildew smell seemed here, in this turgid air, reminiscent of the fresh herbal scent of the deerskin.

"Yes, it's important. I said I'd tell you everything and I will do. My friends . . ." Alec emphasized the *S*, ". . . being kind enough to let me tell it in my own words."

"Let's go over it all one more time, then." Blake settled back in his chair. With an elaborate sigh, Pakenham turned to a new page in his notebook. Kate considered Alec's profile. Richard braced his elbow on the table and rested his chin in his hand, possibly plotting the trajectory of a leap.

Alec squared his shoulders and spoke. "I'm a hereditary white witch, a practitioner of the ancient earth religion. A shaman, if you prefer. And yes, according to some definitions I'm a pagan. When Claire came upon me this morning I was performing the solstice ceremony in the ring of stones. The 'stowe' in Somerstowe means 'holy place' in Saxon, but the stones are much older than the Saxons. So are my beliefs.

"My mother is descended from Elizabeth Spenser's younger brother, who was six years old when they murdered her. Walter Tradescant carried him away to London, saving his life. We didn't return to Somerstowe for almost a hundred years. Where do you think Phillip Lacey got the idea for The Play? From the Spenser who was his gardener. The story wasn't anything the village wanted to remember, not then.

"My father's family is from the Isle of Man, where there's quite a lengthy tradition of witchcraft. My parents and my sisters went back there several years ago to help with a museum of history and mythology, hoping to dispel some of the prejudices. You'd never credit the questions the day trippers ask." He stopped, swallowing fiercely. "I stayed on here, hoping to give something back to my birthplace. To my ancestral home."

"You have," Richard said.

"No," returned Alec. "I let someone murder Melinda. I couldn't stop either attack on Claire even though I cast a protective spell on her. I suppose it was weak because I cast it in the yard outside her flat."

"Or maybe it was weak because it was rot," Pakenham said.

So that's why Alec had been staring up at her window that night. Claire smiled at him. "Why, thank you. Luck, a spell, whatever — I'll take anything can get."

"Who knows all this about witchcraft and spells and such?" asked Blake. "Lacey, I should imagine. Anyone else? Miss Varek, for example?"

"I told Melinda," Alec answered. "As for anyone else — well, I've hardly taken a poll of the villagers. Why should I have done? My family and I, we've never tried to be secretive, just discreet. Some people are polite, some aren't. Most don't care. We live in a secular age in many ways."

"And in many ways we don't," Claire said. Alec made witchcraft sound so ordinary, as though he'd just declared he was a certified public accountant. Not that it was at all ordinary.

Alec frowned. "The blackmailer threatened to expose me not only to the Chief Constable but to the media. The Chief Constable's an old military man, he's made it very clear he expects the officers under his command to have clean noses and spit-polished shoes. He'd ban divorced personnel if he could do, even though that'd mean a depleted force. Last year he demoted a Moslem officer in Chesterfield because he stopped his patrol car to pray during Ramadan. The man was reinstated after suing, but . . ."

"We'd all like to avoid controversy," Blake concluded briskly. Kate leaned forward, her perplexed frown easing into a half-smile. Pakenham shook his head in disgust, as though the entire interview was a waste of his precious time.

"And the media. The same tabloids which supported PC Khan would be over the moon with me — 'village bobby a secret satanist' and such like. And then there are the fundamentalist groups. They'd be demonstrating at headquarters and here as well, demanding my removal." Alec shoved the mug away and opened his hands against the tabletop — *see, I'm unarmed.* "My people have never been devil worshippers. We don't even believe in a devil. We believe evil is in the hearts and minds of mankind. And that any evil you do is returned to you twofold."

"All through medieval times Jews were accused of human sacrifice, among other libels," said Richard. "The Irish Protestants and Catholics have been murdering each other for centuries. Cecil had all but one of the stones in the circle behind the hall toppled, saying they were evil."

"The next to last one fell prematurely and crushed a bystander," Alec said, with a hint of a smile. "That's why the tallest is still standing."

"And Henry VIII's men went roaming about the countryside looting and destroying for God. . . . Well, we could sit here all day citing chapter and verse," concluded Richard. "I've never understood why people choose to live in fear of their neighbors."

Then there was Melinda, Claire thought, who simply chose to live.

"Mind you," added Alec, "there're always folk up to no good — criminals and gangs, or people like Phillip Lacey and Francis Dashwood playing at satanism and black witchery. And whoever put a pin through Melinda's snap, he was playing at a damned malicious game."

Kate overbalanced and almost fell off the windowsill. She caught herself with a quick scramble. Pakenham groaned. Alec reached out a hand to steady her. She got herself seated again without help. "Sorry."

"Alec," Claire said, "I understand now why you were so startled when I asked you if Elizabeth really was a witch. But why did you tell me witchcraft was rubbish?"

"I did that?"

"When you came by my flat to get the letter and the snapshot with the pin in it."

"Ah, then, yes. I meant what the townspeople say in The Play about witchcraft is rubbish. It would have to be, wouldn't it, to reflect the slanders of the time period. The persecution of witches wasn't outlawed in England until 1736, during Phillip's lifetime."

"Enough of the potted history!" Pakenham's pen tapped loudly on his notebook, like a conductor calling his orchestra to order. "Stop going round the houses, Wood, and get to the point. Why did you murder Melinda Varek?

"Sergeant," Blake said, making a "down-boy" gesture.

"This playbill. Is it or is it not damning evidence, Chief Inspector? It's Melinda's handwriting, right, Claire?"

"Yes, it is," said Claire. A bead of sweat formed between her shoulder blades and worked its way down her back like a crawling insect.

Richard leaned back in his chair, arms crossed, eyes bright and unblinking. Blake turned to Alec. "Constable?"

Alec's voice took on an even deeper timbre, resonant with dignity. "Melinda was after writing her novel from Elizabeth's point of view. I knew she'd make a good fist of it, so long as she knew the truth. The truth wants telling, there's enough sensationalism about witchcraft as it is. A popular novel might could reach people in a non-threatening sort of way, in the same way The Play has done. Although The Play, while sympathetic to Elizabeth, doesn't have it right, either."

"When my parents — ah — edited The Play they stayed inside Phillip's parameters, his smug Enlightenment certainty that the supernatural is only delusion and games, even though they knew better." Richard nodded at Alec — *over to you.*

Of course, Claire thought. If Alec and Richard were childhood buddies then their parents must've known each other.

Alec returned the nod. "Melinda knew better. She wanted to know more, so we planned to meet after The Play. The hour was her idea, I suppose because of the belief that midnight is 'the witching hour.' Which it's not, by the by. The place was my idea — my garden, not the rose garden behind the Hall where she died. I intended to teach her a minor spell or two and and tell her about Elizabeth."

Pakenham sneered, "Spells. Hah. Pull the other one."

Claire restrained herself from kicking him under the table. Yes, it sounded crazy. And yet. . . . "When you have eliminated the impossible," she murmured, "whatever remains, however improbable, must be the truth. Sherlock Holmes."

"Who," Pakenham retorted, "I'll thank you to remember, is a fictional character."

Alec eyed Pakenham and shook his head slightly. Turning the man into a newt would only boost him higher up the evolutionary ladder. "Melinda's Elizabeth would've been a fictional character. But fiction can be true."

"And facts can lie," put in Richard.

"Get on with it!" Pakenham snarled.

"Just before the cast party began," Alec went on, "Melinda jumped out at me still wearing Elizabeth's clothes. She gave me quite a turn. She was only winding me up, I reckon, no harm in it. That was her way, wasn't it? But I was a bit nervy with — coming out of the closet, in a way — and I ticked her off for taking it all too lightly. Next thing I knew, she and Richard were rowing. Over me, I thought."

"No," said Richard, "it wasn't about you. It was about us. About there not being an us."

"In any event, I waited for her at my cottage. She never called round. I thought she was narked at me. The next day her car was gone. You know the rest. Now I'm thinking she went down to the garden behind the Hall to pluck roses, perhaps to bring me as a peace offering." Alec cleared his throat.

"Miss Harlow told us your house was dark that night," said Blake.

"I was sitting in the garden trying to collect my wits."

A series of expressions — indignation, disgust, rage — flitted across Pakenham's face as though he was trying them on for size. "Wits? Wits? That's rich. You've been lying to us since day one."

"No, I wasn't talking," Alec returned. "If I'd said I planned to meet her for sex, say, then I'd have been lying. I'd have been lying to tell you I kissed her, because I never did do."

A bulls-eye in the old glass of the window behind Kate made a tiny rainbow just over her head, like an "idea" bulb in a cartoon. Tendrils of hair stuck damply to her forehead and she pushed them back. "Why are you talking now, Alec?"

"As Elizabeth says in Act Two, when she refuses to admit to devil worship, if they're going to hang you in any event, better they hang you for the truth. Pretending I'm something I'm not — or not something I am — is the lie. I'd already made up my mind to put you in the picture today."

"Oh well then, easy enough to say you'd intended coming clean when you're backed into a corner." Pakenham pushed petulantly at the box. "What's this rag then? What fantasy are you going to tell us about it?"

Alec reached out a long arm and swept the box close to his chest. "It's Elizabeth's shroud. Or so my family tradition has it."

"Your family?" Claire repeated, and went on in a rush, "Of course it was your family, not the Laceys — I was leaping to conclusions . . ." Richard's elbow landed gently but insistently in her ribs. "Sorry, go on."

"You're quite right," Alec told her. "This cloth has been in my family for over three hundred years. Elizabeth stitched it in happier days, in her free time when she wasn't working for Lettice Lacey. It was meant to wrap her body when it was returned to the embrace of our mother the earth, so she could be regenerated and reborn. She sewed her own hair into it, enspelling blessing and peace. But Elizabeth died before her time and Walter Tradescant, meaning well, sneaked her body into a coffin in the church crypt.

"A hint of Elizabeth's existence has lingered in the Hall all these years. Only a hint, like a bit of reflected light. I've been fascinated by her ever since I was shown her cloth as a child. One day I insisted that Richard and I follow her reflection up the stairs to the attics. There we found a secret room. Her room, where she could sit and sew and be herself, not what the Laceys wanted her to be."

Like Melinda, Claire thought. Like all of us, searching for our own identity.

"How do you know Elizabeth's motives?" Blake took off his glasses and massaged the bags beneath his eyes.

"She told me."

Blake's fingers stopped rubbing, but he didn't open his eyes. Pakenham's jaw dropped.

"Two years ago," Alec said, "a heating system was installed in the church. The workmen had the floor up and opened the crypt for the first time in almost a hundred years. I looked out Elizabeth's body. Her bones, all cold and colorless. Isolated. Lonely. I should've left well enough alone, I'll grant you that. But I was a bit lonely myself. My family'd moved house, Richard was living with his fiancée in London."

Alec wiped his forehead with the back of his hand. "Also I wanted to test my skills — pride going before a fall, as it says in the Bible. I pinched one of Elizabeth's finger bones — and a leg bone from the cat, for good measure — and took them and the Shroud to the secret room. There I called the ghosts of first the cat, then Elizabeth herself."

Pakenham shut his mouth with a pop. The red in his face was spreading to his ears like a valve inching into the danger zone. Blake hid his face in his hand and shook his head. Claire could almost hear him moaning, *all the detective chief inspectors in Derbyshire and this case falls to me.* Kate overbalanced again. This time she extended a leg and braced it on the back of Alec's chair. He didn't notice.

"The cat's ghost is the more substantial, I suppose because the cat is a less complicated being. He doesn't know where he is or what's happened. Elizabeth does. Her rest may not have been easy, that much was obvious from the reflection. Now, though, she's not at rest at all. I woke her to awareness and to pain." A furrow deepened between Alec's eyebrows. His voice roughened. "I should tell Trevor her bones need burying properly. If nothing else, I should send her away again. But I — I love her. I don't want to let her go."

"And how does she feel about you?" Claire asked gently.

"She's of two minds, I reckon. She cares for me and yet — she's a spirit out of time. She's not at peace." Alec's forefinger traced the stitches on the cloth, tracing out a flow chart of choice and chance and fate. "That's what I meant by 'sin.' Selfishly making Elizabeth's condition worse than it already was. Maybe being afraid to admit to my beliefs was a sin, too.

Not that my people necessarily believe in sin, but this is no time to argue semantics.

"Melinda knew I'd used the shroud to call Elizabeth. What I didn't know was whether she'd told you, Claire. When you took the shroud and said you were after cleaning it . . . Well, I wasn't sure what to think."

"All this is news to me," Claire said.

"If not to me," admitted Richard.

Kate looked from the cloth to Alec's sober face and back again, her teeth sunk into her lower lip. Slowly, Blake put his glasses back on. The bags beneath his eyes were like bruises, purplish-green. Either the whirr of the tape recorder was growing louder, or that noise was Blake's brain on overload.

Another sweat droplet trickled down Claire's back. In the still air the aura of cologne was taking on the rotten tuna-fish odor of skunk. No surprise there — Pakenham's face was telephone booth red. "Oh for the love of . . . Witchcraft and magic — it's all stuff and nonsense! Everyone knows that! Wood's winding us up, playing silly beggars with us, diverting our attention from the real issue. Which is the goddamned fake will!"

"If I wanted to divert your attention," Alec said, "I should choose ideas within your range of belief." He didn't have to add, *narrow as that is.*

"Alec could have killed Claire this morning instead of calling us," Kate pointed out.

"Whose side are you on?" Pakenham snapped.

"The side of the truth." She turned and with a crash and thud opened the window. A few diesel-scented breaths of air leaked into the room.

Pakenham sneered. "The truth is Wood was hanging about the cellars this morning waiting for Claire."

"So then why did he call round for you, if he wanted to kill her?" demanded Richard. "If he'd killed Melinda why lead you to her body? It was his finding Melinda's body that drew your attention to him to begin with, for God's sakes!"

"There you are! He found Melinda's body, didn't he? If that's not utterly damning, what is?"

"Alec was in front of me when someone attacked me from behind," Claire insisted. "I saw him with Elizabeth. I saw her so clearly that at first I thought it was Trillian Nair."

"Shagging a ghost, is that right? What sort of fool do you take me for!"

"Would you like me to answer that?" Richard asked.

Wincing, Blake waved them both down.

Alec's mouth turned up in a lopsided smile. "We've come a long way, haven't we? Elizabeth was done over because the authorities believed in witchcraft. I'm being done over because they don't."

"Oh, we're after doing you all right," Pakenham told him. "And you, too, Lacey, wittering on about honor and literature and such like. The both of you, with your tidy little scheme. Claire, good job you had Kate here or you'd be dead as your flash friend."

"Oooh," said Kate, "you mean I've done something right?"

"So tell me then, Miss Clever Puss, if Wood's not the murderer, if he and Lacey aren't working together, then who the bloody hell is behind all of this?"

"Elliot Moncrief?" Kate asked. "One of the Americans? Rob or Diana Jackman? Maurice Applethorpe, even?"

"They all have alibis, you stupid cow!"

"Be quiet, the lot of you!" commanded Blake.

A loud rap on the door signaled, Claire thought, the end of the scene. She slumped back in her seat and exchanged a look with Richard that for once hid absolutely nothing.

Chapter Twenty-two

The uniformed constable peered warily in the door. "Excuse me, Chief Inspector, it's the vicar, he wants a word."

Trevor's halo of white hair angled around the constable's shoulder. "I do beg your pardon. Mrs. Nair dispatched her Derek to tell me you'd taken Alec in for questioning and I thought he might be needing a character witness."

"Oh absolutely bloody marvelous," groaned Pakenham. "Who else? The butcher? The baker?"

Blake's face was sagging longer and longer, like one of Salvador Dali's painted clocks. "Come in, Vicar. Sit down."

Alec and Richard both stood up. Pakenham waved Alec back down. With a polite smile, Trevor took Richard's chair, leaving him to lean on the back of Claire's. She pressed her shoulders against his hands, wondering vaguely if he did backrubs. Her store of adrenaline, passion, and breakfast fat was dissipating fast. But she couldn't let down, not yet.

"Nothing happens here that you don't know about, is that it?" Blake asked Trevor.

"If I didn't know what was happening on my patch I'd not be doing my job, would I now?" Trevor returned with a smile.

"Wood's been handing us a load of rubbish about witchcraft and ghosts," said Pakenham. "What do you make of that?"

"I've known Alec's family since I came here in the 1950s. His father and his grandfather were both constables. His mother was the district nurse. His grandmother and his older sister taught at the infant's school. They've all professed what they call 'the ancient religion.' I should imagine it's as much modern recreation as tradition, but then, that's hardly my business. What is my business, Sergeant, Chief Inspector, is that there's no malevolence in it. If Alec finds good in it, and practices what he finds, well then, it's not rubbish. On the contrary, more power to him."

"He calls himself a pagan," Blake pointed out.

"So he does," replied Trevor. "I'd like to bring him into my fold, most certainly. And yet when I see so many young people without any faith at all — well, who am I to pass judgement? Every so often I lift up my lamp, and every so often Alec or some other Spenser politely declines to step upon my path. We've reached a balance of powers, you might say."

Across the table Alec nodded. "Thank you. Not all of your co-religionists would see it your way."

"Not all of yours would invite me and my wife to his annual midsummer's eve barbecue," Trevor replied "let alone ask me to offer an Anglican blessing. Yours having already been given, I assume."

Pakenham said loudly, "What a cozy little mutual admiration society! Unfortunately we're a just a bit off the subject, don't you think? Vicar, Wood says he's descended from the Spenser woman in The Play."

"From her younger brother, to be exact. The Spensers have been in Somerstowe longer than the Laceys, let alone the Cranbournes."

"Wood admits to mucking about in your crypt, pinching bones."

"Yes, we had an invaluable opportunity to make an archaeological investigation when the heating system was installed. Alec was drawn to Elizabeth's grave, just as, I suppose, I'd be drawn to the grave of a saint or a martyr. The Christian fascination with relics wasn't invented out of whole cloth. I daresay there's an ancient memory in such reverence, a respect for the physicality of our existence here on Earth."

"Reverence?" Pakenham asked. "He claims to — to. . ."

". . . to have called Elizabeth's spirit?" Sighing, Trevor looked over at Alec. "Yes, I suspected as much. Rather impetuous, my lad, wasn't it?"

"Yes," said Alec.

"It's a terrible story, that of Elizabeth and all the others like her. It makes me ashamed of my own credo, to tell you the truth. But then, I should hate for Alec to be ashamed of his."

Alec looked down into the box. Interesting, Claire thought, how Trevor could minister to him despite their differences.

"Vicar," brayed Pakenham, "Wood claims the supernatural is real!"

"Why so do I, Sergeant. Stop in next Sunday morning if you'd like to hear my formal profession. Alec and I simply approach the supernatural from different viewpoints is all."

"Every turnip in this sodding village is a sodding lunatic!" Pakenham hissed.

"I beg your pardon?" Trevor asked blandly.

Blake's mouth relaxed a bit, as though remembering the concept of the smile. A cool breeze teased the tissue paper surrounding the shroud, making it rustle. Smothering a grin, Kate retracted her leg from Alec's chair. "Father Digby, what we're trying to do here is establish a motive for Melinda Varek's murder. Someone has a secret they don't want publicized. If that secret's not PC Wood's belief system, what else is there? In genealogical terms, have we gone so far out on a limb we've forgotten the trunk of the tree?"

"Well put, WPC Shelton," said Trevor. "What we must remember is that here in Somerstowe the trunk of the tree is the Hall."

"And The Play?" asked Claire. "Or at least the story behind The Play?"

"That, certainly. But — well, I'm sorry Richard, but there's The Play and there's The Play, if you catch my meaning."

Richard's hands flexed on Claire's chair. "I've told them about The Play, Trevor. You knew?"

"Oh yes." Trevor sighed. "Julian told me before he died. Made his confession, you might say, although only in the ethical, not in the liturgical sense. And so he should have done. It's a fine moral dilemma, isn't it? The story behind The Play is perfectly genuine. Indeed, long stretches of it were indeed written by Phillip. That Dierdre and Julian filled in his lacunae. . . . Well, I'm splitting hairs, I'll admit. But the donations of the playgoers made the church heating system possible, and that in turn increased the size of the congregation. I'm sure once the Hall is restored we'll have even more funds, perhaps for that new children's playground or the parish food bank or the clinic, wouldn't you say, Richard?"

"I — ah — I hope so." Richard's hands curled into fists behind Claire's back, making knots behind her shoulder blades.

"Not that proving the truth about The Play would be difficult," Trevor added. "Elliot, for example, found out by chatting up a secretary in the publisher's office. But then, with his deal to represent the secondary rights, Elliot would be keen to keep the secret."

Oh? Claire could just hear Elliot's plummy voice, "I simply adore quaint old things, might I see the famous manuscript?" He'd have recognized the interpolated pages for what they were.

"I've thought the matter over carefully," Trevor concluded, "just as I've thought over the matter of Alec and his family. The first rule for a priest should be the same as that for a doctor — or a conservator, Richard. First, do no harm. I'd do more harm telling about the true provenance of The Play than by keeping quiet."

So the voice of sweet reason, thought Claire, was also the voice of faith. She liked that.

"Even Maurice Applethorpe and his cousins would agree with you there," Blake said carefully, "since the income from The Play is tied to ownership of the Hall. And he would like to own the Hall, I believe."

Nice bait-dangling, Claire told herself. Would Trevor bite? Everyone's eyes, even Pakenham's truculent glare, turned toward him. Behind her Richard's hands might just as well have been lumps of stone.

"Yes, Applethorpe is only interested in The Play as an adjunct to the Hall. That said, he did give me quite a turn one evening. We were sharing a whiskey in the Druid's Circle after one of my lectures — very keen on genealogy, Maurice is — and he was going on about the Hall. I was growing quite nervy, afraid he intended to ask me if I thought The Play was genuine. But no, what he had the cheek to ask was whether I thought Maud Cranbourne's will was legitimate! How absurd!" Trevor laughed.

Richard's hands spasmed. No matter how finely Trevor could split hairs, if he got hold of the truth about the will he'd have to tell. Claire looked from Blake, who was nodding soberly, to Pakenham, who was turning red again. Would Blake play Nigel, who was coming in tomorrow — no, today — as cleverly? Or was Blake's discretion only delaying the inevitable?

"Thank you for coming in, Vicar," said Blake. "We'll certainly bear your evidence in mind. Kate, show him out, please."

Murmuring, "Next Saturday week will be this year's prayer vigil, I'll be suggesting a meditation on the Golden Rule," Trevor let Kate usher him out.

She shut the door behind him. "You heard that, Sergeant. Elliot Moncrief knows about The Play. If he's been getting a tidy commission off the sub-rights he'd be very motivated to keep someone from telling the truth about its origins."

"I'll tell you what we should do. We'll have Wood look into his crystal ball. Knows all, sees all. Bugger all." Pakenham slammed shut his notebook.

End of another scene, Claire thought. Richard patted vaguely at either her shoulders or the chair and paced off across the room.

For a long moment, Blake rubbed his temples. At last he looked narrowly at Alec. "PC Wood, I'm not going to take you in charge. Miss Godwin here says she was attacked by someone else as she was watching you."

"Sir!" Pakenham protested. "He and Lacey are working together . . ."

Blake waved him away like a mosquito.

Pakenham threw his pen into the table, point first. It bounced off the tape recorder. Several words, of which only "doddering old duffer Digby" were intelligible, broke through his clenched teeth and past his contorted lips. A moment later he added tightly, "Thank you for your assistance, Claire."

He thought she was lying, too. "Any time, Arnold." Her face split in a yawn that was close to a snarl.

"As for the rest of your story, PC Wood," Blake concluded, "well, keep yourself available for further questioning. You are not reinstated to duty, not by a long chalk." He reached across and clicked off the tape recorder.

With one last look at the shroud, Alec replaced the cover of the box. His sun-shot eyes turned to Blake. He said calmly, "I'm not going anywhere, Sir. I have another performance of The Play tonight."

A what? Oh yes, the performance. Claire wasn't sure she could still walk, let alone read music. But, as Elliot would say, the show must go on.

"You, too, Lacey," said Blake. "Stay in town."

"I'm booked for the performance as well." Richard paced back across the room and pulled gently at Claire's chair — *let's get out of here before he changes his mind.* She stood up, grabbing at his arm for support. Alec might have calmed down — confession being good for the pagan soul as well, she supposed — but Richard was positively brittle, the muscle of his arm quivering beneath her hand, his jaw stretched taut as a rubber band, his eyes simmering.

No, she thought, Blake didn't have and was never going to get enough evidence to charge Alec and Richard, separately or in tandem, with murder. And yet Pakenham, blast him, was right. When all this came out they'd still be screwed. Because of Melinda. Because of Claire herself. And because of someone who wasn't content with the status quo, someone who'd threatened and finally murdered to change it.

Alec, Kate, Richard and Claire broke into the open air. Alec was the only one who didn't wince at the brilliant sunlight. "Cheers," he said neutrally, and headed not toward his house but toward the Hall, probably to replace the shroud in the secret room. The other three turned the other way. Richard walked backward for a few steps, watching Alec's retreat, then with a tight shrug turned around and fell in beside Claire.

Roshan Nair was setting out a rack of sunscreen. Beside him Elliot inspected a handful of mail. "I say," he called as the trio walked by, "the guardians of our public safety are growing more attractive every day."

Kate offered him a sardonic salute.

Rob and Diana were arranging tables and chairs along the sidewalk outside their door. Janet stood looking into a shop window, shoulders hunched, as though deliberately turning her back on the pub. Everyone was in shirtsleeves. "The weather," Claire said. "It's never rained on The Play."

"Not once," replied Richard. "You might could think it was divine intervention."

She and Kate had been standing in the attic room when Alec came in and said something about the weather and The Play, as though he had some sort of deadline. She saw again the fine dust in the cracks between the floorboards. Chalk dust. Alec had been casting spells there. Making magic. If he could control the weather she had a job for him back home, where the problem wasn't too much rain but too little. . . .

Just because Alec said he could control the weather, she reminded herself, just because he thought he could control the weather or cast protective spells or find Melinda's body with her wedding ring didn't mean he actually could. "I can call spirits from the vasty deep," Shakespeare's Glendower puts it, to which Hotspur replies, "Why, so can I, or so can any man; but will they come when you do call for them?"

Alec found Melinda's body. The weather was beautiful. And Claire was still alive to question his skills. Whether that was all a coincidence or the product of Alec's willpower was simply a matter of perception.

"Funny," she said, "How the concept of Alec — or anyone — making magic seems absolutely normal. Common. Ordinary."

"If he's abnormal, then we need another definition of 'normal.' Have a kip, if you can sleep." Kate swerved and went into the Nair's back door.

Richard walked Claire up the stairs to her flat, waited while she unlocked the door, then glanced around inside. She considered asking him in for a mutual back rub. . . . No. If she touched him he might break. If he touched her — well, she'd like being putty in his hands, but not now. Not until it would be a premeditated meeting of minds and hearts and bodies rather than a distracted ad lib.

This time they managed to kiss without knocking their glasses together. It was like warily touching a hot stove. "Later," Richard said with a wry smile, and walked back down the stairs.

"Later." Claire locked the door. Without bothering to pull out the hide-a-bed she collapsed onto the couch and spread the deerskin blanket out over her.

For a time she tossed and turned fitfully, dreaming of Alec hanged from Pakenham's poisoned pen and Elizabeth Spenser stumbling down dark passages echoing with a *drip drip drip* of blood. But the scent of grass and roses and Richard surrounded her, and eventually Claire eased into a deep, refreshing sleep filled with images of sunlit fields and stone brushed with gold.

Chapter Twenty-three

*C*laire woke herself up mumbling lines from The Play: "This pathetic female, lewd and blasphemous consort of the devil — see how she droops, her countenance pale. She recks well her own guilt though she cannot bring her tongue to speak it — the proof is before us — shall Somerstowe suffer a witch to live?"

Rolling off the couch, Claire staggered toward the bathroom. Poor Elizabeth, she thought inadequately.

She reeled back from the face reflected in the mirror. If she didn't quite look like the wrath of God, she certainly resembled the annoyance of a saint. It was too warm to wear a turtleneck or wrap a scarf around the bruises on her throat, so she took the other tack and put on a scooped neck T-shirt. Letting it all hang out, her mother's generation would say. Or as her own would put it, showing some attitude.

She paused at the bottom of her staircase to scan the sky. The day had betrayed its early promise and clouds were massing in the west. When Kate came hurrying around the corner Claire commented, "Alec must only be able to concentrate on so many things at once."

"He's had a rough go," Kate replied, without committing herself to anything. "I was having a word with the lads — Pakenham's after arresting Alec tonight after The Play."

"He didn't — he hasn't — damn it, he's innocent."

"Plain as the nose on your face, if you ask me. Not that anyone's asked me. Blake's not saying anything at all, just put it about that if one reporter hears about the evidence Alec gave this morning he'll be tearing strips off us, and no mistake."

"So Blake's on Alec's side?" Claire asked hopefully.

"Like as not he's only being cautious."

"Great. Let's get some food."

Dodging the cars and buses clogging the main street, the women dropped into the Druid's Circle for either a late lunch or early tea of pub grub. They were served by Giles and another youth, who were more interested in watching a soccer match than in carrying plates and glasses back and forth. But neither Rob nor Diana was there to enforce efficiency.

Several photographers and reporters walked a holding pattern between the Lodge and the Hall gates, which were guarded by a couple of uniformed constables. Kate and Claire veered up an alley, across a yard, and in through the postern gate in the Hall's perimeter wall.

The first person Claire saw inside was a slightly built masculine figure inspecting an empty birdbath. "Right on schedule," she said. "Just as I'd expect."

"Who is it?" asked Kate.

"Nigel Killigrew, Melinda's ex-husband. Yo, Nigel!"

He galloped across the lawn toward her. "I say, Claire! I was most concerned to hear about last night's misadventure! Are you all right?"

"I'm fine. The bruises look a lot worse than they feel. This is WPC Shelton, my guardian angel," she added. It was a little late to play the "just another volunteer" card.

"Good to meet you," Nigel said, shaking Kate's hand.

He hadn't changed. With his long nose, prominent teeth, and silvered hair swept back from his face he reminded Claire of an aardvark. His Savile Row suit and old school tie proclaimed not only prosperity but propriety. For a brief time he'd complemented Melinda — until Melinda got tired of playing by his rules and went back to her own.

He'd always been scrupulously polite to Claire. "I made my way past the sentries with the help of Detective Sergeant Pakenham. He talked to me briefly last year, after Melinda went missing, and seemed more interested in obtaining the name of my tailor than in finding her. Sad, isn't it, how the days of the gentleman detective are gone forever?"

Kate strangled a guffaw.

"I made an appointment for tomorrow with him and — DCI Blake, is it? Just now I thought I should pay my respects to Melinda, especially since there was no funeral, only her ashes, I understand, returned to her brother in America. I sent flowers. That seemed fitting."

"Would you like to see where we found her?" Claire asked.

"Please, if it's no trouble."

Claire led Nigel toward the end of the lawn and the walled garden. "There," she said, pointing toward the row of rose bushes, none of which looked any the worse for wear for having been dragged from their bed and replanted. In fact, they were blooming away as colorfully as the idealized flowers on a greeting card.

Nigel bowed his head. Claire backed tactfully away, thinking vague poetic thoughts. Was it T.S. Eliot who wrote about breeding roses out of the dead land, mixing memory and desire . . . She looked over the sunlit countryside wondering if Melinda's only family, her much older brother and his wife, had bought some cold, sterile vault for her ashes. Or had they scattered them to the winds as she'd have wished if she'd ever imagined herself dying?

As though in answer, a breeze fanned Claire's cheeks. In the trees behind the Hall the omnipresent crows scolded and then fell silent. Down the slope from the gardens the ring of stones rested impassively. Yesterday she would've thought they were waiting for a congregation that had long ago moved on to other rites. Now she knew better.

"Killigrew has an alibi," Kate said, with no pretense at poetry. "Pakenham did check that out."

It was Nigel's connection with Somerstowe that had brought Melinda here to begin with, but you could hardly blame him for that. Or because Melinda's connection with him made Richard suspect her as the blackmailer. "I know," said Claire. "He's only the straight man."

Nigel cleared his throat and looked around. "Well, then. You're participating in The Play, Claire? WPC Shelton?"

"I'm turning pages at the piano," Claire replied, "and we're both helping with the costumes. Speaking of which, I'm afraid we need to be going."

"Of course. I'm looking forward to the performance. It's been several years since I've seen 'An Historie.'"

They left Nigel standing alone by the garden wall. He wouldn't be solitary for long, though. The gates would open in an hour, and already a throng gathered outside the Lodge and strained eagerly toward the Hall.

Here came Elliot the director, not even remotely the poet, heading toward the back exit. "If something wants doing properly," he announced as he passed, "you have to bloody well do it yourself, don't you?"

"Well, I . . ." Claire began, but he was already gone.

As soon as they walked into the kitchen Claire was surrounded by cast and crew, who asked questions, made comments, and expressed their best wishes for her speedy recovery. She barricaded herself behind the tables heaped with costumes, Kate at her side. Not that anyone expressed anything to Kate. They either looked at her with broad, guileless smiles or pretended she wasn't there. Which was no surprise, with her colleague Pakenham already working the room.

"Do you feel up to turning pages tonight?" asked Priscilla.

"That much I can do," Claire told her.

"I was worried," Janet said. "I figured he got you this time. Tomorrow

Fred and I are out of here, going back home. Enough is enough already."

Behind her Fred opened his mouth and then shut it again, knowing resistance was futile.

"Play's going well, is it?" Pakenham strutted by, his hands folded behind his back, his collar crisp against the flab of his jowls. "I shouldn't worry, matters are well in hand, everything will be sorted tonight. You can even have your party, though there'll be an empty plate at the table."

Kate's expression suggested transfers, demotions, maybe even execution. "Sergeant," she hissed under her breath, "I don't think . . ."

Pakenham turned his back on her and cruised on by trailing not clouds of glory but cologne. "Not to worry. I'll be taking the perpetrator in charge very soon now. Go on about your business."

"Thank you kindly," said Roshan, with a smile as bright as the flame on the match he struck. He lit the AGA cooker and filled the first of no doubt many kettles.

"Anything I can do to help?" Susan asked Claire. "Buttons, bows, mantelpieces?"

"Thanks," said Claire, "Sarita will be along any minute now."

Either Diana was a bit feverish or she'd already dipped into the blusher. "The caverns? I'd never go in there. Don't want bats tangling themselves in my hair, thank you very much."

"I didn't exactly intend to go in there," Claire told her.

"So I'm doing this on my own, am I?" Rob shouted from the hall. "We're catering the cast party as per usual, aren't we? Get a move on — those prats helping out at the pub couldn't find their own arses."

Making a face, Diana turned toward the outside door, "Yes, my lord, anything you say, my lord, I'll fetch the food, shall I, my lord?"

Trevor was just coming in. "May I assist, Diana?"

"No, no," she said with an exaggerated sigh, "I'll have one of the prats help out, won't I? Make them earn their dosh for a change."

Claire wondered how on earth Diana had played Elizabeth. Even if Elizabeth hadn't been quite the sweet innocent of legend, still she'd only been nineteen, not a bitter and disillusioned forty. But playing against type was the equivalent of a vacation. Last Halloween Claire herself had dressed as Vampira, in a slinky black dress with plunging neckline and enough make-up for three Dianas. Not that Steve had had too good an opinion of that outfit, but by then she'd stopped caring about his opinion.

Alec and Richard wrestled a long table from a storeroom through the kitchen and into the back hall, Alec murmuring a litany of, "Sorry, excuse us, mind your step."

They passed Pakenham and in unison averted their eyes. Smirking, Pakenham moved on, telling the Littles, "I'm seeing to matters here . . ."

And then there was Alec playing Walter. Which was like speaking a second language, Claire guessed. He certainly was — well, principled, trustworthy, respectable — pretty much of a Boy Scout anyway. Except when it came to Elizabeth, where he split the difference between Casanova and necromancer. The villagers hadn't consciously protected him, it simply had never occurred to anyone except the blackmailer to make an issue of his belief system. "Well," she whispered to Kate, "even if Alec does lose his job, no one will be hanging him on the village green like Elizabeth."

"Not that Pakenham wouldn't enjoy it," Kate returned.

Sarita herded Trillian and Derek into the kitchen, relieved them of their headphones, and sent them to help in the entrance hall. She handed Claire the length of fabric draped over her arm. "This is an old dressing gown I have altered for you to wear. I am very much thinking it will give the appearance of a lady's wrapper of the period. No corsets."

"Thank goodness," Claire replied. "Thank you."

Richard came back into the kitchen, clipboard in hand, pencil ticking off a checklist. The best case scenario, Claire told herself, was that the Trust wouldn't blame him for the deeds of his parents and would send him elsewhere to work. Whatever, he'd still lose the Hall. Everyone would lose the Hall. Even if Applethorpe and his relatives agreed to keep quiet about The Play — it'd taken on a life of its own, after all, and could still generate income for them — they had no interest in maintaining a four-hundred-year old stone and glass white elephant.

Richard might let her comfort him. Or he might decide she was too closely tied to his loss, too aware of his vulnerabilities. He was no Boy Scout. He was a knight errant, and knights errant wore armor.

Like she hadn't noticed that about him when they first met? With a grimace, Claire turned to the matter — or material — in hand, checking over the costumes and allotting them to their wearers. When it came time for her to dress, she settled for a ribbon in her short hair and a dusting of powder and blush — the audience couldn't see her face, she wasn't about to layer it in Crisco again. And the smell of the stage base turned her stomach.

She walked to the entrance hall with five other people, Fred at point, Trevor and Richard at flank, Alec and Kate in the rear. She noticed the brand-new dead bolt on the cellar door as they passed.

Once again she found herself waiting while the crowd murmured outside like Romans handicapping a gladiatorial contest. "We who are about to die salute you," Claire murmured. She could only hope the killer had already taken his best shot.

Tonight a long table in front of the fireplace groaned with an array of bottles and plates of food covered coyly with napkins. Diana slapped away Trillian's hand. "Yes, Miss, they're little bits of cheese on sticks and such like. No, you can't have one now, you must be minding your pretty frock."

Blake and Pakenham's business suits were conspicuous among the costumes. And conspicuous by his absence, Claire realized, was Elliot.

Richard's mouth crimped with exasperation. "He went off hours ago to collect the master script, the one with his notes written in. He meant for Derek to leave it here last night, but Roshan found it in their kitchen this morning and put it through Elliot's mail slot with the post."

"Can't blame the lad," Kate said, "what with the argy-bargy over Claire. I'm surprised he got home with it."

"Moncrief would be late to his own funeral," stated Rob.

Alec sent Derek running to Elliot's cottage. The boy returned right before curtain time. "I tried both doors, knocked, shouted, did everything save bung a rock through the front window. His Jag's there but he's not."

"If he scarpered," murmured Blake, "he'd take his car. . . ."

For one delectable moment Claire watched a flicker of doubt cross Pakenham's face. Then the smug certainty settled in again, like fog. "He's getting his leg over some bit of crumpet, like as not. He'll come running in at the last minute, making sure we all know just what he's been about."

Claire did expect Elliot to pop out of a closet or down the chimney and whinny, "The Play must go on!" He didn't, though, and The Play went on without him. And, so far as she could tell, without either Elizabeth or the cat.

In the forecourt the lights reflected off the gathering cloud-cover, giving the scene an eerie, otherworldly air. Derek prompted from a regular script, Richard hissed a few instructions from the wings, and the actors, troupers all, strutted their hour and a half on the stage without direction. Or so Claire assumed. She had to concentrate so fiercely on the pages of music — the complete set of pages — that Luke Skywalker and Darth Vader could've dueled with light sabers at center stage and she'd never have noticed.

Then the cast was bowing. The audience streamed down onto the stage. Kate latched her arm through Claire's and elbowed a path through the crowd. Just inside the entrance hall Blake and Pakenham stood in close consultation with two bobbies. Alec ranged up beside them, caught himself, backed off and bumped into Claire and Kate.

Blake looked around. "Well, then, PC Wood. You've been exonerated."

"Eh?" Alec asked.

Pakenham rocked back on his heels, stuffed with satisfaction. "The lad only knocked on Moncrief's door, did he? I thought it a bit much, Moncrief not taking his bows. So I made a recce myself, went round looking in the windows. Then I fetched a constable with a crowbar."

"And?" prompted Richard from over Claire's shoulder. His breath seemed chill on the back of her neck and her skin shrank in dread, not of him but of what Pakenham was about to say.

Pakenham said, "Elliot Moncrief is dead," in the same tone of voice he'd say, *Pass the salt.* "Suicide, with a proper little confession on the desk. I knew he was our killer all along. All the evidence pointed that way."

His words thinned and squealed in Claire's ears. The cold on the back of her neck slid down her body. Her stomach did a sickly little shimmy beneath her ribs. Elliot, she thought. All she could see was his calculating expression in the pub two nights ago. Had she really been in danger from him? She'd never have gone off alone with him, Kate or no Kate.

Elliot killed Melinda? Why? Because she turned him down? There had to be more to it than that. Something about the blackmail letters, probably . . . Claire turned around and collided with someone's chest. It was Richard, his skin beneath the stage base pale, the bronze gleam of his eyes tarnished.

Kate swore beneath her breath. Alec walked several paces in the other direction and peered up the staircase, hiding his expression. Maybe someone or something moved in the shadows, maybe not.

"WPC Shelton," said Blake, loosening his tie, "we'll need you at the cottage to help with the paperwork."

"Yes, sir," Kate said, and looked over at Claire. "Are you all . . ."

Pakenham smirked. "Don't need to nurse maid our little Yankee lass any more, Kate? Big bad wolf's come a cropper."

"Sergeant," snapped Blake, "go make the announcement to the press."

Pakenham unleashed the reporters. The surge of journalistic humanity in the front door drove the actors to the back of the house. Feeling naked without Kate beside her, Claire sprinted past the cellar door, plunged into the dressing room, and pulled off her robe-cum-dress.

Everyone was painstakingly not talking at once. Priscilla was solemn, Susan looked stunned, Diana turned a thin-lipped hot-eyed glare on everyone and fled the scene as soon as she'd changed her clothes. Claire picked up the pink gown and returned it and own wrapper to Sarita in the kitchen. "Roshan and Derek took Trillian home," Sarita told her. "She is tired, poor lass. Thank goodness it is all over."

Sarita wasn't looking particularly thankful. Her plump cheeks drooped and her hands folding the dress trembled. Claire knew how she felt, like a cotton shirt worn too many times without washing and ironing.

It's all over, she thought. It's all over. But she might just as well have been thinking in Esperanto, the words made that little sense to her. The chill on the back of her neck oozed downward like creeping paralysis.

She hurried through the entrance hall, where Rob was cursing a blue streak and shoveling the bottles and dishes back into their boxes. No, there was no need to formally announce that the party was cancelled.

Richard was waiting in the forecourt. No one recognized him in his jeans and sweater, if indeed anyone cared about the actors any more. The audience was separating itself into two entities, a large ameba-like creature with a nucleus of police and reporters which flowed through the gate and up the street, and multiple single-celled units flailing as fast as possible toward cars and buses before they got involved.

Cold hand in cold hand, Claire and Richard followed half a block or so behind the ameba, pacing themselves on Alec's tall form. Beyond the lights of Hall and village the evening was closing in quickly. Once before they'd walked through an uncertain dusk toward a dead body, Claire remembered. Perhaps they'd come full circle, back to the beginning, to the end. . . . She glanced up at Richard's stone-carved face and amended, it's all over but the shouting.

Chapter Twenty-four

*R*ichard and Claire were moving faster on foot than the cars creeping up the high street. Constables in neon-orange vests shouted and gestured, trying to move people along. A chill rain-scented wind, funneled down the narrow street, made Claire's jacket billow like a sail.

The ice-blue lights of police cars and an ambulance strobed nervously on the front of Elliot's cottage and across the red Jaguar. Strips of yellow tape held back the crowd. Various uniformed and suited figures moved in and out of the house and across the lane to the police station. Several took short cuts through Alec's garden and the pungent scents of thyme and rosemary whirled away down the wind.

Richard stopped at the curb. "This is the house my parents always let for the summer. It was a bit shabby, the plumbing would play up every now and then, but it was home. Alec and I, we'd signal each other with torches from our bedroom windows, pretending — ah, God knows what we were pretending, we were bairns, weren't we?"

The grown man who was Alec stood at the front gate, beckoning. Claire squeezed Richard's hand. Together they ducked beneath the yellow tape.

"Richard, come through," Alec said. "Blake wants you to have a look round for the things you sent the blackmailer."

That invitation didn't necessarily include Claire. Even so, Richard tugged her forward. Alec didn't try to stop her but escorted them both past the smashed lock of the front door.

The air inside the house was still and cold, filled with a low mutter of voices. The smells of disinfectant and furniture polish didn't quite mask the ugly stench of mortality. A stack of mail sat on a small table by the door — several letters, a magazine, and a catalog.

A central passage with a staircase extended toward the back of the house. On Claire's left was a dining room, on her right a sitting room. The latter was crowded with people, half of them stooping over and mercifully concealing a human form sprawled next to an antique desk. Muddy footprints smudged the pattern of a no doubt hideously expensive oriental carpet. The script lay on a coffee table next to a silver ashtray and lighter.

Every bit of furniture and every objet d'art in the two rooms and the hall was as tidy and as isolated as though in a stage set. The only items Claire could see that indicated someone actually lived in the house were a row of pictures on the desk. Autographed publicity photos, maybe. She was too far away to make out the names and faces.

"A Du Jardin landscape," Richard said reverently. He was inspecting a painting on a wall above a narrow table filled with small enamel boxes.

"You haven't been here since Elliot moved in?" Claire asked.

"Once, to see the new kitchen he had fitted. He'd rather have guests of the female persuasion."

"I can't remember the last time I was inside," said Alec, "although Elliot and I had a natter or two over the fence."

Richard looked down at the table. "Sheraton. Might be a reproduction. Those snuff boxes are genuine, though." He stepped into the dining room. "Hepplewhite — very fine. The chairs are Charles II. The table carpet is probably sixteenth century."

"Petit point," added Claire, squinting. "A hundred stitches to the inch. Several restored patches. Diana's work, maybe? Or Melinda's. . . ." They were standing there calmly talking about inert objects when the remains of a human life lay in the other room. Again her stomach squirmed.

Richard's jawline was white as the knuckles on a clenched fist. He dodged around the dining table to inspect a cabinet against the far wall. "Well, that's put the boot in, right enough. I posted that eighteenth century oak veneer knife box to London as a blackmail payment. And the Ming porcelain jug with the English silver-gilt mounts."

"So Moncrief asked for specific objects from the Hall?" asked Paken-ham's nasal voice.

Claire, Richard, and Alec turned around to see Blake and Pakenham in the doorway. While the dapper, soulless Pakenham fit right into the rarified atmosphere of the house, Blake looked more than ever like a clerk after a bad day behind the complaints desk, corrugated with fatigue.

"No," Richard replied, "he asked for 'antiques from the Hall.' The jug is a copy, I did well to find it as the original is worth a packet. The knife box is original but worthless, some villain replaced the partitions inside on the cheap. That's neck, to bring the both of them back here."

"Maybe he started asking for money because he realized you weren't sending him anything of value," Blake mused aloud. "He had posh tastes, no doubt about it. Sergeant, the note."

With a flourish Pakenham placed on the table a plastic bag contain-ing a piece of what looked to Claire like good-quality rag notepaper. In spidery handwriting were the words, "My dear Chief Inspector. Little did I realize that when Melinda and I set about teasing the good citizens of Somerstowe it would all come to this. The dear girl let it go to her head, you see. She became a threat. I had no choice but to make her lovely body into compost for the flowers. I meant for it all to end there. It didn't. My plot has unraveled like the Bard's sleeve of care. I'm afraid the tailors and the chefs at Her Majesty's prisons would have a spot of bother rising to my standards. So, farewell. Parting is such sweet sorrow. Elliot Moncrief."

"We compared the handwriting with the notes in that script," said Blake.

"Yes," Richard said dully, "it's his, but it's gone all wobbly."

"There was a glass on the desk," Pakenham pointed out, "and an empty bottle of whiskey in the kitchen. Sucking it down to give himself courage, I reckon. Not that he was of sound mind to begin with."

"You'd have to be round the bend to kill yourself," Alec said, his voice rough, his eyes bleak.

Claire wondered what her own face looked like. Fish-belly white, probably, with bulging eyes to match. The air in the house seemed too thick to breathe, the uneasily mingled odors congealing in her throat. She managed to say, "No. Melinda couldn't have been working with Elliot. He saw that first letter was all."

"Maybe she showed it him as part of the joke," Blake suggested. "Then when the other letters arrived she knew who was sending them and confronted him."

"But why kill her?" asked Claire. "Even if she'd stood up in the pub and announced Elliot was the blackmailer, people would've been mad, yes, but he could've blown it off as a joke. Would anyone even have bothered to press charges?"

"If he saw that first letter then he saw the line about 'the secret behind The Play," Pakenham answered. "That was the real threat. The evidence points right at it, said so myself yesterday."

Claire leaned in closer, enunciating. "Even if Melinda knew about The Play, and we'll never know whether she did or not, why would her reasoning be any different from Trevor's? She wouldn't have told."

"No," Alec agreed, "I don't see her telling. I don't see that at all."

Blake picked up the note and turned it around in his fingertips like a card player considering his next move. "It appears I was wrong. The blackmailer and the murderer are one and the same."

"That's plain as a pikestaff," Pakenham said, puffing himself up. "I'll tell you what happened. Moncrief met Melinda as she left the Hall after the party. She was still wearing her costume, wasn't she?"

"She probably kept it on so she could get into Elizabeth's head," Claire said.

"You think so?" asked Pakenham. "Maybe Wood asked her to wear it, intending to get into it himself, act out a bit of his fantasy, eh?"

"I told you," Alec began, and bit off his sentence, obviously deciding not to waste his breath.

"You're the one said she was plucking roses for you. That's a bit romantic, isn't it?" Pakenham made the word sound obscene. "Or maybe Moncrief lured her to the garden by saying they needed to talk about their blackmail schemes. In any event, there she was. He coshed her, strangled her with a bit of ribbon from the dress, buried her in the garden bed, and was back here in time for a quick shag with Diana. No accounting for tastes, is there?"

"I'll have to review the time table," said Blake. "That's cutting it a bit fine."

"Well then, he needn't have buried her straightaway. Or driven her car to the reservoir until the next morning — all he had to do just then was move it from the car park by the shop. Diana said she went home at first light. We'll check bus and taxi companies, find who drove Moncrief back home."

"That might work, yes," Blake admitted reluctantly, as though he was sorry to find Pakenham capable of logical reasoning. "I'll have a look at the timetable and another word with Mrs. Jackman. She could be covering for him, I suppose, although they're hardly on the best of terms, are they?"

Kate stepped into the dining room. "Chief Inspector, the medical examiner would like a word."

Blake, Pakenham at his heels, walked back across the hall. Kate lingered in the doorway. "I'm sorry. I mean, we have our murderer and all, but it's a bloody mess and no mistake. Literally." She nodded at the other room. "Gunshot wound to the head, fired from less than three inches. Automatic pistol. It was in his hand when Pakenham found him."

"Trust Elliot to make the dramatic gesture," said Richard faintly.

"He had a gun?" Alec exclaimed. "Smuggled it into the country, I reckon, afraid he'd be burgled. Here in Somerstowe, across the lane from the station. He took me for a fool, right enough."

"We passed him leaving the Hall this afternoon," Kate said. "He was dead within the hour."

"Within the . . . It was Pakenham," Claire said. "He was in the kitchen before we got there, swaggering around saying he was going to make an arrest."

"Yes," said Richard, "he was that. And Elliot overheard."

Alec's face was starting to collapse in on itself. "Pakenham was after taking me in charge, not Elliot. Ah, sod it all, I am a fool. All this — blackmail, murder, assault, suicide, illegal weapons — it's happened on my patch!"

"You're not at fault," Kate told him.

"No one's at fault," added Richard.

Before Claire could chime in, too, Alec went on, "Kate, give Blake my respects, but I'm not on duty — this house — it's cold and there's no air . . ."

He edged past Kate and disappeared out the door. Kate turned to watch him. Was he going back to Hall, Claire wondered, to pour his heart out to Elizabeth? Or to the pub, to look for some heart in a glass?

The house was stiflingly cold, trapped in some sort of emotional high pressure-zone. The smell had been bad enough without Pakenham's cologne adding itself to the brew. What is that stuff he wears? Claire wondered. Eau de whorehouse?

"You know where to find me," she told Kate, her own voice sounding choked, and sidled toward the door. She could tell Richard was right behind her without turning around.

Trevor, his dog collar firmly in place, was just coming up the front steps. He murmured something appropriate and slipped into the house. Taking Claire's hand in his icicle-like fingers, Richard led her past the yellow tape, the flashing lights, and the people who lined the fence like vultures. "Eh, mate," called a reporter, "How'd he do himself? Rope? Gas?"

Richard's glance was sharp as a battleaxe.

The man backed off. "No offense, mate."

Across the street the front door of Alec's house slammed shut and a light went on in the sitting room. Yeah, Claire thought, I'd go to ground, too.

The light went off again, replaced by the subtle flicker of a candle.

Richard hesitated, drawn for a step or two toward that flicker, then turning away. His hand squeezed Claire's so tightly she felt her bones creak. Around the corner the main street stretched toward the Hall. Car lights, street lights, lighted windows — they all seemed thin and pale beneath the heavy black lid of the sky

Richard and Claire threaded their way between the knots of people ranged outside the pub. The massive German Shepherd sat by the door like an amiable Cerberus, his leash looped through the handle. At the curb a group of pensioners filed into a van. Inside the shop Roshan was doling out candy bars and soft drinks. A horn honked. Someone shouted. Several of the drinkers laughed.

Richard followed as Claire climbed the steps to her flat. From the landing she could see how all the lights and activity were compressed into a small area in the center of the village. The church steeple on one side and the Hall on the other were barely perceptible shapes against the surrounding darkness . . . No. Headlights swept across the façade of the Hall, reflecting in each succeeding window as though Elizabeth walked through the rooms carrying a torch.

Had Somerstowe looked like this the night Melinda died, Claire wondered, one pocket of life and the world around dark and quiet as the grave? And yet she'd died within sight of the stone circle, which, like the church and the Hall, too, for that matter, was evidence of life and light beyond death.

Life, yes. A fine spray of raindrops brushed Claire's face. She breathed deeply of the cold fresh breeze. But when Richard turned toward her he moved like a robot.

Claire kissed him. Her lips were cold. His were stiff. Their hands and arms collided awkwardly. The physical relationship was moving backwards, wasn't it, from a passionate clinch to a tentative first kiss to this hug, as sexual as hugging your grandmother. "Sorry," he whispered against her cheek.

"There are a lot of people who have something to apologize for, including me. You don't."

He managed a thin smile at that.

Claire pulled away. "Go sit with Alec. Sneak in the back door if you have to. He needs you. You need him. I'll still be here tomorrow."

She thought for a moment Richard would at least try to keep up appearances by arguing with her. But no. That was why she'd fallen for him, after all, because he was honest. "I need you, too. Tomorrow." He let her go and trudged off down the steps. At the bottom he looked up and called, "Thank you."

She waved, and waited until he'd disappeared into the crowd along the street before unlocking her door and going inside.

Her flat was dark and cold. Out of habit Claire inspected her two rooms, She found nothing except a few souvenirs — Melinda's letters, a script, Trevor's umbrella, the deerskin robe bundled at the end of couch. She'd get it back to Alec eventually.

Rain pattered down on the roof. Claire put on her pajamas, made herself some hot chocolate, and sat for a long time looking at Melinda's wedding ring on its bed of cotton. And yet she didn't have Alec's second sight and it didn't speak to her. "You had some things to apologize for," she said softly to it. "You didn't have to die for them. But then, you sure didn't mean to, did you?"

Putting the lid back on the box, she tucked it away. She pulled out the bed, climbed into it, and curled up in the fetal position, trying to get warm. Still the cold lingered bone-deep in her limbs. In her heart.

The investigation was over. She'd achieved her purpose in coming to Somerstowe. Melinda's death was explained. It was even, in a grim sort of way, avenged. She should be happy, relieved, and gratified. Her old life was over. Tomorrow she and Richard could start a new one.

But all Claire could think of was Melinda's cold grave, Elliot splattered over his jewel box house, the blue lights of police cars winking in the sleepless windows of the Hall. And Richard watching over an anguished friend even as his own anguish festered in his gut.

Chapter Twenty-five

Claire stood beneath the taut arch of the umbrella. The Sunday afternoon rain was soft and soothing. The churchyard was meltingly green even in the gloom, its tombstones not objects of fear but assurances of peace. "Little," she read. "Brandreth. Jackman. Hardinge. Stafford." And, on a modest stone to one side, "Julian Lacey."

A bedraggled handful of pinkish-purple lupins lay on the step of the Cranbourne mausoleum beneath the eyes of the decorous Victorian angels on the roof. Claire had seen flowers of that peculiar color somewhere else — the beds in front of the Hall, probably.

On the village green, Priscilla Digby and a couple of other women wearing bright yellow raincoats dismantled the well-dressing panel. They piled a wheelbarrow with the now decayed leaves and flowers and trundled it into the vicarage gardens. Earth to earth, thought Claire. *Compost to compost,* as Elliot had come close to saying in his letter. The return of every prodigal child to his or her roots.

Elliot, she thought, as she stepped up into the church porch. It was like him to make the dramatic gesture, yes. And yet . . .

The weathered wooden door opened soundlessly to her touch. Her shoes made only a slight scuffing noise on the worn stone. The faint creak of the door into the nave was more like a musical note. Closing her umbrella, Claire walked into the dimly lit interior. That faint odor of flowers, candle wax, and mildew seemed an intrinsic part of any church, even a brand new concrete and fiberglass one.

The candles on the altar were burned-out stubs. She tried to dredge up an appropriate quote, the lines from Shakespeare about life being as short as a candle flame, but what she came up with were the much more comforting words of the service this morning.

Then the candles had burned brightly, making little haloes in her glasses, while Trevor preached a sermon about faith. His voice had faltered as it delivered cliché after cliché. His eyes pleaded sincerity to the faces ranged before him. Almost everyone in town had been there, Richard and the volunteers, Nigel, the Jackmans, the Nairs, Blake, Pakenham, Kate, and the police contingent, plus several reporters probably hoping for a scoop between the wafer and the wine.

Alec had stood in the back listening respectfully, his somber face angled not toward the altar but to the floor beneath. He'd been exonerated, Claire repeated to herself. So had Richard, for that matter, although only Pakenham ever thought he and Alec were conspiring.

The killer had paid the wages of sin. Melinda's life and death had come full circle. It was time to move on. Wasn't it?

Claire looked around her. The latticework of the ceiling was lost in shadow. The windows were pale arches in the darkness of the walls, their colorful images shrouded. The effigies along the aisles dozed, beyond rain, beyond death. The silence of the church wasn't like that of the Hall. The Hall brooded on old passions and time past. The church was aloof from time and passion alike. Its fabric was woven with hymns, prayers, comfort, and hope. Claire could almost hear its music. Maybe that was the song Alec had been singing yesterday morning in his own church among the stones.

It was Richard she saw when she looked at the ceiling and the tombs. He'd stopped her after the service, his eyes still reflecting the light of the candles even though the lines bracketing his mouth were cut deep. "I have to lay on a lunch for Nigel and a couple of other trustees at the

Hall."

"A man's work is never done."

"I'll see you later this afternoon, then? I'm thinking it's time we defined our terms."

"I'm thinking that, too. Let me know when."

Claire had made her way back to her flat, where she fixed herself a sandwich and watched Kate and Pakenham argue in pantomime in one window while Blake sat with his cell phone pressed to his ear in the other. When Trillian had delivered Richard's note she'd been ready to jump. More than ready to jump. To run screaming down the stairs and along the high street. She'd cut herself too deep a rut of nervous tension, it seemed, and now she was in over her head.

She forced herself to sit down in a pew toward the front of the church. The wooden seat was so icy she almost shot up again. She set the umbrella down beside her, pulled the note out of her pocket, and spread it across her denim-covered thigh.

Richard and his fine architect's hand, she thought with a smile. Not only was her name printed on the envelope but the note inside was printed, too, its letters looking like the ones on the map of Somerstowe Alec had used to find Melinda's body. "Meet me in the church at two, R."

The church? Why not the Lodge? Was the official delegation camped out there?

Claire heard a creak, as though another door had opened somewhere in the building. A slight stirring of the air brought a whiff of brass polish to her nose. Richard? She looked up. No one was there. Just the old structure settling, she told herself.

Like Alec, she eyed the stone flags surrounding the altar. That one with the iron ring in it, that was the opening to the crypt. Had Walter known the truth about Elizabeth, or, believing that witchcraft was the equivalent of satanism, had he stoutly refused to believe anything of the sort? Well, faith was pretty much wishful thinking in any event. But wishful thinking — perception, desire — could be more important than fact. Especially when it came to something that transcended fact.

In his benediction Trevor had spoken of "God's peace which passeth all understanding." *Amen,* Claire said to herself. In spite of her peaceful surroundings, though, she didn't feel at peace. Maybe she simply hadn't processed everything yet. The future was far from certain, not for Alec, not for Richard, not for her.

The air stirred again, almost imperceptibly. Flowers, polish, wax — the church smelled a bit like the Hall with its lingering odor of potpourri. Except for the candle wax. That was sort of like the scent of stage base, also known as greasepaint. Claire grimaced, feeling again the cloth around her throat, cruelly tight, and her heart bursting from her chest. She'd smelled sweat and greasepaint on her attacker . . . Elliot, she thought. He was the director. He hadn't been wearing stage base. And yet he'd confessed. She must've smelled her own paint exuded in her rush of terror. Weird.

She shifted uneasily on the hard wooden bench, built before people regarded comfort as an inalienable right. She could have sworn she wasn't alone in the church. And she didn't mean the place was suffused with the Holy Spirit, either. She'd gotten used to being paranoid, was all.

You're not paranoid, she told herself, if someone really is out to get you. And Elliot had been out to get her. Claire had been a burr under his saddle since the day she arrived. Everyone assumed she and Melinda had been, somehow, one mind in two bodies — even Richard . . . No. Elliot had searched her room, hadn't he? If he'd plowed through all her notes and all her letters he'd realize she hadn't known what Melinda knew. Which meant his motive had been revenge, pure and simple.

Shaking her head, Claire looked again at the note. Two. Her watch said two, right on the dot. It wasn't as though she had anything else to do, though. Except to think about Elliot making the dramatic gesture even though he knew damn well he wouldn't be around for the applause. About fastidious Elliot killing himself in one of the messiest possible ways.

Claire heard a slight scraping sound. Mice beneath the organ? She peered toward the altar. The dangling end of the embroidered cloth was swaying just a bit, as though in some ghostly draft. Something emanating from the crypt, maybe? Not that she'd ever really believed in ghosts before. Or that magic worked. She'd just enjoyed the stories and thought that there, too, faith transcended fact. That wishful thinking. . . .

Suddenly she went skin-prickling cold. With Elliot's death they were all indulging in wishful thinking, weren't they? They were seeing what they wanted to see — an end to the case. A staged suicide would get the real killer off the hook. It would separate Claire from her faithful bodyguard and leave her sitting alone in the village church.

"Shit," she whispered. Slowly she stood up. The shadows were thick behind the effigies and in the corners, but nothing moved, not even the air. Still the hair rose on the back of her neck.

Someone had held Elliot's own gun on him while he wrote a confession, his hand trembling with fear. People would confess to just about anything under duress. And then — well, it would've been easy enough to shoot and then close Elliot's hand around the gun.

Claire could buy Elliot as a co-conspirator. He had the jug and box. He made regular trips to London, where the blackmail letters were postmarked. And yet the threatening letters had an edge of hatred and resentment that seemed too harsh even for Elliot and his malicious ego-masturbating sense of humor. An edge of hatred and resentment of the status quo that had led — someone else — to murder not once, but twice.

So whom had Elliot thought so harmless he'd agreed to play a game of blackmail with them? Someone he'd not only let into his house yesterday afternoon, he'd let get the drop on him? And as clearly as if he sat beside her Claire heard Richard's voice saying, "He'd rather have guests of the female persuasion."

Of course. She could just see Elliot trying to impress female prey by posturing with the gun, mocking the cliches of machismo even as he bought into them. And not just any female prey, either. If Diana Jackman alibi'd Elliot for the time of Melinda's murder, then he alibi'd her.

Good God. Claire crushed her hand to her mouth. Was it another puzzle, simple once you saw the solution? But she hadn't solved the puzzle. She was back to the one thing that had bothered her — had bothered everyone — all along. Motive. And Pakenham's glib explanation of the income from The Play as the primary cause just didn't go far enough.

The Play, Elizabeth's story, was inextricably part of the Hall. The Hall, Trevor had said, was the trunk of the tree, like a genealogical tree . . . Claire sat back down, landing on the spike at the top of the umbrella. Impatiently she pushed it away. With a small thunk the umbrella's curved handle bumped the armrest at the far end of the pew. Claire barely heard it. She didn't see it. The cascade of words and images doused her mind like a bucket of cold water.

The genealogical tree that mattered wasn't that of the Laceys or the Spensers. It was the family tree of the Cranbournes. Because she'd seen the lupins laid in front of the Cranbourne mausoleum in the back yard of the pub.

Diana's pink dress was initialed "DCJ." A woman often used her maiden name as her middle name after she married. On the way to Bakewell Diana said her family had been in Somerstowe a long time, not all of them in service, either — her grandfather had been a gentleman. But Trevor said Diana was from Leeds and only moved to Somerstowe when she married Rob.

So where had Vincent, the gray sheep of the Cranbournes, gone when he married a maidservant and was cut off from the family? Leeds?

Maurice Applethorpe, from Leeds, had come to Somerstowe for genealogical lectures. He had to know Diana was his cousin. And if he didn't, all he had to do was sit down in the pub and start talking about his connections and she'd be onto him like a duck onto a June bug. And if he started going on about how the Cranbournes had been cheated out of their inheritance by Julian Lacey, about how there must be something wrong with Maud's will, about how much the Hall would bring, sold to a developer . . .

Melinda's letter to Richard. Had he sat down with his mail in the pub then, too? The pub, where you sat and chatted away, your tongue lubricated by alcohol, and assumed your conversations, not to mention your letters, were private. Where the public phone connection at the end of the bar was custom-made for Melinda's laptop, so she could e-mail Claire and tell her she'd learned some interesting things by asking questions in Somerstowe.

Rob and Diana had catered the cast party last year, too. One of them would've had to stay late and clear up. Had Diana been waiting inside the entrance hall when Susan saw Melinda walking through the portico? No, she hadn't. She'd been here, at the church.

Claire looked up, not quite focussing. Ceiling, altar, windows, effigies — all were indistinct, as though she'd taken off her glasses. Damn it, she thought, Blake was right. If any of the Cranbournes, even Diana, thought Melinda knew the truth about the will — even if to them the truth was only wishful thinking — the last thing they'd do is kill her. . . .

One of the effigies moved. Claire blinked. No, effigies didn't stand upright and walk. They didn't emerge from door behind the altar that opened onto the vestry. The vestry, where Trevor kept the old typewriter that had typed the blackmail letters.

"Hullo, Claire." Diana strolled out of the shadow into the dim light of the center aisle.

Slowly Claire stood up. Maybe she didn't yet know Why, or even How, but as surely as she knew her own name, she knew Who.

Chapter Twenty-six

Diana's blond frizz stood out from her head as if electrified. Her oversized jacket gaped lopsidedly over a shapeless sweat suit. Dark smears of eye shadow and lipstick made her face look like a skull. She'd probably been up all night, her mind racing like a rat through a maze.

Claire would've felt a pang of sympathy if she hadn't instead felt a pang of fear.

"I see you got me note," Diana said.

Claire opened her mouth. It was dust-dry. She swallowed and tried again. "The – ah – note I thought was from Richard? You copied his printing from the map, right?"

"Right." Diana took a step closer, blocking the aisle end of the pew. "Seemed only fair, that was the map Alec used to witch up Melinda's body. Takes one to know one, I always say. It's not right, the likes of Alec playing Walter. Walter was a good man, he protected Elizabeth when everyone was getting at her."

"It's a good story," Claire said, taking a step back.

"Dead brilliant. About how the toffs like you and your pal Melinda, all set up proper with your lolly and your posh clothes and your flash manners, how you make the rules for the rest of us. We're good for nothing but fetching and carrying and bowing and scraping. I know how Elizabeth felt when everyone save Walter turned against her."

"Melinda didn't start out with money. She worked hard. She earned it."

Diana's voice was thick, as though her throat was clogged with bile. "Yeh, on her back, I reckon. She had the men queuing up to get into her knickers, didn't she?"

"No, she didn't," Claire said, keeping her own voice even. Getting mad wouldn't help.

"Elliot now," said Diana. "He told me I could've been a great actress. But Melinda took Elizabeth away from me. She'd sit there pushing Elliot to slag me off. 'Our Diana, not two brain cells to rub together.' Men always have to have the young ones, don't they? More ballocks than brains, men are."

Saying something about women sometimes being more ovaries than brains wouldn't help, either. "So – ah – you and Elliot broke up because of Melinda?"

"She sent him off me, she did. Then she died and he saw the error of his ways, like, and we had another go. But I gave him the elbow the same day you came here. He had a spot of bother rising to me standards, if you get me drift."

A spot of bother rising to my standards. That was in Elliot's suicide note, straight, without the double meaning. Again Claire would've felt sympathy for Diana. She thought her affair with Elliot meant she was desirable when what it meant was that she was available. But what Claire felt was the horror of the scene, Diana holding Elliot's own gun to his head and he . . . Had he pleaded with her? Or had he assumed she was too stupid to pull the trigger? Knowing Elliot, he'd said so. Bad mistake.

Diana obviously intended the black eyeliner and false lashes to make her eyes look bigger. Instead the cosmetics made them into small slits. She might not want anything here and now beyond a chance to unburden herself. To confess . . . *Yeah, right.* Claire took another step backward. Was that a door opening? No, that was her own heart thumping in her ears.

She had to keep Diana talking. Over and beyond satisfying her own morbid curiosity at last, maybe Trevor would come in. Maybe Richard would come looking for her, or Rob for Diana, somebody, anybody. "You and Elliot were sending the blackmail letters."

"Yeh. It was me own idea. There was Richard reading over his post in the pub, so narked at one letter he squashed it up then smoothed it out again, quick smart. And me just behind him with me tray. He never saw me. No one ever sees me, I'm just a bit of furniture, aren't I, not worth a notice."

"You realized it was Melinda who sent the letter."

"Thought she was right clever, Melinda did, with all her little hints and lit'ry quotes. But I knew what she was on about. And I saw me chance to make me own back."

"Making money by blackmailing people with what you'd overheard in the pub." Again Claire stepped backward, this time into the rack of prayer books. Its corner gouged her right thigh. Wincing, she eased away.

"Yeh. That little tart Janet and her brother in nick back home, thought no one knew about that. And Fred well, not much to say about Fred, is there? And less about Alec. He's worse than looney, isn't he? I even sent letters to meself and Elliot, too. Wasn't that clever? Mine was true, I had me admirers once. Don't know about Elliot's story, the rock star's wife and all, he thought it'd be good for a giggle."

"Richard wasn't laughing."

"Richard's a Lacey, all prim and proper. Not a bad sort, even so, though why he bothers with the likes of Alec I don't know. No accounting for tastes."

No, Claire thought tartly, there isn't.

"That first letter, that was just a game to Melinda. She could afford to play games. I can't. I asked for pretty things from the Hall — I have a right to them, don't I? Then Elliot said Richard was posting fakes. Said we'd kill the goose that laid the golden egg if we got Richard in wrong with the Trust. Said we should ask for cash, from him and everyone else.

"Elliot thought it was all a game, too. Said we'd save the lolly and have us a party and tell everyone it was us sent the letters. But even seeing Miss Melinda's face at that wasn't worth giving away me money. Every time I went to the shops in Bakewell I'd put it in me own account. Rob never knew he was paying me off to keep quiet about the duty-free beer, did he? The greedy sod and his, 'Where's the receipts, Diana? Why didn't you get the sale price, Diana? So you're a Cranbourne, well la de dah! I am a Cranbourne, mind you, better than the likes of a Jackman any day!" Her lips curved down, hard, like a sickle. "Then Melinda died and I couldn't send any more letters, could I? Just like her, to take me money away from me."

Claire tried to exude calm. "You sent Richard a letter just a couple of weeks ago."

"He thought you sent it, didn't he? Would've given you the elbow and paid up, too, except for that sod Alec — he's hand in glove with the devil himself, that one is." Diana leaned forward. "You and Melinda both, you're nothing more than troublemakers. Everything would've gone down a treat, except for her and for you."

Claire inched backward another half step. Diana was seriously disturbed. If you had to be crazy to kill yourself, you had to be even crazier to kill someone else. "You put that letter beneath Melinda's door, right? Because Elliot picked her to play Elizabeth?"

"Like in The Play, when Cecil finds a doll with thorns in it and accuses Elizabeth. I mean, if Alec can do witchery, why not me? I'm smarter than he is and a Cranbourne to boot. But no, I haven't got the lolly, I'm not good enough. And here comes Melinda, young Melinda, pretty Melinda, perfect Melinda — a foreigner, for God's sakes! A foreigner playing Elizabeth!"

Melinda had worked hard to maintain her façade of perfection, trying to protect herself. She'd done too good a job, it seemed. It wasn't fair. Which was Diana's complaint, that life wasn't fair.

"Melinda wouldn't leave, acted like she never even saw me letter. I thought then she was winding me up, didn't know about the bleeding carpet 'til now, did I? Just as well. The bitch got what she deserved."

"Why?" Claire demanded. "How?"

Diana's red-veined eyes were hot and dry. "Well now, there's a story. As good a story as The Play, except mine's got a happy ending. Started like Elizabeth's, when I went to work for Maud just to see the Hall, just to see Somerstowe. Then I met Rob — well, we all make mistakes, don't we?"

Oh yeah, Claire told herself. We do.

"I sewed and tidied up like Elizabeth did do. I know me way round the Hall better than Richard. Better than Alec with that naff little room in the attics. What he gets up to in there, thinks he's having it off with Elizabeth, doesn't he, but we all know that ghost is a devil. Because that's what witches do, raise devils. Elizabeth was never a witch, she never had any truck with devils. Those rozzers from Derby, Blake and Pakenham, should see Alec off, they should. But no, Alec's a rozzer like them. They all work together, don't they, just like you see in the papers, all bent, every one of them."

Diana's voice was getting louder and shriller. She took a step forward, into the space between the pews. Claire forced herself to stand still, to act — no, she didn't have to act interested. She was interested. And nauseated. And hyperventilating. She tried to breathe normally. Flowers, candlewax, mildew. Sweat and hair spray.

"I did needlework better than anything you Yanks could do. Maud liked me. She was a decent woman, she minded her relatives, said she'd leave the Hall to her brother Vincent's family. Not that she knew I was one of Vincent's grandchildren. A Cranbourne in service? No, I kept that quiet. I told her me maiden name was Cox. I wasn't going to name me true name and have the local turnips slag me off about it, was I? Not 'til I could walk in with the clothes and the cash and tell Rob to take his bloody beer taps and shove them up his arse.

"Then the Laceys got at her, didn't they? And Maud gave the Hall away. Just gave it away like it was worth no more than an old shoe." Diana sputtered, trying to clear her throat. "The mantlepieces, the balustrades, the tapestries, the stones themselves, they're worth a packet, aren't they? People buy the old bits and pieces for their posh new houses, no need to keep the grotty old Hall itself standing. What's the point of that, I ask you? Why the bloody hell bother?"

Claire wasn't going to try and answer that. She edged back another step.

"One day this toffee-nosed twit's sitting there in the pub drinking with Trevor after one of his lectures. Says he's a Cranbourne, Vincent's grandson. Posh suit, Rolex, BMW — he was the business and he knew it too. Maurice Applethorpe, his name was. I minded the Applethorpes, gave us poor relations the elbow, they did, donkey's years ago. But there was Maurice, asking Trevor if there was something rum about old Maud's will. What if she'd really left the Hall to us. He had a buyer waiting for it, planned to sell off the pieces and tear it down and build new houses, ever so nice, and a golf course. All he needed was proof the will was a fake. All we needed."

"We?" asked Claire.

"I took him aside when he was coming back from the loo, told him who I was. At first he went all shirty — his own cousin serving beer and sausages in a pub — then when I told him I might could help, oh, he was polite enough then. It was soon after that I saw Melinda's letter.

"She thought it was funny, winding Richard up about the will. But I knew what she was playing at. 'Willpower,' she said. 'The secret behind The Play,' she said. Because The Play is part of the will, isn't it? She thought she was being clever. I twigged it, though. The song in The Play, 'We gather together thy will to make known.' Get it? 'Thy will to make known?' The Lacey's will? She knew all about it, Melinda did. You could tell by the way she asked questions, by the way she ponced about so proud of herself."

The hymn? Not the quote from Terence? Claire's mouth fell open and she snapped her teeth back together. Melinda's rock — the original blackmail letter — had hit not only Richard's guilty conscience but Diana's resentment, envy, and greed. Somewhere in her stomach she felt her own laugh welling up. Diana's construction was almost logical. Almost. And yet it was as completely wrong as a dog that meowed.

"Melinda was Killigrew's wife, wasn't she? The Laceys handed him a nice little bribe. That trusteeship, like as not, to never notice a fake will. We all know what lawyers get up to, don't we?

"Maurice is all right, though, not like the other toffs — he's me own cousin, isn't he? He said if he had the evidence he'd bring another suit, if he could break the will I'd have me proper share. He'd have thought I was the business, then, if I'd ever had the evidence to give him. I only ever wanted me birthright, mind you. I only ever wanted what I deserve."

It's a good thing most of us don't get what we deserve. Claire's bitter laugh curdled into a wail of anguish. How could this happen? Why? Again she swallowed fiercely and cast a desperate look around the church. The effigies were silent as stone. The altar cross glowed faintly, like a good deed in a dark world. The cloth swayed.

It happened, Claire answered, because perception is more important than fact.

Diana took another step closer, her hand clutching the back of the pew beside her, her eye-slits like the peepholes into a padded room. "You want to know how your chum died, don't you? Why she deserved to die."

Claire forced her voice to stay low and casual. "Tell me about it."

"There was kiss-me-hand Melinda playing me role. Playing Elizabeth. I kept me mouth shut. Had a few drinks at the cast party. Nothing wrong with that, some rozzers to the contrary. Then Rob went down to the pub and looked like ticking off the extra help — never get anyone who can find their arse with both hands, do we? — and told me to fetch the dishes from the Hall. On me own, mind you. Oh, and take the dog for his walk as well.

"I've felt the back of Rob's hand often enough, I didn't give him any back talk. I was carrying the boxes through the portico and there was Melinda, walking through the gardens like she owned them, still wearing her bleeding dress. Getting up me nose with her bleeding dress, all of a purpose. Slagging me off because she thought she was better than me."

She didn't even know you were there, Claire wanted to say. To shout. Melinda had been caught in some vision of her own, maybe working out how best to capture the moment in words — Elizabeth walking down through the garden to the stone circle or on her way to a tryst with Walter. Or maybe Melinda, contrite that her jokes had gone too far, had been musing about how best to mend relations with Alec and with Richard.

"So I tied up the dog and followed her," Diana went hoarsely on. "She was standing atop that pile of rocks, taking in the scene, like — bright moonlit night it was, with the lights from the street making queer patterns on the grass. I said to her, I said, 'No more clever games, me lady, time to come clean, time to tell me all about it.'"

Diana stared over Claire's head, seeing the moonlit night, the garden, Melinda's no doubt puzzled face. Claire thought, if I turn around I'll see her, too. But no. She wasn't going to turn her back on Diana. Melinda was gone.

"'Tell me about the will, the proper will. Your precious husband knew all about it, didn't he? And so do you. You said so in that letter you wrote to Richard. Thy will to make known. The secret behind The Play.' She looked at me like I was talking rubbish, playing me up." Diana's voice rose, scratching hysteria like fingers down a blackboard. "'Tell me the truth! I have to know, damn you, I have to know the truth about the will!' And she fell about laughing. Laughing at me!"

The wail of anguish roiled in Claire's stomach. Melinda laughed because she suddenly saw the train of events she'd set in motion for what it was, a tangle of supposition, an absurd misunderstanding, an illogical deduction. She laughed because she'd always seen absurdity and appreciated it for what it was. She'd always laughed at her own absurd need to hide her truth, afraid she'd be the one everyone else laughed at.

Diana looked back at Claire. Her left hand clutched the back of the pew, her right hand trembled, clenched at her side. Her voice dropped abruptly into a hoarse growl. "She'd pushed me too far, hadn't she? So I pushed at her, to get her attention, like. And she fell. That bloody rock pile's not too steady, is it? She fell."

Claire had stood on top of that pile of rocks. She would've fallen if Richard hadn't grabbed her hand. It wouldn't have taken much of a push.

"There was that posh camera of hers, broken open, useless. Like her pretty head, smashed right in. The blood looked like ink in the dark. She was out cold, I reckon. I shook her. Oh, she was still breathing, all raspy, like. I could've run back to the pub, told them to come quick and help her. And then she'd wake up and tell everyone what'd happened. The rozzers'd come to get me, wouldn't they? And Maurice, without the evidence I'd promised him Maurice wouldn't give me the time of day, not any more.

"It was all Melinda's fault. She spoiled it for me. So I took that little sash from her dress, no more than a ribbon, and I did for her. I knew what I had to do and I did for her, then and there. Me, who she thought was shit on her shoe, I did for her. I had to, didn't I? Melinda had the proof that would give me the Hall and she had any man she wanted and I had no proof and no one."

So here was the truth at last. Every word of it had its own skewed logic and yet every word of it was wrong — Melinda had a concussion, she probably wouldn't have remembered what happened — a sober Diana might have run for help — a sober Diana wouldn't have confronted Melinda to begin with, throwing her own frustrations and resentments like acid. Just as she was now throwing them at Claire.

"I ran back to Hall for some dustbin liners," Diana went on. "Melinda was so little, so nothing, it was only a minute dragging her into the garden. Richard had the rose beds all ready, with tools and a pile of muck to hand. Very obliging.

"The dog slipped his lead and came running up whilst I was digging out the bottom of the flower bed. I thought of Jezebel, in the Bible, eaten by dogs. But he's a good dog, couldn't do that to him. I shied a rock at him. Then I wrapped her up in the bin liners and threw the dirt back on top of her. Dirt, that's what she was. Dirt come to dirt." Diana smiled. She had blood-red lipstick on her teeth. "I wanted to take her ring, but no, peasants like me don't have nice things, do they? Even though she owed it me. I could've had the Hall, couldn't I? She kept me from it. She got what she deserved."

In spite of the chill Claire felt her face glowing hot. Steaming, probably. Eaten by dogs, God. . . .

The dog. Susan had seen the dog running along the street on her way to the midnight vigil. But the woman she'd seen in the portico wasn't Melinda after all. It really had been Elizabeth, agitated, probably, by the horror done in her name.

Diana was still smiling. "I carried the food and the dishes to the pub, locked the dog in, had a wash, and went along to the church, bang on time, made sure everyone saw me. Even that whore Janet. Rob said I was whoring for Elliot, didn't he, and yet when he has it off with a Yankee tart it's only a physical need, like pissing, I reckon."

Yeah, Claire'd heard that one before.

"I said I was ill," Diana went on. "But I wasn't. I felt good. Strong. Stronger than Elizabeth, even, because I fought back. I found Melinda's car keys in her flat along with her computer. I've had a key to that flat for donkey's years, used to char for Sarita. I ask you, a natural born Brit of good family cleaning for a wog. As bad as a wog playing Elizabeth, isn't it?"

Claire knew she'd be wasting her breath asking why race prejudice was any better than class prejudice.

"I'm a good driver, I am, the Derbyshire-sodding-constabulary be damned. I left the car at Ladybower Reservoir and hitched with a farmer going in to market, had him drop me at a motorway service area by

Chesterfield. I hitched from there with a lorry driver. Clever, eh, not to come straight back here?"

"Elliot said you were at his house soon after midnight," Claire said, forcing her lips to form words without letting out her scream.

"Ah, he took a tablet. Always does, says he's a martyr to insomnia — if he ever worked at a real job he'd sleep, right enough."

"You have a key to his house, too?"

"Yeh, he had me in to dust all his pretty things when he was away farting around with producers and actors and other airy-fairy folk. So I slipped in and changed his clock, didn't I, moved it back to one, the time I left the church. Then I woke him up, tried to get him interested. He wasn't up to it. I hear tell they have tablets for that, too, nowadays. But he won't be needing any."

Diana's appearing at Elliot's bedside, Claire thought, had been a victory roll, gloating over a defeated foe. A foe who hadn't even realized she was in combat. "What happened to Melinda's computer?"

"Couldn't get a bloody thing out of it, could I? Just goes to show you she had something to hide, the way she'd nobbled it with passwords and such. Useless bit of rubbish, and not something I wanted lying about — we peasants don't have computers, either, do we? I smashed it up and bunged it in the Littles' stock pond."

In other words, Claire told herself, Diana was completely computer illiterate. . . .

"Everyone thinks I'm a bungalow," Diana spat, "no upper story, see. When that pillock Pakenham said he was after arresting me, I showed him. I showed him good and proper."

Yes, you did. Even though you were wrong there, too. Claire was trembling, every nerve humming like piano wire. But collapsing into a twitching, sobbing heap wouldn't help. Diana had to be getting near the end of her recital. Her speech of self-justification, crowing over Claire because she'd never had a chance to crow over Melinda. "You killed Elliot, to cover up. You went to his house before you went to the pub yesterday afternoon and forced him to write the confession."

"Yeh. It's easy to kill, once you've done it. Like adultery, gets easier every time." Diana's eyes narrowed even further, into spiteful glints. "Mind you, Elliot died because of you, not me. Melinda took away me inheritance. Me birthright. You were after taking away everything else, weren't you? Even when she told you sod-all about the will — thought she was too good for you, too, hah! — still you came here asking questions. Couldn't leave well enough alone, could you? Well, Melinda's plotting came to nothing and yours will, too."

Plotting? Claire repeated. *But neither one of us ever had a clue.*

Diana stepped forward, head down, shoulders coiled. Claire stepped back once, twice. She was almost at the end of the pew. Her left thigh brushed against a fold of the umbrella.

"It was that bitch Kate, W bloody P bloody C Shelton, saved you from the trap I set with the tapestry. Nothing but sodding luck got you out of those cellars alive. And now you're here, walked right in to another trap. Who's stupid, then? Who?"

Claire glanced to her left, toward the main door. Maybe she could outrun Diana. Hell, right now she could outrun an Olympic sprinter . . . The side aisle was almost blocked with the tombs. She'd lose time going around them. Diana could run down the main aisle and corner her by the porch. Then it'd be hand to hand.

Diana was taller, heavier, and stronger. Outside the cellar door she'd had the advantage of surprise, yes, but even so Claire had much too good an idea what would happen if Diana got hold of her now. She could kick, she could scratch — Diana wouldn't feel a thing except her own resentment.

It wasn't worth the effort appealing to Diana's good nature — the woman had worn that out years ago. Reason, maybe? Did she have any left? "Why go to all the trouble of pinning everything on Elliot and then blow it by . . ." Claire wasn't going to say the words. ". . . here? All the hue and cry'll start over again and this time the police'll know exactly who to come after." She flexed her knees. Her jeans made a swishing sound against the black satin fabric of the umbrella. The umbrella . . .

"You're still thinking I'm stupid, aren't you?" Diana's voice was as coolly reasonable as though she was telling a customer the price of beer. "I'll raise the door to the crypt and push you down the steps. Mind you, Elizabeth doesn't deserve to lie next the likes of you, but she's been amongst the gentry all these years, she'll understand. It'll be like one of them ancient sacrifices when all the servants were buried with the king. It's time one of us peasants got hers back."

Claire bent slowly to the left, her hand sliding, fingers outstretched, down the seam of her jeans.

"By the time they find you I'll be gone. I've been creaming money from the till, haven't I? That and me own little account in Bakewell that'll set me up somewheres, anywheres, so long as it's not a turnip patch like Somerstowe. I'll go by me proper name, Cranbourne." She took another step forward, raising her hands. "And I have a button from Rob's jacket here in me pocket, if I put that on your body they'll think it's him, won't they? He's having himself a nap just now, he was alone in the entrance hall yesterday when Elliot died, they'll think he did for the both of you. He'll get what he deserves, a cell, no booze, no whores, no one to knock around, not any more. You know what they say, Claire. Third time's the charm."

Diana lunged.

Ohmygod. The words ricocheted inside Claire's head. She saved her breath to fight. *Ohmygod.* Her hand swept up the umbrella even as she leaped backward.

Her right side smashed into cold marble. So did her left. Swift move, she'd wedged herself between Cecil's and Phillip's tombs. It was all their fault to begin with, yes, maybe it was appropriate she died in their stony embrace . . .

Diana, all eyes and teeth and flying hair, came at her. Claire raised the umbrella. Her thumb found the catch and pressed. With a whoomp the taut-stretched fabric billowed outward. Claire leaned into the outward thrust, leading with the metal spike. From behind the black circle of the umbrella she felt rather than saw it hit Diana.

Diana screamed, ugly and shrill. At least Claire thought that was Diana's voice, not hers. And someone else was shouting too, several someones. Footsteps reverberated off the roof. She was either hyperventilating or the cavalry had come at last.

Hands pushed away the umbrella and pulled her out of her crevice, hands she'd recognize anywhere, any time. Richard. Her knight in shining armor. Or her knight in jeans and a Cambridge University sweatshirt, to be exact. His eyes were blazing. "Are you all right? Alec and Kate are after her, we heard almost the whole thing — are you all right, lass?"

She wanted to smile jauntily and say, "Gee, you're handsome when you're mad." Instead her own voice, tiny and shaky, said, "Oh, Richard."

Somewhere footsteps raced. Somewhere voices spoke. Somewhere a door slammed. But here, but now, Claire dropped the umbrella and threw herself against Richard's chest.

His warm arms enclosed her. "I'm here," he said. "I'm here."

Chapter Twenty-seven

Maybe it was sheer mulishness. Maybe it was Richard's strong arm around her shoulders. It didn't matter. Claire locked her arm around his waist and discovered she could still walk.

Gathering up the umbrella in his free hand, Richard guided her past the altar and around the organ to the vestry door. Inside, Alec was easing Trevor into a desk chair and Kate stood at the open door with a cell phone pressed to her ear.

There was hardly space for them all in the tiny room with its desk, vestment cupboards, and shelves piled with musty books — and the old typewriter. Except for the crucifix above the desk, Claire was reminded of Elizabeth's room in the attics of the Hall.

Past Kate's shoulder she saw a vignette of Olde Englande — green churchyard sod nestled against silvery headstones and the lichened slate roof of the vicarage rising above a wall softened by rambler roses. She didn't see Diana, though, only the blank face of the Cranbourne mausoleum.

Kate switched off and holstered the phone. "Are you all right, Claire?"

"Only bloody just," Richard answered for her. "Trevor? What happened?"

The elderly man waved away Alec's helping hand. "I stepped up to open the door and it flew open in my face. Diana shoved me against the jamb and ran off, never a by your leave or a fare you well. I'm not hurt, thank you, just startled."

"Good show," said Alec. And, to Kate, "Blake?"

"He's sending the lads round the village. No worry, she won't get away."

"Talk about arriving in the nick of time," Claire told them all. Her voice was still a bit shaky, but the wail in her stomach seemed to have receded.

"I stopped by your flat," said Richard. "You weren't there. Trillian said she'd taken you up a note, not a stamped letter, a note left in the basket on the counter. I didn't like the sound of that. I'd been thinking, Elliot and all, it just didn't add up, did it?"

"Call me daft if you like," Alec said, "but Elliot's house last night — the air was wrong for a suicide. There was no — no decision, no ending. His life force left echoes of confusion, surprise, fear."

Trevor nodded. "Daft? Hardly. I felt a similar intuition when I went into the house. Sergeant Pakenham seemed to have the matter well in hand, though, so I didn't say anything."

"The only thing Arnold Pakenham has in hand," said Kate, "is himself. Begging your pardon, Vicar."

Claire managed a thin smile. So did Alec. With an appreciative snort, Richard went on, "I was going into the police incident room when I met Kate coming out. Diana never showed for her interview."

"And we'd just had the forensics report. There were no fingerprints on the gun and no gunpowder residue on Moncrief's hand," Kate explained. "She wiped away her own prints and put the gun in his hand, but didn't press his fingers round it firmly enough. An amateurish mistake."

"She is an amateur," said Alec. "And like most amateurs, she never twigged she's been more lucky than clever, and overreached herself."

"Kate and I met Alec on the high street," Richard concluded to Claire. "He asked Priscilla if she'd seen you whilst working on the green. She had done, said you'd come in here. From the porch we heard Diana going on about the letter Melinda sent me and thought we should have ourselves a listen."

"I can fill in the details on my own," Trevor said with a heavy sigh. "I've seen Diana grow more and more embittered over the years. If only I could've helped . . . Well, you'd best be off." His raised hand wished them Godspeed and counseled compassion at the same time.

Kate settled her yellow I'm-a-cop jacket over her shoulders and waved them out the door. Alec had a civilian windbreaker like Richard's. Claire followed the others out into the rain, grateful for the umbrella. Very, very grateful for the umbrella. Not that anything short of an Uzi would've held off Diana if the others hadn't come running in. Which was one of several things she didn't have time to think about now.

In one sweeping gesture Richard opened the umbrella and raised it toward the sky. Claire saw the English archers at Agincourt lifting their bows, arrows nocked, ready for battle. She saw the field at Agincourt after the battle, the mud churned red with blood.

Raindrops drummed on the taut fabric overhead. When she took Richard's hand she felt his pulse beating in his body almost as fast as the one beating in hers, compelling as a rock band in full cry.

No one spoke as they hurried from the church, across the green, and along the high street. Rain streamed off the eaves, setting the gutters awash. Their footsteps made dull splats on the pavement. A car passed, its tires swishing. Two familiar figures waited in front of the shop. Blake was enveloped in a bedraggled trench coat that made him look less like Sam Spade than a flasher between shows. His colorless eyes blinked out from behind his rain-spattered glasses. "Mrs. Jackman's gone into the pub."

"What's all this about her being the murderer?" asked Pakenham from the depths of his expensive Burberry.

Claire started with the smell of the greasepaint and Diana's initials. Then Alec, Kate, and Richard took up the tale. It sounded even more twisted and sick in their voices than it had in Diana's.

"I see," Blake said with a nod. "Moncrief told us he was asleep when Mrs. Jackman arrived at his house the night of the murder. Said he'd had an early night. Went on for a good five minutes about the heavy mantle of the director — how tiring and so forth — and for another five about provincial villages with no nightlife. It never occurred to him that she changed the clock. Never occurred to us."

"This is all well and good," said Pakenham sarcastically, "but Diana can't drive, can she?"

"Of course she can," Richard said. "She's just not allowed to. She had her license lifted for driving drunk."

"She told me she drove Melinda's car," added Claire. "What more do you want?"

Pakenham stared. "Oh, for . . . She said she couldn't drive, her husband said she couldn't drive, the Digbys said she couldn't drive."

"If you don't ask the right bloody question you don't get the right bloody answer, do you?" demanded Blake. "Come along, Sergeant. PC Wood, PC Shelton. The lads are waiting outside the pub. Let's take her in charge."

"Me?" Alec asked.

"Are you a police constable or not? Off you go!"

"Yes, sir." Alec started off at a run, heading for the back of the pub. Kate sprinted after him. "Wait for me!"

The others followed at a brisk walk, Pakenham muttering, "Diana Jackman, eh? The bitch. Of course it was her. Wants her head examined, doesn't she? I knew there was something wrong with her, knew so all along."

Nigel stood on the corner beneath the expanse of his own umbrella. "DCI Blake? We had an appointment . . ."

"Sorry, Mr. Killigrew," Blake told him as they swept by. "Later."

Claire paused. "We've just found out Diana Jackman murdered Melinda."

"It wasn't Moncrief after all?" asked Nigel.

"She did for him, too," Richard said. "If you'll excuse us . . ."

"By all means." Nigel stepped aside. "Shocking! Simply shocking!"

The rain slackened into what Kate had once called a mizzle, heavier than mist, lighter than drizzle. Somerstowe and its surrounding fields and hills were, literally, a watercolor. The delicate shades of earth and sky blurred one into the other. The contours of Hall, church tower, and houses were defined by a few strokes of stone.

Richard furled the umbrella and tucked it like a swagger stick beneath his arm. His fingers entwined with Claire's were warm, damp, and rock-solid in spite of that beating pulse. Because of that pulse, the same as her own, vital, angry, stubborn as hell.

Britain didn't have the death penalty any more, she thought. Good. Diana was pitiable, why would her death make anything right? And yet . . . *Please, let's get it over with.*

The pub was bright only by comparison with the shadowed day outside. The dark wood of the bar absorbed the light and the horse brasses managed only a sullen gleam. Across the TV screen moved the ghostly images of an old black and white movie. The actors spoke in Elliot's priggish accent.

Only a few people were scattered around the room. When Blake and his invasion force burst in the door every face turned toward them. Behind the bar Rob stood holding a dishtowel and a glass. His troll-like form was repeated in the mirror behind him so that he looked like a pair of bookends. "Where's your wife?" Blake asked.

"Kitchen. Why?"

Pakenham and a uniformed constable dived through the swinging door to the kitchen.

"Here!" protested Rob, and went after them.

"Are you after taking her in charge?" called a reporter from the corner table. Several of his colleagues reached for cameras and notebooks.

Blake strode over to the table where Susan, Fred, Janet, and a couple of others sat over sausage sandwiches. "Yesterday afternoon. Mrs. Jackman left the Hall to fetch the food for the party. How long was she gone?"

"At least an hour," said Janet. "Rob was bummed out, was just about to go looking for her when she came rushing back in with the stuff."

"Mrs. Zielinski," Blake went on. "Miss Godwin says you saw the Jackman's Alsatian running loose the night Miss Varek was killed."

"Well, yes," said Susan. "I sure did. Odd, they never let it out by itself . . ." Her face went chalk-white. "You mean — of course — if it was out, one them was — oh my God. The murderer's not Elliot. It's Diana. She killed him too, yesterday afternoon."

Fred put his sandwich back on its plate as though suddenly wondering what kind of meat was in it. He shot a truculent look at Janet. "So it was safe to stay here after all, huh? The case was over, huh?"

"She could've killed me, too!" Janet's eyes bulged.

"No," Claire said, "she damn near killed me. Three times."

From the rear of the building came an explosion of barking and shouting. Rob burst back out of the kitchen, swearing, his mouth a shell crater in the thicket of his beard.

Blake leaped with surprising agility for the door. It swung open, missing him by inches. Kate stood poised in the opening. "She threw hot water on the dog and it went for us. She's out the back, Pakenham and the others are after her."

Blake wheeled and charged out the front door. Kate whisked back into the kitchen. The reporters jostled each other out the garden door. With one last paroxysm of profanity, Rob threw a vicious punch at a beer spigot.

Through the swinging door Claire saw Alec, one hand wrapped in the huge German Shepherd's collar, the other resting on its head. He murmured in a singsong voice, "You're all right, old boy, just a bit singed on the nose, all that nice thick fur protected you, didn't it? No fear, I've some salve that'll set you to rights, but you'll have to wait a bit." The dog stopped whimpering. With a caress Alec released the animal and loped past the cookers and refrigerators to the back door.

Richard and Claire piled out the front door. Through the thick air Claire saw human shapes converging on the Hall. Muffled cries echoed off the stone walls.

They raced up what seemed like a mile and a half of the high street, past the Lodge, into the gates. Ahead of them the façade of the Hall reverberated with a large crash and several smaller ones. A door slamming followed by frustrated knocking, Claire guessed, peering into the murk . . . She couldn't see because the mist had gathered on her glasses. Impatiently she took them off and folded them into a pocket.

Of course Diana would run here in the end. She'd probably spent hours dreaming the house was hers. Maybe over the last year she'd come to believe it was, that somehow her passions and her crimes had earned it. For what? Claire asked herself. Not to bask in its beauty and its memories but to buy her way out of her own self-hatred.

The blurred shapes of Blake, Pakenham, Alec, and a couple of constables clustered together in the portico. Kate came running down the driveway toward Richard. "She's locked herself in. We need the key."

Richard pulled the keys from his pocket, wrenched one off the ring, and handed it over. "Ta," Kate said, and ran back toward the door. She wasn't even breathing hard, Claire noted. Richard was, though. So was she, and not necessarily from the dash up the street. *Can't we just get it over with?*

The bleachers still surrounded the forecourt, the workmen taking Sunday off. The windows of the Hall looked dark and blank into the wet afternoon, like a sleeper suddenly awakened. A couple of constables trotted around the side of the house. "All the doors are locked, Sir. Should we break a window?"

"No!" Richard shouted.

"Not yet," said Blake. He worked with the key, took it out, inserted it again. He and Alec threw their shoulders against the door and pushed.

"She's thrown the bolt!" called Richard. "Try the kitchen door. Here." Again he pulled out his keys.

Claire seized the umbrella as it fell from his grasp. His damp dark hair was waving like the tendrils of a sea anemone above his pallid forehead and a corner of his mouth was painfully cramped. Was he thinking the same thing she was, Claire wondered, of a woman frenzied with hurt and hate running through the darkened halls — if she can't have her life's desire, then . . .

"Look!" Alec pointed upward.

Something moved in one of the floor-to-ceiling windows of the high great chamber. Claire squinted. Diana? No, it was an indistinct shape, a wraith wavering in the distortion of the old glass. Elizabeth?

"Smoke," Richard moaned. "No. Oh, Jesus, please, no."

Smoke crept up the glass. Light flickered inside the room. Claire's chest seemed to turn inside out with horror. "No!"

A low murmur of anticipation and dread swept across the forecourt. At least a hundred people had apparently sprouted up out of the ground, Claire saw. Some faces she recognized, some she didn't. More than a few people were settling down in the bleachers, as though the scene was the third act of The Play . . . Well, it was, in a way. Every face was turned toward the window and the glow inside. Hands pointed. Cameras clicked.

"Lacey," Blake shouted, "is there anything flammable in there?"

"Oh aye. Paint thinner, lacquer, varnish. Chemicals for cleaning — benzene, potassium p-p-permanganate. Muckle old dry wood and a box of matches ready to hand in the kitchen." The light in the window was nothing compared to the blaze in Richard's eyes, bright as a blacksmith's forge.

Pakenham had his cell phone to his ear. "Fire brigade. Somerstowe. Get a move on."

Nigel's crest of silver hair appeared at one end of the bleachers. "You and you," he announced in the tones of a regimental sergeant major, "go round the village, collect all the pails you can find. And you, bring the garden hose from the shed . . ."

"We'll bring the hose from the back yard of the pub." Susan took Janet's arm and dragged her away.

"There's a tap there, in the portico," Richard shouted. "Another by the garden wall. Another . . . Ah, bloody hell!"

A bedroom window well down the façade from the high great chamber suddenly flared with light. The drapes, Claire's mind said slowly but clearly. Diana's splashed the drapes with something flammable and set them afire, too.

First one, then two smoke alarms started to shriek. Richard sprinted for the kitchen door, shoving Blake and Pakenham aside. He pounded on it, kicked it, and stabbed it with a key. "If you can't have it no one can, is that it? Bloodyminded cow!" The door swung open. He plunged inside. Blake seized his jacket and pulled him back.

Alec ran by them both and disappeared into the house. "Wood!" Blake cried. "Come back here!"

The unmistakable odor of smoke wafted from the doorway. Kate and an assortment of people including Fred and Roshan ran across the forecourt with a hose. Flame leaped in the windows of the high great chamber thirty feet above.

"The house'll be burnt to ruins if we wait for the fire brigade!"

Richard twisted away from Blake and dived inside.

Claire didn't stop to think. Throwing the umbrella down, she ran. Her feet rose and fell as though she was weightless. In slow motion she saw Blake reach toward her. She spun aside and plunged through the door into the house. "Richard!"

Through the dim haze she saw him stop and turn back. *If he tells me to wait outside like a good girl I'll spit at him.*

"There's my Claire. Come along then," he said, and led the way out of the kitchen and down the corridor to the room where the chemicals were stored.

The door gaped open on a mess of cans and bottles. Diana must have swept them off their shelves and onto the floor without waiting to see how many broke. A fierce but tiny blue flame burned in a spilled puddle of varnish, fortunately on stone, not on one of the wooden shelves. Richard and Claire took a canvas drop cloth and smothered the fire.

A constable appeared in the door behind them. "Get this lot outside," Richard ordered him, and with Claire beside him ran on into the depths of the house.

The corridors swallowed themselves, the stairs buckled beneath her feet. Time dilated, so that they spent a week groping their way through just one doorway. The smoke thickened. Claire's lungs burned. Tears of irritation ran down her cheeks. Richard's hand pushed her head down, into the clearer air near the floor. Crouching, they burst into the high great chamber.

Flame danced along the floor and cast diabolic shadows along the plaster friezes as though the room had become an inquisition dungeon. A screeching smoke alarm added just the right sound effect. Richard threw himself at a window, yanking open the latch and slamming the casement upward. Smoke gusted around him. "Here!" he shouted. Answering cries rose from outside and a stream of water hit him in the face.

Wiping his face on his sleeve, he leaned out. "Send up the hose!"

Claire leaned out beside him and gasped for air. Cool air. Damp air. The surging mass of people below looked like berserkers besieging the house.

The nozzle of a hose cracked suddenly against the windowsill beside her, tied onto a long board with numbers painted on it. Oh — one of the boards of the bleachers. Between them she and Richard wrestled the hose in the window. "Switch on!" Richard shouted hoarsely. Water spurted.

Somewhere in the house glass was breaking. No telling how many fires Diana had set. She could be anywhere. So could Alec. . . . Claire's eyes burned and she blinked. The flame before her sank into a dismal puddle of water and charcoal.

Several human bodies burst in the door, driven onward by Kate, who with her blond hair flying loose looked like a pint-sized Valkyrie. Richard thrust the hose at them. When he spun toward the door Claire was right behind him, slipping on the wet floor, her clothes cold and damp, her skin hot. She pulled the bottom of her sweater up and held it across her mouth and nose, making the air she breathed not only harsh with smoke but fuzzy with wool.

They ran by the tapestry frame in the gallery. Richard had basted a new piece of canvas work onto it Friday afternoon, Claire remembered. She'd never looked at it. It'd smell of smoke, its fine old colors would be smudged by smoke, the grit of the smoke would abrade the delicate yarns . . . More was at stake here than needlework.

They were through the gallery and in the far corridor. Richard wrapped the tail of his jacket across his face and felt his way through the opaque fog of smoke, recognizing each door by touch. Claire hung onto his back belt loop, coughing, sniffling, gasping. Funny, it seemed perfectly natural for her to be risking her life for a pile of stone . . . No. For a work of art. For a work of memory and of desire.

In a large bedroom Pakenham was ordering a crew of townspeople and constables, including Rob Jackman, to tear down the curtains and trample out the fire. It wasn't until Claire and Richard had run past that she realized Pakenham was in shirtsleeves, his face dirty, his hair tousled. She'd spot him one redeeming feature then, but only one.

In a small bedroom a fire smoldered on the ancient carpet. Richard and Claire smothered it by rolling the carpet around it.

"Now what?" she wheezed. "Where's Diana?"

Richard's fiery red eyes in his soot-blackened face made him look like a demon. Or an avenging archangel. He turned toward the attic stairs. "This way."

In two of the servants' rooms they found charred wood and scorched fabric. The fires were already out. Alec? Claire asked herself. The windows stood open and the wind was starting to dissipate the smoke. He'd know better than to open the windows if Diana was still setting fires — the fresh air would fan the flames. He must know where she was.

As one, Richard and Claire turned toward the secret room.

Chapter Twenty-eight

They found Alec standing in the closet outside the closed door of Elizabeth's secret room, holding a couple of paint buckets filled with water and a singed drop cloth. He looked around, not at all startled. "Thanks be for a rainy day and indoor plumbing. She's in there."

Elizabeth? Or Diana? "Diana said something . . ." Claire coughed, ". . . about that room. I bet she was spying on you and Elizabeth."

"I hope she learned something, then," Alec returned.

"Let's have her out of there." Richard reached for the sliding panel.

Alec caught his hand. "Feel the wall."

Richard touched the wall. "It's warm."

"She's set herself a funeral pyre," Claire said.

"No, she can't do that. It's not right." Alec peeled off his jacket, stuffed it into one of the buckets, and yanked it out streaming water.

There were a lot of things that weren't right, Claire told herself, and Alec saving Diana's life might be one of them . . . No. Diana's melodrama had come to an end, not with a bang but a whimper. She deserved compassion. She was going to get compassion whether she wanted it or not, damn it.

"Let me," said Richard.

"No. This is mine," Alec told him, and reached again for the catch that would open the door.

It slid aside. Smoke billowed from the opening. Holding the jacket in front of his face, Alec leaped through. Claire picked up the buckets and Richard the wet drop cloth. Between them they drowned and pulverized this fire as well, all the while caroming off Alec's large, solid body half-concealed in the smoke.

With his toe Richard nudged an empty can of benzene out the door. Claire stamped the charred remains of the box of matches into smeared ash. That for murder, that for deception, that for history corrupted — the elements themselves couldn't destroy the truth. Not one of all the truths caught in this room. Which was not a priest's hole but a priestess's.

A gust of fresh air dispersed the smoke. Alec materialized from the haze protecting Diana's sagging body with his own. A length of thin rope hung from a ceiling beam, its end frayed and torn. The other end circled Diana's neck and dangled down the front of her shirt like an ugly necklace. The bench lay on its side against the toppled table.

"She set the fire," Alec said hoarsely, and coughed. "She set the fire, then fixed the rope and stood on the bench. She couldn't have tossed a match into the benzene and kicked the bench away until we were just outside the door. I pulled her down."

Not many men could have torn that rope in two, Claire thought. Alec did have his supernatural moments.

Diana's face flushed an angry mottled red beneath the soot. Only white slits showed between her black-rimmed eyelids. A vicious scarlet welt scarred her throat. She'd identified with Elizabeth to the end, then. To the end of her own bitter near-sightedness.

She trembled violently, her breath a harsh heave and gasp. Alec tried to lever her to her feet. Her body flopped, limbs splaying. Shaking his head — so much for his comment about bloodyminded cow — Richard went to help.

Now came the trial. Now the pretenses and the perceptions, Melinda's as well as everyone else's, would be splattered like road kill across the public pavement. For a moment Claire wished Diana had died here, alone and in pain, as she'd lived alone and in pain.

Then Claire was coughing, hacking up the acrid tastes of fire, brimstone, and hatred. Her ears were still ringing even though the smoke alarms had finally run down. Through streaming eyes she saw shapes wavering at the end of the hallway. Fiends from hell . . . No, they were firemen.

Alec and Richard levered Diana out the doorway into the arms of a couple of paramedics. Tears made tracks like a snail's slime trail down her face. She was swearing in a grating mutter — Alec should rot in hell — so should Richard and a fair number of other people, especially Melinda, who was already there roasting — Melinda was a witch, all witches should be done to death — Somerstowe must not suffer witches to live. Claire bit her lip, pity blending with disgust.

The paramedics and the firemen half-carried, half-dragged Diana away. Their footsteps receded into the house and disappeared. Richard set the table and the bench upright. Alec gathered up a cardboard box from the corner of the room. Oh — Elizabeth's shroud. Either Diana had thrown it down or it'd fallen in the struggle.

Alec lifted the lid of the box and peeked inside. "It's all right. Hang on a sec." He turned toward one of the brick walls, counted up the rows of bricks, and eased one from its crumbling mortar. In the small, dark recess Claire glimpsed a bit of white fabric.

Tucking the box beneath his arm, Alec took the bit of cloth and unfolded it. On his outstretched palm lay two oblong nubbins of ivory . . . No. Two bones, one human, one feline.

Richard inhaled, gargled and sputtered, managed to exhale. His voice rasped. "So you're making an end of it, then?"

"It's come to an end." Alec refolded the cloth — an ordinary hand-kerchief — and tucked the package away inside the box, deep in the folds of the linen shroud.

A shroud, thought Claire. A winding-sheet. A sheet to wrap lovers on a chilly English morning. Poets had been exploring metaphors of love and death as long as they'd had language to spend on it. So Alec had written a new and particularly poignant verse to that neverending poem. It took a mind like Diana's to twist a poem into the trailer of a B-movie.

Together they walked away from the tiny room. What a trio they made, wet, singed, sooty. If Alec looked bleak, Richard looked stunned. He narrated damage and repair in a slurred brogue, ". . . oak floor planks, velvet bed-hangings with applique, smoke-damaged plaster — God," he groaned, caught himself and went on, ". . . windows, how many windowpanes, marble. . . ." They walked into the long gallery and stopped dead.

Tendrils of smoke coiled like will o' the wisps through the shadows . . . That translucent shape wasn't smoke. It glided down the room toward the tapestry frame, growing more opaque with each step. Voices, engine noises, mysterious thumps and bumps sounded faintly in the distance, but here there was no sound except the soft steady cadence of footsteps.

"Elizabeth," Alec said, his voice as husky with emotion as with smoke.

Claire dug her glasses out of her pocket and put them on. The lenses were smeary. Elizabeth was crisp and clear. She wore a dove-gray dress with a white collar and a white cap that barely contained the waves of her golden hair. Her skin was the pink of roses in June. Her sunlit eyes looked out from a heartbreakingly smooth and youthful face. She was carrying the cat nestled against her breast. Its purr made a gentle resonance in the wooden floor. The scent of pomander dispelled the reek of smoke and wet wood.

With a soft thud the cat leaped down. It started washing its face, not at all bothered that every lick of its tongue ripped the fabric of reality. Elizabeth bent over the tapestry frame. Her delicate hands picked up a needle and threaded it. She sewed a stitch, and another, and another. The punk of the needle through the taut canvas sounded like a distant heartbeat.

Alec handed the cardboard box to Richard. He walked forward, extending his hand. Leaving the needle dangling from its thread, Eliza-beth raised her own hands in a gesture partly of welcome, partly of puzzlement and pleading. Her smile wasn't the naive and self-absorbed smile of a nineteen-year old girl. It was the world-wise and world-weary smile of an old woman. Her voice was the melody of a flute. "Ah, Alec, would you have me wait upon you still?"

As one, Richard and Claire turned toward the door.

"Please," Alec asked them, "don't go." He reached out, taking Elizabeth's hands and cradling them between his own. "These are my friends, Richard and Claire."

She looked toward them. At them. She curtsied, her dress rustling. "Good day to you."

"How do you do," said Richard faintly.

Claire managed a similarly faint, "Hello."

Elizabeth's head barely came to Alec's jaw. Even though she looked up at him with her chin thrown back, the tilt of her head and the slope of her shoulders suggested not pride but a sorrow out of time and beyond space. Beyond reason, if not at all beyond emotion. "You have spoken to me of love, Alec. You have taught me the pleasures of love and for that I am grateful, for your gentility eases the memories which burden me. And yet, even then, I am spent, encumbered with those same memories. I would leave this shadow of a life and sleep in the bosom of our mother, and in time be born again and know joy without encumbrance."

"Yes," Alec told her, "I know."

Elizabeth's upturned chin exposed the length of her throat. The fragile flesh was bruised, swollen with the mark of the rope. And yet it was her mind, Claire thought, her spirit, her soul, which were truly scarred by the horror of her death. Melinda now, Melinda hadn't known what hit her.

"We shall yet meet again, you and I, in another life," Elizabeth told Alec. "This life is yours, not mine. My life is but a withered shoot, yearning for the dust. Yours blossoms within your heart at this moment. Do not deny your life in favor of mine, I beg you."

Alec lifted her hands to his lips. "I should never have called you."

"If you had not awakened me then we would not each one have known the other. Should we turn away from love and laughter because neither is perfection?"

"No," Alec said. "No. Not a bit of it."

Richard sighed, his warm breath stirring Claire's hair. She knew what he was thinking. Here they were, two relatively normal human beings, with no entanglements, free to get together mind, body, and soul . . . Well no, there were issues, ones of life and death if you counted Melinda's — not ghost. Memory.

"I'll remember you," Alec told Elizabeth.

"If I should take any image even unto another life, it shall be that of you." Standing on tiptoe, her skirts rustling, she pressed her lips briefly against his and with a smile whispered, "Do not, however, allow my memory to mar your joy of this life."

He smiled back. "I won't."

The cat was batting at the dangling length of thread. The thread glinted red in the shadowy room, like a stream of blood. Pulling her hands away from Alec's, Elizabeth scooped up the cat and stood waiting.

With his right hand Alec sketched a graceful, flowing symbol in the air. His hoarse voice murmured something. Claire heard the feeling behind the words rather than the words themselves, just as she'd hear a particularly evocative passage of music without analyzing what the individual notes were.

Elizabeth's shape wavered and thinned, less like smoke than like sparkling mist. Only her eyes remained distinct.

Alec picked up the scissors sitting beside the frame. He took the dangling needle in his other hand and looked up at Elizabeth. Her eyes smiled at him, lit like a summer's afternoon.

He cut the thread. The tiny metallic snip seemed as loud as a slamming door. In a swirl of light and shadow Elizabeth vanished. *Sympathetic magic . . .*

For a long moment Alec stood considering the place where she'd stood. Then he put down the scissors and the needle. "Richard, Claire, have a look at the canvas . . ." His voice broke. He began coughing, deep, racking coughs torn from his gut and forcing tears to run down his cheeks.

Richard tried thumping his back. But what Alec was trying to cough up, Claire thought, wasn't anything as simple as smoke.

She turned discreetly away and leaned over the needlework canvas. The muted colors depicted Penelope, dressed in a seventeenth-century dress and seated in a seventeenth-century room before a needlework frame, waiting for Ulysses to return either from Troy or from the Civil War battles at Naseby or Marston Moor. Beneath the figure of Penelope was stitched the word, "Faith," and the frayed initials, "ES." Below that monogram was another, freshly sewn in red thread, identical to the first. *Elizabeth was here.*

Oh yes, Claire thought, she'd been here all right. Just like Diana. Just like Melinda. Just like me.

With a strangled sputter Alec caught his breath. "I'm all right," he croaked. "Thank you."

Richard landed a fraternal punch on Alec's arm and backed off. "You thought if you had witnesses you'd have to do the right thing by her?"

"Yes, I did do."

"Conscience is a wonderful thing," said Claire, but refrained from adding, *I could not love thee dear so much loved I not honor more.*

She caught Richard's bloodshot eye and offered him a dry smile. She'd thought he was the last man on Earth who knew what honor meant. She was wrong. But then, unlike Alec, Richard could have his honor and his love, too.

"Alec? Claire? Richard?" A rush of footsteps and Kate flung herself through the door. Her face was daubed with dirt and her blond hair made a halo around her head. "There you are! They brought Diana out, said you were all right, but you didn't show."

Alec squared his shoulders and wiped his arm across his face, which smeared the soot and tears into war paint. "We're all right."

"Right." Kate tried to smooth down her hair.

"Thank you," Alec said, relieving Richard of the cardboard box. "I'll leave this off at the house, see to the dog, be back straightaway, Kate."

"Those broken windows want covering," Richard said. "We should be looking out live embers. The lock's damaged . . ."

Alec shook his head. "I'll see to the Hall. You see to Claire."

I don't need seeing to, Claire thought. So what if she felt as though she'd been beaten, body and mind. So what if her throat was raw, her eyes burned, her nose ran, and she was wet and chilled to the bone, one raindrop away from trembling. She wasn't any worse off than the men.

Now, though, would be a good time to keep her feminist credentials in her pocket. What needed seeing to was her and Richard. Let Alec do his job. That's what he needed.

She took Richard's hand and tugged. With a nod of assent, he went along. They followed Kate and Alec down through the house and out into a cold, drenching, deadening rain shot with the pulsating lights of fire engines and police cars. Inside an ambulance paramedics worked over a twisting and heaving body. Diana. She was screaming, a high, thin, tearing sound like the cry of an animal caught in a trap, a sound sharp enough to cut through the rumble of engines and the thudding of the rain.

Right now Claire didn't care about Diana. Tomorrow, probably, she'd care. Not now.

It really was all over but the shouting.

Chapter Twenty-nine

*R*ichard waved away Kate's offer of oxygen, escorted Claire to the door of the Lodge, and handed her inside like an eighteenth-century gallant handing a lady into a carriage. But he didn't look anything like an eighteenth century gallant. He looked like Richard, the angles of his face whetted and his eyes smoldering.

"Have a shower," he told her. "There're clean pajamas in the dresser drawer. I'll be back soon as may be."

Claire looked at the stack of papers on the table by the door. She'd never asked to see that sketch of Melinda again. That work of art, catching Melinda's vitality, her resilience, her sense of humor. Sometime, Claire promised herself, she'd get that sketch out and appreciate it.

A few steps further on she stopped again, considering the height of the stairs. She'd climbed them before to take bladder breaks during her and Richard's videofests, when they'd sat side by side on the couch touching only intellectually. Which wasn't at all a bad place to start a relationship.

By paying close attention to the positioning of each foot she managed to get up the stairs and into the bedroom.

The four-poster bed was spread up, not actually made. A sweater was draped over a chair and a pair of boots lay turned on their sides below it. The top of the dresser displayed an assortment of litter — receipts, a stack of books, an empty vase, a bit of plaster molding, several coins.

Claire opened the top drawer. Socks, shorts, and T-shirts, more or less folded into piles. She tried the next one. Aha — a pair of silk pajamas in a dark blue pinstripe. And where had he gotten those? From the former fiancée? They looked as though they'd never been worn. Whatever. Gathering up the pajamas, Claire crossed to the window and looked out.

According to the clock on the nightstand it was barely past seven. But outside was gloom, the rain teeming down from clouds heavy as lead. There was Kate climbing into the ambulance. The door shut and it pulled out into the darkness. One of the fire engines left, too. Its headlights flashed across the window, making Claire wince, and then vanished.

Blake was hunched beneath an umbrella — her abandoned umbrella, maybe. They all looked alike. He was directing the ebb and flow of people across the floodlit forecourt, every body casting a tenuous shadow. Only two people still sat on the bleachers, reporters, probably. She wanted to lean out the window and yell at them, "The show's over! Go home!"

Even now, though, the show wasn't yet over. Claire turned around. Yes, she could see her and Richard in that bed, their bodies flexing and loosing together until all the hurt was gone. Except the hurt wouldn't be gone. They'd wake up to unresolved issues.

She went into the bathroom, stripped off her wet and filthy clothing, hung them from a handy hanger, and stepped into the shower. No surprise that Richard's shampoo was mildly herbal, soothing to her burning lungs but not at all sweet.

Claire found the hair dryer hanging from a hook and used the comb from the medicine cabinet. Then, with a shrug, she used the toothbrush, too. This was all very intimate. No reason she couldn't have gone back to her flat or at least asked one of the Nairs to bring her some things. But no, intimacy was one of the issues right now, wasn't it?

As for the other issues — her stomach growled, perhaps with hunger, perhaps reminding her that that wail of anguish and fear still lurked in its depths. Her face in the mirror seemed strange, as though her foundations had shifted and a familiar façade had crumbled.

As she stepped out of the bathroom she heard voices downstairs, Nigel's aristocratic tones contrasting with Richard's slight north-of-the-border lilt. Which was rasping into nothingness. She'd better get to the kitchen and put the kettle on. It was her turn to pour tea and whiskey down him.

The door slammed as Claire started down the stairs. She passed Richard coming up. "Is everything okay?" she asked.

"Oh aye," he said hoarsely. And, looking up and down her body, added, "That it is."

Between the cool air and the smooth silk, her nipples were sending him a real come-hither message. Her shell-shocked face, though, was probably telling him to duck and cover. With a sound that almost made it to a laugh, Claire went on into the kitchen. The bread was in the breadbox, the cheese in the fridge, the tea in the cabinet. A couple of cookies weren't going to cut it. Lunch had been a long time ago.

Yes, a long, desperate, wrenching time ago. At least no one, especially herself, had died this afternoon. Except Elizabeth. Alec had managed to resolve one of his issues — not that a satisfying resolution had been possible. Claire reached for the teapot. Upstairs the shower turned on.

By the time she had the sandwiches toasted and the tea brewed, the noises of the shower and then the hair dryer had stopped. Footsteps on the staircase coincided with a knock on the door.

Alec's voice croaked something. Richard croaked back. The door shut. Through the kitchen window Claire saw Alec walk into the forecourt, then stop and turn back toward the Lodge. Against the backdrop of the Hall his tall body seemed even taller, like a standing stone. He raised both hands. His mouth moved. He was blessing them, no doubt, or maybe even enclosing the Lodge in a magic bubble of time and space, shutting out the world.

The problem, Claire thought, was that she and Richard had brought the world in with them. She loaded the food onto a tray, carried it into the sitting room, set it down on the coffee table.

Richard was kneeling on the hearth lighting a fire. Claire remembered when her mother had given her The Lecture, she'd used fire as a metaphor for sex — it could burn down your house or it could keep you warm and cook your food. Your choice.

If houses both metaphorical and literal hadn't been burning so recently, Claire would've tried the old chestnut, *Come on baby, light my fire.* As it was, she sat down on the couch and opened the bottle of whiskey. "Is Alec all right?"

"He will be, given time." Richard brushed off his hands and stood up. A tiny flame nibbled at the tinder. "He said to throw those twigs on the fire."

"As a soporific or an aphrodisiac?"

"We'll be finding out, I expect. Ah, food. Brilliant."

"Eat," Claire ordered him.

Richard's eyes were less bloodshot now that he was wearing his glasses. He also wore a knee-length bronze-colored robe, exposing trim, strong, shapely calves and feet. He'd look great in a kilt, wouldn't he? And he might not be wearing anything under that robe, either — well, anything other than the T-shirt she could see between its lapels. The cut he'd gotten on his forearm digging up Melinda's body was nothing more than a pink crease. His hair was lying down obediently on either side of a part. If she interpreted that correctly, it meant he was tired, relatively calm, but probably no less determined than she was to see it through.

He poured a dollop of whiskey into her cup as well as his own and recapped the bottle. Its odor was fresh and bracing as a sea wind, complimenting the fragrant smell emanating from Alec's twigs. Claire took a deep drink and discovered she could breathe without wheezing. The toasted cheese sandwich tasted better than frou-frou dishes she'd eaten in five-star restaurants.

Richard folded a last string of melted cheese into his mouth, picked up a second sandwich, set it back down. He refilled his cup with tea and added another drop of whiskey. Did he have a wail of anguish in his gut, too? Claire wondered. The one in hers might have receded for a time but was now coming back three times as strong, like a tidal wave.

Now, she thought. Now we consider the issues. "You didn't confess everything to the trustees this morning, did you?"

"If it all comes out at Elliot's inquest or Diana's trial, then it comes out. I'm not suicidal — my running into a burning house to the contrary." Richard's lips thinned to fatalistic line.

"If I hadn't come here, if Melinda hadn't come here, nothing would be coming out. You'd be sitting here drawing your plans, making your sketches, and writing out your lists without a worry in the world."

"Maybe not the same worries," he said. "But then, I'd be sitting here without you, wouldn't I?"

She was glad he was still thinking along those lines. Even so, her own honor demanded its due. "I never thought my needing to find Melinda would hurt anyone else. Diana, well, she asked for what's happened to her. Alec — he did, too, in a way. Elliot, ditto. But you — you've taken collateral damage and all you've needed is to follow your bliss. Because Melinda and I came here you'll lose that. You'll lose the Hall. The village'll lose the Hall. Psychically Somerstowe is going to look like one of those bombed out towns in Bosnia or Kosovo, all because of Melinda. Because of me . . ." Claire stopped, trying to gulp that tidal wail back down.

Richard set his cup on the tray. "Claire, there was too much going on behind the scenes here. It needed bringing out."

"But you . . ."

"I have asked for it. I thought the Hall was worth lying for. And I couldn't connect with Melinda."

"You and her, that would've been a lie, too. And I'm not saying so just because I want you for myself."

One corner of Richard's mouth and his left eyebrow loosened, hinting at a smile. "Maybe it all happened because of my ancestor who built the Hall. Or Cecil, who lived a melodrama. Or Phillip, who played at writing it out. Fate or free will? Who knows? At the end of the day, it was because of their own desires, their own flaws — because of mine — that Melinda sent me that letter and Diana read it and . . . It's a damned bloody mess, right enough, but you can't blame yourself for it."

"Sure I can. Free will, right?" She tried to smile but the wail filled her throat — oh hell, she was going to cry. She hated crying in front of anyone. She hated looking weak. She hated being weak.

She hated being frightened and yet she'd spent the last few weeks — the last year — frightened first of not knowing and then frightened of knowing, frightened of some nameless criminal and then frightened of Diana, frightened of fire, of the dark, of Richard, even. Because if Melinda had changed her life once, Richard was going to change it again. Either way, by accepting or rejecting her, the rest of her life hinged on this moment. And that frightened her, too.

She sniffed, picked up a paper napkin from the tray, took off her glasses and dabbed at her eyes. "Still got smoke in them," she muttered.

Richard nodded understandingly.

She wasn't fooling him one bit. "I thought when I knew how Melinda died everything would be, well, not all right, I'm not exactly getting her back or anything. But she's the one who'd always tell me, fight the battle and then move on. Let it go. Let go." Claire sniffed again. "It's just that standing there this afternoon listening to Diana telling me, bragging to me, about murdering my sister — it was what I needed, to know why. And yet the why is so wrong, so petty, so stupid."

A tremor started in her stomach and expanded, shaking, rattling, rolling what thin façade of composure she had left. She doubled over in agony, her cry of pain turning into shuddering sobs.

Richard took her glasses from her hand and set them on the tray. He wrapped her in his arms and rocked her against his shoulder. In only a few minutes her sobs dwindled into hiccups. When she lay back against him limp as seaweed he handed her another napkin.

His voice in her ear was smooth below the hoarseness. He'd always been contradictory. That was one of the things she liked about him. "It's not a matter of pettiness and stupidity. It's a matter of perception. The way Diana needed to see herself as Elizabeth, for example."

"It was Melinda who was really playing Elizabeth. You know, the focus of other people's resentments, guilts, desires. The one who's causing your problems for you. Because your problems are always someone else's fault, never your own."

"We all see what we want to see. That's what killed Elizabeth and Melinda both. And Elliot. That's why Diana was after killing you, or, failing that, herself. That's what may bring down the Hall." Richard's sigh shaded into a groan. He laid his cheek against the top of Claire's head.

She sniffed and mopped and for a long moment watched the slightly blurred image of the fire sink into embers. Fire good, fire bad. "I know what those twigs are. Truth serum."

"Oh aye, that they are."

Diana had seen her own passions reflected in Melinda's mirror-like surface, Claire thought. Maybe if Melinda hadn't kept that mirror polished so brightly . . . No, her wounded inner child was no one's business but her own. At least she hadn't spent her last moments consumed by dread, despair, grief. She'd died as she'd lived, both laughing at the world and reveling in it.

Claire managed a wobbly smile. "Maybe Melinda had the right idea all along. Maybe her perception was truer than anyone else's. To fight as hard as you can and then kick back and laugh."

"Oh aye, I can live with that, if you can."

So it really was time for them to start drawing up blueprints for bridges, discussing the options of cantilever or suspension — well, he was the architect, he'd know about bridging chasms, even the metaphorical one between possibility and actuality, between doubt and faith.

She was the librarian. All she could think of, utterly out of context, was the line about a consummation devoutly to be wished. Claire pressed herself so tightly against Richard's side she could feel the texture of the terry-cloth robe through her pajamas. "What was it Elizabeth said to Alec?"

"'Should we turn away from love or laughter because neither is perfection?' She's right."

Richard, though, was no ghost. His shoulder beneath her cheek and his arms around her vibrated with the subtle rhythms of blood and breath. "'Art thou obdurate,'" Claire whispered, "'flinty, hard as steel, nay, more than flint, for stone at rain relenteth.' Or tears, as the case may be."

"Eh?" Taking off his own glasses, Richard laid them down next to hers.

The words of The Play, the words of the letters, all the words spoken in spite and misunderstanding and blessing as well — they'd worked their way through all the words and come out the other side. Yes, Melinda and Elizabeth had been taken before their time. They'd never resolved every issue in their lives. They'd never healed all the hurts. You could die at ninety-nine and you'd still be hurting. You'd still have issues. Seize the day, Melinda would've said. Seize the man.

"I always knew you'd turn out to be a sensitive guy." Claire put her hand behind Richard's neck and pulled him to her. Their lips met, moved, parted. And again, and again. Leisurely kisses, tender, thorough, flavored with the sea spray-and-smoke astringency of whiskey. His long, elegant fingers skated across the silk pajamas, cupping the curve of her hips, tracing the furrows of her ribs and the angles of her shoulder blades, finally enclosing her left breast, so that her breath caught in delight against his mouth.

His lips pulled away. His hand didn't. His thumb was having an inspiring dialog with her nipple — she wasn't sending him mixed messages, not any more. The bronze-green color of his robe made his golden brown eyes look more tigerish than ever. Not that she felt at all like prey.

There was a world outside this little house, this bubble of spacetime, but at this moment the only things that mattered were right here. "It's been a long day," she whispered, opening the placket of his robe and spreading her hands against his chest. Through the thin cotton of the T-shirt his muscles were warm, firm but not at all stiff. If anything were stiff, she'd be finding out real soon now. "Aren't you tired?"

"Yes. Aren't you?"

"Yes. I still noticed that nice four-poster upstairs."

"I pinched it from the Hall. The mattress is new. I've only ever slept there on my own."

"It's time to break it in properly," Claire told him. "Bearing in mind that we're both tired."

"So then," returned Richard, "tonight's not the night I should try proving anything to you?"

"You don't have to prove squat to me." She ran her hands through his hair — there, it was standing on end again, spiky and yet soft.

Richard looked appraisingly at the fire. It had burned to glowing embers, casting a rosy glow over the room. They could leave it. Claire looked appraisingly at the dirty dishes piled on the tray. Nah, leave them, too.

"Come along then," he said, and pulled her to her feet.

The bedroom smelled faintly of smoke, probably from the dirty clothes in the bathroom. Or, Claire thought a minute later, from the friction of cotton against silk. Or, she thought three minutes later, from the even more inspiring friction of skin against skin . . .

Momentary pause, while Richard produced the obligatory foil packet from the drawer of the nightstand. "How old is that?" Claire asked warily.

"I bought it this afternoon," he told her.

"From Sarita?"

"From Roshan. Does it matter?"

"No," she said with a grin. "Let the world know."

He tipped her up and laid her on the bed. The sheets were cool against her back. Richard's body was anything but cool against her front. His shoulders and chest, back and flanks were warm and supple beneath her fingertips, like living sculpture.

He did have a fine architect's hand. As well as an artist's fingertips and a tongue that could've painted the Mona Lisa. "Yes," she sighed, "there, yes." Speaking of following your bliss, she thought, as the sensation flowed from her nervous system to his and back again — "Yes, like that, oh yes . . ." Her voice trailed away into a moan.

In the shadows his face was very serious, very intense, and if he had to stop and cough a couple of times that didn't detract from the heavy breathing. Claire was doing some pretty heavy breathing herself, accompanied by assorted wordless squeaks and gasps. Not to mention a cadence of melodious creaks from the antique wood of the four-poster bed, which fit the occasion just as nicely as she fit Richard.

She grabbed convulsively at the suddenly sweaty skin of his back. With one last harmonic the bed fell silent. For one long precious moment they lay laced tightly together, forehead to forehead, sharing carbon dioxide and a few small residual wriggles, feeling no pain. Letting go.

Then Richard rolled over and collapsed. Claire levered herself up on an elbow, wondering if he was unconscious. Sure, he wasn't going to try and prove anything to her. But then, she already knew that anything Richard set his mind to doing, he did superlatively well.

His eyes gleamed in the darkness. He started to speak, croaked, swallowed, and intoned, "The condemned man ate a hearty meal."

So much for that bubble of spacetime, Claire thought. She'd known it was going to burst sooner rather than later. "Richard, no matter what happens, they're not going to hang you."

"Yes they will, near as dammit. I'll never find another job like this. I may never find another job at all." He waved toward the window.

She followed his gesture. Just above the windowsill the battlements of the Hall looked like old gold filigree against the black drape of the sky. Losing the Hall would be to Richard like losing Melinda was to her.

With a sigh she folded herself into the crook of his arm, shaping herself against his side. He wrapped his arms around her. "Sorry," he whispered, his words slightly slurred. "I spoiled the moment."

"No," she told him. "That's the point of the moment. No matter what happens, I'm here."

"Good." Richard's eyes closed. His breath lengthened into a gentle snore.

Claire watched the angles of his face soften and his mouth relax. It wasn't that the past was gone, she thought. The past would always be there, if not physically then psychically, preserved, conserved, restored. It was that she and Richard could now face the future together.

Smiling, Claire spun down into sleep.

Chapter Thirty

"And what is so rare as a day in June?" Claire quoted silently as she shut the door to her flat. When it came to weather, at least, Monday was more than making up for Sunday.

Even while Richard made and fed her breakfast this morning she'd sensed him going back into bunker mode. Yes, the ashes of the fire were cold on the hearth. But the birds sang outside and the windows of the Hall sparkled like laughing eyes. . . . Which was just the problem.

She'd made it back to her flat two minutes before Pakenham pounded on the door. Maybe he'd actually gotten his hands dirty at the Hall yesterday, but today he was back in his usual fashionable if lumpy suit and tie, smirking at her wet, dirty, smoky sweater and jeans.

She'd told him the story — the church, Diana, the Hall — and sent him off to harass whoever was next on his list. Pakenham got in the last word, though, by ordering her to appear at the police incident room at one.

Glancing at her watch, Claire hurried down the stairs. Roshan, just climbing into his red Royal Post truck, waved cheerfully. His knowing smile was a matter-of-fact "Good for you!"

Claire cringed as she stepped from the postcard-perfect day into Blake's stark command post. And yet she'd known all along she was going to wake up from the IMAX night before and have to face a scratchy black and white morning after.

In the back room Richard was already sitting at the table with Blake and Pakenham. When Claire sat down beside him he offered her that same resigned smile she'd seen last night. Ignoring Pakenham's snicker, she touched his arm. Hard as stone. He might just as well be a statue on the Hall's upper balustrade — a pigeon could land on his head and he'd never notice. Last night his stiff upper lip had turned out to be surprisingly tender. Last night the clean, spare lines of his armor had cracked to reveal baroque flights of passion. Today both tenderness and passion were unaffordable luxuries.

The door opened. A uniformed woman constable looked into the room . . . Good God, it was Kate. Seeing her in smart navy blue and brass was like seeing Clark Kent transformed into Superman. "Mr. Killigrew is here, Sir." She stood aside for Nigel, then slipped in and sat down herself.

"Thank you for coming, Mr. Killigrew," said Blake. "I thought as Miss Varek's former husband you should be present at the conclusion of the case."

"Very kind of you." Nigel seated himself on Claire's other side.

The conclusion of the case, she thought. The end of her old life and the beginning of her new. For better or for worse and all that.

The door opened again. Alec was still in civilian clothes, khaki pants and a tidy shirt and sweater combo. His clear hazel eyes were shadowed like an overcast day. He'd just lost his love, Claire reminded herself. That his relationship with Elizabeth was doomed from the start didn't matter. Surely Blake wasn't going to take away Alec's work as well — yesterday he'd sent him into action quickly enough. If nothing else no one still suspected Alec of murder, conspiracy, or black magic. Although, judging by Pakenham's disdainful sniff, that last was still on his agenda.

With a taut smile at Kate, Alec sat down between her and Richard. The two men exchanged a quick, silent conversation, ranging from *how's the love life then* to *don't let the bastards wear you down,* using only the angles of their eyebrows, the shapes of their mouths, and the tilt of their chins.

Once, thought Claire, she'd been able to talk like that with Melinda. And now — well, considering how profoundly she and Richard had communicated last night, soon they'd be able to speak telepathically.

The bags under Blake's eyes looked like thunderclouds, dark and heavy. With a sigh he loosened his tie. "Right. Mrs. Jackman is in hospital in Derby. A filthy bruise on her neck, smoke inhalation, a few burns and scrapes. She was cutting up so rough they sedated her and admitted her to the psychiatric ward. We interviewed her there early this morning."

"She looked like a dog's breakfast and no mistake." Pakenham patted down the oily strands of his hair.

Shaking his head, Blake went on, "What Mrs. Jackman told us agrees in every particular with your version of the — ah — confrontation, Miss Godwin. She still seems to think that everyone in town, from her husband to the vicar, was conspiring against her. And she hated Miss Varek with a passion."

"Yes." There was passion, Claire added to herself, and then there was passion. Yesterday had run the gamut.

"I got on to Applethorpe this morning," said Pakenham. "Yes, Diana told him she was on to something about the Cranbourne will, but she never came through with it. As to why he never mentioned this to me, the pompous ass said, 'I told you I discussed the matter with my relatives, what more do you want?' I should do him for obstructing the police."

"Leave it," Blake said. "He's not worth the effort."

With another sniff, Pakenham flipped several more pages in his notebook. "Wood, Shelton, Lacey. Digby. The temporary help at the pub. Everyone has the same story. All straightforward and aboveboard. I thought so all along."

Kate hid her face with her hand.

"Diana knew quite well that WPC Shelton was no volunteer," Pakenham went on. "She said again and again, 'I'm not as dense as everyone thinks I am.' Stupid self-righteous tart. First she murders Moncrief in a perfectly obvious fashion, then blows the gaff in front of four witnesses. She's one of those people that dense she doesn't realize how dense she is."

Every eye in the room focussed on Pakenham's smug smile, waiting for the punch line. Except for Nigel, who was staring off into the far corner of the room. "So the motive was jealousy exacerbated by greed," he said. "What a shame. A dashed shame. Can't be helped, though, can it?"

No, Claire thought, it can't. After a powerless life Diana had tasted power, corrupt though it was. After a life of frustration she'd thought her dreams were in her grasp at last. She wasn't the first person to believe that money could buy class.

Kate looked at Alec. Alec looked at Richard. Richard looked at Blake. "What happens now?"

"Mrs. Jackman will be able to stand trial, no worry there. We'll be needing you to stay on, Miss Godwin. I assume you have no problem with that?" The corner of Blake's mouth, barely visible beneath the curtain of the moustache, almost twitched into a smile.

"None whatsoever," Claire returned with a smile of her own. Even though working out the practicalities of staying on depended on what happened now.

A block of sunlight lay in a glowing square on the floor. The odors of roses and baking scones filtered through the open window, along with a symphony of birdsong that suddenly had a mocking edge to it. Richard sat with his knees and elbows close to his body, under siege. "It all goes back to the letter Melinda wrote me. Diana got the wrong end of the stick, thinking Melinda was going on about Maud Cranbourne's will when she was actually going on about me and about The Play."

Claire's sideways glance met Alec's coming the other way. So Richard was going to force the issue. Well, better a quick execution than a long lingering death of a thousand cuts.

"Diana," Pakenham said, "is the only person in the UK who doesn't know The Play's a fake. Aren't I right, Killigrew?"

"I say," murmured Nigel. "One has one's professional ethics."

"Everyone in this room knows the truth," Kate told him.

"Well then — ah — yes, I'm quite aware The Play is . . ." Nigel coughed discreetly ". . . not what it appears. If Maud had consulted with me before she published it, I should have attempted to dissuade her. However, she did not. I assure you I never told Melinda. If she knew, she found out from Moncrief. He did quite a bit of business with theatrical publishers."

"The Play has a genuinely old pedigree," suggested Alec. "Now that it's an accomplished fact, so to speak, maybe the specific details no longer matter."

"I quite agree. I see no reason for anything about it to come out at the trial. If Mrs. Jackman doesn't know the full story, well then . . ." Nigel spread his hands, inviting Blake and Pakenham to join the conspiracy.

Blake's moustache crumpled and his eyes crossed. He was no doubt visualizing robbery, murder, illegal weapons, and drugs infiltrating the public schools. "Play? We saw a couple of performances. Not the kind of thing that would give Andrew Lloyd Webber a sleepless night, now is it?"

"Not at all," Kate said brightly.

Pakenham shrugged. "Forget the bleeding Play, then."

"How odd," added Nigel, "that you'd mention Sir Andrew. Among Moncrief's letters was one from Sir Andrew's secretary saying thank you but he has no interest in buying rights to The Play. I always thought Moncrief was reaching a bit with that. Nothing ventured, I suppose." He reached into the inside pocket of his expensive but understated suit — no hope Pakenham was taking notes on style — and produced a leather-bound memo pad. "I'll see to organizing new representation for 'An Historie,' shall I? And perhaps a new edition citing Julian and Dierdre Lacey as editors."

"Please," Blake said with a shooing motion.

Claire considered Nigel's affable anteater face. She could see why Melinda had been attracted to him — and why it had all gone wrong. Whatever, she gave him a grateful half-smile. But The Play wasn't the major issue. Blake had only nibbled at Richard's bait.

The block of sunshine stretched across the floor almost to her feet. She could sense its intimation of warmth. Back home this time of year she'd be gasping in the sun-blasted heat, huddling beneath a ceiling fan during the day and only emerging vampire-like after dark. Here, though, warmth and sunlight were a blessing to be savored immediately or lost. Like love, she thought, glancing at Richard.

His eye flickered, aware of her thought, probably even agreeing with it. For him, though, the day was cold and dark. He was standing on his balustrade, guarding his post, even though raindrops were trickling down the back of his neck. Beyond him Alec's profile was less sharp but just as cold and damp.

"So that's that then," Pakenham said, slamming shut his notebook and capping his pen. "Nothing left but the paperwork and the trial. A job well done, wouldn't you say, Chief Inspector?"

"Hang on," began Kate. "What about Al . . ."

"No." Richard's voice cut through hers. "That does not wrap everything up. You've not put Alec back to work. And there's the matter of Maud Cranbourne's will, which may be a minor point of order to you but is a whacking great spear point to me."

Blake inhaled. It was Nigel who answered. "Richard, why should the matter of Maud Cranbourne's last will and testament figure in Mrs. Jackman's trial? I realize she and Applethorpe wanted to challenge it, but there are no grounds whatsoever for a suit. Maud's will is in perfect order, dated two days before she passed on and witnessed by Trevor and Priscilla Digby."

Every jaw in the room dropped, one after the other, like dominos. Claire spun around to Richard. His eyes gaped as widely as his mouth. What little color had been in his face drained to a flat greenish-white. She closed her hand on his arm. The tension ebbed so abruptly from it she expected him to slide bonelessly under the table. Even his hair seemed to collapse.

"I beg your pardon?" Blake managed to say.

Nigel scooted back a bit, no doubt wondering why everyone looked as though they'd just been goosed. "Maud Cranbourne left Somerstowe Hall to the National Trust. Mr. Lacey — Julian Lacey — well and truly succeeded in convincing her of the value of the Hall as an historical structure. All the legalities are in apple pie order and always have been, if I do say so myself. If Mrs. Jackman thought otherwise — well, she's in a psychiatric ward at this moment."

"The Cranbournes found a will in Maud's desk," Richard choked out.

"The preliminary draft signed by your parents the week before her death? How very kind of Julian and Dierdre to help Maud prepare it. The conveyancing of a major property such as the Hall can be quite complicated. Being aware of this, Maud sent me the will as soon as the Digbys signed it so it would be on file in my office. And not before time."

Claire closed her mouth. She didn't leap from her chair and turn a cartwheel or leap on Richard and smother him with kisses. She didn't kiss Nigel either, tempted as she was. Did he suspect what Dierdre and Julian had intended with their "preliminary draft?" Maybe so, but his ethics would never let him voice a mere suspicion. How casually the good gray lawyer had slain a fire-quenching dragon. Go figure.

"It's a tragedy, isn't it," Nigel concluded, "that Diana murdered Melinda for something that didn't even exist."

The will? wondered Claire. Or Melinda's perfection.

Pakenham threw his pen down. "I'll be damned." Alec and Kate shared quickly suppressed grins.

The color flooded back into Richard's face, which eased from stunned to simply dazed. He put his hand over Claire's and squeezed. "Oh aye, but tragedies eventually come to an end."

"Right." Blake unbuttoned his cuffs and rolled up his sleeves. His arms were meaty, more suited to cleaving logs or pigs or even heads than stitching the subtle shadings of a murder case. But he'd tied this one off, even so. Almost.

He leaned forward. "Whilst I was in Derby this morning I stopped by Chief Constable Figgett's office."

Alec braced himself. If he'd been standing up he'd have clicked his heels together. "Sir."

"I played Figgett the tape of your interview, including the vicar's endorsement at its end. I commented favorably on your conduct yesterday during the fire and the apprehension of the suspect. And I reminded the Chief Constable that the Derbyshire constabulary just lost D.C Khan's religious discrimination case. We don't need another one boiling up on us."

Pakenham snorted. "Khan may be a Paki, but at least Islam is a real religion. Wood here . . ."

". . . is a practitioner of the Native British religion," said Blake, turning up the volume. "I understand being a practitioner of the Native American religion is no bar to service in the American police."

"It sure isn't," Claire said.

"What do you expect of Yanks!" said Pakenham scornfully.

Blake's volume went up another notch. "The Chief Constable and I agreed that another scandal would do us much more harm than good."

"The reporters are already on to Wood!" Pakenham shouted. "That jiggery-pokery with the ring and the map . . ."

Blake turned a bland eye on Pakenham's scowl. His voice dropped almost to a whisper. "Why Arnold, you wrote in your report that your questioning of PC Wood suggested to you a possible scenario for the night of the murder, and that your superior deductive abilities then turned up the body. Or did I mis-read an official document?"

Pakenham's eyes bulged. He subsided to a low sputter like a teakettle on the boil.

In an impressive display of self-control, Alec kept a straight face. "So I have my job back then, sir?"

"Yes," Blake told him. "Be discreet, eh? Ask the padre round to do the honors before your party."

"That's not why I have him in," said Alec, "but yes, sir, I've only ever meant to be discreet. Not secretive, discreet. Not deceptive, private. Thank you, sir."

Blake removed his glasses, pulled out his handkerchief, and started polishing. "Sergeant Pakenham."

"Yes," said Pakenham truculently, and added a beat later, "Sir?"

"After I played the tape for the Chief Constable, my second matter didn't need discussing at all. Remember, Figgett's an old-fashioned sort of chap. He asked if my sergeant always behaved in such an insufferable and vulgar manner. Like a common little oik, is the way he put it. It doesn't look good, he said. Have to maintain our standards, he said. The public can be troublesome enough as it is, he said. Mind you, he was probably over-reacting just a bit after having to concede the matter of PC Wood."

Pakenham's jowls sagged in horror.

"I had no choice but tell him the truth, Arnold, that your behavior to PC Wood and Father Digby was entirely typical. And of course I had to mention how your putting it about that an arrest was imminent led Mrs. Jackman into murdering Elliot Moncrief. The Chief Constable then suggested transferring you to a position as a file clerk, where you needn't be dealing directly with the public."

Pakenham gobbled, but nothing coherent came out of his mouth. A look of utter glee bounced along the line of faces from Claire to Richard to Alec to Kate and back.

Having wiped Pakenham away, Blake replaced his glasses. "WPC Shelton."

"Yes, sir?"

"I need a sergeant to help me clear away this case. Seeing as how you've made a good fist of it all, I've recommended your promotion."

"Yes, sir!" said Kate, with a triumphant look that would've gutted and flayed Pakenham if he hadn't already been slumped deflated in his chair, his suit looking two sizes too big for him. He didn't even glance up when Kate and Alec exchanged a high-five discreetly below the edge of the table.

Now that was a punch line worth waiting for. "You go girl," Claire told Kate, with a judicious pump of her clenched fist.

"Well played," Richard said to Blake. Even Nigel smiled.

So it wasn't that Blake didn't have any backbone. He simply didn't want to change horses in mid-stream. Fair enough. Still he'd been looking for an excuse to demote Pakenham and reinstate Alec. Blake, like everyone else, wasn't what he'd first seemed. Everyone in the real-life play, the tragedy of Melinda Varek as visited upon Somerstowe, had been playing a role.

Richard stood up. Claire could almost see the armored carapace he'd left behind sitting ghost-like in his chair. "Thank you, Nigel. Thank you, Chief Inspector, Ser — WP — Kate. Give me a shout when you need me to testify. I'll do what I can as a public-spirited citizen and all. Claire . . ." She was right behind him. His momentum carried Alec and Kate out the door as well.

Behind them Nigel asked, "By the way, Chief Inspector, why did you ask me in for an interview yesterday afternoon?"

"Just crossing the t's and dotting the i's," Blake told him.

"Well now, I've made a profession of that," replied Nigel.

Richard paused in the outer office to take a deep breath. Alec nudged him with his elbow. Even with its fragile edge of regret, his grin stated, *oh ye of little faith.* What he said was, "Tomorrow is Midsummer's Day. I'll be laying on a barbecue as per usual. Claire, Richard, you'll be there?"

"With bells on," Claire replied for them both.

"A midsummer barbecue would go down a treat," said Kate plaintively.

Alec stared a moment, then did a classic double-take, "Oh! Yes, Kate, please, by all means, join me. Us."

"My pleasure," she returned with a demure flutter of her lashes.

Richard and Claire shared a pleased look. Maybe the shadows still lingered in Alec's eyes, but the sun would be rising soon.

From the back room came Pakenham's whining voice. "Killigrew, I'd like to retain you to file a discrimination suit."

"On what grounds?" Nigel asked incredulously.

"Detective Chief Inspector Blake here is discriminating against normal English males of good family background — I attended Winchester, I won't have your treating me like a common . . ."

Blake's voice fell like the blade of a guillotine. "Leave it, Arnold, or I promise you'll find yourself a litter ranger in Manchester. Wood! Shelton! We have papers to sort! Mr. Killigrew, if you'd be so kind as to leave me your card."

Bumping companionably in the doorway, Alec and Kate went back inside. Richard and Claire went the other way, out the door and into the light.

"Are you all right?" she asked.

He shook his head. "If only my mum and dad had asked to see the will, if only they'd sat in at the reading — well, why should they, they knew what it said — the time difference to Canada, my mum needs telling straightaway . . ."

"Richard," repeated Claire, "Are you all right?"

"Oh aye," he stated with a dazed smile. "Gobsmacked, mind you. Limp with relief. But quite all right, thank you."

Claire grinned. "Not too limp, I hope. We need to celebrate, don't we?"

"Oh no, not so limp as all that," he assured her, his smile spreading into a grin of his own. "You're expecting a dinner, I suppose. Wine, candles, roses . . . Well, we should miss out the roses."

"No," Claire told him. "We have to have roses."

"Roses, then. That's enough for you, is it? Or are you wanting me to get out my sketch book as well?"

"I think we have to have the sketch book, too," she told him.

His grin broke into a laugh. The laugh exploded into a war whoop. Richard danced a Highland fling up and down the sidewalk, then swept Claire into a waltz. The dazzling sunshine might as well be frost compared to the light that illuminated his face and spilled out to brighten hers as well. Together they sailed onto the high street sharing the giddy grins of people who've just stepped off a roller coaster.

They almost danced over the Digbys. Trevor smiled tolerantly at their apologies. "Is the case closed, then?"

"Yes. Oh yes, it is," answered Richard, catching his breath but not his gravity.

"I'm so sorry," Trevor went on. "I never connected Diana Jackman with Vincent's granddaughter Diane. She said her maiden name was Cox and that her folk were originally from Kent."

"No need to apologize." Claire assured him.

Priscilla settled her shopping bag on her arm. "Call in for a coffee when you're free. We're thinking of setting up a museum in that empty shop once the police leave. The true story of Elizabeth Spenser. The story behind The Play. Your design skills would be helpful, Richard. And Claire, perhaps you could make a copy of Elizabeth's shroud."

Even they assumed she'd stay, Claire said to herself. Her and Richard's posture betrayed all — they were clinging together as though their bodies had been magnetized. "I'd be glad to. But why can't you use the original cloth . . . Oh. Alec's going to bury her in it."

"Yes," said Trevor, "he called in last night and we had a very meaningful discussion. He greeted the idea of the museum with enthusiasm, and will talk to you, Richard, about photographing the cloth before the — the ceremony. A private one, he said. As seems only fitting."

"We still have her lovely altar cloth," added Priscilla.

"I'll do all I can," Richard said. "The true story needs telling."

Across the street Rob Jackman propped open the door of the pub, stared balefully out into the sunshine, and vanished back into his den. The dog draped itself across the threshold and laid its chin on its paws. A couple of reporters sat down at the outside tables and offloaded their cameras.

"I'll have a word with Rob," said Trevor.

Priscilla shook her head. "A terrible tragedy."

"Yes," Claire and Richard said, simultaneously and wholeheartedly. Hand in hand they walked on up the street to the gates of the Hall, which stood wide open once again.

Birds caroled merrily and children laughed. The twin beds of flowers lining the forecourt looked like a double rainbow leading to the pot of gold that was the Hall. Workmen scrambled over the bleachers, breaking them down into their component parts. Claire imagined these workmen's ancestors taking apart the ancient Norman castle and dismantling the gallows on the green. "All the world's a stage," she said.

"And all the men and women merely players," Richard replied. "We've made our curtain calls now. And even though they're not, thank God, going to strike the set after all . . ."

". . . the show's over," concluded Claire.

The Hall basked in the sun, stone glowing, windows shining, all passion if not spent at least redirected. The pile of building stones seemed half-absorbed by the green grass at the end of the lawn, like the ancient tombstones beside the church or like the megalithic circle beyond the slope of the hill. Banks of red and pink roses spilled over the walls. "Good bye, Melinda," Claire whispered.

And Richard concluded quietly, "Thank you."

Fred trundled a wheelbarrow of burned and broken bits around the corner of the building. "Richard! The glazier needs to talk to you about those smashed windows."

"Richard!" called Janet from the kitchen doorway. "Should I just use soap and water on the floor in the entrance hall?"

Susan trotted briskly across the forecourt, dodging the waving boards and tubing, and offered Richard his clipboard. "The smoke damage on the fireplace in the high great chamber isn't too bad. Should I try some more kaolin and benzene?"

"Richard," Claire said, getting into the spirit of things, "should I pick out that monogram on the Penelope canvas or do you want me to leave it in, with proper attribution, of course?"

Richard waved away the clipboard. "Fred, Janet, Susan — I'll sort things presently."

The volunteers retreated, trading bemused smiles.

"Well then," Richard said to Claire.

She threw her arms around him and kissed him. His lips in reply were flexible, creative, and promised glories to come. Somewhere behind the Hallelujah Chorus playing in her mind Claire heard the workmen cheering. Fine, but she had no intention of taking a bow.

When they parted she was beyond dizzy, approaching ecstatic. Her glasses were skewed across her face. Richard adjusted them.

His eyes shone with the same burnished sunlight reflected from the windows of the Hall. Funny, Claire told herself, she'd come here thinking she was a stranger in a strange land, only in the end to come home.

Together she and Richard turned toward the Hall, the intersection of past and present that was the gateway to the future.

About the Author

Lillian Stewart Carl grew up in Missouri and Ohio and has lived for many years in North Texas, in a book-lined cloister cleverly disguised as a tract house. So of course she's developed a taste for exotic locales and otherworldly happenings.

She started out writing science fiction and heroic fantasy and is now writing contemporary novels which blend mystery, romance, and fantasy/paranormal themes. Her books always feature plots based on history and archaeology, and explore the way the past lingers on in the present — especially in the British Isles, where she's visited many times.

She has a husband, two sons, a tabby cat, and an assortment of houseplants she views as rentals — her thumbs are ink-stained, not green. When she's looking for an excuse not to work she knits and needlepoints, reads, and listens to music, especially Scottish rock 'n' reel.

Lillian is a member or former member of SFWA, MWA, RWA, Sisters in Crime, Novelists Inc., and the Author's Guild. For more information about her other novels and short stories, please visit http://www.lillianstewartcarl.com.